ISBN-E-book: 979-8-9902554-5-6

ISBN-Paperback: 979-8-9902554-6-3

Fire and Water

The Protector's of Power Series
B.M.Light

For those whose who feel like life's chains keep them locked away.
Grab those chains and break free.

Playlist

The Phoenix- Fall Out boy

Bad Things (With Camila Cabello)- MGK

War of Change- Thousand Foot Krutch

Over You- Daughtry

Better Than Me- Hinder

This is War- Thirty Seconds to Mars

Hear Me Now- Bad Wolves, Diamante

I'm Gonna Love You- Murphy Elmore

Something To Feel- Dixon Dallas

Falling- Harry Styles

Nightlife- Livingston

Me Myself and You- Braden Bales

50/50- Knox

Go To Hell-Letdown

1

Aiden

"Aiden! You need to get up for school!" I barely hear my aunt's voice echo through the house. Her words filtering in through my sleep-clouded ears.

"Go away. I want more sleep." I mentally think towards her as I doze back off.

"Aiden!" My aunt says in a sharper tone while opening my bedroom door. But I again ignore her, covering my head with my dark gray comforter.

"I swear, teenagers are the worst. So lazy." She says as she stomps into my room and over to the window before pulling open the gray curtains, letting the morning light shine through the glass.

"Aiden Rivers, you get your ass up out of that bed right now, or I will drag you out. You're going to be late for school." She scolds as she smacks at my bare foot that's poking out from under the comforter to get my attention.

I groan as I roll over on my back, threading my fingers through my hair. "Fine! Geez, I'm up."

"Good. Now move it. I'll be damned if you're going to be late on the first day of your second semester." She says as she rests her hands on her hips. Her long black hair tossed over one shoulder while her light brown eyes stare daggers in my direction.

"Okay, okay. I'm getting up." I say again as I roll out of bed and make my way to the main bathroom to get my shower.

As I wait for the water to warm up in the shower/tub combo, I turn around, facing the mirror to glance at my reflection. My sleep tousled short, reddish-brown hair, and my mismatched eyes—the left green, and the right brown—stare back at me.

"You're gonna be sixteen tomorrow, and then the countdown begins." I say to my reflection.

I glance down at my bare arms as anticipation fills my chest, wondering when the first signs of my abilities will begin to manifest. Wondering when the tattoo-like markings that will let everyone know what kind of power I have will appear on my skin.

When I was younger, Uncle Matt told me about people developing abilities anywhere from the ages of sixteen to eighteen and how they could be part of a major group in our society called The Protector's of Power. I've seen them around town over the years and they are amazing at what they do.

Powerful and brave. People with elemental abilities that can range from fire, water, earth, wind, electricity, and metal. They all have the desire to make our world a better place and to help the less fortunate and the powerless.

It's unsettling to know that there are still people around with no powers at all. Forced to live as a normal human in a world where everyone else is stronger and faster than you. It's even scarier knowing that there are people out there who can and will use those powers to hurt others. To destroy entire towns with little to no thought about the lives they just took. I shiver at the thought of that group.

The Parasites.

This other group exists for those who fight the onset of their powers and are essentially controlled by their abilities. It's like having a living entity under their skin. I shake my head to clear that thought as I look back in the mirror with a sly grin. I've always dreamed about all the different powers I could develop and how I could use each of those powers to help people, to protect them.

When I turn sixteen, my clock begins, and after that, I have a two-year window to see what powers I will fall into because once you turn eighteen, your chances at having powers become non-existent.

"Aiden, are you dressed yet?" I hear my aunt yell from the kitchen.

"I'll be right out, Aunt Viv!" I holler back as I peel out of my sleep clothes and hop in the shower.

After a quick breakfast of scrambled eggs, sausage, and toast, courtesy of Uncle Matt, Aunt Viv pulls into the parking lot of my high school about thirty minutes later. She quickly leans over the center console to press a kiss to my cheek before I can get my hand on the door handle.

"Aunt Viv, come on, I'm not twelve anymore. Just a simple 'goodbye' is all I need." I scoff.

"Well, too bad; you're my favorite nephew and I'm gonna give him a kiss on the cheek to wish him luck on his second year of high school."

"I'm your only nephew, Aunt Viv." I say as I roll my eyes.

"All the more reason to spoil you."

She gives me a small smile, but it doesn't reach her eyes and at that moment, I know who she's thinking about. My parents. Avery and Cole Rivers.

My parents disappeared without an explanation not long after I was born. Cole left a note saying they hoped one day I would understand, and he asked his brother to raise me in their place.

With the pained look on Aunt Viv's face weighing on my chest, I lean over the console and return her kiss. "Thank you, Aunt Viv. I'm sure today will be great. I'll see you after school."

She gives me a wobbly smile as I exit the car and walk into the brown-brick building while shaking my head. I know that I will do almost anything for that woman, and even though I give her a tough time on things, she knows deep down that I love her and will always cave to her.

As I make my way towards the rows of lockers, I see my best friends, Ivan Grant and Grayson Lukas.

"Hey, guys. Long time no see." I smirk.

"Oh yeah, such a long time. I mean, this summer just lasted forever." Ivan's voice drips with sarcasm as he pushes his eye-brow-length black hair away from his face and his silver-gray eyes shine with mischief.

Gray laughs at him as he adds, "Yeah, it's not like we totally didn't hang out every day during summer break."

"You're lucky I like you two." I say as I shove past my best friends and ruffle Gray's mousy brown hair. "Come on, we're going to be late for class."

I head into the first classroom and take a seat in the middle of the second row as Ivan and Gray follow behind me. Ivan sits a desk ahead of me while Gray takes the one to the left of him near the window.

Ivan turns around to look at me and then at Gray with a sly smile on his face. "Here's to the first day of the next two longest years of our lives. May the schooling be quick and the powers be strong." He lifts a fist in the space between us, waiting for me and Gray to chime in.

"I agree with that!" I smile while resting my fist against his.

"Yeah, me too, on the schooling at least. My family has been lacking in the power department for years, so I'm not holding my breath on that one." Gray says.

"Hey, you could be the one to bring it back. So, don't count yourself out just yet, man." Ivan says.

Gray shrugs his shoulders and we see our teacher, Mr. Jaffe, walk in the door, followed by a few more students. The three of us settle into our seats as the newcomers do the same in what desks are available throughout the room.

I bend down to get my notebook out of the front pocket of my royal blue backpack and when I set the notebook on the smooth surface of my desk; I see a girl standing in front of Mr. Jaffee. She's talking to him while pointing to a piece of paper she places on top of the binder on his desk and I get the feeling she's a last-minute addition to the class.

Mr. Jaffee nods his head and gestures for the girl to take a seat. When she turns around, my breath freezes in my chest. Her dark brown hair is up in a high ponytail and her eyes are a bright sky blue, and her smile alone could power a city block. I can't help but stare at her.

As she takes her seat to my right, I hear Ivan cough before he turns to her with a bright, cocky smile that for a second, makes me want to punch him in the damn face but the words that come from him makes my mouth dry out.

"Hi! My name's Ivan, this guy here is Gray, and the dude who needs to pick his jaw up off the floor, is Aiden Rivers." Ivan winks at me as he turns back around in his seat while Gray punches him in the arm.

At least one friend is not out to embarrass me.

"Nice to meet you, Ivan. Gray." She says with a nod to them while pushing a stray piece of her dark brown hair behind her ear.

She locks eyes with me and I instantly snap my mouth shut. The sound of my teeth clicking together fills my ears and I barely hear Ivan's chuckle when she speaks again, her eyes locking on mine.

"My name is Maya Harper. It's nice to meet you too, Aiden Rivers."

Before I can think of anything to say, Mr. Jaffee claps his hands together, forcing our attention forward and on him as he says with a smile, "Okay ladies and gentlemen, welcome to your first class of the day, World History. I hope we all can have a smooth and informative semester. Now let's begin."

He turns the fluorescent lights off so we can see the PowerPoint shine on the whiteboard and our first lesson of high school begins.

The first three classes flow without issue, and we make it to our lunch break. As soon as Ivan, Gray, and I find a table in the corner of the room, my head whips to my big-mouth friend.

"You really had to out me to her? 'The dude who needs to pick his jaw up off the floor is Aiden Rivers.' Really, man?" I say in a mocking tone.

"Hey, you were the one ogling her, not me." Ivan says as he takes a bite out of his pizza.

"Just wait until either of you like a girl; I'm going to embarrass the shit out of you." I shoot back.

Ivan leans back against the concrete wall with a snort as his silver eyes shoot to Gray and says, "Sure, whatever you say, man."

Gray looks at the food on his plate like it's the most interesting thing in the world, ignoring the both of us completely.

"Who do you–" I begin, but the sound of a tray sliding against the metal table cuts me off.

"Is this seat taken?"

I look over my shoulder and I see her. Maya. Face bright with a smile while looking between me, Ivan, and Gray for approval.

Ivan clears his throat as he takes another bite of his pizza and he hooks his thumb under his chin and acts like he's forcibly closing his mouth. I understand the gesture for what it is and I flip him off. He smiles again as he takes his spot against the wall, smugly devouring the remaining pizza from his plate.

"Uh, no, Maya. Please, sit down." I say while gesturing to the empty seat across from me.

"Thank you." Maya says, and she takes the spot right next to me and I feel my cheeks heat from her proximity.

"So, how's your day been so far?" I ask.

From what I saw of her schedule, we only share a total of two classes. World History in the morning and then biology in the afternoon, just before the school day ends, and for some reason, I am genuinely curious about her day.

"It was good. There are a lot of things to remember and study, but I like a challenge." She beams.

"So where did you move from, Maya?" Ivan asks. "Gray here tells me you're a last-minute transfer."

I shoot a look towards my friends, but Ivan just stares Maya down, his silver-gray eyes boring into her blue ones.

"My dad thought it would be best to finish up the school year here. He went to this school, and he wanted me to have the best education I could get."

I watch as Maya holds Ivan's gaze for a heartbeat, but then she looks away and I get the feeling that there may be more to the story than she's letting on. And again, like the damn watchdog that he is, Ivan must pick up on the same thing.

"You sure that's the only reason?"

"Ivan! I didn't get that information for you to grill her on things that are none of our business." Gray bites.

Ivan's eyes flick to Gray for a moment before they slide back to Maya's. She takes this moment to pull her shoulders back and get into her unbothered demeanor.

"If you must know, my dad thought that if we moved here, great things would happen that would benefit me. Benefit our family." Her gaze slides to mine before meeting Ivan's again. "And I think Dad may have been right."

Before I can wrap my head around what she just said, the warning bell rings, signaling that lunch is about over and to start cleaning up.

"I'll see you in bio, Aiden." Maya says as she stands, taking her tray with her to throw away the trash, before walking out the cafeteria door.

"I like her." Ivan says.

"I didn't know I needed your approval." I growl.

"Hey, I'm older than you." Ivan begins, but I cut him off.

"Oh, come on, by one month!" I snap.

"Again, I'm older than you, so yes, you need my approval. It's the way it is with brothers."

I roll my eyes and I look at Gray, who is the youngest of our group, his sixteenth birthday being in September. "Then good luck when you get a girl, dude. Since it's a *brother's* job to approve your relationships, you have two coming after ya." I say.

"Oh, I don't–" Gray begins, but Ivan throws an arm around his neck and grins down at him.

"Don't worry, man. You'll get there one day and when you do, you'll have so many hotties after ya that I'll have to beat 'em off you."

Gray gives him a small smile as Ivan takes both of their trays and walks toward the trash cans on the way out of the cafeteria, leaving me in their wake. I find myself shaking my head at them as I throw my own trash away, continuing with the rest of my school day and being a horribly distracted bio partner for Maya.

2
Gray

I figured out I was gay about six months after my fifteenth birthday and I really wish I had the balls to tell my friends that I'm into guys, so they will stop teasing me when it comes to going out on dates with girls. And I want to tell them, but I'm terrified that they will have the same reaction as my father. That they'll tell me that I'm just going through a phase and I will get over this *thing*, and get back to a *normal sexuality*.

A few months ago, my feelings were put to the test when I was out with Dad for a police academy reunion with a buddy of his. He brought his daughter, Tracy, along too. And I mean yeah; she was nice and all, and Dad tried to get me to talk to her, but I was more interested in looking at the retired police chief's son instead. His muscles filling out the varsity jacket that shows he's a football player for another local school, and his laugh that was just starting to change from a light squeak to a deeper tone makes my heart race in my chest.

The guy, Ethan, after I finally worked up the nerve to talk to him while standing around the punch bowl, came right out and told me he was bi when I noticed a pride flag earring stuffed into the right lobe of his ear.

I take a sip of my punch before I speak. "My name is Gray. It's nice to meet someone that is able to show what he is to everyone around him." I tip my cup in the direction of his earring.

"You can't? You're talking to me and seem to be pretty open." Ethan says as he drags his eyes down my body, causing shivers to race down my spine.

"The only one I'm open with and that's just in very minor aspects is my mom. My dad," I say, pointing over my shoulder to him drinking heavily with his buddy by the appetizer table, "he's completely against it. Thinks it's just a phase I'm going through."

Ethan's blue gaze bores into mine as he pulls me behind a standing banner of the police county logo that's next to the punch table, so we are out of sight of our parents.

"Have you been with a guy, Gray?" Ethan asks as he caresses the back of my neck.

I swallow at the feeling of his hand on my neck. "No. I mean, I kissed one, one time, but that was a while ago."

"I could help you with that." Ethan says as he leans in closer to me, but for some reason, I freeze.

I want this. I know I do. I want to my first sexual experience to be with someone who knows what they are doing, but something stops me. Before I can really figure out what that is, Ethan is pressing his lips to mine, and it feels...wrong. I try to push past the feeling, forcing myself to kiss him back, and I finally feel myself start to get into it. Opening my self up to let him deepen the kiss if he wants to.

"Let's go somewhere a little more private, Gray." Ethan growls, and I just nod numbly.

He pulls me through a door that's behind him and into an empty hallway before pinning me against the wall. His larger body looms over me as he crushes his lips to mine again as he palms my slowly growing erection through my jeans. His hum of approval of my reaction to him makes me feel just a bit bolder, and I let my body, my mind, take over.

As I begin sliding my hands to Ethan's side, a pair of silver-gray eyes flash in my mind and blood pounds in my veins in response. But Ethan has blue eyes, the silver belongs to...no. Anyone but him. Anyone but Ivan. He's not into guys. He loves the girls' attention he gets at school.

I'm just about to shove that thought to the back of my mind so I can focus on this cute guy in front of me when I hear a voice that makes my heart freeze in my chest.

"Grayson Lukas, get your ass in here right now." Dad growls, his voice slurring from already hitting too many drinks and it's not even been an hour.

Ethan pulls away from me. His unamused gaze sliding from my dad and back to me while I smooth out the wrinkles of my dress shirt, trying to compose myself.

Ethan shakes his head. "Damn, you're right. Your dad's a total tool. Good luck with that, Gray." He scoffs and walks away like nothing even happened.

Before I can even peel myself off the wall, Dad's shoving me against it, forearm braced on my collarbones so he's careful not to leave bruises.

"I thought I told you I'm not going to allow my son to fuck another guy. You are straight, you hear me, boy?"

"I hear you." I whisper, but I don't agree with him and that's the part he misses. Just because I hear him, doesn't mean he's right.

"Good. Now get your ass back in here and talk to Tracy. She's a nice girl. Maybe you can even slip out and mess around with her instead of guys." Dad slurs as he pushes off me and staggers back into the dining hall.

I let loose a shaky breath and just before I walk back in to talk to this girl that I have no interest in at all, my phone lights up with a text message and my lips curve into a real smile. I didn't have this on my face when I was talking with and making out with that asshat earlier.

Ivan

> Hey man. Anything fun going on right now? I'm bored out of my mind.

Me

> No. I'm at my dad's reunion party and it sucks balls big time.

Ivan

> Can you sneak out? I'm sure Aiden and I can meet you somewhere.

Me

> No. Dad's drunk like usual, so I have to drive him home or call Mom to get us.

Ivan

> I wish my old man had another car or I'd come get you. your old man's an asshole

Reading his texts has my eyes welling up with tears. Ivan has heard how mean my dad can be, but he doesn't know the full reason behind it. Right now, though, I don't want to be in the same room with Ivan or else I'm going to see if I have the same reaction to him in real life as I did in my mind.

I send him a thumbs up emoji and I stuff my phone back in my pocket and force myself to walk back in the dining hall and make fake nice with Tracy like my dad ordered me to. But as I stand next to her, I can't help but think I'm talking, touching and even kissing the cheek of the one guy I can't have.

Ivan.

3
Aiden

The next day, I wake up to find my room looking like a Party City just exploded in the confines of my four walls. Balloons, streamers, and a banner that says 'Happy Birthday' in varying, bright colors hang above my desk.

"And the torrent of Aunt Viv begins." I grumble as I take in all the decorations littering my room.

She has always gone overboard on my birthdays and I know she will for as long as I allow her. I think even if I had my own place, she would figure out a way inside just to decorate for me. I smile as I roll out of bed, on time for once, and not needing to be yelled at to get up.

After I get dressed for school, I go into the kitchen and find that Aunt Viv has made my favorite breakfast. Chocolate chip pancakes topped with whipped cream and sliced strawberries.

"Good morning, my birthday boy." Aunt Viv beams as she dances around the island to pull me in for a hug and kisses me on the cheek.

"Morning, Aunt Viv."

As I sit down at the island to eat, Uncle Matt comes into the kitchen from the dining room. When I look over my shoulder at him, I notice he tugs his sleeves down over his arms and I catch the barest hint of something white against his skin but the book he holds in his hands grabs my attention before I can think anything of it.

"Happy birthday, Aiden. Your aunt and I talked last night, and we agreed that this is something we thought you would like to have." Uncle Matt says while he places what looks like a photo album in front of me.

I look back at him as he stands next to Aunt Viv, pulling her into his side while his right arm lovingly rubs her back.

"A photo album?" I ask incredulously as I look over the book in my hand.

"Open it." Aunt Viv urges.

I sigh as I open the cover and when I see the first picture, my head whips around to my aunt and uncle, then back down to the album in front of me. I see the only picture I have of my parents. The one where Avery must have just had me. Her auburn hair slicked with sweat, but her face is bright with love and exhaustion, and I am wrapped in a baby blue blanket, crying in her arms.

Cole is standing over her shoulder, his dark brown hair wild like he was raking his fingers through the strands; but I can see how proud he is of us in the way he looks at his wife and at me. My heart aches at the sight of their faces and I wonder, not for the first time, why they left me.

As I turn the pages, I see more pictures of them, all smiles and laughing, whether it be at a picnic or Christmas parties. One picture is of Uncle Matt and Cole standing beside one another, beers in their hands, while standing in front of the same grill that sits out back on the patio now.

They look so much alike, but Uncle Matt's smile is bigger and Cole is a little taller than his brother. I notice the bright blue and black lightning bolt tattoos that crawl up Cole's arms and neck, only to end right below his jaw. I know that with his markings going up that high; he is a powerful lightning wielder and my chest swells with pride, knowing he was so strong and that he was part of The Protector's of Power.

Maybe that's why they had to leave me. Maybe they had a mission for The Protector's of Power and then they died.

I look over my uncle in the picture and I notice his bare torso and arms and I start to wonder why he didn't get any powers. Before I can voice that thought, Aunt Viv comes around to make me flip the final page, and it's of my parents, but the other two men and the woman in the picture are ones I do not recognize. Cole's arms, which proudly show his lightning tattoos, are linked with Avery's, and her own flame tattoos delicately travel the expanse of her forearms.

Then my attention moves to a man with black hair on Cole's left. When I look into his brown eyes, I get the feeling he's older than he looks, but it could be the black tribal-looking tattoo crawling down his neck and disappearing into the collar of his shirt that makes him look different. There is a woman on this man's arm. Her blonde hair and blue eyes shine brightly and she looks just as distinguished as the guy next to her. Then the last guy, his blonde hair and green eyes, stare back at me, and I realize that his skin is empty of any markings, but I get the feeling not to count him out in a fight.

"Who are these people?" I ask.

"Just friends of your parents." Uncle Matt says as he looks at the picture.

"That was taken a few years before Avery and Cole got married and had you." Aunt Viv says.

"Really?" I ask as I glance back down at the picture before me. I drag my eyes away as I meet my aunt and uncle's gaze and with a pleading look, I ask, "Why did they leave? What happened?"

Uncle Matt lets out a frustrated and tired sigh. "We... don't know."

I stare at him as he gets lost in the fabric of his sleeve. Like a memory takes hold of his mind and he's reliving it.

"Bullshit. You do. Why can't you tell me?" I snap.

"Aiden, please. I don't want to have any arguments about them, especially on your birthday. I will say this; I'm sure they had their reasons, and I trust their judgment." Aunt Viv says as she looks to Uncle Matt and he gives her a swift nod.

"Alright, fine." I say.

I stand from the island when I notice that it's almost time to leave for school and Aunt Viv unties her apron and tosses it on the counter before she walks over to grab her purse from the rack next to the front door.

"Aiden." Uncle Matt says, his voice tight and firm.

I stop in my tracks and look back at him, waiting for him to continue.

"Don't ever use that tone with me again. We all have our reasons for doing things we did in our lives. One day I hope you will understand, but for now, you have to worry about your own life and what may happen at any time over these next two years."

I let a defeated breath flow through my nose and I nod my head once. "I'm sorry, Uncle Matt. It won't happen again."

"Good. Now get to school." He says with a tight smile on his face.

When I get to school, I'm not surprised to find Ivan and Gray near my locker, but who I am shocked to see standing beside them is Maya.

"Morning." I greet all three with a smile and a small wave.

"Morning." Maya says. "I heard from a little birdie that today is your birthday, Aiden." She says as she looks towards Gray and he looks anywhere else but my direction.

"Sorry, she overheard me and Ivan talking about going over to your place tonight after school." Gray explains.

"That's okay, Gray." I pat my friend on the back as I turn to Maya. "Thank you, Maya." I grin, and then a thought hits me. "Would you like to come over and celebrate with us? I know my aunt will have plenty of food made for an extra guest."

"Sure." She says without thinking much about the offer.

I grab my notebook from my backpack and write my address down on the top corner of the paper so I can still use the page later for notes and hand it to her.

"I'll see you after school then." She says as she pockets the paper and in one swift motion, she rises on her toes, kissing me on the cheek before she darts into the classroom across the hall.

I stand there dumbfounded for a moment. She just kissed me. The most beautiful girl in the school kissed me.

"You still there, Aiden. Do I need to send out a search party for your brain?" Ivan chuckles as he smacks me on the back.

"Screw you, man." I say as I shake my head and toss what I don't need in my locker.

"Just making sure she didn't short-circuit ya." Ivan smirks as he and Gray walk into the classroom.

Later that evening, Uncle Matt, Aunt Viv, Ivan, Gray, Maya, and I are all gathered around the dining table. Aunt Viv fixed her famous parmesan chicken and roasted potatoes along with a homemade marble cake with white buttercream icing.

The two-layer cake shows symbols representing the various abilities of The Protector's of Power, alongside the question, 'What will yours be?' written in red icing. On the top in the same red icing is *Happy 16th Birthday, Aiden*. Everyone sings Happy Birthday—which I always feel awkward sitting for—then we have our cake and just talk for a while until it's time for my friend's parents to come and pick them up.

After everyone leaves, I help Aunt Viv clean up the kitchen and help her with the dishes. As I'm drying off a cake pan, my aunt bumps her shoulder with mine and she's wearing a wide smile on her face.

"So, Maya was cute." She teases in a sing-song voice.

My face heats as I meet my aunt's gaze. "Yeah, she's alright, I guess." I say, trying to play it cool.

"Oh, my gosh. You are just as bad of a liar as your uncle is." She laughs. "If you like her, you need to tell her, Aiden. A girl always likes a guy who is true with his feelings."

I finish drying and putting the cake pan away and when my aunt hands me the other one; she doesn't let go until I meet her gaze again.

"And in case you didn't know, she likes you, too. I caught her looking at you several times."

"Okay, yes, I like her. I've been thinking about asking her out, to be honest." I grumble.

"Well, do it. I can take you all to the movies this weekend. Or you can walk the mall and buy her something with your allowance." Aunt Viv offers.

I smile at her ideas, and that's exactly what I do. Once I worked up the nerve a week later, I ask Maya out. When she happily accepts my offer, I take her to the movies, where Aunt Viv and Uncle Matt chaperone, sitting just a row behind us. I know at least my uncle doesn't watch a single moment of the movie because I feel his gaze singe the back of my head. But I realize that as long as I have Maya at my side, I don't worry about it too much. She makes everything better, no matter what's going on around me.

The more dates we have, the more at ease we become with one another. And while we are in front of my aunt and uncle we only hold hands and kiss on the cheeks, but when we are at school, I find her in between classes and I go to one of our favorite corners by the emergency exit and we kiss each other senseless, but she controls where my hands go, which is no higher or lower than her waist.

"I love you, Maya." I whisper one day in the midst of our heated kiss, and my heart freezes in my chest.

Is it too early to say this? Mid-August to mid-October is not long enough for me to be stupid enough to say something like that. She pulls back from me so she can see my face and I hope she can see the truth in my mismatched eyes. She lifts her left hand to caress my cheek and I lean into her touch.

"Aiden." Maya begins.

"I'm sorry, it was too soon. You don't–" I begin, but she cuts me off.

"I love you too." She says with a bright smile.

I lean in to kiss her again and her soft moan fills my chest, but I force myself to pull back before I push for more from her. She swipes her thumb over her ruined lip gloss and I give her a smug grin.

She rolls her eyes and then she smiles up at me while wiping her lip gloss from my mouth. "My birthday is tomorrow. Why don't you come over to my place and celebrate with me and my parents?" Maya asks.

"Okay. I'd love to." I say with a grin.

The warning bell rings before I can think of leaning in for another kiss, and I sheepishly glance over my shoulder before looking back at her. "We better go before someone catches us."

"Why do I get the feeling that you don't really care if anyone catches us?" She asks with a raised eyebrow.

I chuckle and lean in for that kiss I was holding myself back from taking but pull away before she can thread her fingers through my hair.

"You're right, I don't really care, but I know you would, so I'm trying to honor that."

A cute tint of pink flushes her cheeks and I pull her from our little hiding spot and down the hall toward her locker. "I'll see you tomorrow." I give her one final peck on the cheek and force myself to walk away.

4

Aiden

The next night when Aunt Viv drops me off at Maya's house, I toy with the bow of her present, a simple necklace with the October birthstone dangling from the center, resting inside the gift-wrapped box on my lap.

I go to open my door, but my aunt stops me with a quick kiss on the cheek. "You two are so cute together; have I told you that?"

"Only every day since I started taking her out." I say with a half smile.

"I feel you two are good for each other. Just take it slow, and I know everything will work out for you two."

"I will, Aunt Viv." I say as I finally make my way out of the car and onto Maya's front porch.

When I hear Aunt Viv drive away, I knock on the door and a man who I assume is Maya's father answers.

"Hello, Mr. Harper. I'm Aiden Rivers."

"Ah, yes. Maya's told me all about you. Please, come in." He says while waving me in with a forced smile.

"Aiden!" Maya calls from the couch and she jumps up to meet me in the middle of the living room.

I wrap my free arm around her and turn my head just in time for her kiss to land on my cheek. I hear her small intake of breath at my reaction and I hold her for a moment before angling my mouth next to her ear, my breath causing a ripple of gooseflesh to bloom in its wake and I feel pride fill my chest knowing that I did that to her.

"I won't let you look bad in front of your parents. If anything, I will be the one to kiss you if you want. That way, they'll hate me and not be disappointed in you."

"Aiden." She whispers back.

"I care about what people think about you and how you perceive yourself." I say and then I pull away, releasing her from my embrace. "Here, for you. Happy Birthday."

She looks from me to the gift in my hand and takes it with a loving smile and I know it's from more than just the gift. I give her a wink as she opens it and her cheeks go from an embarrassed flush of pink to an expression of wonder at the necklace in the creme-colored box.

"Oh, Aiden, it's beautiful. Thank you." She leans in for another hug and she whispers in my ear. "Kiss me."

I pull her back enough to place a gentle kiss on her lips and I immediately hear her father clear his throat at my actions. I pull back from my girlfriend with a knowing chuckle that only she can hear. I mouth 'told ya' before glancing over at her father for a moment.

"Sorry, sir. I got caught up in the moment." I say by way of apology.

He makes a noise deep in his chest like he wants to call me out, but Mrs. Harper calls from the kitchen that dinner is ready and Maya pulls me with her into the dining room.

Dinner goes by in a flash, and while it's tense between me and Mr. Harper since I kissed his daughter in front of him, Mrs. Harper at least tries to make friendly conversation as we eat.

After we finish dinner and sing *Happy Birthday,* I ask Mrs. Harper if she would like my help with the dishes, which she happily accepts.

"So Aiden, tell me, have you gotten your powers yet since turning sixteen?"

"No, not yet. But it's still early, so we'll see." I say with a shrug.

Then, as I hand her another dish to dry, she leans into my side and says, "I saw what you did with my daughter."

I panic for a moment and I think about every single interaction between me and Maya tonight, and I'm not sure what she's referring to.

"When you first came in. I watched you two from the little window there." She says as she points to a window built into the wall of the kitchen. I didn't notice it at first because I realize that there is a panel she can close if she wants privacy. "Tell me, did you plan that little kissing stunt, or was it just all a simple coincidence?"

I chuckle as she takes the plate to dry it and I look back into the soapy water to search for another plate. "Yes, I planned that. I told Maya that if she wanted to kiss me to let me do it that way, you all would hate me and not be disappointed in her."

"I like you. You're a true gentleman, and I love that for my little girl. *But* that doesn't give you free reign over her. You two are still in high school and have a long while before you are adults, and I expect you to be a *gentleman* to my little girl. Am I clear?"

"Yes ma'am. My Aunt tells me the same thing."

"Good." Mrs. Harper says.

We finish up with the dishes right as Aunt Viv pulls up to take me home. I wanted to take Maya on the front porch to say goodbye to her in a little more private setting, but her father was adamant about not letting her out with me. So, I settle for a quick hug and a kiss on the cheek as I walk out the front door.

Ivan

I decide not to go to Maya's birthday party, one because she didn't invite me, but two tonight is the night my old man and I spar in the basement so my body can be ready for when my abilities develop.

My family line usually manifests metal or earth abilities, so the body needs to be sound in order to handle the strain the power puts on the muscles. Hence, my intense training sessions three times a week. The only difference this time is I invited Gray over to train with me. I don't know why I did, but when he noticed me looking into Tae Kwon-Do and Jiu-Jitsu techniques on my phone during lunch one day, he seemed interested.

I'm sitting on the couch in the living room, wrapping my knuckles in athletic tape, when I hear a car pull into the driveway. I watch through the window as Gray hops out of his mother's car, then he waves goodbye to her before shutting the door and running across the grass and onto the porch.

"Dad! Gray's here!" I shout down to my father as I pass the door to the basement while making my way to the front door so I can open it for Gray.

"Yo, Gray. Thanks for coming over, man. You are going to love this." I smile.

"My dad's been trying to get me into sports, so this may be just the thing to get into." Gray says, but I can hear a bit of a sour tone to his voice.

"Come on, we got a whole setup in the basement. Just wait until you see what my old man has built for me."

I lead Gray down the unfinished plywood stairs and into the bare concrete walls of the basement. A punching bag hangs in the corner to the right, and a bench press is on the opposite side with free weights in all different sizes resting beside it. There is a treadmill against one of the walls near the back, and finally mats are laid throughout the room to practice hand-to-hand fighting techniques.

"Wow. This looks cool, Ivan." Gray says in awe.

"My dad made most of the weights here. Being a metal wielder comes in handy a lot more than you realize." I say with a smile.

"Right, you are my boy! And if you're anything like your old man, you will fall into the same power. Now enough yappin' and let's get to fightin'."

Dad tries to grab for the back of my neck, but I move at the last minute to block his attack with a solid hit to his forearm and I ram my elbow into his nose when I see that he's open for my own attack. He recovers quickly and then he bull-rushes me into the adjacent wall while landing a few well-placed punches to my side before I bring my hands down like a hammer to knock him in the back of the head.

He backs away from my attack and that gives me the opening to try to land a solid punch to the face, but when my fist connects with his cheek, I almost feel the bones want to pop in my hand.

"Damn it, Dad! No fair! Stop making metal under your skin." I whine.

"I never said these fights would be fair, son." Dad grins.

I shake my hand out to ease the ache as I glance over at Gray and give him a small, pained smile. "See, it's fun." I grimace when I try to roll my hand into a fist and the ligaments in my fingers bark in pain.

"Yeah. Looks like a blast." Gray says while rolling his eyes.

"It really is, Gray, when you're taught the right ways." Dad says. "Ivan, why don't you show Gray here some of the easier grapple moves while I get some water for all of us." Dad instructs while he points to another set of mats in the corner of the room.

"Sure. Come on, Gray." I say as I make my way over to the mats while pulling my shirt over my head. Gray follows my lead, but he keeps his shirt on as he patiently waits for my next instruction.

"Okay, so right now, let me show you how to get out of a rear choke." I say.

When I walk in front of Gray and put my back to his chest, I see a flash of panic fill his eyes and I give him a soft smile.

"Don't worry. You're not going to hurt me with what I'm about to show you." I say. "Now put your right arm around my throat."

He pauses for a moment more before he finally relents and wraps his right arm around my neck. At the last possible second, I grab his forearm and I sit into my stance before I swipe my left leg behind his right and I easily drop him onto his back on the mat.

"See? Nice and easy." I grin.

"That was fast." Gray says from below me.

"Yeah, and that wasn't even as fast as it can be." I say as I grasp him by the hand and help him back to his feet. "Now it's your turn."

"What?"

"Yeah. You do the same thing to me now." I say as I pull him into my chest.

When his body collides with mine, something flutters in my chest for a moment. Before I even allow myself to think what the hell this is about, I shake my head to push the odd sensation away as I lift my left arm and quickly wrap it around his throat. And just like I showed him, Gray drops into his stance and puts me on my back quicker than I even thought possible. In my shock at his strength, I grab his shirt on the way to the floor and he ends up falling on top of me.

Our faces are inches from one another's. So close that I can feel his breath on my cheek, and I can see that his eyes have the barest hint of honey brown in random areas, giving some variation to the dark brown coloring that I never noticed before.

"Why the hell do I care about his eyes?" I ask myself.

But before I can tell him to get off me, Gray suddenly leans into me and my eyes widen when I feel his lips press into mine. That fluttering comes back to life in my chest, begging me to act on something I don't understand.

I feel Gray start to pull away, but before he can even move, and before I can comprehend what I'm doing, I'm chasing after him, threading my fingers through his hair, and pressing my lips against his. I barely hear Gray's raspy intake of breath before something drops against the floorboards upstairs.

The sudden noise seems to snap us both back into reality, and we quickly scuttle away from each other. Both of us panting from whatever that was. I swallow hard and just stare at my best friend. I can't even begin to comprehend what just happened before something flashes across Gray's features and he's on his feet.

"I'm sorry." Gray whispers before running upstairs and out the front door.

I race after him up the stairs and I rip open the front door a moment after it closes to watch as he runs across the yard and down the street. "Gray! Come back!" I yell.

"What happened? Did you hurt him, Ivan?" Dad asks as he walks out of the kitchen to join me by the front door.

I look back at my dad, and I shake my head. "I don't know."

"What happened?" Dad asks again.

I pause for a moment, but the look in my father's eyes tells me I can be honest with him and in this moment, I need someone with a level head to get me out of my own. So, with nerves wracking my body, I tell him what happened.

"Do you like Gray in that way, Ivan?" Dad asks after a moment.

"I don't know. I didn't even know that Gray really went that way." I say. "I mean, he never talks to girls, but I just thought he was shy."

"I'm sure you'll figure out something, son. I'm not going to tell you what to do; you have to figure that out for yourself. But know that whatever you decide, I will support you in any way I can." Dad says.

I can only nod as I look back over my shoulder and hope that Gray got home safe.

5

Gray

When Ivan texted me that he wanted me to join him for a workout, I figured I would lift weights with him and ogle him silently from a distance. I did not expect him to pull me into his chest or to put me on my back in a way that made my heart skip a beat or I never would have come over.

I almost had a panic attack when he told me to try to take him down, but something in his silvery gaze seems to smolder when he looked at me. Like he's feeling something that he's not completely understanding, either. Or it could just be me pining over a guy I have no shot of having. And with him being shirtless is not helping matters either.

When Ivan's arm wraps around my throat, my breathing hitches and I react on pure instinct and remember what he just showed me a few minutes ago. I sweep his leg out from under him and when he falls backward, he's caught off guard by how fast I moved and he's grabbing onto my shirt, pulling me down with him, and we fall on top of one another, my hand braced on his smooth, slightly defined chest.

His eyes lock onto mine and it's like he's trying to memorize my irises or it could be just me imagining it because I'm doing that with his. He has little streaks of black running through the grey that make his eyes look exactly like steel. His breath caresses my cheek, and that makes me react. I lean in and press my lips to his and the heat that flares in my blood makes me feel like I'm soaring and plummeting at the same time.

I try to pull back, but to my utter shock, Ivan chases me. Threading his fingers in my hair and pressing his lips to mine. I let out something that's close to a breathy moan as I feel myself harden at his actions towards me, but before I can even think about pressing my mouth deeper against his, something clatters from upstairs and we break apart and scatter to opposite sides of the room. My heart is pounding in my chest and this is nothing like I experienced with Ethan. I have a damn heartbeat between my legs and in my head and I want to tackle Ivan and do it all over again.

As that thought crosses my mind, I know a look of panic floods my face before I'm saying, "I'm sorry," and rushing out of Ivan's basement and running down the street toward my house a few blocks over.

Luckily, my dad's not home and I run right into Mom as I burst through the front door.

"Gray, Honey, what's wrong?"

"I...I..." I stammer. Can I even talk to her about this? Will she even understand? God, I wish I could talk to *someone* about how I feel.

"Gray, please talk to me. You act like you've seen a monster." Mom says gently as she leads me over to the couch while running soothing circles down my back.

"You may view me as the monster." I whisper.

"Grayson! Why would you say that?"

"Because, Mom! I kissed Ivan this evening."

She looks at me like I've grown a third eyeball and I shake my head as I begin to get up off the couch, but her hand on my arm stops me.

"How did he react?" Mom asks. "How do you feel about it?"

I look back at her in shock. She's never asked me about how I feel about my feelings towards other guys.

"Do you like him?"

"Yeah." I sigh. "But I don't think he likes me that way. I mean, he loves the girls' attention he gets at school."

"Have you told him?" Mom asks.

"No. And I can't. If this kiss didn't mess things up between us, I don't want to ruin our friendship over something I can't have with him since he's not even bi."

"Well, only you know how he may react." Mom says, giving me a loving kiss on the cheek. "And don't let your father's words get in your head. I want you happy, Gray. I won't try to tell you any different, because I don't know what it's like to love someone the way you do. But I do know love is love and I want that for my son."

"Thanks, Mom." I say with a small smile, but even when I go into my room, I won't admit anything to Ivan about how I feel about him. I'm just too terrified of how he'll react.

Ivan

The next morning at school I find Aiden and Maya waiting by our lockers, but I don't see Gray, and his absence makes my chest constrict to the point of pain.

"Did he make it home last night? I should have tried to call or text him, or his parents."

"Good morning, Ivan." Aiden says with a wave in my direction.

"Morning." I say as I look over his shoulder like Gray will just appear out of nowhere.

"You okay, Ivan?" Maya asks.

I shake my head. "Have you heard from Gray?"

"Yeah. He said he's not feeling well, so he's going to be skipping class today." Aiden says.

I'm glad that he made it home, but I'm pissed that he messaged only Aiden and not all of us, like we normally do in our group chat. And I'm pissed that he's running from something he did, and before I can even talk to him about this whole thing.

"Okay. Hopefully, he feels better soon." I say as I walk into our first class of the morning and try to keep my shit together for the rest of the day.

Once I get home later that evening, I run into my room, pull my phone out of the front pocket of my jeans, and open a private text message to Gray while I sit on the edge of my bed.

Me:

Gray we need to talk about what happened man.

I see that he read the message, but I don't get a response from him. I let out an aggravated sigh as I message him again.

I wait for a few minutes, just staring at my screen, but this time I don't get a read notice on my message.

"Damn it." I growl as I lock the screen and toss my phone on my nightstand.

"Still nothing from Gray?" Dad asks from my doorway.

I jump at the sudden intrusion and silently scold myself for not hearing him come by my door.

"No. He's ignoring me. And he wasn't in school today either."

"I would just give him time, Ivan. Maybe he's still figuring things out for himself, too." Dad offers.

After he leaves and as the black screen of my phone stares back at me, I suddenly know what I'm going to do tomorrow if I see Gray at school.

The next morning when I get to school, I see Aiden, Maya, and finally Gray, but I brush right past him with a dark chuckle and walk over to one girl I have had my eye on this year. I mean, yeah, she's cute. I don't think totally my type, but she will do for what I have in mind.

"Megan, hey." I say, trying to sound all cool and collected.

"Ivan." She chuckles nervously.

"Hey, I was wondering, would you like to go out on a date with me? Say tomorrow night?"

"Oh, my God. Yes!" She giggles. "This is a dream come true! You are so hot."

I mentally roll my eyes at her flirting, but when I look over her shoulder and glance at Gray, I see exactly what I wanted to see. Shock and a hint of hurt in his brown eyes.

You don't wanna own up to the move you made buddy, then I'm going to act like nothing happened.

"Well, you're pretty cute yourself, Megan." I give her my best sultry smile and she practically melts in front of me. "I'll pick you up tomorrow night at seven."

I give her my number and walk away from her, passing right by Aiden and Maya with a smile, but I completely ignore Gray this time. I can almost feel his eyes on my back and it takes everything in me not to turn around and yell at him for leaving the way he did and for ignoring *me.*

During lunch that afternoon, I eat outside in an effort to stay away from the prodding eyes of Aiden, but I should have known better. The nosey asshole follows me outside and sits across from me at the picnic table.

"What is your problem with Gray?" He asks with a raised eyebrow.

"Nothing. We had a fight the other night and I'm not talking to him right now." I reply as I take a bite of my sandwich.

"What the hell was the fight even about?" Aiden presses. "It's not like you to hold a grudge. If someone pisses you off, you usually throw some hands and then it's all over."

"It's none of your business, alright." I snap as I quickly finish my sandwich and stand to my feet, gathering the empty wrapper before walking over to the trash can to throw it away. "Just stop asking questions, dude."

As I'm walking away from a dumbfounded Aiden, I pull out my phone to text my dad and tell him about my plans tomorrow night so he can make arrangements to drive me on this date with a girl I know nothing about.

As I step out of my old man's car the next night, I walk up to Megan's house to pick her up for our date at a local eatery. I actually find myself having a good time with her. She tells me that after she's out of high school she wants to be a veterinarian because with the water-wielding ability she has, she will be a great asset in surgery.

"I'm sure you will be amazing at whatever job you get, Megan." I say.

"What are you going to do after high school?" She asks.

"I don't know. I haven't gotten my powers yet." I tell her as I rub my hand over my bare forearm.

She reaches out to caress my hand, and I freeze at her touch for a moment. I take in the feel of her skin brushing against mine for just a heartbeat longer before I act on something that I had playing out in my mind all afternoon.

I lean over the table and I press my lips to hers for a heartbeat, two, three, before pulling away. I see the blush creep into her cheeks at my action and the feeling that I have blooming in my chest lets me know exactly what my next move will be.

After paying for our meal and taking Megan home, I ride with my old man in silence for a few minutes before his voice is filling the space around us.

"So, did this impromptu date show you what you needed to know, Ivan?"

I think for a moment and I look at my dad and nod. "Yes, it did."

Once we get home, I make my way up to my room and I send one final text message of the night.

Me:

Gray. I'm just gonna act like nothing happened the other day. I'm still your best friend and I am going to act like it. Now it's up to you on how you act with me. Night man.

I don't even look for a read message, I just lock my phone and turn in for the night.

When the next morning comes and I go to school, I act like nothing was even bothering me. I go back to my normal self. Arms slinging over Aiden's and Gray's shoulders, giving Maya a wink, which makes Aiden want to punch my lights out, and I keep it casual with Megan.

I do keep an eye on Gray for the next few days and he's finally coming back out of his shell around me and I feel a sense of familiarity settle in my chest and maybe even something a bit more.

6

Aiden

After the odd fiasco with Ivan and Gray, the rest of the school year goes by quicker than I thought it would. We celebrate Ivan's seventeenth birthday at the end of July and so far no powers have manifested from any of us, but we hold on to hope that it will happen soon with the one year we have left.

Once Uncle Matt is finished cleaning the pool, I send out a mass text to our group chat to invite everyone over.

Me:

> Hey! Uncle Matt said the pool is open for business. Y'all wanna come over for a swim?

Gray:

> I am there!

Maya:

> Yay

Ivan:

> Sounds good. I'll be there

About an hour later, we all gather out back, sitting at the large oval glass table on the stone patio, as we wait for Uncle Matt to uncover the pool and skim the top for some stray leaves that came off the cover. As soon as he gives the thumbs up for us to dive in, I jump to my feet and pull my shirt over my head.

"Finally! Let's go guys." I say as I take a step away from the group.

Maya slips out of her floral cover-up, her orange one-piece bathing suit hugging every curve in a way that my hands are itching for. I take a breath, forcing myself to look away from her before I react to the slowly building desire in my blood. My eyes then land on Ivan's tall form as he unfolds himself from the seat, takes off his sunglasses and tugs his own long sleeve shirt over his head then tosses it on the arm of his chair. What I see staring back at me makes my jaw drop.

I turn to Maya and she is just as shocked and speechless as I am, but when I look at Gray, he is just quietly taking in Ivan's muscular arms. Watching the beginnings of rippling muscle that he's been working on the last few months flex under his skin.

"Ivan, when did that happen?" I finally ask.

I take in my friend's naked torso, at the tattoo-like markings of gray, black, and bright white, with hints of orange that resemble chains. They spiral from the middle of his chest, snaking their way across his collarbones, where they then come to the apex of his shoulders before branching off in two different directions. One way extends down his biceps and wraps around his forearms, stopping just before his wrists. When my eyes travel back up to the top of his shoulder, the images then crawl up his skin to the middle of his neck.

"Three nights ago. I didn't want to show you all until my old man could help me control it. For the first few hours, I was doing nothing but dropping pieces of metal all over the house." He chuckles and I take in the gold rings around his steel grey irises. The sign he didn't fight the onset of his abilities and he's part of The Protector's of Power.

We all watch as Gray finally stands and slowly walks over to Ivan. His eyes fixed on the tattoos. Gray lifts his hand as if he wants to touch Ivan's skin, to trace those markings, but Ivan's snort of what sounds like annoyance makes him stop short and he snatches his hand back, clutching it to his chest like the sound bit into flesh.

"I know. I'm gonna have to beat *everyone* off me now. These tats make me too irresistible." He says with a smirk playing on his lips, and Gray laughs nervously.

I roll my eyes at Ivan and pull Maya along with me to the pool and help her up the ladder so she doesn't slip. When Maya's form dips below the water's surface, I begin to climb the pool ladder after her. I pause, looking back over my shoulder to see if Ivan and Gray are following, but I notice that Ivan is standing ramrod straight. The muscles in his slowly broadening shoulders and back are rigid as Gray steps closer to Ivan, slowly inspecting his wielding tattoo.

"You two jumping in or what?" I shout before I let myself think too much about their interaction. Maybe Gray just likes the design and wanted to study it.

This seems to break whatever it was between them, and Ivan smacks Gray on the shoulder as he runs across the length of the patio, leaping off the side, and races across the yard. As Ivan gets closer to the pool, he makes an iron pole right before us; the metal leaking out of his hands just before hardening into something solid.

When I think he's about to run right into the pool, he shoves the pole into the ground and pole-vaults into the pool. The force of him crashing into the water sends waves over Maya's head, the spray drenching me and forcing some of the pool water out over the side before the waves finally calm down.

"Ivan! I'm going to get you for that!" Maya shouts as she swims over to him to splash him in the face a few times.

"I'll help you with that, Maya!" I grin as I dive from the top of the ladder and swim in behind Ivan to put him in a firm chokehold, pulling him under the water for a moment before letting him back up to the surface.

"Gray, get in here and help me with these two!" Ivan laughs as he goes to splash Maya again.

Gray grins and scrambles up the ladder, diving in the pool with us where he comes after me from under the water and grabs at my ankles, knocking me off my feet to pull me under the water.

After he lets go and we break through the surface, I shake the water out of my hair like a wet dog and I give Gray a moment to wipe droplets from his face before I go after him.

"Oh, it's on now, Gray! Maya, don't go easy on metal boy there!" I laugh as we all have this mock fight in the water and we track how many times we can pull the other under the surface.

By the end of the night, Ivan wins, much to my dismay. I still say he cheated a few times and used his metal underwater to either trip us or make us heavier and easier to pull under. He denies it, of course, but we laugh it off since we are all still having a blast either way.

After Ivan and Gray's parents pick them up, I am on the front porch, sitting with Maya on the wicker loveseat, waiting for her dad to come and get her.

"I had a great time today. Thank you for inviting me over." Maya says while tucking a strand of her dark brown hair behind her ear.

"I'm glad you came over." I say as I lightly run the middle finger of my left hand over her forearm.

Goosebumps flare to life on her skin and I feel an odd sense of pride flow through my veins that I was able to get that kind of reaction out of her.

"And Ivan's power." She begins, her voice shaking at my touch, and I reluctantly pull my hand away.

"Yeah. It was pretty badass."

"I can't wait to see what powers you and I fall into." Maya says as she looks at her hands, turning them over in her lap like they hold the answers to her inquiry. "I always wonder which one I will get."

"Me too. The waiting game is driving me nuts." I say as I drag a hand through my hair. "But what makes it a little easier is that I know whatever power I get, I'll be able to help people with it. To keep them safe." I look down at her, and she lifts her head up to meet my gaze. "To keep *you* safe.

Pink flushes her cheeks, and she looks away from me with a shy smile playing at her lips. I hook my index finger under her chin, gently coaxing her head up to look at me for a moment before I press my lips to hers. She takes a sharp breath in through her nose as her hand comes up to rest in the middle of my chest. I know she can feel how fast and hard my heart is beating against my ribs for her.

Before I can deepen the kiss, her father's car pulls into the driveway; the roar of the engine causing Maya to jump in my arms. I reluctantly back away from her, but I can't help the smirk on my face when I hear the little whine bubble from her throat.

"Remember, Maya, I want your father to hate me, not you." I say as I stand and help her to her feet and down the stairs to meet with him on the sidewalk.

Her father gives me a stiff nod, and he walks away with Maya at his side.

As the weeks go by, Ivan is getting better and better with his metal abilities. He's working out more, so he's able to handle the extra strain that his power apparently puts on his body. Which makes sense, I guess. He needs to be able to be strong enough to lift whatever shape or weapon he makes.

This year I notice we have a new student join us at the last minute and as soon as I meet this guy's gaze, I am instantly on alert. I don't know what it is about him, but his whole presence feels like trouble. His jet-black hair is pushed back and off to the side, covering the left side of his face.

But those eyes.

Hard, lethal-looking brown eyes stare back at me. I see what looks like a healing bruise around his right eye and as I look further over his face, I notice his lip is split, too.

"That's Mason Jasper."

I turn around to see Gray walking up to us, his eyes landing on Mason.

"He's a transfer from another county. On his last transfer, actually from what I read. No other school wants him. He's always getting into fights and barely attends class." Gray explains.

"Then he better stay in his fucking lane." Ivan growls.

I look over at my friend, and I see liquid metal drip from his fingertips. A few drops splash onto the floor before he closes his hands in a tight fist, stopping the flow from his palm.

"I'm sure he will, Ivan." Gray says softly.

"Yeah, and if he doesn't, then we have the big bad metal guy to beat his ass." I joke, trying to lift the tension from Ivan's shoulders.

"Damn straight." Ivan snaps.

The next few days thankfully go by without incident from Mason yet. But I think him beating me up would hurt less than going through yet another birthday and not developing abilities.

7

Aiden

Maya's seventeenth birthday comes around in October, and her parents throw her a small party. Only me, my aunt and uncle, Ivan and Gray, are invited. But I don't mind, that means I can dance the night away with her in my arms and I don't have to share her with another stranger. I mean, Gray danced with her and Ivan is currently spinning her around the dancefloor, but they feel like my brothers, so it's different. They aren't going to make a move on her like some other asshole would.

After I grab a quick drink from the punch bowl, I bring Maya one as I cut in on her and Ivan mid-dance and apparently mid-conversation.

"May I have my date back, please?" I ask with a smile.

"Sure. Thanks for the dance, Maya." Ivan grins as he gives her an exaggerated bow and steps away.

"You're welcome, Ivan. You're an amazing dancer." Maya says with a bright smile.

"I keep telling Grayson that, but he doesn't believe me." Ivan replies with a nervous chuckle while searching for his friend.

"Well, you'll have to show him then." Maya says while taking the punch from my hand and taking a sip while giving him a wink.

"Maybe you're right." Ivan says as he gives me a pat on the back before walking away.

"Hello again, beautiful." I say as I wrap my arm around her waist and begin to slowly sway back and forth with her as the tempo of the song changes to a soft melody.

"Hi. Are you having a good time?" Maya asks as she drains the rest of her punch and sets her cup on a nearby table.

"As long as you're with me, I'll always have the time of my life."

Ivan

As I'm dancing with Maya, the quick tempo keeps us moving around the dance floor along with her parents and Aiden's aunt and uncle. I notice over her shoulder that Gray is leaning against the wall, plastic cup in hand, watching us. But I get the feeling he's watching me.

"You okay, Ivan? You've been kinda quiet." Maya asks as she looks up at me. She tries to look over her shoulder to see what I'm staring at, but I turn her at the last second.

"Yeah. I'm good. Just can't believe you're seventeen now." I lean in closer as the song fades into a slower ballad.

"Yeah, it's hard to believe how fast time has flown by." Maya says.

I hum my agreement near her ear because that just happens to be where my mouth ended up, but when I flick my eyes up, they land on Gray and I swear I see a flicker of hurt flash in his brown eyes that makes my chest ache. Ever since I've gotten my powers, and when he traced my tattoos when no one was looking that day on Aiden's patio, we've been awkward around each other. A stolen glance here. A quick tender touch from me, at least, from time to time. But nothing like that night in my old man's basement or that caress from this summer.

"Shit." I whisper.

"What's wrong?" Maya asks as she finally looks over her shoulder. When she sees who I've been looking at, the grin that spreads on her face makes my heart freeze in my chest.

"What's that smile for?" I force myself to ask.

"You tell me." Maya challenges while stepping away from me a bit and crossing her arms.

I pull her back into me as the next song comes on and thankfully, it's a quicker beat again. "I—" I begin.

What can I tell her? Do I even understand what it is I feel for Gray? But then, as soon as that thought crosses my mind, I know in my soul what I feel for him. I notice Aiden grab a cup of punch and he starts to make his way back toward us and I know he's about to cut in on my dance with his girlfriend.

"I'm in love with Gray." I blurt out before Aiden comes up to us.

I know Aiden doesn't pick up on Maya's knowing wink after I stupidly said I *keep telling Grayson I'm a good dancer*, but her words ring in my ears, *Well, you'll have to show him then*. And I know her words hold a double meaning that only she and I share.

I didn't intend on saying anything to her about how I feel, but damn it, when his eyes landed on me dancing with her and the flash of hurt that flared in his eyes, it was like a knife to my chest and I couldn't help it.

I've never told anyone, other than my old man, about my feelings for Gray, but with Maya, she gave me the strength to finally make that leap. To finally let him know that I'm not going to be afraid of this anymore.

The music changes to a faster pace as I reach him, and I stand in front of Gray, extending my hand to him.

"Would you like to dance?" I ask, but my voice cracks a bit at the nerves fluttering in my gut.

At first, he looks at me like I've grown a third eye before his eyes glance over the dancefloor.

"Ivan, I don't—" Gray begins, but I cut him off.

"Or we can go in the hallway if you don't want eyes on us. I seriously don't think anyone will care, but if that's what you want, we can go." I chuckle before I say, "I don't care; I just want to share a moment with you. To have a *real* moment with you." I admit.

Gray nods, "Okay. Let's go in the hallway."

I grin like a damn fool as I grab his wrist, leading him through the swinging door and into the hallway. As the door shuts behind us, the music becomes a muffled sound, but at the same time, the silent hallway is just as loud with only me and Gray in the space.

"So what do you mean by having a *real* moment with me, Ivan?" Gray asks as he leans against the wall while looking me up and down.

I smirk as I scrub my hand over my face. "I know for the last two years, I've been brushing you off. I've been keeping you just on the cusp of friendship. But I've seen the looks you give girls that come up to say hi, and when I compare them to the looks you give me." I shake my head. "The way you *touch* me, Gray, no matter how fleeting, I know you'd never touch a woman that way. And to be honest, I don't want you to touch anyone else but me. I don't want to be touched by anyone but you." I say.

"You don't mean that, Ivan." Gray says as he starts to push off the wall to walk by me.

"Yes, I do." I grab his shoulder and pin him against the wall.

"I thought it was just a phase or something I was going through. But I *tried* to actually go out with a girl once, you know that. And you want to know what I thought about when I kissed her?" I say as I push in closer to him, my nose almost touching his. Gray doesn't say anything, so I answer for him. "It was you, Grayson. All I could think about was how it would feel to have *your* lips against mine again instead."

"Ivan." Gray whispers, but to my ears it sounds like more of a defeated sigh.

"Tell me you don't think the same thing."

Gray reaches out a hand, his index finger lightly tracing the chain link design of my wielding mark on my skin. The sensation is like a bolt of electricity and it goes right down my spine, ending between my legs, making me hard for him in a way that I've never been with a woman before.

"You want to know who I thought of as my anchor when I developed my powers?" I ask and Gray looks at me with confusion shining in his brown eyes. "It was you, Grayson. I made myself focus all the pain, the heaviness that was weighing my body down, and my fear on this handsome face of yours. Because I knew with these powers, I could protect you from almost anything."

"We won't be accepted—" Gray begins, but I cut him off.

"I don't give a fuck who likes it or not. I want you and that's all that should matter. So, I'll ask this, Grayson Lukas, do you want me just as much as I want you?" I ask as I press my hips into his, letting him feel just what his proximity, what his touch, does to me.

His moan does me in and I trace my nose up the column of his throat, over his Adam's apple, and over the ridge of his chin where I am staring into his brown eyes. I arch an eyebrow, letting him know I am still waiting on his answer.

He swallows before nervously nodding.

"I want to hear it, Grayson." I growl as I lightly wrap a hand around his throat. His eyes flare, but this time instead of hurt, it's with shock, and something more. Desire.

"I want you too, Ivan." Gray says as he lifts his hands, resting his palms on my chest. "I've wanted you since I kissed you in your dad's basement."

"That's all I wanted to hear." I say as I lean in to press my lips firmly against his and they feel just as good as that first time in my old man's basement.

His hands trail up my neck, then into my hair as he rocks his own hips against mine and I feel he's just as rock hard as I am. I find the button on his dress shirt and just as my fingers are about to start pushing them through the holes, the door opens behind us and Aiden fills the doorway.

"Oh shit! Sorry!" He begins, but then his eyes take in who I am kissing and they go from embarrassment to utter shock, and I feel a protective heat flare in my chest.

"You got a problem with who I'm here with?" I growl.

Aiden lifts his hands, palms towards me, and backs away a step. "No man. I don't. Honestly, I've been kinda wondering about you two, but I just thought you were just tight friends. But now it makes sense, so I'm happy for ya." Aiden says, then while hooking his thumb over his shoulder, he adds, "We are about to eat dinner and cut the cake. You two wanna join us?"

"Yeah. We'll be out in a minute." I say.

Aiden turns around, but before he walks back through the swinging door, he looks back with a smile. "And be who you want to be out here. If anyone says anything, I'll kick their ass for you." Then he walks away.

I look back over my shoulder at Gray and I see a slight flush to his face and I can't help the chuckle that bubbles from my throat. "What's it gonna be, Grayson?"

He thinks for just a moment before he takes my hand with a smile and we walk out onto the dancefloor and celebrate Maya's birthday. Eating dinner, cutting the cake, dancing, and taking pictures. All done together.

8

Gray

I'm quiet as Ivan drives me home. Still reeling from what happened tonight. The guy who I have been secretly pining over for the last two years actually likes me back. I feel over the moon right now that I can't really put words to all the emotions fluttering in my stomach. I look over at Ivan as he drives. His left hand on the steering wheel, his right on the shifter. I swallow at the memory of that hand around my neck just an hour ago.

As we turn down my street, I reach out to run my fingers through the close-cut hair at the nape of his neck. He sucks in a quick breath before glancing over at me and giving me a bright smile.

"I love it when you touch me, Grayson."

A corner of my mouth lifts, loving that I have this effect on him. "You do, huh?" I tease as I trace my index finger over the line of the chain link tattoo on his neck.

I want to run my tongue over those marks. To drive him to the breaking point before shoving us both over the edge as we take turns sinking into each other. Before I can form those desires into words, Ivan pulls up to my house and all the lingering desire fades in a heartbeat.

There's a single light still on, telling me that my dad is still up, and my chest tightens with a twinge of apprehension.

Ever since Dad was forced to retire after he was shot while working with the sheriff's department a few years back, he's taken to drinking to drown himself in his sorrows. He's never drunk enough where he doesn't know what's going on around him and forget about it the next day, but drunk enough where he has no filter at all.

After Dad caught me with Ethan, he makes sure that I do 'man's work.' Getting my hands dirty while helping him work on the car when it needs maintenance, mowing the grass, fixing things around the house, and even going to the local jiu jitsu sessions.

The jokes on him though, I love doing all that 'mans' work, because, guess what, Sherlock, I'm still a guy, no matter who I like. But I do my best not to look at any guys. To not check them out, but when it comes to Ivan, I can't keep my eyes off him.

Ivan lets the engine run as he puts the transmission in park and motions for us to get out of the safety of the cabin. As I close my door and walk to the front of the car, Ivan grabs me, caging me against the hood. I stare in shock when I feel his hand caress my face.

"Where did you go? You have that look on your face like you were thinking about something." Ivan asks.

I chuckle; he knows me much more than I thought he did. "I was just thinking how sexy those wielding marks are on you and how I'd love to trace each and every one." I say, trying to bring the mood back up.

"While I like the sound of that, I know what you were thinking. Your old man doesn't know, does he?" Ivan asks, his steel-grey eyes staring into mine.

"He does but he—"

I am cut off mid-sentence when Ivan leans in closer, pushing me harder against his car and kissing me soundly on the lips. I stand in total shock for a moment before I snap and thread my fingers through his hair. His growl of approval tumbles from his chest and down my throat.

I move one hand from the back of his head, wanting to slip it under his shirt so I can trace the muscles of his defined stomach and chest. I get to the hem of his shirt when I feel his own hand move to stroke me through my jeans.

"Ivan." I whine, actually freaking whine like a needy little thing, which is something I am not used to at all, but with Ivan, he brings out different sides of me I never knew existed.

"Just wanted to give you a little teaser of what it will be like with my hand wrapped around you while I make you explode with pleasure." He whispers against my ear.

I feel myself harden at his words. I know he feels it just like I do and the smirk that flashes on his face makes my knees shake and pressure build low in my back.

"I'll stop. For now." Ivan croons as he releases me and steps back. "Only because, the first time I make you come, I want you in my bed, and not with your old man staring over my fucking shoulder like a creep."

I look over his shoulder, and my stomach drops at my father staring at us through the window of the living room. His face is red with anger and my mother stands just over his shoulder, her face filled with shock at the scene, but I also notice a hint of fear in her eyes. Ivan sees it too, and he grabs my hand, practically dragging me up the porch to my own house. Dad opens the door and I can tell he's about to say something to Ivan, but Ivan's words cuts him short.

"I brought Gray back safe and sound, and I expect to see him tomorrow the same way, Mr. Lukas." Ivan says in his most chipper, unthreatening tone, but I hear the threat for what it is and so does my father when his glassy eyes narrow on Ivan.

Ivan then slaps a picture into my palm and I notice it's the one we took from the party. He snuck a kiss to my lips when Maya had the camera in her hand.

"So you can remember me when we aren't together." Ivan says with a wink.

"Get in here and get in your room, Gray." Dad snaps.

"Good night, Grayson." Ivan smiles as he backs away from the porch so I can enter the house and close the door behind me.

I start to make my way towards my room when Dad's voice stops me.

"I don't want you seeing him, Gray."

"Dave, shut up." Mom snaps. "Gray, go to your room, please." She adds gently.

"Mom."

"Go. I'll be there in a minute."

I take a breath and I go to my room just as I hear Ivan's Mustang drive off, and a part of me wishes that I could have gone with him, but I know for a fact that Dad will not let me out of this house and live on my own until I'm eighteen.

About thirty minutes later, Mom comes in and sits beside me on my bed while gently rubbing my shoulder.

"So, it's true? Ivan likes you too?" She asks, her voice shaky.

I nod, not trusting myself to speak right now.

"Your father isn't going to let this be easy for you. But you probably already know that. So just don't give him anything to work with until you can be your own man."

I look up at my mother, shock filling my chest.

"Mom, I—" I say, but I can't make words form in my head.

"I'm glad that you found Ivan. If it had to be anyone, I am glad it's him. I've seen how protective he's been for you and Aiden over the years and from what he said tonight, oh, that got under your father's skin." She smiles. "I haven't seen him that amped up in a long time."

"Thanks, Mom. You may not agree with my love life, but thank you for being agreeable to it." I say.

"It's not my life to have a say over; it's yours, Gray. And as long as you're happy, that's all I want for you."

Tears prick at my eyes and Mom pulls me into her loving arms while pressing a kiss on the top of my head.

"Good night, Gray. I love you, my son."

After mom leaves and I get a quick bath, I find myself looking at the picture Ivan gave me and his words replay in my mind.

You were my anchor.

I pull up Google on my laptop and I search for the definition of a wielder's anchor, and what comes up makes my chest swell with happiness and pride that the thought of me was able to help Ivan in the best way possible.

9

Aiden

Two days after Maya's party, I asked Ivan and Gray to meet me at the forest we found a few years ago so we can have privacy to talk about what happened between them the other night. I'm still reeling a bit, but yet as I look back, I'm stupid for not seeing it sooner. I just want to make sure they are alright and to let them know that I still think of them as my brothers, no matter what.

Ivan's Mustang pulls up beside Uncle Matt's Subaru that I borrowed and he and Gray get out and walk over to the little campsite we made where we all sit on the make-shift log stools. Ivan to my left and Gray on my right, the cold fire pit sitting in the middle. Just like old times.

"Hey." I say.

"Hi." Gray says.

"Yo, what's up?" Ivan asks.

"Nothing really. I just wanted to see how y'all are doing?"

"We're fine, Aiden. It's not like we came out and said that there were aliens walking the planet." Ivan chuckles.

"I'm sorry. I just, I didn't see this coming. But now that I think about it, I realize that it was there between you two all along. I just want you to know that I still consider you my brothers, no matter what." I say as I glance at both of them to make sure they are hearing my words. "We are stuck together as friends and there is nothing you can do to get rid of me." I smile.

"Thank you, Aiden. We appreciate that." Gray grins.

My phone suddenly starts ringing, and I glance at the screen.

Mr. Harper.

I answer it on the third ring. "Hello, Mr. Harper."

"Aiden." The firm tone of his voice sets me on edge and I put it on speaker when I feel Ivan tense up beside me.

"What's wrong?" I ask.

"Maya is asking for you. Please come by the house. She's asking for you to be her anchor."

Her anchor. She's getting her abilities, and she wants me to help her through it.

"I'll be right there."

Without a word, Ivan, Gray and I all jump into our respective vehicles and race over to Maya's house.

It seems like it takes forever to get to her place, but I am finally in her driveway. As soon as I slam the door to Uncle Matt's Subaru, her father opens the front door, and I rush through the threshold.

"Where is she?" I demand, my eyes searching the house for her.

"I have her out back. I don't know what power she's developing, so we wanted her out of the house." Mr. Harper says.

With Ivan and Gray on my heels, we venture out into the backyard where I see Maya lying on a chaise lounge. Her moans and cries of pain filling my ears.

I rush over to her and slowly pull her into my chest. "I'm here, Baby Girl." I croon.

"How did you—" She begins to ask, but I shake my head, telling her not to talk.

"Your dad called me." I smile.

I begin to let her out of my embrace so she can lie back on the chaise when another wave of pain wracks her body and I immediately pull her to me again and I sit behind her, letting her back rest against my chest.

"Aiden, please." She pants. "Let me go. I don't know what power I'm getting. I don't want to hurt you."

"I'll be fine, Baby Girl. I'm here for you. Just try to relax." I whisper as I slowly rub her left arm in an effort to calm her down.

"How long has she been like this?" Gray asks.

"About ten minutes." Mrs. Harper answers.

"So we have a while to go, I assume." Mr. Harper adds.

"Then it's a good thing I'm comfortable because I am not moving from here until it's all said and done." I promise.

As the minutes tick into the first hour, Maya's groans and yelps of pain become more and more frequent, but I hold her tight to my body. Keep telling her she's going to be okay. That it's going to be over soon. I have to keep her body and mind calm to the point where she's accepting what's going on. I refuse to let her fight this and become a Parasite. To become like Mason. I'd die before that happens to her.

As the second hour begins to creep onto us, Maya begins to sweat. I see the beads of it on her skin, erupting out of each and every pore. Gray brings over a washcloth without a word and I gently blot Maya's face to dry it, but what I wipe away is immediately replaced by more. She moans loudly again as she clutches her chest and tries to wiggle out of my embrace, but I place a gentle kiss on her temple while tightening my arms.

"You're okay. Just relax."

After I pull my lips back from her skin, I realize that I don't taste the saltiness of her sweat like I thought I would. It takes me all but a heartbeat to figure out what power she's getting and before I can even voice the thought; she screams the most pain-filled scream of the evening and she grabs for my forearm that's wrapped around her waist. And when she does, I feel how her power can save lives just as much as it can destroy them.

She's a water wielder, and with her right hand gripping my forearm, she's both giving and taking the water from my body. The sensations happen back to back to back, and I can't fully comprehend one before the other takes place.

"Aiden, let her go!" Ivan yells.

"No." I grind my teeth against the pain in my body.

"Aiden, please." Maya begs. "I don't want to hurt you." She screams as she fights through another wave of pain.

"You won't hurt me, Baby Girl." I whisper. "But you need to focus on whatever you're feeling and control it. You got this." I hiss a breath as her power begins taking the water from my body again. "You chose me as your anchor; now use me like one. Center yourself, Maya."

The next sound from her throat is a growl of determination instead of pain. She uses her left hand to grip my thigh, grounding herself while taking slow, deep breaths. I can tell when she starts to get a hold of her power because it feels like the remaining water in my body is floating within the cells. I feel like I am on the verge of passing out from dehydration, but I force myself to hold on to consciousness. For her, I would hold on to anything I could to stay with her. She lets loose another breath and I feel the water fill my body, giving life back to the cells that were almost destroyed.

"You did it, Honey." Mr. Harper says as he crouches by the chaise and taking his daughter's right hand and giving it an approving pat.

I am taken aback by the delicate flowing pattern of white, blue, and bits of gray on her right forearm. It looks like water was splashed on her skin and it dried as a reminder of what her power is.

"You were amazing, Baby. Good job." I praise.

"Are you okay?" Maya asks as she spins in my arms, hands splayed across my chest, eyes searching my face.

"Yeah. I'm good." I give her a lazy smile and hope she can't see the exhaustion that is filling my body from what her power did to me.

"Okay." She lifts her right hand to caress my cheek as she gives me a sad smile and somehow I know that she knows I'm not as fine as I'm leading her to believe. "Thank you for being my anchor. I hope I can return the favor one day soon."

She leans in and before I can even think to stop her, gives me a sound kiss on the lips. Her father clears his throat and Maya pulls back with a sheepish grin. I find the energy to shake my head at her as she slowly lifts herself off me and into her mother's waiting arms.

"You should rest, Maya. That was a lot to go through." Mrs. Harper suggests.

"Yeah, and we should take Aiden home, too." Ivan offers.

"I can drive the Outback home if you want, Aiden." Gray says.

I nod at Gray and weakly toss him my keys as Ivan helps me to my feet so he can walk me through the house, but before Maya's mother takes her to her room, I make Ivan stop walking so I can get Maya's attention.

"I'll be sure to call you when I need an anchor too, Baby Girl. We're in this together, right?" I ask.

She nods as her mother ushers her through the house and Ivan makes me walk out the front door to take me home where I flop into bed and I immediately fall asleep before my friends even close my bedroom door.

10

Maya

It's been three days since I developed my water abilities and Dad has been training me non-stop. He says that it's important I get the hang of such a resourceful power quickly, and especially since my left forearm is still bare.

Dad said that I am becoming something special, and if it wasn't for the sensation that's been pulling in my chest for the last few hours, I would tell him he's full of shit. But I can feel something in my Soul Power is churning and pulling to the left of my body.

I'm out in the backyard, which has now become my training grounds as long as weather permits. If not, I train in the garage. God forbid if I damage something in the house. I roll my eyes as I create and shoot a geyser fifty feet in the air, then immediately make the water molecules evaporate from the air as if nothing was there a moment before.

"I want that geyser to one hundred feet by the end of the day, Maya." Dad barks.

"Gee Dad, a little praise would be nice." I mumble.

"What was that?" He snaps.

"Yes, sir, I hear you." I say.

"I don't want to hear backtalk from you, missy." Dad growls.

"Harry. Go easy on her. I mean, she's already doing better than I was at her age." Mom says, her own water tattoo cascading up both her forearms.

"She's got to be strong, Rita." Dad says. "She's part of it; I know she is."

"Harry, I think we would know if she is." Mom says gently. "Maya, why don't you call Aiden and see if he wants to hang out for a while? You *deserve* a break." She glares over at Dad.

"Okay." I say as I rush into the house before Dad can say anymore to stop me.

I pick up my phone off the table and I call Aiden.

After three rings, he answers and his voice fills my heart. "Hey, Baby Girl. What's up?"

"Hey, you wanna hang out for a while?"

"Sure. Actually, I want to show you something anyway." Aiden says, "You mind if Ivan and Gray come too?"

"Sure. The more the merrier."

"Great. I'll pick you up in fifteen minutes." Aiden says.

I hang up the phone and I rush into my room, grab a clean set of clothes, then dash into the bathroom to get a shower and put fresh makeup on.

Fifteen minutes later, Aiden arrives in his uncle's Subaru as promised. I wave goodbye to Mom because Dad apparently is still outback sulking at my departure, and I walk out the front door and slide into the passenger seat.

"Hey, Aiden." I smile.

"Hi, Babe."

"So, where are you taking me?" I ask.

"It's a surprise. But It's one I think you'll like." He says with a smirk.

I feel the anticipation build in my chest, but at the same time, I feel that Soul Power pull happen again too. I squeeze my left hand, trying to will the sensation away. It lessens, but never fully dissipates. I begin to think that I need to tell Aiden what could be going on with me, but I feel the car slow to a stop. The hum of the tires against asphalt turns to the quiet roll over something softer, and I find myself surrounded by a forest.

"Where are we?" I ask.

"The guys and I found this a few years back and we come here when we need some privacy and somewhere quiet for a while." Aiden says while looking over at me. "Come on. Ivan just pulled up."

I look over my shoulder and Ivan's dark green Mustang pulls up beside the Subaru. I smile as I open the passenger door while Aiden walks over to my side, threading his left arm behind me and resting his hand at the small of my back. His touch is always so careful, so mindful of where he places his hands. It makes me feel safe, and I relish in that feeling.

Ivan and Gray stand before us in much the same way as Aiden and I, but Ivan has his partner pulled close to his chest with his arm slung over his shoulder, both of them wearing loving smiles.

I'm glad that Ivan finally told me about his feelings for Gray and that I was the one to give him the push he needed to stop dancing around the elephant in the room when it came to the two of them.

I give Ivan a knowing smile as I tug at Aiden's hand. "Show me what is so amazing about this forest."

Aiden nods as he wraps his fingers in with my own and he leads me deeper into the forest, with Ivan and Gray following a few steps behind.

As we make our way through the trees, it's so quiet. I don't even hear any birds singing in the treetops. But the silence is welcoming. When we walk through the line of pine trees and into a hollowed-out space, I see a little setup of what looks like a campsite. Four logs that have been cut into makeshift stools that surround a fire pit that has been constructed from cement pavers.

"I remember when we first made this stuff." Gray says as he sits on one of the logs.

"Yeah. Took us all day, but it was fun. We were almost too tired to enjoy it, but Aiden insisted we at least light the first fire to break it in." Ivan says, taking his spot next to Gray.

"Hey, you were going on vacation the next day, Ivan. I wasn't going to wait a week before enjoying our hard work." Aiden chuckles as he playfully shoves his friend on the shoulder, almost knocking him off the log he was sitting on.

Ivan then bounds to his feet, a wicked smile forming on his lips, and if I didn't know Ivan, see the twinkle of mischief in his steel-gray eyes, I would be afraid for Aiden right now. But Aiden just smiles back at him, beckoning for Ivan to come at him in a friendly fight.

I just shake my head as I take Ivan's spot next to Gray. "Can you remind me why we hang around them?" I ask as Ivan makes a thin metal pipe and hooks it behind Aiden's knees, taking him to the ground.

"I think it's because, for some reason, we love those dumbasses." Gray jokes. "And when it counts, they are there for us."

I nod my head, "Yeah, they are." I say as my chest begins to pull again, my left side going numb for a heartbeat before going back to normal again.

I can't help the little groan that bubbles in my throat and I hope that the shouts and laughter from Ivan and Aiden are enough to drown it out from Gray's ears, but I feel his broad palm flatten against my back.

"Hey, are you okay?"

I internally groan again, but this time it's not from the pain in my chest.

"Maya, what's wrong?" Gray pushes again.

I sigh. "I think I'm getting a second power."

"We need to get Aiden over here, then." He says as he lifts his head to see where the guys are.

"No. I don't know what I'm getting. I don't want to hurt him again, Gray." I whisper. "I know I could have really hurt him the other night when my water ability developed. When I got it under control enough to use it, I could feel Aiden dying. I was pulling every molecule of water from his body. What if I get electricity or fire? I don't want to hurt him again."

"But Maya, that's why you chose him as your anchor." Gray pauses. "Do you know why they use anchors?"

I shake my head. All I know is when you develop a power, you need an anchor to get through the process. I was just going to have Dad help me, but he insisted on Aiden being there and I just agreed with no other thought other than making the pain go away.

"Anchor's are picked because that person is one you would never want to hurt and you want to use those powers to protect them from others. That is what helps you get your abilities under control for the first time." Gray says. "It is what keeps you from becoming a Parasite."

"How do you know so much?" I ask.

"After Ivan told me that he thought of me as his anchor, I did some research on it, and that's what it told me."

I nod as I lift my gaze to find Aiden and Ivan still sparring with one another across the clearing. The pain flares in my chest again and I know I want nothing more than his arms around me again. To help me in to this new power.

"Hey, Aiden." I shout, letting some of the fear fill my words.

As soon as my voice hits his ears, he and Ivan immediately stop mid-punch and rush over to me.

"What's wrong?" Aiden asks as he kneels before me.

"I'm going to need you for an anchor once more." I show him my bare left arm. "I'm getting a second power."

Aiden nods and he lifts me off the log and sits down against a nearby tree, pulling me to his chest, his mouth so close to my ear.

"You do what you need to, Baby Girl. I'm right here."

And that's what I do. With Aiden grounding me, his quiet praises and loving touches when I feel any pain, I somehow know how I need to connect to this second power, letting my water and what I now understand is wind, co-exist in my Soul Power as one.

Aiden

It's rare for someone to have two powers, but it's not impossible. And here is Maya, my girlfriend, becoming something so rare right in front of me while I hold her close to my chest.

While I am ecstatic for her to be something so special, something so important to our society, I can't help the tinge of longing for my own powers.

Both Ivan and Maya have abilities and I am still powerless, and the closer we get to the end of this year, the more I start to dread it.

11

Aiden

I have five months left. Once I turn eighteen, I'm done for. I'll be powerless for the rest of my life.

As that thought starts to take root in my mind, I slowly begin to dip into bouts of depression. Most of the time when I'm around Ivan, Gray, and Maya, I can cover it, but when I'm alone, it hits me. Gripping my chest like a vice, and one word flares in my mind:

Failure.

At times when I can't take the confines of my bedroom, I drive to the forest and aimlessly walk around. The idle sounds of the wind rustling through the branches of the trees, the chittering of squirrels, and the chirping of birds fill my ears and help ease the heaviness in my mind. That is, until even the forest becomes quiet and those raging thoughts come rushing back in.

My parents were a few of the strongest people in The Protector's of Power group, from what I understand. So how can their son be powerless? I shake the thought from my head once more when I see a white rabbit dart in front of me and disappear through a thick line of trees that I've never noticed before. So, in an effort to keep my mind from spiraling again, I follow after the animal, and I'm glad I did.

With a small smile pulling at the corners of my mouth, I walk to the middle of a hollowed-out grove and I immediately know that Maya would absolutely love this place. My steps are lighter when I begin to imagine the look of awe on Maya's face when she sees this hidden gem in the woods. As I make my way back through the forest, I make mental notes of how to get back to this clearing, occasionally breaking a branch as a marker of sorts.

As I hop into my new truck, a maroon Colorado; an early birthday gift from my aunt and uncle, and begin to make my way back home; I don't feel the boulder of worry that was in my chest when I first came here tonight. It's not completely gone, but it's a river stone in my gut now instead of a boulder. Present, but not crushing.

Once the sun is shining again after a few days of rain, Maya and I take advantage of the warm weather and are alone for once out in the backyard. I lead us hand in hand to the oversized hammock that I strung up between two poles, mainly for her, since she loves to feel like she's swinging while lying down. I settle in the blue and white pinstripe fabric and pull Maya down against my chest.

She leans in pressing a firm kiss to my lips before settling down against my body, hands splayed across the left side of my chest while her thumb lovingly moves back and forth over the fabric of my shirt and we just settle into what I think is a peaceful silence, but I should have known better. This woman knows me too damn well.

"You've been awfully quiet lately. What's going through your mind, Babe?" Maya asks.

"It's nothing." I say, trying to bury my worry, my fears that I apparently suck at hiding.

"I know you better than that." She lifts herself off me and settles her weight over my stomach, positioning herself just high enough to still be modest, but low enough that it still drives me crazy.

She then leans in and presses a tender kiss to my lips while running her hands through my reddish-brown hair. I am just about to do something bold and brush my tongue against the seam of her lips in a silent request for me to deepen what she started, but she must know the thoughts on my mind, because she pulls back, her teeth scraping across my bottom lip as she moves. I have to force a growl back down my throat as she sits up on my stomach again, but no matter how far away she is from my hips, I feel myself beginning to harden in my jeans to the point of pain against the zipper.

"Maya." I growl.

"Nope, you don't get any more until you tell me the truth of what's going through your mind." She says as she begins to play with her water ability between her fingers like it's second nature for her.

The water droplets dance like they are suspended mid-air and rolling from finger to finger, then gliding up her arm, over the light blue and white swirling water splash tattoo that wraps daintily around her right wrist and ends in the middle of her forearm. My eyes also take in the white and gray wisps of what look like clouds dancing up her left forearm in the same manner.

I sigh and I tilt my head back as I close my eyes for a moment. "Fine. I'm terrified that I'm down to my last few months for my chance at developing powers, and you won't want to be with a powerless guy."

Maya is quiet for a few minutes, and I open my eyes to find her looking at me. The sun shining down on her long dark hair, gives her natural highlights and making her look so much more beautiful than she was even a moment ago. I stare into her blue eyes, the little golden ring that again tells me she is a part of The Protector's of Power since she didn't fight the onset of her abilities, show nothing but love for me and it fills my chest with my own for her.

"I don't care if you have powers or not, Aiden. I love you for you." Maya says as she leans in to kiss me again, as if sealing the declaration she just made to me. She starts to pull back, but I grasp the back of her neck with my right hand, digging my fingers into her flesh.

"You love me, Maya Harper?" I say, my voice dipping low.

"Yeah, I do. I mean, how can I not? You're hot as hell." She says as she bends her head to kiss the skin on my bare forearm. "Those eyes of yours alone are enough to make me swoon. I get my two favorite colors. Green like the blades of grass or the summer leaves filling the trees, and brown that reminds me of my favorite hot mocha coffee from Starbucks."

"Wow, you must love me a lot because I know how much you adore your coffee." I chuckle.

"I love you even more, Aiden. I am not going anywhere. I want to spend my life with you, that is, if you'll have me."

"Do you even have to ask that, Baby Girl?"

Before I can move her body lower, to show her just how much I want her to be a part of my life, show her how she makes my body come alive; the backdoor opens and Aunt Viv's voice filters through the backyard.

"Kids, it's time for dinner!"

I reluctantly let go of Maya's neck as she gracefully gets out of the hammock and waits for me to join her and lead her into the house so she can have dinner with us.

12

Aiden

When my eighteenth birthday rolls around, I am not as hurt as I thought I would be. With Maya at my side, I still feel like the most powerful guy in the room. And that's saying something because Mason was yet again kicked out of school for getting into a fight with a student when they pointed out that he had red rings around his brown iris'.

Parasite.

The word echoes in my head. I've never seen any of them in the flesh, but from what Mason acted like, I don't want to meet anymore. He looked like he could and would kill any one of us if we just glanced at him the wrong way. He would always go around setting things on fire for no reason other than he could, and no one could stop him.

Once he was out of the area, Maya and a few other water wielders would put his fires out. Pride bloomed in my chest that she was able to help out where she was needed the most, even though it took a while with his fire burning hotter than usual due to his power fighting against him.

As the school year comes to a close for a final time and we all graduate in May, I find myself getting ready to take Maya out on official dates since we no longer have school to worry about, but taking her to the forest right now just doesn't feel right. So I wait and instead decide to take her out to the movies for tonight's endeavor.

I walk down the hall from my bedroom and I find Uncle Matt waiting for me in the living room by the front door. The keys to his car held tightly in his hands and he has a stern look on his face.

"This is your first unchaperoned movie date with Maya; don't make me regret letting you take her out."

"Yes, sir." I say, picking up on his hidden meaning.

"Good. Now have a good time at the movies." Uncle Matt says enforcing that's the only thing we should have fun with.

"Oh Matt, come on. Lighten up on him." Aunt Viv says. "You were his age once with me." She adds as she places a kiss on his cheek.

"Exactly. I was his age once."

"I'm going now. I don't want to hear y'alls escapades in the backseat of a car. Oh God, it wasn't in this Subaru, was it?" I ask, only half joking now that I think about it.

"No. Your uncle had an older Corvette from his grandfather." Aunt Viv says with a smile.

"Oh, good." I sigh as I walk toward the front door.

"But that didn't stop us from a good time." Uncle Matt croons as he kisses his wife deeply. "Hence why you're taking the Subaru. I'm not giving you a *bed* for easy pickings."

"Oh, that's gross! I'm leaving now. Text me in two hours if it's not safe to come back home." I jest as I slam the door behind me.

I pick Maya up from her house fifteen minutes later and she openly kisses me on the lips right in front of her father and I freeze under her body. She hasn't been the first one to kiss me in front of her father since she came into her powers a year ago.

"Maya." I say, with confusion in my tone.

"Let's go." She says a tad briskly as she makes her way to my uncle's Outback.

I quickly walk behind her so I can open the passenger door and help her into the seat. As I walk around the back of the vehicle and open the driver's side door, I pause, glancing up, only to find her father staring daggers at me. Before I can ask what his issue is with me, Maya calls my name and I drop into the driver's seat and drive away. I may have let the tires squeal a bit on the pavement just to get under his skin.

When we arrive at the theater and I buy us drinks, popcorn and snacks, I find us a set of seats near the top of the row so we are secluded but still have a good view of some chick flick that Maya wanted to see. I don't care what it is as long as my girl has a good time and I'm by her side.

I interlace my right hand in hers while I drape my left arm around her shoulder to keep her close to me, and I feel the tension ease from her muscles. I keep my caresses of her body gentle, and I even give her a light kiss on the cheek here and there until she thankfully ends up being all smiles and back to her normal self by the end of the movie.

Once we leave the theater and get into the Outback, both of our demeanors change once we are forced back into reality and we just sit in silence for a bit. The thought of how her father was acting now that there is nothing to distract me, is eating at my brain.

"What was going on with your dad today? I've never seen you that mad at him before." I ask as I take her hand in my own, bringing it to my mouth to press a gentle kiss to her knuckles.

"He... it's nothing. We just got into an argument about colleges, that's all." Maya says.

I can tell that whatever she and her father got into is still weighing on her, and I think about a few months ago when she distracted me from my own inner turmoil, so I decide to return the favor.

I wrap my left hand around the back of her neck and I pull her towards me ever so gently, where she knows there is always the option to say no. To pull away and I'd allow it.

But instead of pulling away, she leans into me, into my kiss, and it feels as if fire floods my veins at the eagerness of her lips against mine. I break away for a moment, long enough to push the driver's seat back and lift her into my lap. As she settles across my thighs, she takes a sharp breath as she finally feels what she does to me against her skirt-clad center. I pull her mouth back down to mine, needing her to be as close as possible to my body and she moves her hips once across the building bulge in my jeans and I groan into her mouth.

"Maya. Please stop that. I don't have condoms with me." I say, but I can't stop my hand from reaching for her breast, anyway.

"Aiden." Maya pleads as she crushes my hand against her breast while tilting her head back at my touch.

Just as I start to knead and tease her pebbled nipple through the fabric of her shirt, her phone starts to ring and she freezes in my lap. "Oh no. Please, no." Maya begs.

"Maya?" I ask, a twinge of fear filling my voice.

"Please take me home." Maya snaps as she moves off my lap and sits back in the seat as she answers the still-ringing phone.

I pull the seat forward and try to subtly adjust myself before I make my way back to her house, but something in my gut doesn't feel right.

I pull up to Maya's house and before I can even put the car in park she gives me a lightning-quick kiss on the cheek, and for a split second I see a tear in her eye before she rushes from the passenger seat and into the porch. I jump out of the car just as the front door slams and locks in my face.

"Maya!" I shout as I pound on the front door. "What's going on?" *Did I push you too far tonight?*

Just as that thought hits me, I take a step backward, then another until I make it down her porch. I look up to a window that's above me and I see her in the window frame, tears streaming down her cheeks, and it breaks my heart.

"Please tell me what I did, Baby Girl." I yell again.

I watch as she moves from the window and my heart leaps, thinking that she'll come down and talk to me, but instead of my girlfriend, I see her father filling the doorway.

"I want to see Maya. I need to talk to her." I demand.

"No. I don't want you to be around my daughter anymore." He snaps.

"Why the hell not? What did I do to her, to you, to say that?" I growl.

"That is something she will tell you when she's able to."

"Oh, that's bullshit!" I fume. I look past him into the house, "Maya! Please, Baby, what is going on?!"

"Get out of here, Aiden!" Her father yells again.

I swallow hard at his words and the only reason I even listen is because I love the girl hiding in this house and I don't want her to see me pummel her father to a pulp for keeping her from me. So, I turn on my heel without another word, and I make my way back home.

Thankfully, it's quiet when I get in and I make my way to my room where I flop onto my bed, pull out my phone and open the text thread for Maya.

Me:

Maya, Baby. Please talk to me. Did I do something that made you feel uncomfortable? You seemed to be into it tonight. Talk to me Baby Girl. Let me fix whatever I did wrong.

13

Aiden

Fourteen days go by without a word from Maya.

I fight with the need to text her, to call her, to race over to her house and demand she talk to me. But I try to hold on to the sane part of me that knows it's not healthy to act that way. She has to have her reasons, right? She just needs time to talk to me, that's all.

As I am sitting at the dining table later that night with my aunt, uncle, Ivan and Gray, I notice that the guys are smiling and whispering to each other.

"What are you two whispering about?" Aunt Viv asks.

"You tell them; it was your idea after all." Gray says with a wink.

"Okay. Gray and I moved in together last week. We just moved in the last box this morning." Ivan announces.

"That's great, you two!" I say, forcing a smile.

"How did you afford to do that, Ivan?" Uncle Matt asks.

"My dad helped me. When I was working for him during high school part-time, I was saving my money and when I graduated, he said he would match whatever I had in my savings account. My dad took my relationship with Gray better than his parents did, so I wanted us to be on our own as soon as I could make it happen."

Ivan says as he wraps his arms around Gray's shoulders and presses a quick kiss to the top of his partner's head.

"Good for you, Ivan. That was a smart move." Uncle Matt praises.

Just as we finish eating dinner, my phone dings with a text message and my heart soars in my chest.

Finally.

I lift the phone from the table and what I see filling the screen makes me see nothing but red.

Maya:

> I can't be with a powerless guy, Aiden. It's over.

I barely hear the voices of those around me as I storm out the front door and I just run. I run across town to her house.

To her now vacant house.

She moved away.

She broke my heart, and she moved away.

She lied to me, shattered my heart and fucking broke up with me over a damned text message over something she *promised* me she didn't care about.

I sink to my knees as I look at the darkened house. The for sale sign is still buried in the yard with a sold sticker plastered diagonally across the center. Silent hot tears stream down my face and neck as I scream into the night, letting all my frustrations bleed through.

I'm powerless.

I'm weak.

Who I thought was the love of my life just ripped me apart on the very thing that I was terrified of.

I hear Ivan's Mustang pull up behind me, and footsteps echo around me when they walk over, but I don't care. I just continue to scream, and cry and curse the world at the shittiest hand I have just been dealt.

Gray leans down next to me, putting a firm hand on my shoulder and he gives me a warm smile, letting me know that he's willing to listen to me.

"She left because I'm powerless." I sob.

Gray shakes his head in disgust. "She didn't deserve you if she left because of that. She thought she could still love you without powers, but it must have been too much. It's her loss, Aiden. Not yours. One day she will realize it, and it's going to be too late for *her*."

"I agree with Gray. She fucked up and I, for one, am never letting her get near you again. Near *us* again. We don't need that toxic shit. She played you like a damn fiddle and no one does that to my friends and gets by with it." Ivan growls.

Ivan and Gray help me to my feet, pulling me away from the now-empty house. As Gray opens the passenger door to the Mustang, he pulls the seat forward so I can slip into the back. When my ass hits the leather and he clicks the front seat back into place, my mind goes deathly still.

I slowly close my eyes and I imagine mental bricks forming in my mind and around my heart. I decide then and there I am never letting anyone get close to me again. It hurts too damn much.

So I just sit in the backseat of Ivan's Mustang, listening to the sound of the tires rolling along the pavement and will brick by brick to form a protective wall around me that's impenetrable.

When Ivan pulls up to my house, I don't say anything when Gray exits the car and pulls the seat forward so I can slip out. I don't speak when I numbly open the front door and walk inside, past my aunt and uncle and into my room. I don't even bother in taking my jeans off. I just collapse into bed and wish this was all a nightmare, but I know better. This is my fucked up reality now and I don't want anything to do with it.

14

Ivan

When I drop Aiden off at his house, I just stare at the front door through my windshield, my engine idling in the driveway. He was deathly silent for the entire ride home, and I know that's not a good thing. He went from hysterics to a deathly calm too quickly.

I saw this happen to my grandfather when I was younger after he lost his wife in a freak car accident. He became a shell of himself and was just going through the motions of life, but not really living it; and I refuse to let that happen to Aiden. I refuse to let that bitch break a good person just because she couldn't live with a powerless guy.

I feel something brush against my arm, a thumb tracing one of the chain links of my wielding mark that is branded into my skin. The touch brings me out of my protective thoughts and I look to my right, where I find Gray staring back at me. He gives me a small smile and I will my body to relax as I sigh through my nose.

"We've done all we can for him tonight, Ivan. Let's go home." Gray says.

"Yeah." I nod as I back out of the driveway and drive to our home.

Just that simple word, *home,* makes my chest swell with happiness and pride and the memory of how I told Gray what I did for him, for us, plays in my mind.

When we graduated, I went to my dad and asked him to help me find a house that I could rent for Gray and I. Once I found the perfect house and signed the leasing agreement a week later; I grab my phone from my pocket with the keys still dangling from my hand and I text Gray.

Me

> Hey. I have something I want to tell you tonight. Can I come by your place for dinner?

Grayson

> Sure? What is this about?

Me

> You'll find out soon, Babe. See you in a bit. Love you. *blue heart emoji.*

When I drive up to Gray's parent's house later that evening in my new green Boss Mustang, I'm giddy with nervous energy. I'm sure Gray will say yes to moving in with me, but I know his father is going to blow up, I just don't know how badly.

I park on the curb and as I open my driver's door; I pat my right front pocket to make sure the keys to the house are still there. Of course they are. I'm worrying for nothing.

I walk up the porch and just as I'm about to knock, the front door opens and Mrs. Lukas greets me with a warm smile.

"Hello, Ivan. Please come in. Gray is in the kitchen helping me with dinner."

"Thank you. I'm going to pop in and see him for a minute." I tell her and she nods as she makes her way into the dining room to, I assume, set the table for us.

I stride into the kitchen and Gray is standing in front of the stove whisking something in a pan. His tight fitted green shirt hugs his body and I watch the muscles in his back flex as he works. I could just watch him all damn day doing random shit and I would walk around with a perpetual hard-on all the time. He turns to grab something off the island and his eyes lock with mine, making him let out a startled yelp.

"Ivan! You scared me. I didn't hear you come in."

I walk around the island towards him and I pin his body against the counter, bracing my arms on either side of his hips. "I didn't mean to scare you, but I loved watching you being in your element." I lean in, dragging the tip of my nose over his cheek before pulling back just enough that my lips brush his when I talk. "I love watching you do anything, honestly."

"I know the feeling." Gray chuckles low in his throat.

I close the distance between us with a bruising kiss, knowing mainly his father can walk in here at any moment. I'm not an exhibitionist in the least, but when it comes to that asshole, I love throwing it in his face of what Gray and I have together. Just as Gray's hips rock into mine and I feel how hard just one kiss already has him, we hear his father's growl as if on cue, rumbling off the walls of the kitchen.

"Quit that fucking shit before I lose my appetite."

"Sorry, Dad." Gray mumbles as he gently pushes me away, but I catch the flash of hurt in his eyes.

"I'm not. You think I like seeing you kiss your woman?" I shoot back with an eye roll.

"Ivan!" Gray hisses under his breath in warning.

"We'll that's the problem right there. You don't like women, do you, boy?" Mr. Lukas asks, his words slurring a bit.

I chuckle darkly. "This is going to make your head spin, old man. I like both."

"Dave, leave them alone. Dinner's almost ready." Mrs. Lukas says, pulling her asshole husband out of the kitchen.

"Why do you always have to push his buttons?" Gray asks as he opens the oven to pull the lasagna out, but he pauses, searching for a hand towel that's hidden behind me.

"'Cause it's fun to fuck with him." I laugh as I move toward the oven, willing a thick layer of tungsten metal to cover my hand. "Here, let me get that for you." I offer as I pull the baking dish from the oven.

"I love it when you do that."

"What, pull a dish out of the oven?" I ask, arching an eyebrow, but knowing he's talking about something different.

"Yeah. We'll say that." Gray chuckles. "Can you take it in the dining room? I'll bring out the salad and the dressing." He instructs as he picks up the bowl he was whisking when I first walked in.

I nod and take the dish into the dining room and before I set it down; I make a small elevated cooling rack so it won't burn the table.

"That's very handy, Ivan." Mrs. Lukas says with a smile.

"Thank you. Being a metal wielder has many uses." I say as Gray sits the salad and dressing down next to the lasagna.

"Oh! I didn't even think to tell you to get a pot holder before setting that down, Ivan."

"Don't worry. I got you, Babe. I'm not completely dumb when it comes to being in the kitchen." I say as I run my now normal hand down his arm.

"Let's eat." Mr. Lukas grumbles, snatching the metal spoon from Gray's outstretched hand.

Anger flares in my chest and I want to snatch the utensil back from him or make it melt in his hands just because I can. Gray must see the thought spiraling in my head because I feel his hand slide to the small of my back for a fleeting moment before he takes his seat across from his mother, but one down from his father. I take a seat on Gray's right, leaving that chair empty beside the insufferable old man.

After we all fill our plates and are several bites in, Mrs. Lukas breaks the silence. "So, Ivan. Gray told us you were the one who wanted this dinner. It's so nice to spend some time with you and get to know you better."

"I feel the same way." I say, looking at Gray, then over at his mom before shooting daggers at his dad. *Nope, don't want to get to know you, buddy.* "But I did actually have something I wanted to ask Gray tonight."

Gray looks at me with confusion lining his gorgeous brown eyes. I take a breath as I pull out the keys that have been burning a hole in my pocket since I've gotten them, and set them on the table in between our hands. Gray scrunches his eyebrows before glancing over at me.

"You have a set of keys?"

I shake my head. "*We* have a set of keys to our own place a few blocks away from here." Gray's eyes snap to mine at the same time his mother's cry of surprise rings in the air.

"Ivan, what are you saying?" Gray asks, voice shaking.

"I really have to spell it out for you?" I chuckle. "I want us to move in together, Grayson."

"Absolutely not!" Mr. Lukas shouts, slamming his fist on the table, making the plates, silverware and glasses rattle. "My son is not moving out and living with a man."

"I'm not asking you." I snap. "Gray is eighteen, and he's able to answer for himself. I just gave you the courtesy of hearing it in person rather than your *son* just disappearing into my bed one day."

"Get out! I'm not listening to your queer shit anymore! My son is *not* gay!" Mr. Lukas roars.

"Dad!" Gray shouts and his father looks at him with anger rolling off him in waves. "I *am* gay! I have been gay since I was fifteen! Stop ignoring the elephant in the room and accept it! Mom has!"

In that moment, I am so proud of my man and *finally* standing up for himself that I want to kiss him right here, right now and really give his homophobic father a show.

"You walk out that door, Gray, and I don't ever want to see you again." Mr. Lukas growls.

I freeze where I stand at his words. I know Gray loves his mother and even his father to an extent, but I didn't really think he would completely kick Gray out of his life. Before I can even think about whether I want Gray to have to choose between me and his old man, Gray's grabbing the keys from the table, then whipping his attention to me.

"I'd love to move in with you, Baby." Gray says and even with what just happened around him, his smile is the brightest I've ever seen it.

"Let's get out of here, then." I say before turning to his mother. "You're welcome to come over anytime once we get settled."

I grab Gray's hand and when I walk him out the front door; I feel like I'm the local commoner stealing away the prince in the middle of the night from his evil king.

As we settle into bed for the night, Gray rests his head on my bare chest while he tenderly traces my chain link markings with his index fingers, and I can't help the shiver that rockets down my spine at his touch.

He smirks at my reaction as he presses his lips to the middle of my chest before looking me in the eye. His brown eyes search mine for a moment and I know he can still see I am fuming over what happened tonight with Aiden, but there is also a question lingering in his eyes and I don't like that thought one bit.

I let my own smirk play on my lips a moment before I flip him onto his back and roughly pin his wrists above his head, pushing them deeper into the mattress. I relish in the primal feeling as the look of shock quickly morphs into desire over his handsome face.

"Get that damn thought out of your head, Grayson." I order.

"What thought, Ivan? I have a few going through my head right now." He teases with a raised brow.

I press my lips to his for a few heartbeats before I trail a few kisses down his neck, but when I get to the soft spot where his neck and shoulder meet, I sink my teeth into his flesh. Not enough to break skin, but enough for him to feel, and the groan that echoes in the room goes right into my ears and down my spine, making me harden to the point of pain in my black boxers.

I kiss the hurt I just inflicted on his skin before I work my way back up to his lips again. When I pull back, we are both breathing heavily and humming with need. Before I act on the growing desire between us, I call him out on the one thought I know is floating around in his head.

"I will never choose anyone else but you. I know I've said this before, but I want you to completely understand it tonight. I don't give two shits that you're powerless. I know that's what was going through your mind right now, and I am going to drive that thought right out of your head to the point that nothing else will fit except you and me."

"Show me just how much you love me, Ivan." Gray pleads as he grabs my erection through my boxers and I growl.

"Remember, you asked for it."

I force his hand away from me, and I slide down his body, kissing my way past the strong V of his waist, hooking my fingers in the waistband of his sleeping pants before pulling them down his hips and tossing them to the side.

His impressive length stands at attention between us, and I wrap my hand around him. Stroking, teasing, and bringing him to that edge, but keeping him from the release that I see glistening at his crown.

"Ivan." Gray groans, flexing his hips into my fist, and I know my man wants more.

I dip my head between his legs, taking him deeply into my mouth with long; slow tugs. Gray moans as his fingers thread through my hair and I give him a few more hard pulls before I pop off him.

"Ivan." Gray whines.

"That's not how I want to hear you say my name, Grayson." I growl.

Reaching to the right, I open the drawer of my nightstand and pull a condom from the box I stashed there. After ripping the foil wrapper in half with my teeth, I slide it over my shaft before squeezing out a dollop of lube onto my hand and spreading it over me.

Straddling Gray's hips, the tip of my erection brushing right where I know he wants me, I brace my arms on either side of his head, and when I lean down close to his ear, I can't keep the possessive growl from my voice.

"Remember when I told you the first time I make you come, I wanted you in my bed?" I feel Gray shiver under me and I chuckle. "This is the night for that, Grayson."

I ease into him, allowing his body to adjust to the size of me. Pulling back to the tip and sliding in a bit more on the next slow thrust, again and again until I'm fully seated in his tight hole.

"Ivan!" He shouts as his legs wrap around the small of my back, pulling me even closer and deeper.

When I hear my name pouring from his lips, I know his only thought is how I feel against him, inside of him and loving him fully. I claim his lips with harsh abandon as I wrap my hand around his throat in just the way I know he loves to be handled.

His fingers claw at my back as I feel his release begin to build, and with one final thrust of my hips, his orgasm erupts between us.

"You're so gorgeous, Baby." I praise as I keep riding him through his release. "You're doing so well."

"Ivan! Don't stop. Please." Gray whines breathlessly, tilting his head back into his pillow as his hips move to meet each of my thrusts, somehow forcing me even deeper and he cries out. "Yes! Right there!"

"Come for me again, Grayson."

And this time, when he obeys my order, I fall right behind him. Praises, curses and growling names fall from our lips as we lose ourselves in one another time and time again.

15

Aiden

Three Years later

I drive over to Maya's house, *eager to pick her up for our date tonight. I walk toward the porch, the lights from inside spilling out onto the* concrete *around my feet. When the door opens, I pull the bundle of purple flowers out from behind my* back *as Maya's form fills the doorway. Her eyes glance from the flowers then to me, and her loving smile then turns wicked. She backs away from me and as I take a step towards the house to stop her; it goes dark a heartbeat later and I'm standing in the middle of her lawn on my knees, staring up at the vacant house.*

The for sale sign spirals down from the sky, almost impaling me from the force as it plummets into the ground. The sold sticker slapped across the sign gleams brightly at me, as if mocking me. Footsteps echo on the driveway behind me. I spin around, *noticing the smug look on Maya's face, laughing at my reaction to her empty house.*

"I never loved you, Aiden. I just wanted you as an anchor to hold on to when my powers developed. I could never be with a powerless guy, no matter how cute."

I wake with a jolt from the nightmare that's been haunting me for the last three years. My breath rushing out in harsh pants as I try to get my bearings again. The navy blue comforter tangled around my legs, and the cool air around me prickles against the sweat on my bare chest. No matter how hard I try, I can never get her damn face or voice out of my head and I'm left with nothing but these nightmares.

I scrub my face with my right hand and groan at the trembling muscles that flutter under my skin. Another sound suddenly blares at me and I jump at the noise filling my bedroom.

I look over on my right and sitting on my black faux wood nightstand is my alarm, and it's blaring at me, letting me know it's seven thirty in the morning. I reach over to the still blaring alarm and pound my fist into the off button with a solid thud.

"Why did I let Aunt Viv talk me into going to college?" I groan.

Aunt Viv and Uncle Matt gave me time to get over everything, or so they thought. They gave me two years. But when it was clear that I was going to do nothing with myself other than work the bare minimum to afford my truck payment, and my share of the car insurance and cell phone bill, Aunt Viv put her foot down and made me go to college to make something of myself. I didn't have the heart to tell her I didn't care.

So like always, she played against that soft spot I have for her and I finally broke down and enrolled in what I am sure will be mind-numbing college courses, for at least an associate's degree in Business where I can maybe get a high-paying job in some Fortune 500 company with accounting or something, and today I'm thankful this is my last semester and all this schooling shit will be over.

I force myself to roll out of bed and I make my way to the bathroom where again like a broken record; I turn on the shower, pull the white curtain closed, wait for the water to warm up, and just look at myself in the mirror.

My reddish-brown hair is cut closer to my head, but long enough in the front that I can somewhat style it. If I ever felt like doing that. I've been working out with Ivan and Gray more, so I've built up more muscle over time, though I'm still nowhere near as bulky as Ivan, but I can hold my own in a fight with him. What I lack in strength, I surpass him in not giving a shit how I win. I just fight dirty until I do. I wait for him to give me an opening and I snap like a snake.

I use to always leave the fighting and protecting to Ivan, since he's a walking weapon with his metallurgy abilities, but I got tired of leaning on people, of being weak. So that is the one thing that I focused on. Figuring out how to fight on my own against those with powers. Mostly up-and-coming Parasites that single out the powerless or those just coming into their powers and don't know how to use them yet. I mostly do it when I can't sleep at night. I walk the streets and I look for those that need help. Plus, the violence helps with my own anger and depression.

Aunt Viv hates that I come home bloody or have to have bones reset more than I like to admit, but it's actually Uncle Matt that I hear at night after they think I've fallen asleep, telling her to leave me alone and let me deal with things in the best way I can. I get the feeling that he somewhat understands what's going through my head now. That I need to be something, even if it's someone else's punching bag for a while. It's my messed up way to protect someone and helps me forget my own personal pain at times, too.

As I stare into my eyes, the mismatched green and brown are dull, calculated, and haunted. Even more so since that damned nightmare this morning. I have been sporting a five o'clock shadow for the last year, keeping just enough on my face to make me look older and rougher, but not enough to give someone something to hold on to in a fight. I shake my head as steam begins to fill the bathroom and I jump into the tub before I run out of hot water.

After finishing my shower, I wrap the towel around my hips and make my way into my room again. I pull a pair of dark wash jeans out of my closet, a black t-shirt, and one of my favorite orange hoodies and get dressed just in time to smell that breakfast is ready and waiting.

I grab my black backpack that is sitting next to my desk from the floor and walk down the hall, where I find Aunt Viv standing at the counter next to the stove, joyfully humming to herself as she's cooking. A timer dings and she pulls the waffle from the waffle press and places it on a plate where one is already waiting for its twin to take the empty space next to it. She hears me walk into the kitchen and she sets the plate on the island for me while drizzling maple syrup over the buttery crust. I watch as each crevice fills with the sugary, sticky liquid and Aunt Viv tops the plate off with a scoop of whipped cream with a satisfied huff.

"The waffles look amazing, Aunt Viv. Thank you." She's the only one who gets my real smiles anymore, and I make sure to give them all to her without a thought.

She turns around and her own smile brightens up her face. Her black hair is pinned up with one of those claw-looking things that women wear, and the little tuft of her hair bounces around as she flits through the kitchen to pour more batter into the waffle machine.

After she closes the lid and waits for the batter to cook, she wipes her hands on her pink and white polka-dot apron so she doesn't get her purple blouse dirty, even though there is a dusting of pancake mix on the collar of her shirt, and she turns to look at me.

"You're welcome, Aiden. Now hurry up or you'll be late for school." Aunt Vivian says, her light brown eyes shining with love.

I look at the stove clock and the pale white font shows it's eight o'clock and I have to be at school at eight-thirty, but thankfully it's a ten-minute drive for me. I quickly devour my waffles, then walk over to the dishwasher, where I deposit my dirty plate on the top rack. I turn to give my aunt a kiss on the cheek before I grab my keys off the hook and walk out into the garage. I push my fist against the button fixed on the wall to open the garage door as I press the unlock button on the keys to my maroon 2018 Chevy Colorado. Once the garage door is open, I throw my backpack in the bed of the truck, drop into the driver's seat at the same time I insert the key into the ignition and turn it over. When the engine roars to life, I back out of the garage and make the drive to my first day of of my last smester of college.

The drive to the University of Colorado is a bit slow from the morning traffic, but I arrive with time to spare. I jump out of my truck and grab my backpack from the bed and then walk into the tall red brick building with the flood of other students. I pull my class schedule out of my pocket which consists of just three classes today, Algebra II, Business Management and I chose Abilities 101 as an elective for credit purposes and the fact that apparently my high school teacher, Mr. Jaffee is teaching that class made me choose it even more.

I make a note of what classroom I need to look for first before making my way through the school. When I find the classroom, I lean against the wall with my backpack resting on the floor between my black and white Converse-clad feet and wait for the professor to arrive.

As the minutes tick by, I start to hear some roughhousing, then laughing and shouting down the hall. I look to my left and I see a few of the university football players toss around a football. But it's not an ordinary football. No, this one is made of fire. Before I signed up for classes here, I had a feeling to look at the sports roster and there was a name on the football lineup that stood out. I couldn't place it at first, but now after seeing that flaming football, the color of it, the deep reds, oranges, and traces of black, I know for sure who the co-captain of the football team is.

Mason Jasper.

I haven't seen him since high school when he was on his last transfer attempt. I was hoping I'd never see him again after he was kicked out, but alas, here we are.

The group of three other players are all tossing the fiery ball around as they continue to obnoxiously laugh, and race through the halls. Mason then pulls the flaming football into his hands from another player and gestures for someone with the last name of Newman printed across the broad shoulders of his jersey to step back a few paces, where Mason can make a pass to his teammate.

Rhett Newman. I remember seeing that name on the roster, but I've never met the dude before in my life.

Just as Mason hurtles the football across the hallway, I feel someone walk up next to me at the same moment that Rhett misses the pass. The ball comes flying for me and whoever just came into my space. I instinctually move in front of the figure behind me, like my human body will protect us from this asshole's ungodly hot fire, but I can't help the automatic movement.

I hear Gray curse behind me and my stomach plummets to the floor like a stone. I turn and start to push Gray down on the ground, using my back to keep the flames from reaching my friend, but just as I feel the hairs on the back of my neck start to singe from the heat, the football fades into red hot floating embers that still burn through my shirt but doesn't harm me or Gray.

"Come on, man! Watch out for us non-powered people!" Gray yells as his brown hair falls in his face and he drops the papers and notebook he was holding when I went to try to shove him down.

"You better pick up your papers, you weakling." Another player sneers as he kicks up a small gust of wind to blow Gray's papers further from his grasp.

As Gray scrambles after the papers, Rhett laughs manically as he makes little pebbles drop from his hands and he throws them around the floor, trying to make Gray slip on them.

"Alright, that's enough!" I say, coming to Gray's defense and grabbing his arm before those damn pebbles can make him fall flat on his ass.

"What are you gonna do about it?" Mason asks as he squares up with me.

He looks me up and down with an irritated glare, then a small fire flickers to life in his right hand as a wicked smile forms on his face. His black hair, which looks blue in areas under the fluorescent lights above us, hangs close to his brown eyes. I finally notice what someone was talking about back in high school. There is a hint of a red ring around his iris that gives his eyes a harder edge, and the sight of them sends chills down my spine. It's like they can burn a hole right through my chest. I then notice the black and dark gray flame tattoos that travel up both his arms and disappear into the sleeves of his football jersey. No color at all. Just the solid dark markings of a Parasite.

Before I can think of a comeback to his challenge, I hear another voice from behind us and Gray releases a thankful sigh as Ivan comes up and practically shoves me out of the way to stand before Mason.

"You got a fucking problem?" Ivan asks as he's holding onto a piece of metal in his hand.

It looks like a crowbar, but smaller and flatter. He bounces it in his hand like he's contemplating the best way to use the weapon against the Parasite in front of him and won't think twice about using it if provoked again. Ivan's black hair is cut close to his head in a faded style and his steel-gray eyes with the gold ring around his iris are focused and filled with challenge. The sleeves of his burgundy hoodie are pushed up, proudly showing off his chain link tattoos along with the corded muscles of his forearms that flex each time he bounces the metal rod in his hands. Mason gives Ivan a dirty look before letting an evil smirk at the three of us play at his lips as he walks away with the rest of the football team trailing after him.

Once we know they have left for good, I bend down to help Gray pick up his papers that are still scattered across the floor. Ivan blows out a frustrated breath as he reabsorbs his metal rod into his left hand. I stare at his hands for a moment with a twinge of jealousy filling my chest. If I just had a drop of power to be able to put Mason in his place, that would make my day.

"You two okay?" Ivan asks as he extends his hand to help Gray off the floor.

"Yeah, just those assholes making our morning hell. I'm fine." Gray says as he places his hand on Ivan's shoulder, giving it a quick squeeze before dropping it to cradle the books in his hands.

"Try not to let them get to you. I know it's easier said than done but trust me, it'll be better that way." Ivan says as he glares over his shoulder in the direction the team went.

"Yeah, says the guy with abilities and us boring humans that have to take his shit." I scoff.

"Oh, I wouldn't be able to fight him." Ivan says quickly. "I hear his fire is abnormally hot. I think he'd melt through even the thickest metal I could make like it was paper."

"I just wish I had just a drop of *something*, to be able to put people like him in their place and not just be something they can push around." I groan.

Ivan knows what I do at night when I can't sleep. Knows that I try to fight back but ultimately get my ass handed to me every time, but he never tells me I'm stupid, only reckless.

"I was holding on to hope that maybe I was just insanely late in getting any abilities, but with turning twenty-one tomorrow, I just need to stop worrying about it and get on with my life. Whatever that may be now."

"You know, having powers is not as glamorous as you think it is." Ivan begins.

"Oh yeah. Tell me just how bad it is." I scoff.

"Well." Ivan begins as he tosses an arm around Gray's neck, pulling him close to his chest. "Once you show what power you have, you are automatically enrolled into classes that will show you what jobs will be out there after you finish whatever schooling you plan on doing. Then you become a living manufacturing plant, to be honest." Ivan complains.

"Oh yeah, having a solid, well-paying job that you're naturally good at. Such a bummer." I say sarcastically while rolling my eyes.

"Can't you decline those jobs and do something different, Ivan?" Gray asks.

"You think I work at my old man's metal plant because I like it?" Ivan asks.

"We'll I thought you did it because it was an easy way to get a job and get out from your old man's place." I ask.

"Wow, you all really need to get into that Ability 101 class." Ivan says with a touch of annoyance in his voice. "You can decline them to a point, but if you have the top four powers, you have to go at least twice a month and work for twelve or fourteen hours."

The top four powers. Fire, Electricity, Water and Metal. The fundamentals of life. Even I know the importance of each of those powers. A group of people with electricity can charge the huge generators at the electric plant and power a whole county for a month. People with fire can either work for the fire department along with the water wielders to help extinguish the fire or to conduct controlled burns for a number of reasons. Water, of course, has almost unlimited possibilities. The fire department, the electrical plant for kinetic energy, hospitals for clean sterile water, and the list can go on and on.

"Oh wow, that sucks." I say. "Good thing I don't have powers, then. It's hard for me to just get to work on time. I'm only on time for school today because I had my nightmare." I say, and I instantly kick myself.

"You had that one again?" Gray asks gently, knowing which one I'm talking about.

I nod my head. Every time I think back to that day, something just doesn't feel right. We had such a great time at the movies and just a few days before she was showing me how she was getting better with her powers and then she does a complete one-eighty and ends everything with me over a damn text. I tried to blame it on myself. On me moving too fast that night, but even that feels like a lie. She was into it before her phone rang. It's almost like there was something bigger at play that she didn't want to tell me about.

There is only one day during the year that I allow the walls to come down. Only one day that I make my way back to that once special place in the forest that is now my reminder of what I lost and I let the beauty around me clash with the pain and sorrow in my heart. I shake my head to clear those thoughts and make myself focus on the rest of the school day ahead of me.

After I work through my two main classes for the day, I decide I don't want to know any more about abilities since Ivan just gave me a shit-ton of information, so I skip my last class of the day and head home.

When I pull into the driveway, I find the house is empty, so after I drop my backpack off in my room, I make my way into the kitchen and raid the pantry for a bag of chips and snag a cherry Dr. Pepper out of the fridge before flopping my ass on the couch. I toe my converses off and cross my legs at my ankles as I dump a handful of chips on my chest. The orange color of my hoodie making the sour cream and onion-flavored chips stand out in stark comparison to the fabric. I intend to scroll TikTok, but my fingers find my photo gallery and pull up the one single photo that I keep close to the top.

The one of my parents holding me as a newborn.

Days after my life went to hell-in-a-hand-basket, I threw the photo album that my aunt and uncle gave me for my sixteenth birthday deep into the back of my closet, but I took that single picture with my phone, just so I could keep them close. I don't know why I did that, to be honest, but I can't make myself delete it from my phone now.

As I look at the photo, nothing about it obviously changes, but *I* feel different. I feel out of control and nothing in my life is going the way I wanted. The way I imagined it would.

"Why didn't you all stay?" I ask the photo and not for the first time. "Did you know I was going to be normal, and you all didn't want that?" I whisper as I look at their smiling faces and at my crying, infant self.

My eyes linger on the tattoos of my parents. The delicate golden-red flame-like tattoo on my mother's arms and the bluish-white lightning bolt of my father that goes up his arms in harsh jagged lines. As I stare at the photo, I see something flash out of the corner of my eye, but it's too quick to even distinguish a color. I almost think I imagined seeing something at all when I hear the garage door open. Aunt Viv must have gotten back from the grocery store. So I quickly finish the remaining chips on my chest, dust the crumbs from my hoodie, and replace the chip bag in the pantry all before she walks in the door.

"I'll help you with the rest of the bags, Aunt Viv." I offer, stepping into the garage with her.

After I get all the bags from her trunk, I help Aunt Viv fix dinner. I actually like cooking when I'm in a good mood and I'm getting better with each meal I make, but I'm nowhere near as good as my aunt. She tells me I'm doing great even when I accidentally overcook something, but she coaches me on what I did wrong and I correct it on the next attempt.

When we serve dinner that night, we all chat about how our day went. I, of course, leave out the fact about almost getting into a fight with a Parasite, but I let them know that my day went well. Uncle Matt offers to clean the dishes as well as the kitchen for his wife, and I take that opportunity to start on my homework from today's classes for a while before turning in for the night.

When I pull the comforter up to my neck and close my eyes, I am almost immediately pulled into what seems like a dream, but I am aware that I am dreaming, which is weird, but I can't make myself open my eyes. All I can make out is darkness around me and I occasionally see flashes of orange and a bluish-white light fill the darkness around me. Almost like bombs are detonated in the air, with no sound at all coming from them. I can feel this dream is coming to an end, and with one final flash of orange light, I hear what sounds like a fire crackling in my right ear.

I jump up from my bed and look around the room. It's dark and I hear the cricket that is chirping outside my window, the sound of the forced air flowing from the vent in my ceiling making up the nighttime sounds.

"That was weird." I say to myself as I settle back into my pillow, pulling the comforter closer to my head and letting my eyes close for the second time tonight, and finally a dreamless sleep takes me into her slumbering fingers.

16

Aiden

No other dreams come to me throughout the night, and I wake up to the sound of my alarm the next morning. When I turn over to pound my fist into the off button, I open my eyes and I see colorful streamers and confetti all over my room.

Somehow, Aunt Viv did all this while I was asleep. How she does it every year and not wake me, I will never know. I smile to myself and I put a shirt on so I can walk over to the bathroom because, like always, I know what she's up to. I grab the doorknob and I brace myself for whatever she has planned, which sometimes involves a confetti bomb, but not always. So I never know what I will get from year to year.

"Happy Birthday, Aiden!" Aunt Viv cheers when I open my door. Her arm spread wide on either side of her head and doing a jazz-hands motion for further emphasis on her excitement.

"Thank you, Aunt Viv. The confetti was a nice touch." I say with a smile.

"You're welcome. Now I just have to clean it up later, but it's fun making the mess." Aunt Viv says brightly.

"It's okay. I'll clean it up." I offer. "I don't have anything to do on this boring, nothing special, just a typical Saturday." I say, trying to hide a smile.

"You are so bad." Aunt Viv says while shaking her head, chuckling to herself as she walks down the hall and into the kitchen to give me privacy while I use the bathroom and brush my teeth.

As I turn the water in the sink to wash my hands before grabbing my toothbrush, I feel a slight pain in my right temple. I grab at the sudden hurt and hiss through my teeth, but my breath catches in my chest when I start to dream again, but this time, I am wide awake.

The bathroom around me fills with what looks like shapes of trees, but I can't make out what kind they are. Flashes of orange and bluish white light erupt from all angles around me and I hear a fire burning off to my right. When I turn my head in the direction of the sound, it's all gone in an instant and I'm back in the bathroom, the steam from the running water fogging up the mirror.

I shake my head and wonder for the first time if I am going crazy. I shrug these weird images off as my brain finally catching up from all the shit I've dealt with and maybe from the few good blows I've taken to the head as well.

Deciding to leave my room as is for now since Ivan and Gray usually come over to celebrate the day with the family, I go into the kitchen where I see Uncle Matt, who is still in his green pajama pants and long sleeve dark yellow shirt, standing in front of the stove cooking breakfast that consists of eggs, sausage, rolls, and hash browns; my second favorite breakfast after waffles. A steaming plate is already waiting for me at the island and there is a green envelope sitting next to the plate with my name on the front, written in Aunt Viv's elegant cursive font.

I open the envelope to find a birthday card and on the front is a big-headed basset hound with a party hat strapped to his head. When I open the card, it sings *Happy Birthday* to me and there is one hundred dollars cash in the form of twenty's inside.

"Go to the mall and get what you want, kiddo." Uncle Matt says with a bright smile as he sets a plate down on the island for Aunt Viv before walking around the island to stand next to me. "Happy birthday, son." He says while giving me a hug.

"Thank you, Uncle Matt." I say, returning his smile, and then look over at my aunt. "Thank you too, Aunt Viv. For everything." I say, tilting my head back to the hall, hinting at my room again.

After I eat with both of them, I grab my keys off the hook and walk out in the garage to jump into my Colorado and head to the mall. When I find a parking spot, I head into GameStop to look for a PC and PlayStation 5 game that I want. Once I find what I'm looking for, I head to the checkout counter and I find a kid that barely looks old enough to be working, and by the dead-eyed look in his eyes, I can tell that he doesn't want to be there either.

As he wordlessly scans my games, I start to feel like someone is watching me. The little hairs on the back of my neck stand on end and I turn to look toward the entrance, but I don't see anyone. I quickly finish paying and then I decide to walk the mall a bit and just do some window shopping, but no matter how hard I try to ignore it, I still can't shake the feeling I'm being followed, and the person is just out of sight.

I finally come across a music store and I walk around in there for a bit. As I am getting to the rock & roll section, I see a figure dressed in dark tones: a black shirt, dark blue jeans, a black baseball cap low over their eyes, and aviator sunglasses to cover their face further, walk in and head over to the right side of the store. I can tell by the walk that this person is a man, and somehow I know this must be the prick that's been following me around.

I decide to stick to the center of the store so I'm not cornered by him. I make it seem like I have no idea he's in the store with me and I just discreetly watch his movements out of the corner of my eye. When this figure walks by the line of shelves on my left and comes down the aisle directly behind me, panic builds in my chest. I do not want my back to this guy. So I turn to face him through the shelves. I don't even make it look like I'm just browsing. I'm done with him and his stalking. I look right at him through the slots in the shelving unit and my expression says everything I need it to without words.

I fucking see you, buddy.

After a few tense moments pass of me staring into his dark blue aviator sunglasses, I get the sense he won't hurt me, but I just don't like a strange person behind my back who's been following me around the mall.

I then see him take a CD case from the back pocket of his dark jeans and place it on the shelf. As he pushes the case toward me, the wood of the shelf and the plastic of the case grind against one another, and I can tell from the side it has personal graphics on it. I snatch the case off the shelf with my left hand and when I do; I hear something rattling around inside it. I pull my eyes away from this dude's sunglasses to look down to read the cover. It's a plain white background, but the image on the front makes my heart freeze in my chest.

In the middle of an orange scroll-like banner is a message written in bold black ink.

Aiden, you can trust me.

How does this random person know my name? I look back up between the shelving unit, but he's nowhere in sight. My heart sputters in my chest as I quickly make my way to the main entrance to the store, but I don't see this figure walking in the mall anywhere.

"How the hell did he get out so fast?" I ask myself.

I decide then and there that I don't want to be in the mall anymore. I don't want to be where his prying eyes may still be on me. So, after stuffing the CD case into the pocket of my hoodie, I briskly walk through the mall to make my way to my truck. I can't help but glance over my shoulder every once in a while to see if the bastard has come back to watch me again, but I don't see him or anyone else.

When I exit the main doors to the parking lot, I run to my Colorado and I'm thankful I was able to find a close parking spot. Once inside, I feel the semblance of safety flood over me and I remember the CD case in the pocket of my hoodie. I pull it out and I throw it up on my dash. The case sliding against the faux leather is so loud in the cab that it makes my skin crawl with the sound, but I just find myself staring at it. The white cover and the font that sits on the orange banner seems to be beckoning me to open the case.

I take another look around to see if I can spot the figure and while I don't see anyone walking around the parking lot right now, something tells me to still get away from the mall. So, I listen to it and I go to the only place that I know I can find privacy. The forest.

When I pull up to the edge of the tree line and throw the transmission into park as random raindrops spatter on my windshield, so I stay in the cab and kill the engine. I pick up the CD case again and I still hear something moving around in it. When I open it up, I find two necklaces inside. One necklace is a little yellow bolt of lightning, and the other little pendant looks like an orange and yellow flame. But what's weird is, I swear that same fire I heard crackling this morning in the bathroom echoes in my mind when I look at the little pendant. I laugh humorlessly as I shake my head to clear my thoughts.

"What the hell is this? Some kind of fucking joke?" I ask myself out loud.

"No, it's not a joke, Aiden."

I hear a male voice respond to my question, but not with my ears; it's like it came from inside my head. I turn in all directions to look around me to find the source, but no one is around me. The only thing that I hear is the chirping of birds that are hidden in the trees.

"Who the hell are you, and how the hell do you know my name?" I growl with a mix of anger and fear in my tone.

"That will come all in good time, Aiden. But for now, I need you to trust me. I believe in the next few days you will become what The Protector's of Power have been waiting on." The voice says simply.

"The Protector's of Power? What the hell is going on? How are you talking to me? Is this the guy from the mall? Did you put a speaker on me somewhere?" I ask, firing off question after question.

"I will say this. You will be gaining abilities soon, but you must not–" The voice begins in a serious tone, but I laugh and mentally cut him off somehow.

"Now, I know you got the wrong guy. I'm twenty-one, and I'm not getting any abilities. So you're barking up the wrong Aiden tree." I say.

"Your parents are Avery and Cole Rivers, aren't they?" The voice asks, but his tone tells me he already knows the answer.

My heart stops in my chest at the mention of their names and I start to get angry at the tone of this voice, like he knows he struck a nerve. "How the fuck do you know my parents?" I ask with cold anger.

"Ah there, you see? I know I have the right, *Aiden."* The voice replies with a bit of an 'I told you so' tone. *"I understand this is all confusing now, but in* time, *it will all make sense. The main thing now is you can not fight what is about to happen. The fate of everyone with an ability hangs in the balance."* The voice says, getting serious again near the end of his words.

Just as I am about to ask him again just who he is, I feel him leave my mind, which is a disorienting feeling.

"What the hell just happened? How did he know my parents?" I ask myself.

I look at the CD case and the necklaces in my hand for a moment. Then, without missing a beat, I hit the automatic switch on the driver's window and I toss everything out in the dirt.

"Like hell I'm listening to that crazy asshole. He's probably a Parasite trying to play mind games." I say and I drive off, leaving the CD case in my rearview mirror.

I drive home in silence, but the words of that voice are still creeping in my mind. *'Something The Protector's of Power has been waiting on'* and *'the fate of people with powers hangs in the balance'*. I shake my head to clear my thoughts of his words just as I pull up to the house and park my truck in the garage.

I walk in and see Aunt Viv sitting on the couch with her legs folded up under her; the phone tucked up against her ear with one of her friends while she's painting her nails. I wave hello to her and sit at the dining room table to unpack the games I got from the mall. As I throw the shopping bag away, I feel my phone vibrate in the back pocket of my jeans and I see the text from Ivan.

Ivan:

> Gray and I will be over soon. I just finished a shift at my old man's factory

Me:

> That's cool dude. I just got back from the mall. Take your time.

Aunt Viv finishes her call and joins me in the dining room a moment later. She picks up the game cases to inspect what I bought and turns her nose up.

"How can you go from horror to what is that, a Sims game?" Aunt Viv asks incredulously.

"Cause they are both fun." I say with a smile as I take *The Last of Us part II* and *The Sims 4* back from her.

She smiles at me as she walks back into the living room, and I decide to join her since she's off the phone. I get up from the dining room chair to go into the kitchen to grab a Dr. Pepper first before joining her when I feel something that I swear feels like a tickle in the back of my brain and then I hear a ghostly chuckle echo in my mind.

"The streamers are nice, but the confetti's a bit much, *though."* The voice says with a touch of humor. *"Happy birthday, by the way, Aiden."*

I stop dead in my tracks, trying to process what I just heard, and then I finally put two and two together. This bastard is in my room.

After that thought forms in my mind, I dash across the house and throw open my door, not caring how it flings back into the wall. I find myself grinning now that I know I have this asshole cornered and I can finally tell him how much of a fucking creep he is and drive my fist into his face, but I freeze.

My room is empty.

I instantly look at my window but I notice the curtain is still closed and not moving one bit like it should if someone pushed it aside, and I know there's no other way to get out of this house without going to the front or back door, which is directly across the living and dining room. So, there is no way in hell this dude got by us. My eyes scan the room again and when they land on my desk, my blood runs cold.

On the black, wooden surface, staring back at me, is the CD case that I threw out the window of my truck before I left the forest.

17

Aiden

As I stare at the CD case on my desk, my heart pounds against my sternum, and my frustration hits an all-time high. It's like the orange and white homemade cover is mocking me, saying 'you can't get rid of me that easily.'

"How the—?" I begin, but I notice my aunt come up behind me out of my peripheral vision. I quickly throw the CD case in my desk drawer before I turn to face her.

"Aiden, you okay? You took off like something had you." Aunt Viv asks while looking around my room to check and see if there is a problem.

Something did kind of have me. I say to myself. "Sorry, I thought I left my window open." I lie.

"Well, go slower next time. It's not like it's gonna rain all of a sudden." Aunt Viv replies, giving me a look that flat out says she doesn't believe me one bit.

I nod at her and as we are walking away from my room; I glance back at the drawer where I threw the CD case for the time being and take a breath before I close my door. As we make our way back into the living room, Ivan pulls up in his dark green Mustang. I walk over to the front door to open it and wait for my friends to come in.

When Ivan puts the Mustang in park, he and Gray hop out at the same time and they race to the front door. I chuckle as Gray kicks his right leg out to trip Ivan with his foot. He doesn't fall down, but he stumbles a few steps while his arms windmill at his side to keep from falling completely on his face, which gives Gray time to get to the door first.

"Happy Birthday, man!" Gray says while catching his breath, a brilliant smile on his face that he was the first one to say the birthday wishes.

"You tripped me, Gray!" Ivan pants out as he walks up to his boyfriend on the porch.

"You just tripped over your own feet, you heavy metal lug." Gray says with a mischievous smile.

"I'll show you heavy metal." Ivan says, while making a small metal paddle with his left hand.

Gray sees this and a look of 'oh shit' floods his face and he takes off past me and into the house, his laughter trailing behind him while Ivan chuckles darkly and runs in after Gray. I shake my head and silently laugh to myself at the banter between them, happy for the distraction from a few minutes ago.

I shut the door and head into the living room, where I see Ivan has caught Gray. His large hand gripping the back of Gray's neck and my friend has a wicked smile on his face.

"You wanted a pinata, right? I'm sure Gray has lots of candy." Ivan jokes while he gently taps the metal paddle to Gray's stomach before playfully pushing him away and face-first onto the couch. "But seriously dude, happy birthday." Ivan says, looking at me while reabsorbing the metal material.

I pull Gray up off the couch and we all go into my room to play the new games I bought this morning while Uncle Matt, who has arrived with groceries, starts dinner. Ivan, Gray, and I take turns playing; each time one of us is eaten by a monster ridden with cordyceps, we swap controllers.

"Your aunt always goes wild on the decorations every year." Gray says as he looks around the room while I take his controller for my turn with Ivan.

"Yeah, she does. But deep down, I like it. It's something she's done since I was little, so it's no shocker when I wake up to it. But this time she added confetti which is gonna be a nightmare to clean up, but I told her I would do it in a bit." I say while waving my hand over the small shimmering dots on the beige carpet.

"You're a good nephew; I would have just left the mess." Ivan says while the game is playing a cut scene to toy with one of the blue streamers in his right hand before flicking it toward me.

As the streamer lands on my foot, I reach out to rub my knuckles against Ivan's head and he tries to duck away from my hand. I grin wickedly as I leap over toward him and put him in a headlock just as the cut scene ends and an undead monster jumps from the ceiling and lands in front of his character.

"No, you're gonna make me die!" Ivan says while fighting to get out of my grasp and grabbing the PS5 controller to fight off a fungi-ridden monster at the same time.

About an hour and a half later, Aunt Viv calls us for dinner and there is a lineup of steaks, baked potatoes, and steamed vegetables on the island.

"Thank you, Uncle Matt and Aunt Viv. This looks amazing." I say as I eye the still-steaming food in front of me.

"Anything for my nephew, now let's eat!" Uncle Matt exclaims with a bright smile.

We all load up our plates and file into the dining room while we talk about what's been going on with our classes. Ivan and Gray are mindful and leave out the altercation we had with Mason and the football team the other day, and I am careful to not talk about my run-in with this crazy mystery guy from the mall who seems to be able to...the only word that makes sense is, teleport from place to place.

Once we finish with dinner, Aunt Viv and Uncle Matt go into the kitchen and when I hear the strike of a match, I know they are bringing the cake out next. It's a simple cake with my favorite colors of blue and green on it for the edging and in the middle, it's the same alternating colors to spell out 'Happy 21st Birthday, Aiden' in Aunt Viv's cursive font.

Everyone starts to sing *Happy Birthday,* and I feel awkward like most people do, but once I see the fire dancing on the blue number 2 and the green number 1 candles, I start to zone out. My eyes only focusing on the flames. I then feel that now familiar tickle in the back of my mind and the mystery voice whispering,

"Don't fight it."

Once my subconscious hears the cheering that signals the song is over, I quickly blink back into reality and blow my candles out.

"Happy birthday, Aiden!" Aunt Viv says brightly and gives me a hug.

Maybe I'm going nuts. Or maybe there was something on that CD case. Was I drugged? I ask myself, but it feels like a lie. *This guy knows more than he's letting on. I just don't know what it is yet.*

Once we had our fill of cake, Aunt Viv insists on Ivan and Gray taking a few extra pieces for themselves before they leave. I walk my friends to the porch, thank them for coming over, and I watch Ivan's Mustang roar down the road. I shut the door and I go to my room so I can clean up the decorations like I had promised my aunt earlier, but no matter how I try to keep my mind on other things, I find myself thinking of everything that happened today. The necklaces, the voice in my head, and the broken images I've been seeing that I almost feel are visions of the future.

I continue to pick up my room like I'm on autopilot, not really paying attention to what I'm doing, but going through the motions all the same. When I finally notice the trash bag is filled with streamers, I take the bag out the back door to toss it in the trash can. The sound of the lid slamming shut makes the squirrels chitter in surprise as they scramble higher into branches of the nearby trees at the sudden noise.

Then I go back into my room and I vacuum the confetti out of the carpet, sometimes using the crevice tool to get closer to the furniture. After I finally get it all cleaned up about forty-five minutes later, I sit on the side of my bed while looking at the drawer I tossed the CD case into earlier. I shake my head as I stand, flinging open the drawer and snatching the case out of the hollow space and I slowly sink into my desk chair, the springs creaking at my weight when I sit down.

I look at the font again and I hear the two necklaces tumbling around in the case. I let out an aggravated sigh as I open the case and I take them out one at a time. I study the shapes of the lightning bolt and the flame as they swing on the ends of their cheap gold-plated chains. The longer I stare at them, the more I have this weird sense of familiarity come over me, and the odd need to wear them around my neck.

"What the hell. I'll put 'em on." I say and I can hear it in the tone of my voice, that I am just fed up with the day.

I fasten the necklaces around my neck and they both fall to the center of my chest, resting on the fabric of my gray t-shirt and glinting in the light from my small desk lamp every time my chest rises when I take a breath. I glance at my clock on the wall and it's almost midnight, so I fist the pendants in my right hand, tuck them under my shirt, and turn in for the night.

18

Aiden

I feel the wind around me, but I can't make out much detail. Everything is fuzzy, out of focus, and my ears just pick up on muffled noises around me. When I look to my right, I pick up on the sound of fire crackling from a huge inferno blazing somewhere in the distance, the buzzing and crackling of electricity to my left.

I see figures run over to me, but they are just black silhouettes against the orange, and the blueish-white flashes filling my vision. I try to get my eyes to focus more on the things around me and I finally start to see something come into focus. I see the outline of something gigantic, so large I can't even put a measurement to it. I make out that it's something cone shaped and I can see pipes and wires going in all directions. I begin to lift my hand to point at this thing in front of me when I hear my alarm clock blare at me from somewhere in the distance and it gets louder as I come back to consciousness.

I sit straight up in bed, trying to catch my breath, as I'm still reeling from the weird dream. A bead of sweat trails down my back as I put my head in my hands for a moment and then look around to make sure I am still in the safety of my bedroom.

"It was just a dream. A weird one, but a dream." I say breathlessly.

After a few moments, I realize that my alarm is still yelling at me to get up, so I turn it off and I begrudgingly get dressed for school. As I fasten the button of my black jeans, I walk into my closet to grab a white long-sleeve shirt and slip it over my head and I slide the sleeves up to my elbows while I sit on the corner of my bed to tie my shoelaces.

After I tie my right shoe, I move to my left foot and I suddenly feel my right arm get hot. It feels like a burst of heat flows over my skin, from my wrist to my shoulder, almost like I'm next to a heater that just turned on. But I'm nowhere near a heat source, and we don't have the HVAC on right now since it's a mild day out so far, so there would be no heat anywhere in the house. Before I can really think too much of it, the feeling is gone.

Maybe my sleeve pinched a nerve or something. I think to myself.

I shake my head to brush it off as I grab my backpack off the floor and I take the egg sandwich that Aunt Viv made off the counter and eat it on the go.

When I get to school, everything goes smoothly. No issues with Mason and the football team, and the coursework seems to be easy this week, so that helps the day go by quickly.

After I have a quick lunch with Ivan and Gray in the cafeteria, I walk into my last class of the day, which is the same one I skipped the other day, Abilities 101. I find that this is the only class that I share with Ivan, so I meet up with him and we sit at neighboring desks.

"Here are my notes from the other day; I figured you'd want to catch up." Ivan says, now knowing I skipped class.

I nod at him and then turn my attention to the front of the room and on the whiteboard, written in big, blocky blue letters is,

THE BIRTH OF THE PROTECTOR'S OF POWER.

I instantly remember this voice saying a similar term and my chest fills with anticipation. I nervously wait for Mr. Jaffee to come in and see what he has to say about this group. But it's not Mr. Jaffee that walks in, it's a woman. She's middle-aged, her blonde hair is up in a bun on the top of her head, and wearing a beige pantsuit with a cream button-up top. I scrunch my eyebrows in confusion, but before I can even think to ask where Mr. Jaffee is, she shuts off the lights and begins her lesson.

"Good afternoon, class. Today we will be talking about the birth of The Protector's of Power." Mrs. Jaffee says.

She presses a button on her keyboard and the picture of her PowerPoint change and it asks 'When did it all start?' with blue question marks all over the screen.

"Research has shown that various elemental power wielders existed as far back as 1822. And as most of you should know, once someone develops their ability, they stop aging as quickly as normal humans. The average age of someone with abilities is about one hundred and fifty years old. And if someone wielded more than one power, it's said they could live well beyond that." Professor Jaffee explains, and that makes me wonder just how old my parents were before they left.

"Over the years and years of research, we found that the abilities have not changed very much compared to the ones that we have now. Metal like Ivan here, Earth like James, and Fire like Jaiden." The professor continues while pointing to the various students.

I look behind me at Jaiden, and he gives me a small nod. Since our names are similar, I think back to when I told the voice he had the wrong guy, but that thought sits like a bunch of rocks in my stomach. Just uncomfortable and wrong. Somehow, even I know now this strange voice does have the right person, but why? Professor Jaffee begins talking again and I force myself to focus on her.

"Back in that time, though, The Protector's of Power would not use their abilities as openly as we do now. If they did, they would be tried as a witch or something evil, because there were so many conspiracies and misunderstandings during that time. So, with the fear of being killed, there are only a handful of documented people with abilities that came forward and when they did, most were in groups thinking that the power of numbers would keep them safe, and most of the time it did. However, those who did not have a large gathering behind them decided to hide to preserve their lineage."

She presses a button on her remote and the screen changes and the picture she shows next makes my heart stop, but I am not completely sure why, but something about it is familiar.

"While we all know about abilities in today's world, people have been slowly going back into hiding because of this machine that has been made by a group called The Parasites, which from the last piece of documentation we have is being governed by Victor Powell, the brother of–"

I stop listening to her as I zone out again. I think about the dream I had last night and I notice the shapes are almost exactly the same as my dream compared to what's staring back at me from the PowerPoint. I am brought back to the present when I feel Ivan's hand on my shoulder.

"Dude, you okay?" Ivan whispers.

I focus on Ivan with a dumbfounded look on my face. I wordlessly nod to him and realize I am holding my breath. I shake my head slightly and take a shaky inhale through my nose.

"If you're fine, then stop holding your pencil in a death grip." He says while nodding his head toward my right hand.

I look down to see my knuckles are white and the pencil is on the verge of being snapped by my fingers. After I set the pencil on my notebook, I notice that tingling feeling in my right arm again, but I brush it off as the blood starts to move through my limb since I'm no longer choking the pencil to death.

I shake my hand out to try to get the blood moving again when the inside of my right wrist starts to itch. I glance at it and I swear I see a dark little flame pop up on my skin, but then it disappears as Professor Jaffee turns the lights back on and my attention is pulled back to the room around me. I feel Ivan's hand on my arm again and he has a look of concern on his face, his hard silver-eyed gaze trying to search for answers.

"You sure you're okay, man?" Ivan asks again.

"Yeah, I haven't been sleeping well the last few nights." I say truthfully.

I haven't been sleeping well, and it's because of these stupid, trippy dreams, and this voice messing with my head. Ivan gives me a look like he wants to say more, but he doesn't for the rest of the lecture.

"You know you can talk to me about anything, right?" Ivan says as we start to walk out of the classroom, and I hear the concern in his voice.

I nod at his words and I try to quicken my step to get out of the room faster, but when I walk by the image of this machine, that's still on the whiteboard, I pause for a moment. Something about this thing gives me chills. I don't even know the name of this monstrous contraption, but it scares the absolute fucking shit out of me, and as I continue to stare at the image before me, I get this one thought in my mind.

Destroy.

19

Aiden

When I get home after school later that afternoon, I say hello to Aunt Viv before I make my way back to my room where I toss my backpack on the floor, promising myself I will do homework in a little bit, once I can clear my head of what I learned in that damn Abilities 101 class.

I head back to the kitchen and offer to help Aunt Viv with dinner. I realize that this is the only semblance of normalcy in my life right now. I feel like I'm in my own little world when I am cooking. Just me, the flame from the gas stove and the pan. I am in control and it sits like a comfort in my chest. I even find myself smiling when I start to sauté the vegetables and I don't burn them.

"You're getting better at cooking, Aiden. I'm proud of you." Aunt Viv says with a smile as she pokes me in the side. "I knew I'd get through that tough shell one way or another." She says as a joke, but I can pick up on the undertone of understanding.

"You are the only one that can, Aunt Viv." I say with a sad smile, as the reason for these walls haunts me again for a moment before I shove them back down.

I figured that if I stopped caring about things, just go with the flow of life, stay in the shadows and don't get invested or involved in people, then no one can use that type of vulnerability against me again.

After dinner, I try to get some homework done, but my thoughts are clouded by the image of that odd machine and I only get halfway through my assignment. I let out a frustrated sigh as I slam my textbook closed.

"The hell with it. It'll still be here tomorrow morning. I'll finish it then." I say as I turn in early for the night.

When my head hits the pillow, I almost instantly fall into a restless sleep that is filled by my recurring nightmare.

I am back in this strange forest, and this time the sounds around me are clearer. The sound of fire crackling and popping as it consumes the materials around it, the trees and grass, giving it more fuel to burn. The violent arcing buzz of electricity sparking, and the sound of voices yelling, but I can't make out the words. It's almost like they are screaming at me.

I look over, and the only thing that's in focus is this huge metal machine. I'm able to take a few heartbeats to look at it and I can estimate that it stands about twelve feet in height. The cylindrical tower with wires and tubes coming out of every available spot stares back at me. I start to look down at my right arm that's itching and burning, but before I can focus on what may be there, I feel that mysterious voice tug at the back of my mind.

"Don't fight the change that's coming. You may be our only hope."

"What if I don't want any of this?" I yell into the void of the trees. *"I didn't ask to be part of this!"* I think to this voice.

I feel the voice leave my mind in a flash and the images around me cut to black.

I jump up in my bed with sweat beading on my forehead. I glance around the room and while I don't feel I slept a wink, the morning sun is beginning to shine in my window. I glance down at my wrist again and I swear I see that faint black outline that resembles a flame, like I did yesterday. I don't get the chance to really focus on it when I hear Uncle Matt out in the hallway talking to Aunt Viv about something.

I turn to the door for a moment to see if he's going to come into my room and when he doesn't; I glance back at my right wrist and the marking is gone. I almost think about skipping my classes today, but I know I would have more questions on that than I am willing to answer right now. So, I take a breath to compose myself and get ready for school.

When I get to school, I am antsy for some reason. Like I can't wait for the day to be over, which is not usually me. Again, I usually just go with the flow, but now, it's like a huge damn inconvenience to be here and I don't know why.

I meet up with Ivan and Gray by the Mustang and give them a small wave before walking past them without another word, but I know they follow me into the school and only stop when I arrive at my first class of the morning.

Ivan looks me up and down for a moment with concern etched into his features before he opens his mouth. I know he's about to ask me something, but is cut short when the professor opens the classroom door. I take the distraction and I quickly walk into the room to get away from my friend's prying eyes.

I may be present in class, but I barely pay attention to anything that's discussed. I find myself drawing this flame symbol that reminds me of the pendant on the necklace that is still hiding under my shirt. I'm not an artist in the least, but my subconscious can't help but think of it.

After I quietly eat lunch alone in my truck, I finally walk into my last class of the day, Abilities 101. As I take my normal seat, I fold my arms in front of me on the desk and rest my head in the middle of them, trying to build the energy to get through this last class.

Ivan drops into his desk next to me, but I don't lift my head to greet him.

"Hey man. Are you okay? You've been weird all day. You know you can talk to me about anything, right?" Ivan presses, not for the first time this week.

"I know and I'm fine." I say as I tilt my head to the side so he can see my face, but I don't lift my head from the semi-comfort of my folded arms. "I've just been having this stupid nightmare and I can't shake it, so I haven't been sleeping well." I say, still telling him the truth, just not elaborating on it.

As Mrs. Jaffe dims the lights and turns the projector on, I prop my chin on my forearm to look at the screen and seem at least halfway interested in what she's about to lecture on, but what I see on the screen makes my whole body freeze. I slowly lift my head while my stomach drops to my feet, and it takes every ounce of my self-control I have not to jump up out of my desk and run out the door. It's the machine from my dreams, and in big red letters, I see its name for the first time.

The Siphon.

"Okay everyone, listen up; this is important here. This *machine*, as I will say nicely." She spits the word like it's the most vile thing she's had in her mouth and her voice waivers for a moment before continuing her explanation about this monster.

"This is the very contraption that is responsible for injuring and even killing people with abilities. This class is, The Siphon. It was built many years ago by Victor Powell, and it was designed to forcibly remove the powers from its helpless victims."

I try to keep the professor's voice in the background, but as I continue to look at this machine and think back to my dream, I can almost see the images overlap one another in my mind. As I stare at the image of The Siphon in front of me, I begin to feel my entire right arm get hot again. But this time the feeling blooms like a wave over my whole body for an instant. Like someone just threw me in a sauna with my clothes on and shut the door. The room feels too stuffy, too crowded all of a sudden. Without another thought, I grab my backpack and leave the room.

"Sorry ma'am, I'm not feeling well." I say and I walk past her without a word.

I briskly walk to my truck, get in and slam the door, gripping the steering wheel until my knuckles turn white as I try to get some sense of control back.

"What the hell is going on?" I ask myself out loud.

I glance at the clock and it's 4:30 in the afternoon, so I decide to drive to the forest so I can try to get my bearings before I go home. When I arrive fifteen minutes later, I find a hidden section to pull my truck into, throw the gearshift into park, and just let the quiet stillness around me become my white noise.

Part of me wants to reach out to this mystery voice, but I have a feeling that he won't tell me shit. So, I just try to think about the few things that I do know from the dreams.

One, I have this deep-seeded need to destroy this thing now that I know what it is and what it does. I don't know how I know I want to destroy it, but I do. It makes me sick to my stomach to know it steals the powers of someone. That has got to be excruciating.

Two, apparently I'm *very* late in getting powers, I guess? I can only assume that's what's happening to me. What I still don't understand is, why me? What makes me so special? How can I be strong enough to destroy this fucking monstrosity when I haven't had years to hone my power?

I finally notice that it is getting darker and I realize how much time has passed during my mini meltdown. I glance at my dashboard clock and the green digital numbers read 6:30 pm, so I take a cleansing breath and drive home. I help Aunt Viv with dinner again while Uncle Matt sets the table and all three of us eat with mild chatter.

After we finish dinner, Aunt Viv goes to get dessert out of the fridge and I start to feel hot and flushed again. I do my best to hide it and take a sip of my coke, but even with the ice cubes making the liquid cooler, it does nothing to calm the heat under my skin. When I sit the cup down, my wrist starts to itch again and I scratch at it absentmindedly.

"Aiden, you doing okay there?" Uncle Matt asks as he looks from my wrist to my eyes.

I think about lying to him, saying that a bug bit me, but I'm just mentally exhausted right now. I slowly shake my head. "No, actually, I'm not feeling well. I think I'm gonna go lay down." I say truthfully.

I get up from the table, but I do force myself to at least take my plate of half-eaten food to the kitchen sink, then I walk into my room and shut the door while leaning against the faux wood. I take a breath and close my eyes for a minute, but when I feel the slight pinch on my chest from one of the few hairs being pulled out of the root, I slowly open my eyes as I pull the collar of my shirt down to find the two necklaces still around my neck. I grab at the chains and I jerk them in a quick motion, breaking the clasp to lift them in front of my face.

I still want to deny what is happening to me and what I have been seeing. All this is, is just a mental breakdown I'm having from these last three years being bottled up deep inside me and finally coming to a breaking point.

I toss the necklaces on my desk and they slide a bit against the wood until they come to rest next to my forgotten homework. I shake my head and I take a step toward my bed, but I feel something almost constrict in my chest and then the tingling and the heat hits my arm again.

Biting back an aggravated growl, I decide to try to lie down for a bit because I have a feeling that I'm gonna need every ounce of sleep I can get.

20

Aiden

I wake up a few hours later, drenched in sweat. The whole right side of my body, from the side of my head all the way down to my little toe, feels so hot. It's like I have a roaring fire licking against my skin, and the static tingling that follows feels like every nerve ending on that side is asleep, but I still feel every ounce of pain.

Looking over at my alarm clock, the digital red font shows it's a little past midnight. Before I can even think about rolling over and going back to sleep, the heat in my body flares to life again.

I need to cool off. I think to myself, hoping that a cold shower will help ease this searing heat under my skin.

When I force my body to move, my nerves sing with pain from the numbness and I suck in a breath at the sensation. I swing my legs over the side of the bed and when I try to stand, my right knee almost buckles underneath me and I realize that I can't feel my leg at all due to the tingling. I grind my teeth together as I make my wobbly leg hold me because I know I need to get to the bathroom if I have any hope of coping with these sensations wracking my body.

Once I make it to my bedroom door, I slowly open it and, after checking to make sure that my aunt and uncle's door is closed and their light is off, I quietly stumble my way across the hall.

I enter the bathroom with a relieved sigh and I flick on the small light over the toilet to give me just enough light to see by and pull the door closed before another wave of heat hits me. As sweat begins to roll down my bare back, I start to think about the mystery voice, and not for the first time today, but I shake my head. I don't need a ghostly voice that won't give me any answers right now.

I quickly strip out of my sweatpants and I force myself to get into the shower and turn the faucet on. When the water sprays from the showerhead, it feels so good on my hot skin that I almost let out a moan at the chilliness that hits me. But as soon as I start to feel just a little better, the heat flares even hotter, as if it's mocking the cold water that patters against my body. With an aggravated growl, I turn the faucet until it's all the way to the coldest setting, but the water does nothing to cool me down. It's only a tapping sensation against my skin now.

I brace my right hand against the wall of the tub as the molten lava in my veins feels like it's moving backward and begins to build in the center of my chest. It almost feels like the power is creating a ball behind my ribcage for a moment before it strikes out like a snake, moving down my right arm and into my fingers. At this sudden rush, my legs give out and I have no choice but to slide down the wall, sitting under the flow of water from the showerhead.

I reach up to try to turn the faucet even colder, but when I remember it's as cold as it will go, I let a frustrated sigh escape past my lips and lean my head back as I feel the water drip from my hair and down the bridge of my nose.

"One day soon, *I hope to return the favor and be your anchor, Aiden."*

Maya's voice fills my mind, and I scoff at the memory. "Yeah. A lot of good that fucking promise is doing right now, huh?" I growl with venom filling my voice.

I close my eyes just as another wave of pain hits me in the chest like a punch, almost like it's feeding off the negative thoughts that just filled my heart. Panic begins to fill my mind, and I finally let myself think of the strange male voice.

"Hey Mystery Guy, you awake?" I whisper breathlessly while thinking of this dude's voice. "I kinda need you here."

I wait for what seems like a lifetime, but I don't get a response from him, and that terrifies me before I feel a wave of anger fill my chest.

"I knew he wouldn't be here for me." I growl as the thought to protect my body, to fight back against what's happening fills my mind.

I feel another hot, piercing pain bloom in the center of my chest and my breathing gets quicker as a response.

"Fight back." I hear the words in my mind, almost like a mocking whisper, laughing at me.

I roll over onto my knees, curling up almost in a fetal position with my head resting against the bottom of the bathtub. As the burn gets so unbearably deep within my chest, I ball my left hand into a fist. Wanting to pound it against the fiberglass floor of the bathtub because I am desperate for a different sense of pain compared to the one that floods my brain now.

I lift my fist, ready to bring it back down, when I feel a little tickle in the back of my mind, and his forceful presence stops me.

"No Aiden, do not fight this. Just breathe. Focus on the water." The voice says.

"I can't feel it anymore." I whisper as water drips over my lips. "I'm too hot."

I'm starting to feel exhaustion set in, but I'm relieved that I have someone with me, even if they are in my head. Another heat wave of pain hits me. It's almost like a hot poker is being stabbed in the center of my chest and it's all I can do not to scream out. I feel the voice in my mind again, but it takes me a moment to focus on him.

"Aiden, Aiden!" The voice says urgently, trying to get my attention.

"Sorry, kinda hard to focus here with the pain." I say, trying to distract myself with sarcasm.

"Aiden, try to focus on that heat you feel in your chest and force it into your right hand." The voice instructs.

I scoff at the idea, but at the same time, if that will help the pain, I will try it. I focus on the fire that I feel flowing in my veins and try to imagine that feeling going toward my hand. Just when I thought things couldn't get worse, I am given the metaphorical bird.

Immense pain blooms from the middle of my chest so fast and hard that it takes my breath away. I instantly stop pushing whatever this is to my hand while letting out a groan that is laced with anger, frustration, fear, and exhaustion.

"Come on Aiden, you can do this. You're stronger than you think." The voice whispers in my mind.

I start to say I'm so tired, but I suddenly think of that machine I saw today in class, and in the visions I've been having. The Siphon. Somehow, I know that I am the only one who can destroy it. I don't know how or why, but I am. I also know that I can't let these people get hurt or killed anymore.

Almost like this voice can sense my thoughts, he gently prods my mind, as if urging me on.

I somehow find the energy to give a lazy smile at this voice. "I get through this; you are so gonna tell me your name dude. 'Mystery voice' ain't gonna cut it anymore."

I close my eyes, thinking about the fire in my veins one more time. When it begins to move, the heat builds up again in my body, but this time I'm prepared for the onslaught of pain. I hold my chest with my left hand while pushing this feeling out toward my right hand. Power rushes out from the center of my chest, down my arm, then into my hand and I can't stop the yell that escapes my throat, but it's over as quick as it came.

As the pain ebbs, I notice that even the heat and the numbness are gone. When my body starts to feel like it's my own again, I can feel the cold water I was so desperate for beating on my skin. But I don't move. Fearing that if I do, something will happen and I just want a few minutes of peace, so I keep my eyes closed, trying to gain some strength back.

The voice gives a little tug on the back of my mind and I wait for him to speak. *"Well done, Aiden. Now, look at your hand."* He says, his tone light with relief.

When I open my eyes, my hand comes into view and I am shocked at what I see dancing quietly in my palm. A bright orange flame. Once I get over the shock, I realize it's not burning me at all and I suddenly have a thought pop in my mind. I slowly move my hand under the still running water from the shower head, expecting the flame to be doused with the water, but it continues to live just as well as it did in the air.

"Normal water can't put out this flame. Only water that is created by an ability can." The voice replies.

I actually find myself fully smiling at this information. I glance down and notice the little black image of the flame on my wrist morph into something wholly different. Like a caterpillar turning into a butterfly.

In the dim light of the bathroom, colors of red, orange, and black travel up my arm almost like a snake, with embers flicking off at random points as it wraps around my forearm. I watch in silent awe as it keeps moving up my arm, encircling my bicep before traveling up past my shoulder. I can tell it goes higher, but I can't see how high, but I know when it finally stops moving over my body, coming to a stop in the center of my chest; almost setting into place on my skin and I know it's part of me now.

I glance at the flame still flickering in my hand, and I can feel the power flowing through me constantly. Moving from my chest and down my arm to continue to feed the element and it's such an odd sensation.

"This is so weird, but awesome at the same time. Too bad I'm too exhausted to care right now." I let my head fall back against the wall. "But how do I turn it off?"

"Just think about the flow of power you feel and keep it to the center of your chest."

I do what he says, focusing on the flow of fire I can feel in my arm and imagine pulling it back to the center of my chest. As the current gathers back to my core, the flame dies in my hand a moment later.

When the cold water starts to make me shiver, I peel myself off the floor of the tub while reaching up to turn the faucet off. I slowly climb out of the tub and grab a towel so I can dry off. Part of me wants to look in the mirror. To turn on all the lights to see what my new marking looks like, but I'm terrified that the color will stay as dark as it looks. And I refuse to look at my eyes right now. I fought against this power and I just don't have the energy to see the result of my actions tonight.

I wrap the towel around my hips as I open the door, peeking my head out and looking toward my aunt and uncle's bedroom. I breathe a sigh of relief seeing their door is still closed and the light is still off. Once I know the coast is clear, I walk out of the bathroom and quietly go back to my room so I can find clean clothes to put on before I collapse face-first onto my bed. I lie there a moment before I manage to roll over to my left side, so I can be just a little more comfortable, but I don't even bother to pull the covers over me. Just thinking of that simple movement fills me with exhaustion.

I then, for some insane reason, wonder how long I was in the bathroom, so I coax my right eye open to look at my clock. The digital red font reads 2:15 am. I groan, knowing I was in that bathroom for two hours, fighting the onset of this new power, and now mentally kicking myself for even wanting to know.

I'm totally screwed. But I'm too drained to care, and it's not like I'm going to go all Godzilla on the house. I don't think I have the strength to do it even if I wanted to.

Before I can pass out into blissful slumber, I hear the mystery voice once more in my mind.

"My name is Seth." He says, and I can tell somehow that he's smiling.

Through the haze of my exhausted mind, I finally comprehend what this voice told me. "Well, nice to meet you, Seth. Now if you don't mind, I'm gonna pass out here. We'll talk more in the morning." I say as I fall into a dreamless sleep.

21

Aiden

When my alarm wakes me the next morning, I roll over while reaching out blindly with my right arm to hit the snooze button with my fist, but I don't get out of bed. I instead rest the crook of my elbow over my eyes to block the sun I can see shining through the window behind my eyelids. My body feels more sluggish than usual and the slight ache in the center of my chest, the power I can feel flowing in my veins is all the reminder I need to know last night was real.

I lift my right arm from my face, but I don't allow myself to look at the coloring of the tattoo. I need to see everything all at once now that I am awake. I need to know if I am a threat to everyone around me because the flames that I feel living under my skin I know can cause catastrophic damage if used the wrong way, but at the same time, it won't hurt me.

Before I open my bedroom door, I throw on a long-sleeved shirt, just in case I walk past my aunt or uncle in the hall. Once I hear that they are in the kitchen making breakfast, I rush into the hall bath and close the door behind me, but I don't turn on the light just yet. I just stand there in the darkness for a moment.

No matter what your eyes look like, or the color of the marking on your skin, you will do the right thing. You will protect those around you, even if it's from yourself.

I give myself the mental pep talk before I pull my shirt over my head and my right hand finds the light switch and I flip it on. As the lights over the mirror fill the small bathroom, the sudden change makes my eyes sting as they adjust to filter in the light. Once I can get my eyes to focus on my reflection, I make myself look at my tattoo.

The bright, crisp colors of red, orange, and sharp black make up the spiraling flames starting from my wrist, curling up my forearm, and my shoulder, where it branches out to the middle of my chest. The same spot that I felt all the pain stem from last night. Then I look back to the top of my shoulder, where the tattoo crawls up the side of my neck, stopping just under my jawline, and I breathe a sigh of relief.

Bright colors of The Protector's of Power and not the dark, muted tones I was fearing that would make me a Parasite.

I focus on my mismatched eyes next. My brown eye has a gold ring around the iris. Proof that I indeed have abilities now. I chuckle as I scrub my left hand over the stubble on my chin.

"Well, looks like I'll have to be hiding this for now." I say as I glance at my right arm again.

I notice that my left arm is still blank and I know that I must be getting another power. I wonder, again not for the first time, why am I getting these powers so late in my life? And until I can figure that out, or finally have Seth tell me, I have to keep everyone in the dark and make sure my tattoos stay hidden until that time comes.

After sliding into a pair of jeans and pulling a black long-sleeve shirt along with a purple hoodie over my head, I check to make sure the hood covers my neck completely before grabbing my backpack off the floor near my desk. I also slip on a pair of dark sunglasses to hide my eye before leaving my room and walk towards the garage door.

"Good morning, Aiden!" Aunt Viv says, "I have breakfast ready for you."

"Sorry, Aunt Viv. I'll get something from school; I'm running late." Which isn't a total lie. I am running later since I was staring at myself in the mirror this morning. "I'll see you later! Bye." I say as I dash out the garage door and into my truck.

As I arrive at school, I surprisingly get there with a few minutes to spare, so I go to the cafeteria to get a quick sausage burrito to eat on the way to my class. When I walk into the building next door, Ivan and Gray walk in behind me and I slow my pace for them to catch up with me in the hall.

"Morning." Gray yawns.

"Morning. You look like shit, Gray." I say.

"I was up most of the night studying for my computer programming class. I have a test this afternoon and I am stressing about it."

"You're going to do fine, Grayson." Ivan croons as he pulls Gray in for a loving kiss.

For a moment, I just look at them. Take in the gentle way that Ivan holds his partner close to his body and the way Gray seems to almost melt into Ivan's side. I know that same feeling of pure love on a deeper level than I want to recall right now. I find myself ripping the sunglasses from my face and pushing the palm of my right hand into my eyes. As if the pressure there will force the haunting memory of *her* away.

"Ivan's right, Gray." I say as they finally pull away from each other. "You are the brains of our group, and I wouldn't sweat a test that I know you studied your ass off for." I glance over at my friends and I give Gray a reassuring smile.

Ivan stiffens when his eyes lock onto mine and I remember that the sunglasses that were supposed to still be on my face are dangling between my fingers and I swallow a curse at my forgetfulness.

"Dude! When the hell—"

Ivan is cut off mid-sentence when Mason walks right into the middle of our group. I flick my eyes down to look at the floor as I make sure to tug my right sleeve closer to my palm while I use my left hand to make sure my hoodie is still covering my neck. But my movements only make Mason look at me more.

When I feel his eyes bore into me, I force myself to lift my head so I can stare right back. I know from the way his dark eyes shine that he can see the gold ring around my right eye glimmer under the fluorescent lighting.

His expression goes from arrogance to anger in an instant as he steps closer into my space and shoves me against the wall. I can feel my flames come to life under my skin as he looks me up and down, like he's sizing me up and trying to figure out if I am a big threat to him or not. I have to grind my teeth together so I can focus on keeping this new power locked to the center of my chest and not let it flow down my arm but at the same time, I want to show him that I am not the weak human I was the last time we interacted.

Ivan squeezes in front of me, and he gets right into Mason's face. "You got a fucking problem, buddy?" He growls.

Mason gives an evil smile toward Ivan and then his gaze flicks over to me again before he says, "If there weren't professors around to try and stop me, I'd show you my fucking problem."

He lets his fire dance in his palms and I notice it is darker than mine. The red is so dark that it almost looks like blood and there are traces of black running through the flame at times. When I feel the heat pour from his hand, I know it would hurt like hell to be burned by it.

"Mr. Jasper. Step away from that student." A random professor says with fear making his voice shake.

Mason chuckles darkly before he looks from Ivan to me, then finally to Gray before walking away.

Once he's out of sight, I collapse against the wall, leaning my head against the plaster as I let a sigh of relief out through my nose.

"What was all that about?" Gray asks as he steps closer to Ivan, his eyes scanning him to make sure he's alright. "I hate that douchebag."

"Just a damn Parasite thinking he can walk over people because they fear his ungodly hot fire." Ivan snaps.

As the word 'Parasite' hits me, images of last night come flooding back into my mind. Thoughts of how close I was to actually fighting this power, and that little voice taunting me, makes my heart freeze in my chest. I was so close to becoming something like Mason before Seth stepped in and coached me through it.

"You okay dude?" Ivan asks, his steel-gray eyes searching mine and lingering on my right eye a heartbeat longer before taking Gray's hand. "Come on, we got class."

I nod, "Yeah, man. I'm good. Thank you, like always, for stepping up and threatening to kick ass." I say, while trying to make light of the situation.

He gives me a hard look that says he's not done with me before he walks away.

22

Aiden

When lunchtime comes around, I grab something from the cafeteria before I head to the library to see if I can find anything on dual powers and this machine. I'm just about to go down the A section for abilities when Ivan walks in through the door and marches over to me.

He grabs me by the shoulder, drags me over to a light oak table before pulling a chair out and shoving me down to sit in it and taking one for himself.

"Dude. What is going on with you? And don't even try to tell me nothing is wrong." He snaps while putting his elbow on top of the table to point a finger at me. "I see the gold ring in your eye, so I know you have powers now."

I sigh as I nod and pull the sleeve of my hoodie up to my elbow, showing off the bright flames snaking up my forearm.

"When did this happen?"

"Last night." I say.

"At least you didn't fight it." Ivan says with relief. "From the gold ring and the bright colors, you're part of The Protector's of Power."

I glance down at the tattoo for a moment before I look back at him, "I almost did fight against it, Ivan." He stills at my confession.

"I didn't understand what was going on. It hurt so fucking much, I just wanted the pain to end, but—" I pause, not knowing if I can say anything about Seth right now. "But I did have some help at the last minute and I was able to finally get control before it got out of hand."

"You can tell him about me, Aiden. Your friends may be able to help you more than I am allowed to right now." Seth says.

"I had help from Seth." I blurt out.

"That's good. I'm happy that someone was able to—" Ivan pauses as the name seems to click in his mind, "Wait, did you say Seth? As in Seth Powell?"

"I guess. He didn't tell me his last name."

Ivan then jumps to his feet and starts to pace the floor in front of me while running his hand through his hair. "I can't believe the great Seth Powell is talking to you. And don't take this wrong, but why are you getting powers all of a sudden?"

"The hell if I know. Ever since my birthday last week, I've been getting these dreams, almost like visions. I think I'm destined for something big; I just don't understand it yet." I say with a frustrated sigh.

"I know some people have the ability to see the future, but it's not clear most of the time." Ivan replies.

Then, out of the corner of my eye, I catch something moving behind a shelf. At first I'm afraid it's Mason, but I catch a glimpse of brown hair and I breathe a sigh of relief. Ivan looks over his shoulder and he chuckles lightly before shaking his head.

"Stop hiding, Grayson." Ivan says in a teasing tone.

Gray sheepishly steps out from the bookshelf and walks over to the table. "Well, it looks like I'm the odd one out now, huh?" He says while looking at my right arm.

"Grayson." Ivan scolds. "You are not the odd one out, Babe. We still need your smart, beautiful brain. Besides, you have the two of us to protect you now." Ivan grins while giving his partner a quick peck on the lips.

"Ah, about that. I still need you to protect me, Ivan. I don't know the first thing about how to use this power." I say while waving my right arm in the air.

Gray's eyes trail a line down my right arm and then over to both of Ivan's before landing back on me. "Why do you only have one tattoo, Aiden?"

"I guess I'm getting two abilities. Remember when—"I pause, again thinking back to her. *God, why can't I get that face out of my head?* "I'm getting two abilities." I say matter-of-factly.

"Seth is talking to him." Ivan quips.

Gray's head snaps to his boyfriend's before his brown-eyed gaze lands back on me. "Seth Powell?! He's alive?"

"I guess. The dude didn't tell me his last name." I growl, now getting irritated that they both seem to know more than I do. "Why would you ask me if he's alive?" I add while rolling my eyes. *I don't think I can talk to ghosts, can I?*

"You don't know?" Gray asks in shock.

"Oh, that's right, you skipped that first class." Ivan says, while lightly smacking me on the head. I give him a playful dirty look and he continues explaining. "He is the founder of The Protector's of Power. He helped build the powerful community we know today back in

1925. From what records say, he's what's called a Mimic. He can copy any ability and use it as if he was born with it. Mimic's are even rarer than people with two abilities." Ivan says.

"Records also show that he disappeared about twenty-one years ago when he had a falling out with his brother, Victor. We know there was a huge fight between them and all records pointed to him being dead." Gray explains.

I feel Seth come into the back of my mind and I can somehow tell he's laughing at my thoughts. "What's so funny?" I ask out loud while looking a little bit over my right shoulder.

Ivan and Gray both look at me like I just grew a third eyeball. I touch my left temple and smile. "Seth is laughing at me." I say.

"It's just funny that you think a dead guy is talking to you." Seth laughs.

"He said he thinks I'm dumb to think a dead guy is talking to me." I say out loud to my friends, who are still looking at me like I just lost my marbles. "He can talk to me through my mind. I'm guessing it's a Mimic thing?" I say, my voice trailing off in a questioning tone.

"When do you think you'll get your second power?" Gray asks.

"I have no idea, and that kind of terrifies me. This hit yesterday out of nowhere." I say as I tell them all about what happened last night. About the pain and fear, and how I just wanted it all to stop.

"I understand that." Ivan says. "When I got my metallurgy abilities, I felt like I was being crushed. Metal is heavy, after all, but my dad has the same ability, so he kind of coached me through it." Ivan then looks over to Gray and gives him a small smile while running his nose over Gray's temple. "It did help that I had Grayson in my mind as an Anchor." Ivan croons and Gray shivers at his partner's touch. I look away, but only to give them a moment of privacy.

When Ivan mentioned his father, for the first time, I wish my parents were here. They have abilities and know what the onset feels like and could help me like Ivan's dad did. But I shake that thought out of my head, because no matter what, I am alone in this and I have to get through it myself.

"Hey, when you think you're getting your second power, we can help you, Aiden!' Gray says. "Ivan and I can be your anchors."

"No, Grayson." I say sternly. After seeing the look of hurt on his face, I take a breath and rub the back of my neck. "Sorry Gray, but if it's the power that I think I'm going to get, it will be dangerous for anyone to be around me."

"What power do you think it's going to be?" Gray asks.

"I think it's going to be electricity."

"I can make something to protect us, and I can figure out a way to ground you." Ivan says.

I smile at my friends and for the first time, I'm not as afraid of these powers and what they may mean in the near future.

"Okay. I'll let you two know when I feel it's going to happen."

23

Aiden

The next day thankfully is my day off from school, so I try to catch up on some sleep that I have been sorely missing out on, but Aunt Viv has other ideas.

"Aiden." Aunt Viv sings as she knocks on my door while opening it at the same time. "I have laundry for you to put away."

I groan as I turn on my left side to face her and she sets her laundry basket down on my desk to deposit the clean clothes at the foot of my bed. I toss the covers off my body and I sit up to run my right hand through my hair, not thinking about my naked torso until Aunt Viv's sharp intake of breath fills the space between us.

"Aiden Rivers! What is that on your skin, mister?" She scolds.

Shit.

"I uh, decided to get a tattoo." I say while turning my arm over in an effort to keep her searing gaze on the *ink* than my eyes, where I know the golden ring shines around my brown iris.

"What's going on, Vivian?" Uncle Matt says from the doorway after apparently hearing his wife yelling at me. His gaze darkens for a moment when he also notices the marking on my skin. "Why didn't you tell us you got a tattoo, Aiden?"

"It was just a random thing I did. I didn't think I needed your permission." I snap.

Uncle Matt gives me a warning glare as he says, "You don't need permission to do anything with your body, but we do expect the courtesy to at least let us know if you do something this drastic while under our roof."

Even though my aunt and uncle are still pissed at me for going to a 'tattoo shop', they don't give me too much more grief about the issue. While I'm relieved that I don't have to hide my tattoo, the lie of how I got it still sits like a stone in my stomach.

As I'm lying in bed five days later, something feels off. It's like I feel a vibration under my skin on the left side of my body. At this strange feeling, I think of Seth and he's there in an instant, his calming presence flooding my mind.

"You will be fine, *Aiden. You have good friends with you and I will be here too. You just need to reach out to me."* Seth says gently. *"I will warn you though, the second power is usually the hardest. Because you have two forces trying to merge in one soul, so they have to find space, but that's what makes people with two abilities stronger."* Seth says, trying to give me courage.

I listen to his words as I walk into the bathroom to look at my reflection, and I give myself a swift nod before jumping in the shower. Once I'm dressed, I head into the kitchen to have a quick bite to eat. I devour the eggs, sausage, and toast that Aunt Viv made, all the while still being careful to keep my eyes averted or not look at her for too long, and then I am out the door.

I pull into the parking lot at the University and as I'm walking up to the door that odd vibration rattles the left side of my body again. I take a breath and try to will the sensation away as I open the door and find my friends waiting for me in the hallway.

They both fall into step on either side of me, Ivan with a sharp nod and Gray with a friendly smile. I look at both of them for a moment before I feel that buzzing sensation ring through my bones again.

"Hey, are you two still willing to help me out with the second one?" I whisper so I'm not overheard.

"You don't even have to ask, buddy." Gray chimes in.

"Do you think it will be tonight?" Ivan asks in a serious tone.

"I don't know. Maybe." I reply as I rub my right hand over my left arm, trying to calm the sensation in my body, my flame tattoo peeking out from the sleeve of my hoodie with the movement.

"Dude, we will be there; don't even worry about it." Ivan replies with a small smile.

I nod my head at my friends, at my anchors, with appreciation shining in my eyes, and I know they will do anything they can to help me through this.

"Call me if you need to leave before the day is over." Ivan orders.

"Okay. I will." I say as we walk away from each other to go to our respective classes.

As the morning goes on, I feel the vibration slowly getting worse. It builds deep in my chest, just like my fire did before it strikes out like a snake toward my left shoulder. I find myself rubbing my arm at times to distract my brain from the sensation and when our lunch break rolls around; the movement gets more aggressive to cope with the discomfort. When I sit down at the metal table that Ivan chose, I am already eyeing the door that leads to the parking lot and the thought of leaving fills my mind.

"Come on, man. Let's get out of here." Ivan says, after seeing how uncomfortable I am.

He looks at Gray and motions for him to get our backpacks from the floor before he practically lifts me to my feet. I don't fight his hold as the three of us start to walk out of the cafeteria.

As we walk by a metal trash can, my left knee gives out, making me stumble a step, and my left arm brushes against the can. At the quick point of contact, electricity loudly buzzes around me and snaps at the metal, causing the can to rock in place for a moment before it settles down.

"Shit!" I grimace as I glance down at my arm, at the blueish-white electrical currents dancing over my skin for a few seconds before it disappears.

I look over my shoulder and a few people that were in the vicinity stare at me with an odd curiosity on their faces, because normally people in college don't have to deal with the onset of their powers.

This is when I know it's absolutely time to leave before I hurt someone by accident.

Ivan must come to the same conclusion because he's pulling me toward the door with an urgency filling his long stride.

"Come on, you two, let's get out of here; now." Ivan pulls something from his back pocket and I barely hear the jingle of his keys as the familiar pain begins to build in my chest again. "Gray, you drive my car to Aiden's place for me."

Gray nods as he catches the keys that Ivan throws his way.

Once Ivan and I make it to my Colorado, Gray tosses our backpacks in the bed of my truck and as Ivan drives me to my place, I silently pray that my aunt and uncle aren't home.

Mason

Sitting at a table in the corner of the cafeteria, I quietly watch the whole scene play out with Aiden as some kind of static electricity crackles around him while his two friends lead him through the door and out into the parking lot.

"Huh, so the old man knew what he was talking about when he insisted we enroll at this worthless university." I say with, a dark, amused tone.

"I still don't understand how you can doubt Victor and Avery." Rhett replies with a hint of annoyance at me.

He gives me a wild sideways glance while stabbing at the food on his plate. The sleeves of his black hoodie are pushed up to his elbows, the dark shades of gray spheres and harsh lines of his tattoos that look like a rock slide are on full display showing off his power to make and control the dirt and rocks of the earth. I give Rhett a smug look as my only response to his statement.

"Not a blind follower." A rough, ghostly voice whispers in the back of my mind.

I can feel my flames lurking just under my skin and I nod inwardly to my only comrade that I can somewhat trust, as long as I don't push them too far.

"I'm just not the type of Parasite groupie that has blinders on." I snap while getting up from the table to walk over to my beautiful girlfriend, Dani Glass, who just walked into the cafeteria.

"Whatever, man." Rhett replies, shaking his head and taking another bite of his food.

I take in Dani's presence. Her dirty blonde hair, light blue eyes that are finally starting to lose their red tint from the drugs and alcohol leaving her system, and a still somewhat slender frame that is slowly starting to look healthier as each day passes.

"Hey, Baby." I croon deeply, pulling her into my body and soundly kissing her on the lips for the whole student body to see.

I hear someone whisper, "Gross, get a room" to my left. I quickly turn my attention to the younger guy, who immediately schools his face to a look of indifference from the disgusted one he had on it a moment ago. But I don't let it go.

"What did you say, prick?" I sneer with anger, letting my dark red flame play on my fingertips.

"Protect." Whispers my flame.

"Mason!" Dani yells while grabbing at my arm as if to pull my power away from the guy.

I look over at her and reluctantly back off, but I toss a medium-sized ball of fire in the middle of the table, making the trays of food, sheets of paper, and books catch fire before I finally walk away.

"Was that necessary?" Dani asks in annoyance.

"Yes." My flame and I answer almost in unison as I drape a protective arm around her shoulders and walk out of the school, not even bothering with Rhett and the rest of my classes.

Aiden

We pull up to my house fifteen minutes later and I am relieved to see that the driveway is empty, so I know my aunt and uncle are still out of the house. When Ivan puts the transmission in park, another painful vibration hits me in the chest again, and I can feel that I'm about to discharge another electrical current again.

I begin to shove against Ivan. "Move it. Let me out, Ivan." I order.

He quickly exits the cab and I hear him say something to Gray when he pulls the Mustang behind my truck as I stumble out of the cab and into the grass near the driveway. I take a few more steps away from my friends before the pain grips my body again and I collapse to my knees in the middle of the yard.

I barely make out the sound of footsteps behind me and before I can yell at whoever it is to stay away, Ivan's face appears to my left, and he shoves something cold and solid into my hand.

Pressure builds in my chest again and I know it's that internal snake getting ready to strike. Grabbing onto what I now know to be a copper rod, like the lifeline that it is, the electrical snake strikes, and it discharges again, but this time, the bolt arcs down the rod and into the ground.

I look up at Ivan, our labored breath mingling with each other's is the only sound between us for a moment as the shock that his copper rod actually worked in keeping the electricity from arcing off my body.

"Let's get you inside, man." Ivan says.

I can only nod as he helps me to my feet and leads me into the house where I collapse onto the couch, my back sinking into the cushions and my feet hanging over the arm. Ivan sits in the oversized beige chair in the corner of the room while Gray goes into the kitchen to get each of us a bottle of water.

"Thanks, Gray." I say while taking the offered bottle and taking a few hearty chugs. I didn't realize how thirsty I was until the water touched my lips.

Gray then offers a bottle to Ivan, who politely declines. Gray sets the two bottles down on the coffee table and perches himself on the arm of the chair while gently rubbing a hand over the back of Ivan's neck. Even I can tell it's Gray's silent way of making sure his partner is okay and to ease the still-tense lines of his shoulders.

"Thanks, you two. Especially you, Gray." I say. "It's dangerous for you to be here right now and you didn't run. I appreciate it, man."

"I'm here for my friend. I can't do anything special other than making sure you don't go to the dark side." Gray says half-jokingly. "I mean you could fry me like a hamburger right now and this is just the beginning of your power it seems. I can't imagine the full force once this is all done and you have full control." Gray continues, with a hint of awe in his voice.

"I've never been around someone with two abilities. My family wasn't blessed like that." Ivan says.

"Why is it so rare for someone to have two abilities?" Gray asks while looking at Ivan.

We are quiet for a moment since this is something that is not really taught in high school or even at the university. Then, after a few moments, I feel Seth come into my mind and I repeat what he tells me.

"According to Seth, it's because it's not natural for two separate powers to operate in one body. They have to be compatible for one, and the one wielding them needs to be strong enough to handle them." I say. "Seth already warned me this is gonna be tough and yeah, even though you all are here, I'm still terrified." I admit, and I cover my face with my right arm, not wanting to see their own fear of my possible failure.

Ivan gets up off the chair and he pulls my arm down with a grip that says 'don't fight me' and when my eyes meet his, I see determination in their steel-gray depths.

"Don't be afraid, Aiden. I have this feeling that you are going to be doing great things, and Gray and I will be there to help you as much as we can." Ivan says.

"I don't want to hurt you two." I groan as I feel another wave hit me like a ton of bricks in the chest.

I get up from the couch with the copper rod in my hand and walk away from my friends until the metal discharges me with a loud crack in the space around us.

"You can't really do anything to hurt me much. I can cover my body with metal and I can give Gray here a shield. So we are good dude. You're not getting rid of us that easy." Ivan says after the electrical pulse fades from the air.

I smile at Ivan's words and at Gray's eager nod in my direction. Then, a moment later, I hear my aunt's car pull into the driveway. Panic fills my chest as another wave hits me quicker than I anticipated. It seems to feed off the panic in my mind, making the arc stronger, and the lights in the house surge for a moment as a result.

"Shit, dude, we gotta keep your emotions in check. Go to your room; I'll handle your aunt. Ivan, you go and stay with him." Gray says in an oddly commanding way.

"Oh, have I ever told you I love it when you get bossy, Grayson?" Ivan croons.

"Now's not the time you, Lug Nut. Get out of here." Gray snaps.

I lead Ivan to my room and he shuts the door behind us as I sit on the bed and he takes a seat at my desk. I watch in silence as he opens his right hand to make a thicker rod for me. The metal flowing out of his palm in a thick, almost molasses consistency, then hardening into the copper rod a moment later.

"Just in case you break that one." Ivan says with a smile.

"That's honestly weird to watch you do that." I say. "I've never paid attention to how you use your ability." I say as I start to feel that odd pull in the center of my chest get stronger again. "I think it's about to get worse soon." I say as I rub my chest as I look into Ivan's eyes.

"Feeling the Soul Pull, huh? That's the best way I can explain it." Ivan says. "It's when your ability is trying to figure its way out of your Soul Power and through your body."

"Yeah, I guess." I say as a wave hits me and this time I feel it pull from the center of my chest as it starts to go toward my shoulder and the entire left side of my body feels like it's filled with a thousand bees buzzing under my skin.

Just as Gray opens my door, another arc comes off me and I can't help the yelp that bursts from my throat at the loud snap. My grip tightens on the rod in my hand, but I feel something crumble around my fingers. Like Ivan said, from the electric shock coursing through the metal, the rod rusts and burns in my hand.

"And that's why I made a thicker one. I will make it thicker each time you rust one." Ivan says in a cool tone as he hands me another rod before making another one to have at the ready.

24

Aiden

This is the one thing that scares me the most about this whole power thing. Just like last time, I have no sense of time. I can't figure out how long I've been at this and I can tell that Ivan nor Gray will clue me in on it.

I can't stay still anymore. I start to pace the floor of my room and each time the pain builds and pulls in my chest; I sit on my bed and let the metal that Ivan made ground me. He even made metal plates for me to put my bare feet on when I sit down to keep the arcs on me and not branch out into the house. I'm not even sure when I kicked my shoes off, but my bare feet on the metal helps me ground a bit better.

Sweat drips from my brow as faint whispers begin to fill my mind and what they tell me, what they beg me to do, sends chills down my spine.

"Keep fighting. Keep fighting back; it will help with the pain." The voice whispers in a manic, echoing laugh.

I think back to Ivan's words, that he felt I was destined for great things and this helps me focus on the rod in my hand and allow the electricity to arc down the metal.

It feels like a lifetime has passed by. Ivan has made four more plates and three more rods, all thicker than the previous one. At some point, I must have stripped off my shirt because I only have my black shorts on now. This is the first time that Ivan and Gray have seen my flame tattoo on full display, and the look on Ivan's face when he sees how high up on my neck it travels makes my gut clench. He knows as well as I do that how high the marking goes means how strong the power will be.

I shake my head as the electricity begins to consistently flare from my left arm and my back, but they don't arc toward the pole this time. They keep a closed circuit on my skin before disappearing under the surface, only to reappear a moment later in a new area.

As I take slow breaths to cope with the exhaustion that is slowly filling my limbs, my wrist starts to itch like it did with my fire. I look down and there is a little black lightning bolt forming on my skin. At this little image, I become even more aware of the pressure building in my chest and I hear the taunting voice again whisper eerily in my mind.

"Fight me, fight me Aiden. I know you want to."

I jump up with a burst of anger and annoyance filling my veins and I rear my arm back with a desperate yell and I punch a hole in the wall next to my closet with my left hand.

I leave my fist in the hole and lean my forehead against the drywall. "Get out of my head, damn it." I whisper while breathing heavily, not moving from my position.

I open my right eye enough to notice Ivan has pulled Gray behind him at my outburst and I can see the panic flood both of their faces.

"Ivan, get ready to... protect Gray. I think I should try to release it." I say, thinking back on what I did with my fire, and then everything calmed down.

I feel the pull in my chest again and it's all I can do not to scream out. "Now, Ivan." I manage to grunt out.

At my plea, Ivan erects a thick copper wall, and he makes sure that Gray is behind it. Once I know my friends are safe from me, I can't hold back this power anymore. I peel myself off the wall while dropping the pole from my hand. I imagine the electricity that I feel writhing inside me flow through my veins and the power moves from the center of my chest, over my shoulder, down my arm, and into my fingers, in a violent rush that I swear would make my arm explode.

A loud crack of electrical power echoes through the room as it arcs out of my hand and toward the door. When the current collides into the drywall over my bedroom door, all the lights in the house go out at once before flickering back on a few tense moments later. My legs all of a sudden feel weak with the burst of energy I just let loose and I lean against the wall near my closet again, trying to catch my breath.

The vibration in my left arm begins to fade and I watch as ghostly blue and white jagged lines start to climb up my skin from the underside of my wrist going all the way up my arm to my shoulder and neck before curving into the center of my chest to meet up with the flame that already lives there on the other side. The harsh, jagged lines make it look like I have a living lightning bolt on my skin.

"You okay, dude?" Gray asks popping his head out from behind Ivan's wall.

I nod as I slowly walk over to my bed and sit on the corner. I put my head in my hands to get my bearings, both tattoos catching my eye.

After a few minutes, I feel Seth in the back of my mind, and I think he's about to tell me I failed because I was so close to fighting back...again.

"Yes, you were close to losing; I'm not going to beat around the bush, but I think your friends really helped pull you through. Your thought to protect them helped you focus on what you needed to do." Seth says.

"It's so weird." I think to Seth for the first time without verbalizing my thoughts to him. *"It's like they have a mind of their own."*

"That's because they do. That is what makes people go mad. The abilities become parasites, controlling the host." Seth says.

At this information, chills run up my spine. I couldn't imagine hearing something that creepy all the time.

"That is why we have that initial burst of power. That expels the sentient being and the powers are then ours to control." Seth says.

Ivan walks over to me and puts his hand on my left shoulder. I lift my head from my hands to look at him and with the expression on his face, I can pick up on the loaded question he wants to ask, but is too afraid to verbalize it.

"I'm fine. I'm still on the good side. Don't worry." I say with a weak smile.

"You had me wondering there for a bit, dude." Ivan replies while looking down at my new wielding mark.

"I was worried too." I admit quietly.

"Those are so badass, by the way." Gray says while walking over to us and pointing to my arms.

They don't take up the entire expanse of my skin, just encircling my arms like a snake and defining the muscles, which right now, makes them look bigger than they are. I am by no means out of shape, but I am not as built as Ivan is.

"We're going to let you get some rest, and we need to do damage control here, too. You want us to bring back some takeout?" Gray asks.

"Yeah, that would be great. Besides, hanging out with my best friends doesn't sound that bad after an ordeal like this." I say as I look around the room at the holes in the wall from my fist and from the bolt of lightning over my door. The charred plaster still smoldering a bit from the contact.

When Gray and Ivan leave, I lie back on my bed and as soon as my head hits my pillow, I instantly doze off. After a few moments, a plain gray chamber begins to come into view and I feel someone standing behind me. I turn around and I am met with the black silhouette of a human figure. I can tell it's male from the larger build and from the way they walk. Even though I can't make out any features, I somehow know it's Seth.

"I wanted to check in on you to see how you are doing." Seth says, using what I can tell is his real voice.

"I'm tired. And I'm also still on edge on how damn close I was to giving in and listening to that power." I say with shame in my voice and I look away from Seth. Even though I can't see his face, I don't want him to see the failure in mine.

"Try being a Mimic." His simple reply makes my head snap back to look at his silhouette. "I had several in my mind all at once and I almost gave in. It's human nature to feel the need for self-preservation, to protect yourself no matter the cost. But we must have a strong mind to face the fear and the pain so we don't lose ourselves." Seth says.

I stare at the black figure of Seth, and I smile at him. "Thank you for that." I say, suddenly not feeling so bad.

Seth chuckles. "Now go get some rest because soon you will meet me in person and start your training."

"Training?" I ask.

Seth's silhouette vanishes without an explanation and I'm left alone in the gray room. After a few beats, I start to see images of the visions I've been having appear on the walls like a silent movie, but this time, things make more sense to me. The fire crackling in the distance and the snap of electricity arcing around me and near the huge metal construction of The Siphon. But what I still don't understand is, why me?

What can I do that Seth, a Mimic, can't?

25

Aiden

I wake up a few hours later to the sound of colorful curses flying from Ivan and Gray while they are playing a game on my PlayStation 5 and losing horribly to a horde of undead monsters.

"I hope you all are having fun there." I say with mock annoyance.

"Oh come on Gray, quit cheating!" Ivan yells.

"You're just a sore loser, Babe!" Gray replies.

"Sorry, Aiden. We got bored watching you sleep." Ivan says as Gray kills off a monster with a shotgun to the face.

"Your aunt and uncle have no clue about anything. When we left, no one was home, and we got back in time for Gray to patch the walls for you." Ivan says while pointing behind him where he knows the damage was.

I look around the room and I notice a little bit of wet paint still over the door where my electricity connected with that part of the room and also on the wall next to my closet where I punched it to try to block out the voices.

"Thank you." I say to both of my friends.

"I told Gray I knew there was a reason we kept him around. He is great at fixing the stuff we break." Ivan jokes while putting Gray in a headlock.

Gray breaks out of Ivan's grip and the brightest grin I have ever seen him make appears on his face at Ivan and me.

"I hear that behind every great Protector of Power, there is a human that helps them in the background." Gray says.

"Where the hell did you hear that?" Ivan asks, rolling his eyes.

"From me, I just made it up." Gray says while jumping Ivan and pulling his arm behind his back.

I just watch my friends wrestle on the floor, and I shake my head at their bantering. When Gray goes to pin Ivan on his back and straddle his hips, I look away before I hear Gray press a quick kiss to his partner's lips. I don't give them any flack for showing their affection towards one another because I know I did it enough around them when we were younger. But on the other hand, I don't want to feel like the third wheel here.

"Come on, you two, let's play that game for a bit." I laugh as they finally untangle themselves from one another and we play until we begin to smell dinner cooking from the kitchen.

The next day comes and goes without issue and I am careful to hide the new tattoo from my aunt and uncle, keeping the long sleeve of my left side down to hide it. Ivan and Gray come back over to play video games and hang out like yesterday didn't happen.

I am lying sideways on my bed while Ivan is in my desk chair, and Gray is sitting cross-legged on the floor in front of him, both with a controller in their hands while they watch a cut scene from the game. I trace the bright blue and white edge of the lightning bolt that peeks out from my sleeve and I start to think about what has happened to me in the last few weeks. And while I feel stronger, I have no clue how to use or control these new abilities, and that scares me.

"I know that look. What are you thinking about, Aiden." Ivan says, reading my quiet demeanor.

I try to brush him off, and I push both sleeves up to my elbows in an effort to push back the thoughts in my head, but he pauses the horror game just as the fungal-ridden monster is about to jump at his character, and now I have both Ivan and Gray staring at me.

I take a breath and look at them both before I speak. "I feel stronger, but yet I have not one clue how to use these abilities. I've never been around anyone with powers outside of you, Ivan." I refuse to say *her* name still. "Aunt Viv and Uncle Matt don't have them." I say. "So I don't have the slightest clue in what to do."

After a moment of silence, I continue with what has been plaguing me since yesterday. "I'm supposed to have training with Seth soon, but what about in the meantime? I can't hide these forever." I say while waving my hand down my arms that scream, *I have powers now.* "I don't want to put you two in the middle."

"You will not be putting us in the middle of anything." Gray says.

"Do you want me to show you some things for now?" Ivan asks. "It shouldn't be much different from how I am able to use my metal."

I look at Ivan like he's grown a third eye, but then I smile at him. "Yeah, show me." I say.

"Okay. Have you pulled your abilities since you've gotten them?" Ivan asks.

I shake my head. "No, I haven't. I don't really know how to." I say with a little embarrassment heating my cheeks.

"Let's pull your fire to your hand. Since you got that one first, it may be easier for you to control." Ivan says.

I think about the first night and how my fire was dancing in my right hand. I feel that pull from the center of my chest, the Soul Pull as Ivan called it, and that makes me back off. I rub a hand over my chest while Ivan looks at me questioningly.

"I...something feels weird. I still feel that Soul Pull as you call it." I say as I continue to rub the center of my chest.

"Oh, you will feel that all the time. This is the source of everyone's power. You may feel it a little more than I would because, one, I'm used to it, but, secondly, since you have two powers, you may feel it stronger than I do. But that is normal. Try again." Ivan says, urging me forward.

I take a breath as I nod at my friends. I focus on my right hand again, and when the pulling sensation flares to life in my chest, I force myself to push through. I feel a surge of fire flow from my chest then down my arm in a rush that threatens to take my breath, and just when I'm about to pull it back to my center, I see a bright flame finally dancing to life in my hand. It's higher than I wanted though, probably about two and a half feet off my hand, but I called it for the first time on my own.

"Yeah! Look at that dude!" Gray says with excitement.

"Now, just keep doing that and you will be able to control it better. That's how I learned. Just bring it forward and turn it off." Ivan says.

"How did you do that and not have tons of iron bars everywhere?" Gray asks while looking at Ivan with a confused brow.

"I can also absorb metal just as well as I can make it, so I just cleaned up my mess." Ivan says while shrugging his shoulder. "You should be able to do that with fire and the electricity too, Aiden."

"Seriously?" I ask, whipping my head from the flame in my hand to look at my friend.

"Yes, but don't do that just yet. You can still hurt yourself." Seth warns.

I nod slightly at Seth's voice, but the thought of being able to do something like that both horrifies and excites me at the same time.

26

Aiden

After school the next day, which thankfully goes by without incident from Mason, I make it home and go right to my room to start on *homework,* but when in reality, I'm practicing with my fire like Ivan taught me.

Each time I call my fire to my right hand, the easier it gets and the more I can understand how the power flows through my body.

I work on changing the size each time I bring my fire forward. I make the flame dance about five feet in height from my hand, and when I cut the flow of power with a simple image of a valve being closed, it dies with a whoosh from my fingers. Then I imagine only opening that valve halfway and a smaller flame bursts to life no bigger than a softball in my palm.

Thirty minutes later, I hear Aunt Viv cursing in the kitchen before she calls my name. "Aiden! Come here a minute if you're not busy."

"Coming!" I holler back as I kill the fire in my palm and make sure that my left sleeve is pulled down to my wrist. I haven't told my aunt about my other 'tattoo' yet, so it's best to leave that hidden for now.

I walk out of my room and go into the kitchen to find my aunt trying to get the pilot light on the stove to catch.

"This old thing won't light again. Can you watch it while I get some kindling for the pilot light?" Aunt Vivian asks.

I nod my head, and she walks out into the garage with an aggravated huff. I look at the stove and I know it needs a flame to catch the gas vapor. As I step closer to the burner, I focus on pulling my fire from my core, but instead of igniting my whole hand like I have been doing, I think about the flame going toward only my pinky finger.

I feel the Soul Pull, but it's a little stronger this time because I'm forcing this power into a smaller point of release, but I make myself push through the uncomfortable feeling. After a few moments, my flame dances on my fingertip and I let a small smile tug at the corner of my mouth at my accomplishment.

As I hear the garage door open, I gently put my finger next to the pilot light, and with a sharp whoosh, the gas ignites into a blue flame. I shut off the flow of fire from my fingertip and I pull my hand away just as Aunt Vivian comes into the kitchen. She looks at the stove and back to me in confusion.

"The pilot light finally caught." I say, hoping she didn't hear the way my voice cracks a bit at the lie. "Good thing I was here to watch it."

"That's why I wish we could get an electric stove. I hate this old thing." Aunt Viv complains as she grabs her skillet and starts to fix dinner.

"Very good Aiden. I'm proud of you." Seth says.

I smile at his words and I can even feel his approval from what I was able to do. So, I turn to Aunt Viv and I decide to help her finish with dinner.

Later that night, I think of my electricity and maybe I should practice with it for a while too. I try to pull it forward and while it comes right away, it still arcs off the top of my shoulder with a violent zap, and the lights flicker in the house from the sudden power surge.

A heartbeat later, I hear my aunt and uncle talking through my bedroom door.

"Matt, what was that?" Aunt Vivian asks.

"It may be the fuse, Viv. I'll go look." Uncle Matt says in annoyance.

"Oh shit, I can't do that here right now. I have to be out of the house and away from other electrical currents. At least until I can control it." I say out loud to myself.

I call it a night of practicing with either power and I decide to see if Ivan has any ideas on how I can control my electricity better.

The next day at school as I pull into a parking spot, Ivan and Gray are already waiting for me by his Mustang and I grab my backpack from the bed of my truck as I begin to walk with them into the main building.

"Good Morning, Aiden." Gray says with a smile.

"How ya doin' man?" Ivan asks while smacking me on the shoulder.

"I'm good. I was practicing last night and I'm getting better with," I pause and shake my right hand to indicate my fire. "but I'm still not able to use my left side without arcing. I almost made the whole house surge last night because I wasn't grounded with a copper rod."

Ivan nods for a moment, and his brows scrunch in thought. "I have an idea. Give me a little bit to figure some things out and I'll get back with you on that."

"Okay. Thanks, man." I say as we walk inside the main building of the school and go our separate ways for our respective classes.

Just as I turn a corner, I pass right by Mason on the other side of the hall. I instinctively pull at my sleeves to make sure my tattoos are covered, and he immediately tracks the movement while giving me a menacing smirk. I try to quicken my step to get into the classroom and away from him, but before I can even put my hand on the doorknob, a maroon-colored ball of fire, no bigger than a baseball, flies in front of my face. It collides with the brick wall in a shower of flames and embers as it devours the papers that were taped to the wall a moment ago but are now ash on the floor.

With just that small amount of fire, I can feel just how hot he can make his flames. The skin on my face and neck is almost constricting from the quick burn and it didn't even touch me, so I can just imagine that it would hurt like a bitch to actually have his flame burn flesh.

Anger floods my chest once the shock of the attack fades. Does he know about my developing powers and thinks he can coax me into an easy fight? I might not know how to fight with my powers yet, but I can still throw a damn right hook and break his nose.

Just as I am about to confront him, the door that I was rushing for a moment ago opens and the professor looks between me and Mason before giving the latter a weak scolding stare as he ushers me into the classroom and away from the threat in the hall. Mason only chuckles darkly before walking away with his hands in his pockets.

After I have lunch later that afternoon, I have a few hours between classes so I figured I would just go back to my truck and maybe privately practice with my fire again when I see Gray leaning his back on the passenger side door and his foot is resting against the tire.

"Gray, what are you up to?" I ask as I approach.

"Come with me." Gray says with a smile.

He leads me around to the rear of the college grounds and over to an empty shed that's nestled into a little patch of overgrown weeds and shrubs.

"What are we doing here?" I ask as Gray walks into the 12 by 12 space.

I look around and I notice that the only light source is from the skylight in the roof. The dingy and dirty glass letting in only enough light to see with. I can somehow also tell that this shed has no electricity it in and I find myself smiling at my friend.

"Again, Gray Lukas, you are the brains of our little group." I say.

"You can't short circuit a building that has no electricity running in it." Gray grins like he just struck an oil well.

"But what are we doing here?" I ask again. "You can't really help me here, Gray."

"No, but I have an idea." Ivan says from the doorway.

I turn to see him setting a box of something on the dusty floor of the shed and the clinking of glass fills my ears. Ivan then leans against the door frame with his arms crossed over his muscular chest and the grin that plays on his lips makes his face light up with pride at his idea.

"And just what idea do you have, Ivan?" I ask as I mirror his stance.

He bends down to open the box, and he pulls out a clear glass light bulb. "You are going to power this bulb without blowing the fuse." Ivan says like it's a simple task.

I look at Ivan like he's a madman, but deep down I know this would probably be the best way to learn how to control this ability. Ivan hands me the bulb and then makes me a copper rod to help me ground myself.

"Go on. Light one up." Ivan instructs as he motions for Gray to stand by his side near the door.

"Fine." I sigh.

I sit in the middle of the floor, crossing my legs and I concentrate on calling my electricity. Which, thanks to the rod, I am able to keep the current in my hand.

Two hours later and breaking about a hundred bulbs, my body is starting to ache and tire from using my power so much, but I am determined to at least try to light one, just for a second. So I decide to try once more, concentrating on how the electricity flows through my veins, and while it's erratic and quick-tempered, I can feel it flow through my body like my fire does. Slithering just under the skin.

I try to ease the power into my thumb, index and middle fingers that are currently holding the bulb and I almost get the filament to light without breaking, but I hear Gray knock something over and I jump which makes the lightning arc from my arm, breaking the bulb and sends the current racing toward the opposite wall from my friends.

Ivan quickly erects a copper wall around him and Gray before the bolt touches them and after I know they are safe, I throw the broken bulb into the box and collapse onto my back with an aggravated growl echoing off the wooden walls of the shed.

"Damn it, why is this one so fucking hard?" I whine while throwing my right arm over my face.

"Do you think it can be because of the type of power it is? Even normal electricity is hard to predict." Ivan says.

"That and because with it being a second power, you have to focus a little more." Seth says, tickling the back of my mind.

"This is gonna be a long day. You got anymore you can confiscate, Ivan?" I ask.

"Seth gave you info, didn't he?" Ivan asks, ignoring my question.

"Yeah. I just have a lot going against me here. The fact alone it being a second ability is already a little harder, plus the type like you said." I tell him.

"Give me an hour and I'll be back with more bulbs." Ivan says.

Mason

I watch from my hiding place in the brush as Aiden and his friends walk into the shed. I noticed the smaller of the three scoping out this place about an hour ago, so I decided to follow him, somewhat curious about what these three are up to.

"Good thing we are alone, or the pet would report back to him." My flames gravelly voice whispers in my mind, speaking about Rhett.

"Tell me about it." I reply under my breath.

I quietly stalk closer to the shed and I find a crack in the wall to look through and what I see makes me quietly chuckle to myself.

"How the hell is this dude going to be an issue for Victor and his insane plan? He can't even control his powers. This has got to be the biggest joke I have ever heard." I think to my fire.

I shake my head and walk away from the shed as Aiden breaks his one hundredth bulb. I am not going to bother with this weakling anymore; he's not even a threat.

Avery got it wrong.

27

Aiden

While we are waiting for Ivan to get back with more bulbs, I have a thought.

"Gray, can you back up to that metal door? I want to see if I can control it without trying to force it into anything." I ask.

Gray backs up toward the door and notices a rubber mat on the floor, so he decides to stand on that while watching me silently. I take a breath and close my eyes, focusing on the connection I have to my abilities. Somehow I know that deep down my connection to my fire is different from my electricity if I concentrate on it hard enough.

I call my fire forward and I pay attention to how it feels when I'm pulling it from my Soul Power. I focus on how it flows across my chest, down my arm, and into my hand. I begin to feel Seth lurking in the back of my mind, but I try to ignore him so I can focus on the task at hand.

I cut the connection to my fire and while taking another breath; I attempt to bring forward the electricity. I feel the power pull from my chest, but instead of the flow like lava, this sensation is like a striking snake. It snaps toward the left side of my body and as soon as it hits my shoulder; it arcs out with a loud crack, and I quickly cut off the connection. I think back to when I was first getting this ability and how I was able to at least keep it to myself when I was grounded with the help of Ivan's copper rod.

I wonder if I can do that myself? Like attracts like, *right? Maybe I can have this power going in several directions at once.*

I then try to call the lightning again, and this time, I visualize two threads branching from my Soul Power. One going to my leg and down to my foot, and the other toward my arm for me to use. I feel the electrical current hum around me a moment later, but I'm not hearing the loud crack of the discharge off my shoulder.

I feel Seth in my mind again and I can tell he's brimming with excitement. I open my eyes, turning my head to the left and there is a little ball of electricity bouncing in my hand. Every once in a while, an arc of lightning skitters down my arm, but it's staying around me.

Gray comes out from his hiding place behind the door with a huge smile on his face. "You did it, dude! I don't know how, but you did!"

"I was just thinking of how Ivan was able to help me ground and I thought that maybe I could do that to myself." I explain.

I start to walk toward Gray with my power still flowing down my arm, but when I pick up my left foot, I hear a loud crack of electricity and I watch in horror as the arc flies toward Gray. I don't think about my next actions, I just move.

I instantly push my fire to my right foot while imagining rockets using a flame to make them move, and that helps me run faster. At the last possible second, I somehow beat the electrical current and find myself standing in front of Gray, my palms flat against the wall behind him while my arms cage in his head and his nose almost pressing into my chest. I feel the electrical current connect against my back a heartbeat later with a small jolt, and I can't stop the yelp at the shock as my body reabsorbs the current.

Gray looks at me with fear in his eyes and I know my face is showing the same.

"You okay, Gray?" I ask softly, still shocked that I was able to get there as quickly as I did and to take the lightning back into my body.

Gray's face instantly morphs from fear to teasing as he takes in how close I'm standing to him.

"I didn't know you liked me that way, Aiden. But I will say, Ivan does not share what's his." Gray smiles fiendishly.

I fight to not roll my eyes at him. "Well, does Ivan know that you look at other men?" I playfully challenge.

Gray shakes his head at me and pushes me away, but his expression morphs again to shock. I look over my shoulder and I see a white trail of smoke drifting from my back at the point of where the electricity collided with my skin.

I take off my hoodie, noticing the hole in the center and the charred edges that are still smoldering.

"You okay, man?" Gray finally asks.

I turn around so he can look at my back and I hear him chuckle a little.

"What?" I ask, looking back over my shoulder at him.

"Yeah, man. You're good." Gray says while taking a picture on his phone.

He turns his phone around to show me what was once a crisp white undershirt, is now charred and fraying at the edges of the hole, but the skin on my back is unscathed.

"That is still so odd to see." I say in disbelief.

"You're telling me!" Gray says with an energetic tone.

Ivan finally comes back with more bulbs and he stops in his tracks at the sight of my shirt, and he looks between me and Gray with a shake of his head.

"I leave you two alone for one hour, and you get into trouble." Ivan scolds, but at the same time, he tries to hide a smile, which fails miserably.

"Hey! We got bored." Gray quips back with a smile towards me.

I explained to Ivan what I was trying to do and how I was able to protect Gray. Ivan's stance changes from worry at my story to a sense of ease at how I was able to protect his boyfriend when he wasn't there. I do, however, leave out Gray's little jab earlier. I may do stupid things, but I'm not totally dumb. Ivan would still kick my ass for even talking to his man that way.

"Well, I'm glad you were able to protect Gray." Ivan says as he moves toward his partner and gives him a kiss on the top of the head before turning his attention back to me. "Did you still want to practice more?" Ivan asks.

I think about it for a moment, then I smile and nod. "Yeah. I want to try to figure this out. There has got to be different ways to ground where I can still move around." I say.

"We'll let's get started." Ivan says while handing me a light bulb.

I take the bulb and go to the middle of the room, away from my friends. I decide to try to ground in my leg again, just to see if I can control the current. I imagine the current flowing from my chest and branching out into my leg and arm at the same time.

Once I feel the energy hit my hand, and the little arcs of current flowing across my arm, almost like the lightning bolt of my wielding mark is coming to life, I slowly let the power climb up my thumb, index, and middle fingers and into the socket of the bulb where I hear the filament heat up and bend. I stare in awe at the lit bulb in my hand and I try to not let my joy overpower the current, but when I hear Gray's cheer of excitement, it startles me and I end up overloading the bulb anyway, making glass explode with a sharp crack.

"Good job, man!" Gray exclaims. "Sorry, I made you overload it, though."

"It's okay. I'm happy I was able to get it to light at all."

I start to think of another way to ground myself as I light another bulb, this time being careful not to overload it.

"Hey Ivan? Can you make a wall around you and Gray? I want to try another grounding idea." I say.

"Sure, dude." Ivan nods as he makes a thick copper wall around himself and Gray.

Ivan is closer to the outer edge than I'd like, but I figure he can make something to cover his face if needed. So, I focus on the electricity in my veins and I ground it to my left foot. As I pick that foot up to take a step, I try to switch the current over to my right foot, but when I try to imagine it jumping over, it doesn't happen and I end up arcing off my shoulder again, the current striking the copper wall right next to Ivan's face.

I pull the power back to my chest and I run over to my friends. "Ivan! Are you okay? I'm so sorry!" I say, and I don't even hold back the fear in my voice.

"It's okay, Aiden. It didn't get me." Ivan says, his eyes still wide on how quickly the arc rushed him and how close it was to his face.

After the initial rush of adrenaline fades from my body, I begin to feel lightheaded and find myself leaning against the copper wall for support.

"Hey guys, I'm gonna call it quits for today. I think I may have overdone it." I say, while trying to catch my breath.

"It's okay. You did a lot today. You should be proud of what you were able to get done. It probably doesn't feel like much, but you were able to control it, even if it was just for a little bit." Ivan says.

"Thank you, man. I appreciate that more than you will know." I say as we walk out of the little shed.

I trail behind Ivan and Gray and I catch little bits and pieces of their conversation. Gray is so expressive with his hands and Ivan just quietly listens like he always does. Gray must accidentally let it slip just *how* I protected him and I am on the receiving end of a glare that could kill if his eyes could shoot daggers, but Gray's touch and a whispered word in his boyfriend's ear makes him look away.

When we make it back to the parking lot, I am just about to climb into the cab of my Colorado so I can drive home when I see Ivan grab the back of Gray's neck and before I shut my door; I hear Gray's sharp laugh echo through the air before he jumps into the passenger seat of Ivan's Mustang.

Ivan looks back at me through the windshield and he gives me a smug smirk and I know that he will get back at me for *trying to take what's* his, even though he knows it's a joke. So I just flip him off as I start the engine of my truck and drive home.

When I pull into the garage fifteen minutes later, I notice the time is about three-thirty in the afternoon and the house is empty, so I decide to go to my room and try to rest a little bit before it's time to help my aunt with dinner.

I wake up a little bit later, and I glance at the alarm clock on my nightstand. The red digital font reads five-thirty in the afternoon, and I pick up on the smell of food cooking on the grill out back on the patio. I hear my aunt humming a tune from the kitchen, so I get up, fix my unruly bedhead, throw on a t-shirt, and join her.

Just as I hit the entry to the kitchen, Uncle Matt is walking through the open sliding glass door that leads to the patio so he can put the hot dogs out on the grill.

"Hi, Aiden. I wondered where you were." Aunt Viv asks.

"Yeah, I fell asleep when I got home from school." I say as I scrub the back of my neck with my right hand.

I see she is in the middle of peeling potatoes, so without thinking, I grab a paring knife with my left hand to help her and she glances at both of my arms. It doesn't dawn on me until her eyes widen at what she sees on my left arm and my stomach clenches. Both tattoos of flame and lightning are on full display, but before she can utter a word, we hear a loud whoosh of fire and Uncle Matt yells from out back.

"Oh shit! Get the fire extinguisher!"

Aunt Viv runs out to the garage while I go out back with Uncle Matt. I watch in horror as the fire dances on the grill and gets higher from the grease and the oxygen in the air. I watch for a moment while it starts to lick at the bushes near the house and I know if they catch, then the whole house might go up.

I rush over to pull Uncle Matt away from the grill when I remember how Ivan told me he can absorb metal and I think of how I was able to absorb my electricity earlier today. So, without a second thought, I take a step toward the grill.

"Aiden, no!" Uncle Matt yells while grabbing my right arm to pull me back.

"Just be careful, Aiden. You can get hurt even with fire. The best hint I can give you is to try to mix your fire with that flame and then act almost like a vacuum to pull them both in." Seth says.

"Aiden, what are you doing? Get away from the grill!" Aunt Vivian screams as she brings the fire extinguisher from the garage.

"Please, just trust me." I say in a surprisingly calm tone.

I look at the flames again and notice they are a darker color than my flames. I reach down to turn off the propane tank and then I call my fire to my hand. I hear my aunt and uncle's shocked reaction to my own flame, but I try to ignore them.

I think about my flame getting larger than this natural version and I let them mingle with one another. It's easy to see where my flame ends and the natural one begins due to the color difference.

Once I have enough of my flame covering the other, I start to pull my flame back towards me. I feel the bite from the natural flame's heat go into my hand and snake its way up my arm from the inside, and I groan in pain. Just as I feel the fire start to creep into my shoulder, a thought comes to me, like a little voice that says to stay away from my Soul Power.

So, I pull it into my chest while being mindful to keep it away from that invisible core, and I watch as the fire on the grill finally disappears. My body feels like it's on fire on the inside, but it's not as bad as the night I first developed my flame, but it still hurts.

My body then begins to shake and I struggle to catch my breath, and it's then that I realize I didn't recover enough from my little experiment session earlier and I start to feel myself getting tired. Seth's presence blooms in the back of my mind again, and I reach for him like a lifeline.

"Now imagine your fire merging with this natural flame, taking it over and devouring it." Seth instructs.

As soon as I think about my fire eating the natural flame, it happens all at once. My flame becomes this ravenous creature, devouring the other version, instantly snuffing it out. Once the burning in my body fades and I collapse onto one knee, a fresh wave of exhaustion hits me. Beads of sweat drip down my forehead and I'm still trying to catch my breath. I hear someone take a step toward me and I have forgotten that Aunt Viv and Uncle Matt just witnessed all this.

"Aiden?" Aunt Viv asks in a soft voice.

Even though her voice is soft, I can hear the fear and confusion in it. I look over at them as I shift my weight from my knee to sit down and try to give a lazy smile.

"Are you okay?" Aunt Viv asks.

"Yeah, I think so." I say, still a little out of breath, while weakness weighs my limbs down.

"When did you get abilities?" Uncle Matt asks in disbelief.

"About two months ago, right after my birthday." I say.

I show them my arms, and I watch as Uncle Matt's face goes ghostly white at both of my wielding marks.

28

Aiden

“No. It can't be.” Uncle Matt whispers.

“What's wrong?” I ask, getting my strength back suddenly as adrenaline courses through my system again.

He looks at me for a second before asking, “Have you met with Seth?”

“Matt, you know he's gone.” Aunt Vivian interrupts.

“No! He's not. He went into hiding after I lost—” Uncle Matt snaps but then pauses.

“Hold up, you know Seth?” I ask, cutting off my uncle before he can say anything else.

“Yes, I know him. He was, I mean, he's my best friend.” Uncle Matt says.

“Yeah, I've been talking to him since my birthday. He helped me through getting my abilities.” I say.

“Has he told you anything else?” Uncle Matt presses.

I shake my head in response.

“Of course, he's keeping you in the dark about certain things,” Uncle Matt says with a hint of annoyance.

"You know more than you're letting on, Uncle Matt. What's going on here?" I ask, pleading for him to tell me more of what all this means.

I notice the looks between Aunt Viv and Uncle Matt. Her expression is filled with sadness while his is filled with anger.

"Let's take this inside." Uncle Matt says as he helps me to my feet.

We all walk inside and sit around the dining table. Uncle Matt looks me in the eye and gives a small chuckle, apparently just now noticing the golden ring around my irises, and then he looks over to Aunt Vivian who has a tear in her eye. He gives her a small smile and looks back at me.

He takes a breath while pushing up the sleeves of his shirt to his elbows. He then grabs a napkin from the dining table and dips a corner of it into a glass of water.

He starts to wipe away something from his skin. I then understand he was covering his skin with what I am assuming is Aunt Viv's makeup. The more he wipes at his skin, I slowly begin to see sharp and jagged lines appear. He stops at his elbow where his sleeve is still bunched up and I take in the image before me with wide eyes. I realize that he has lightning bolt tattoos on both of his arms, but they're not as colorful as mine or Ivan's markings. Uncle Matt's are stark white in color, almost like scars.

"You have abilities? Why didn't you tell me, or ever use them?" I ask in shock.

Uncle Matt takes a deep breath and runs his right thumb over his left wrist. "I had electricity, like you." He whispers.

I instantly pick up on the past tense and I can't help but to ask again, "You had electricity?" I ask, fearing his next words.

"They were taken, just before you came to live with us." Uncle Matt says.

I start to have flashes again of The Siphon, and I shake my head to clear the images from my mind.

"Why?" I ask.

"Wrong place, wrong time. And Victor knew that hurting me would hurt Seth and your parents the most." Uncle Matt says with anger in his vacant eyes, almost like he's reliving that moment.

I jump up from the table and reach for Seth and I begin talking out loud. "Why the fuck didn't you tell me any of this, Seth? Don't you think I should have known?"

"I didn't want to tell you anything until I knew for sure you were the one we were waiting on, plus if you didn't know about Matt's powers or lack thereof, I shouldn't be the one to tell you. That's Matt's story to tell." Seth says.

"Okay, he had one point. He didn't want to tell me about you; that is your story to tell." I say to my uncle. "But what do you mean about if I was the one or not?" I direct this question to Seth, but Uncle Matt answers it for me.

"You have to be able to at least control your abilities a little bit before you're told anything, Aiden." He says.

"I have my fire down, but the electricity is a bit hard. I can't ground the right way yet." I pause, suddenly needing to know this one piece of information right now. "Does this have to do with The Siphon?" I ask.

Uncle Matt's face floods with knowing and I reach out to Seth so he can hear what I'm about to say too.

"If it has anything to do with that machine, I will do whatever it takes to destroy it. I've been having something like visions, and I know I am the only one that can destroy it." I say with a hint of anger in my voice. But something inside makes me feel that I may not walk away from this.

"And even if it means giving every ounce of my own powers and possibly even dying, I will make sure this thing will *not* hurt anyone again." I say with determination and putting the people that I love the most in my life first, like I had three long years ago.

Uncle Matt looks at me and after the declaration I just made hits home, he gives a small smile, but I can tell it has a touch of sadness at what may come to pass. After a few tense moments, he looks from his pale lightning bolt tattoo and then over to me.

"You said you were having a hard time grounding?" He asks softly.

I nod. "Yeah. I finally figured out a way to ground, but I can't move around or I discharge and arc all over the place." I reply. "I tried to ground in both feet, but since my electricity is only on my left, I can't move it to the right side of my body." I add.

"That makes sense." Uncle Matt says with understanding in his tone. "Since I only had one ability, I was able to switch sides and ground in different ways." He explains.

"Yeah, that would be helpful if I could do that." I say with a touch of annoyance.

Uncle Matt smiles and looks at me. "I think I can help you figure out a way to ground. Do you trust me?"

I give him a look that says 'are you kidding me?' "Of course I trust you, Uncle Matt." I say with a slight chuckle.

"Alright. Let's go outside." Uncle Matt says while getting up and going out the sliding door.

I follow him and Aunt Viv trails behind me and sits on one of the patio chairs while Uncle Matt makes his way to the middle of the yard and I walk over to join him.

"Okay. You can visualize your abilities, right?" He asks. "Or at least I could, when I had them." He adds with a touch of longing.

I nod and give him a small grin. "Yes, I can see them if I think about them."

"Okay." Uncle Matt says while taking a breath and clasping his hands together. "So one thing you can do is, instead of splitting your power to go toward your leg and then your arm, you can keep it near your Soul Power." He says while pointing to the middle of his chest. "But don't keep it attached." He warns.

I look at him with furrowed brows; the question lingering on my tongue, but he explains before I can ask the question.

"It can short circuit, so to speak. I did that once, and it knocked me on my ass. Bruised my Soul Power, and I had a hard time using my abilities until it healed." Uncle Matt explains.

"I remember that day." Aunt Viv says with a giggle. "You were trying to show off with me, because you were finally getting the hang of your power, and you were trying to make something for me. The next thing I knew, something sparked off you, and you were on the ground a few feet away from me."

"I was trying to make you a heart, Vivie." Uncle Matt says with a loving smile.

"Okay, this is nice and all, but reminisce on your own time." I snap.

I realize how rough my tone was from the hard look my uncle throws my way and I try to give a small smile, but that only makes him shake his head.

"Sorry, Uncle Matt. It's just so frustrating to have all this thrown at me all of a sudden. And to have this deep need to destroy this thing that I don't understand at all." I say as a way of explanation.

Uncle Matt takes a breath. "I can't say I know what you're going through fully, but I know how it can be hard to control a power you don't understand." He says. "So, that's why you have me to teach you." He adds with a smile on his face again.

"So, what can I do differently?" I ask.

"Try to ground on your rib or something, but not your heart or your Soul Power." Uncle Matt says.

I nod at him. "I had a feeling to keep things away from that. When I took those flames in from the grill, I felt the need to keep them away for some reason."

"Wow, Seth really has kept you in the dark about things." Uncle Matt says with shock, filling his words.

I am about to ask him what he means by that, but he puts his hand up to stop the question on my lips. "I'm sure he wanted to know what instincts you had." Uncle Matt offers.

"That had better be the reason." I say, but I also push that thought toward Seth and he gives a light chuckle in my mind as if I had hit the nail on the head.

"So go ahead and try to ground that way, Aiden." Uncle Matt urges me.

I take a breath and close my eyes and I visualize my electricity snaking from my Soul Power while splitting in two. I sent one tendril toward my left arm and I keep a short one near my last rib on that side. As it latches on the bone, I feel the energy snake down my arm and into my fingers.

I hear the low hum of the current on my skin and I open my eyes to see the blue arcs dancing down my arm, but they are not discharging. I look over at my uncle and he has a tight smile on his face, like a half-victory. He then takes his right hand and almost shoos me away, telling me to take a step back. Fear fills my heart at the thought of discharging so close to him.

"Can you go back toward the house?" I ask. "I don't want to hurt you in case it didn't work."

He nods in understanding and he walks up the three steps to the patio, stands on a rubber mat near the top of the steps and nods at me. I release a calming breath and close my eyes. I lift my right foot and take a step backward, then I close my eyes tighter and slowly lift my left heel, trying to drag this out as long as I can, but when I'm finally forced to lift the toe box of my shoe, I freeze with my left foot in the air a few inches off the ground. The silence seems to go on forever and then I hear Uncle Matt laughing and cheering suddenly.

"You did it, Aiden!" He exclaims.

I open my eyes and I look to my left. I still see the electricity dancing down my arm, bridges of the bluish-white current silently going into my bicep and coming back out near my elbow, but staying connected to my body.

A huge smile takes over my face and I jump off the ground to do a fist pump in the air in celebration, and again, I do not discharge at all.

"Oh, Aiden, I am so proud of you, sweetheart." Aunt Viv says when I finally join my aunt and uncle on the patio.

She brings me in for a hug and I quickly pull my power back in so I can return the embrace.

"I'm proud of you too, Aiden." Uncle Matt says while patting my shoulder. I see a bit of longing in his eyes for his own power, and I give him a small smile.

"Thank you." I say.

Later that night I am lying in bed in only a pair of shorts, no use hiding my markings anymore, and I call my electricity to my hand again. Now that I know how to ground, it's almost like second nature to me. I practice making the bolts appear on one finger and then bouncing that spark from one digit to the other. After a few minutes, I hear a knock on my door before my uncle comes into my room. He sees the blue bolt on my ring finger and when I bounce it to my thumb; he smiles.

"You know you can actually make that a ball and throw it where it would explode on impact." He says with a look that tells me he's done the same thing hundreds of times before.

I sit up in bed while I tuck my left leg under the other and I look down at the current still dancing in my hand. Then I pull that back and call my fire and I let go of a frustrated sigh.

"This is such a pain in the ass, Uncle Matt. I feel so behind. I mean, this is the kind of shit people go through when they're sixteen. When they're still young and they have the time to figure out how to use their powers." I say with a touch of anger at my situation. "Not at twenty-one, when I'm trying to work my way through college and get a normal life going." I add.

Uncle Matt takes in my words and I can tell he wants to help me understand, but the look on his face says he won't give anything away. He looks down at my wielding marks again, and as his eyes travel up the length of my arms, I can tell he finally notices how high they climb up my neck when his eyes blow wide for a moment before he schools his features.

"I just don't understand why they waited so long to come out for me." I say, not really asking him directly, but voicing the question that's been in my mind ever since I first got my fire.

"That is something for Seth to talk to you about." Uncle Matt says softly.

"Why does Seth have all the answers?" I whine. "Why am I still being kept in the fucking dark so much?"

"I will say this," Uncle Matt begins. "there is a story that's been passed down for generations and it's life-changing to our people. But that's all I'm gonna say." He says while putting his hands up to signify he's done talking and not to press anymore. "I will say this; you are going to be a very powerful man, Aiden. Those markings traveling up that high on your neck are proof. Trust in your instincts and in Seth's training."

He gets up to leave and when he's standing by the door; he pauses to look at me once more.

"I know your parents would be proud of you, Aiden. I know you think they left you because they didn't want a powerless son." I look at him in utter shock that he knew my deepest fear. "But just know that wasn't the reason at all." Uncle Matt says with a hint of anger in his eyes, and then he walks out of my room.

29

Aiden

Two days pass and I haven't asked Uncle Matt about his cryptic statement to me from the other night. I figured that would come in time, plus I have bigger fish to fry at the moment than my flighty parents.

I go to my classes on Monday morning and I have no issues at all, which I am glad of. I actually don't even see Mason or Rhett, which suits me just fine.

As I am walking out to my truck later that afternoon to go home, I see a hooded figure by a line of trees near the parking lot and I feel Seth's presence tickle the back of my mind. I toss my backpack in the cab of my truck, lock the doors, and walk over to him. Seth is careful to keep his face shaded in the black hood and something in me tells me not to say his name out loud.

"So, to what do I owe the pleasure of this meeting?" I ask mentally, while giving him my best act of formality.

"Smart ass." He retorts. *"Get in the car."* He says as he nods to a white 2017 Hyundai Sonata.

I get in the passenger seat while he slips in the driver's side and drives out of the parking lot of the university. I make mental notes of where we are going so that I know where I am next time I have to come here. It takes about thirty minutes to get to his house, which is a large two-story grey concrete home with immaculate black metal beams that contrast the off-set rooms of the house. The solid brown front door is set back into a little alcove while the right side of the house is set forward a bit and is completely covered in shades of dark grey stone.

The windows that adorn the front of the house are gigantic, at least eight feet, but yet I can't see into the rooms. So, I assume they have some kind of one-way film on the inside.

"Nice house." I say while looking at the home through the windshield of his car.

"Thanks." Seth says briskly while using his real voice for the first time.

Seth gets out of the driver's seat, still careful to keep his hood up, and I follow him to the porch. I watch as he unlocks the door, steps in, and motions for me to follow. I glance over my shoulder to make sure no one is looking, but I don't know why. I shrug the thought out of my mind and walk into his house.

The inside is just as well designed as the outside. The tall ceilings of the foyer echo with our footfalls. I see what would be a dining room to my left, but it's bare of any furniture other than the chandelier hanging in the middle of the ceiling. To my right is a living room where a leather couch, a matching loveseat, and two wing-back chairs take the space. The black coffee tables and end tables sit near the couch and a flat-screen television is set up on an entertainment center on the longest wall to complete the room.

Seth walks into the dining room to the left while taking his hoodie off, revealing his blue t-shirt underneath, and hangs the hoodie on the coat rack by the doorway, while he runs his fingers through his blonde hair before flicking his green eyes over his shoulder to see if I'm going to follow him. Two things I notice about Seth that's odd are one; his arms are void of any power markings. But I don't ask him about it at first, thinking that maybe he covers them like Uncle Matt did with his. Secondly, if I remember what Ivan told me about this guy, he's well over a hundred but doesn't look a day over forty.

Pushing that fact to the back of my mind, I follow him into the empty room, but I don't pay attention to where he goes. I am too busy looking around at the empty space that holds only one personal decoration, and my heart stops in my chest at the sight. It's of my Uncle Matt, Aunt Viv, Seth, and my parents. All are smiling at whoever is holding the camera like they don't have a care in the world.

The sound of water trickling behind me catches my attention, so I turn thinking that Seth is getting something from the kitchen that I noticed was in the back of the house, but instead, I am met with a large stream of water coming at me from Seth's direction.

Panic fills my chest at his action and I instinctively call my fire to my right hand and imagine a wall in front of me. Once the wall comes alive between us, the water is boiled away, leaving only steam behind.

"What the hell, Seth?" I yell.

I look to where Seth was when he sent the water stream at me, but I don't see him. I then hear a footfall from behind me and Seth is practically in my face. He draws his left arm back to punch me in the jaw, but I put my forearms in front of me, making an X shape to block him. His right fist comes at me from my peripheral vision and I take a step back to avoid it.

The sizzle of electricity fills my ears and, for an instant, I think it's my own power, but I can feel it's still slumbering in my Soul Power. I look toward the sound and Seth's left arm is rearing back to punch me again. I notice that as he gathers more and more electricity in his hand, a similar wielding mark to my own appears on his skin. White and yellow jagged lines of lightning crawl up his arm as he makes a large yellow ball of electricity, acting like he's about to throw it at me.

I barely have time to ground myself and call my own electricity to try to cancel his out. As I move to deflect his attack, I can't cancel his electrical current out fully and the different voltages collide, causing a shockwave that pushes me back across the floor a few feet.

"What are you doing, Seth?" I growl as I shake off the static of his electricity from my skin. "Have you lost your damn mind?" I ask while swapping over to my fire, since I can control that a bit more at the moment.

Seth doesn't answer me and instead gives me a sly smile before he disappears from my sight. I stare at the empty space before me, completely dumbfounded for a moment.

I knew this asshole could teleport. That explains how he got out of the mall and into my room so quick.

I make myself take a breath and listen for him to make his next move. My ears strain in the silence of the room and I have to ignore the rushing of the blood in my ears. A heartbeat later, I hear his breath to my right and I instantly turn toward him, creating a wall of fire and I try to make it hotter than the first time.

Just before the wall is complete, Seth appears before me with a fist made of solid rock and I know he is trying to punch me in the face again, but he hits my wall first and I hear him hiss in pain from my fire burning through his rocky fist.

When my gaze lands on his forearm, I notice what looks like boulders appear on his skin that seem to replace the lightning that was there just moments ago. We lock eyes and he teleports from my sight again and I turn around in circles in hopes of catching his next attack.

I then smell the mineral scent of water, which would normally strike me as odd, but now, knowing Seth can make water, I know this is his next attack, and it's coming from behind me. I instantly pull back my fire and call my electricity without much thought on grounding, just acting on instinct to do what I need to so I can use that power in a seamless transition.

Seth is at the far end of the room and he throws a powerful stream of water toward me. I visualize my electricity snaking its way up the stream. When it's just seconds from reaching Seth's hand, he drops his connection with the water and my current tries to go with it, but I push it forward and make it connect with Seth's still damp hand.

The zap of the bolt making the connection fills the room and I hear Seth scream in pain before he drops to one knee. I stand there, panting for breath, my body shaking from the adrenaline coursing in my veins from the fight, and wait for his next move.

Seth chuckles lightly while looking at the hand that just got shocked. "Not bad for your first fight. I'm happy with your instincts and how you were able to catch on quickly."

"This was a test?!" I yell. "You scared the fucking shit out of me!" I say while bending over and putting my hands on my knees. It feels like someone just popped a balloon in my chest and the stress of the fight leaves me in an instant.

"If I told you what I was doing, you wouldn't have used your instincts. You would have held back." Seth says, but his tone makes me feel like I should have known that would have been his answer.

I back up to the wall, sliding down it to sit on the floor, no longer trusting my legs to hold me. I rest my arms on my knees and lean my head against the wall while trying to will my heart rate to slow down. After a few tense moments and I don't feel as riled up, I lift my head to look at Seth, who is now standing in front of me with a slight grin playing at the corner of his mouth.

"So, now what since I passed your little test?" I ask, still giving him a hard time on it, but I try to give him an understanding look.

"Now the real training starts. You should be able to use both powers at the same time, so we need to work up to that." Seth explains.

I can't even imagine using both powers at the same time right now. If I use one too much, I feel exhausted. But this mock fight has me completely drained, and it's all I can do to keep my eyes open right now.

"One thing that I think will help you is to meet your partner in all this. Then I can tell you both what your roles are and what's to come." Seth says.

I remember from my visions that I had help in destroying The Siphon, but I could never make out who they were.

"When am I going to meet this dude?" I ask after a few moments as I slowly feel the strength fill my limbs again.

Seth chuckles as he looks down at me. When he offers me his hand and pulls me to my feet, I notice that his skin is free of any markings again, which I find odd, but then on the inside of his wrist, I see what looks to be a medium-sized circle. As I look closer, I see that the circle is made up of all the elements that a person can wield.

Fire, electricity, water, earth, wind, and metal. Those six symbols make up the circle that shows he does indeed have abilities. Seth leads me into the living room and I follow him on still rubbery legs, so he puts an arm out to steady me and I begrudgingly take it. I'd rather have some help than faceplant onto his living room floor.

"You will meet *her* today. She'll be here in a little bit." Seth says as he helps sit me down on his couch and he takes one of the wingback chairs beside me.

I lean forward, elbows resting on my knees, while scrubbing my hands over my face to try and rub the tiredness from my eyes as I anxiously await this mystery girl to arrive. I hate to bring anyone else into this mess, but it sounds like we both may be needed to do whatever it is we need to do.

I then start to feel my eyesight blur a bit and I know now it's a vision coming to me.

I stare at the beige carpet as it turns to a forest floor. I see this machine in front of me. My fire burning to my right and my electricity humming to my left. I then hear my name being called, but at first, it's muffled, almost like it's underwater, and I can't make out the melody of this person's voice. As this version of me turns toward the sound of this voice, she comes into focus for me. Her hair is a short dark brown, but the familiar blue eyes that hold love and fear at the same time *collide with my mismatched ones. My heart drops at the image, and I am violently thrown back into reality.*

I somehow find renewed strength in my body and jump to my feet. In two long strides, I am in front of Seth, grabbing at his shirt, bunching the fabric in my fist, anger flaring in my heart once again; but there is also a touch of fear.

"Tell me it's not true!" I yell. "Tell me that someone different is coming through that door, Seth!"

30

Maya

After I developed my powers back in high school and my dad forced us to move away, Seth made a mental connection with me and told me that one day he will bring me back here to begin my real training. I didn't know what that meant at the time, and I didn't care. I was too heartbroken and angry to care about anything other than trying to forget the love of my life.

Yesterday, Seth told me it was time to come back so I can meet the person I will be helping in this strange endeavor that he's been keeping under lock and key for the last three years.

As I pull up to the large home made of concrete and black metal columns, I exit my Volkswagen Passat and make my way to the front door. When I realize the door is unlocked, I walk right in. But instead of the calm quiet that was outside, I am met with harsh shouts and loud zaps of electricity filling the air.

"Tell me it's not true! Tell me that someone different is coming through that door, Seth!"

That voice is so familiar and my chest constricts to the point of pain, but it can't be. He didn't have powers when I last saw him.

I round the corner into the living room and I see a tall, muscular man with short reddish-brown hair pinning who must be Seth to a wall with a hand around his throat. Electricity and fire are both pouring from the tops of this guy's shoulders, and I hear his harsh words echo in the air. Without seeing his face, I know for a fact who is standing in front of me, and it both breaks my heart and terrifies me at the same time.

"I don't want her help, Seth!" Aiden roars.

I've never seen him angry before. Pissed off at times, yes, but this is red-hot anger and the power that is pouring from his body is uncontrolled. I've never been scared of Aiden before, but now, I feel my water edge to the surface, readying to snuff out his fire if he attacks me with it.

Seth must sense my presence and my anticipation of a fight, because his eyes land on my own for a moment before Aiden turns his head to look at me over his shoulder.

"Well, Aiden, it doesn't really matter if you want my help or not. It looks like we both are a part of this mission." I say nonchalantly, like his rage doesn't bother me in the least.

I don't know why I say what I do. I think it's a coping mechanism I've built over these last few years. Act indifferent, so no one knows just how much the last three years have messed me up.

Aiden finally lets go of Seth to look at me head-on, his powers fading like wisps of smoke from his shoulders. I again take in his bulkier build, and I think back to when we were in high school. He was fit back then, but now, he's all muscle, and the wielding marks on his skin make him seem so much more dangerous, but at the same time, I want to run my fingers over the images and commit them to memory like he used to do with my own markings.

I notice that his hair is shorter on the sides, and a bit longer on top and I suddenly itch to run my fingers through the strands again, but when I look at his face, at the five-o'clock shadow on his chin, at the hard lines of his jaw, I know this is not the same Aiden that I once knew. And I'm to blame for this drastic change.

While his eyes are still his normal mismatched of green and brown, they show the gold ring around the iris that shows he's part of The Protector's of Power, but they lack that lightness and life that used to be there. They are nothing but cold and calculating now.

After a few tense moments of us just staring at one another, Aiden steps toward me and my heart constricts in my chest. My body suddenly remembering all the times that he touched me and I want it so badly again that I almost moan in pain, but the words that he growls next make the feelings fade like a single water droplet in a drought.

"I'm out of here. I'm not working with a fucking hypocrite like you."

Okay, I deserve that, to an extent, but he doesn't know the hell I went through these last three years. I was forced to move away. I didn't have a choice in the matter, but he probably won't listen to me, not now at least. He's too pissed, which again I understand, but if I could just get him to listen to my side of the story, then everything will make sense.

"I'm not doing this, Seth. You either find a different partner or I'm doing this on my own." Aiden calls over his shoulder.

"Aiden! Come back, we need to talk about all this!" Seth says while trying to stop him.

"Nope. I'm not working with her. End. Of. Story." Aiden says as he walks out the front door.

"Well, that went off without a hitch." I deadpan after I hear the door slam shut, and it's just me and Seth in the foyer.

Seth drags a hand through his hair and blows out an exasperated sigh. "I had a feeling breaking you two up would blow up in my face once you came back into the picture."

"Well, it's too late to go back and change it now. Even I still hate you for that too, by the way." I say, while crossing my arms.

"I know. But I know your father told you some things, but as for Aiden," Seth pauses while looking at the front door. "We weren't one hundred percent certain he was the one we were waiting for."

Aiden

"Tell me it's not true!" I yell. "Tell me that someone different is coming through that door, Seth!" I scream as I allow my powers to flow from me and I somehow know to let them release from the tops of my shoulders in just enough warning for him not to mess with me, but yet I can't keep my powers under control due to the anger boiling in my blood.

Seth is quiet for a moment, realizing who I saw in my vision, and just as he is about to say something, I cut him off.

"I don't want her help, Seth!" I scream again, with conflicting reasons why I don't want her involved.

We then notice movement in the foyer. My screaming must have concealed the door opening, and I see those beautiful blue eyes that three years ago I could get lost in and held my heart so dearly before she shattered it into pieces. Her hair is shorter, cut to just above her shoulders, but I know I could still grab it in my fist if I wanted to.

"Well Aiden, it doesn't matter if you want my help or not, we are both a part of this." Maya replies with a haughty tone.

I let go of Seth's shirt and I just stare at her with so many conflicting emotions constricting my heart. I watch as she looks over my body, her eyes lingering on my tattoos for a moment longer than necessary, and I lose it.

"I'm out of here. I'm not working with a fucking hypocrite like you." I growl as I walk past her. It takes everything in my body to keep walking and not allow myself to touch her, even if it's only a fleeting touch.

She left *me*. She couldn't love a *powerless guy*, so just because I now have powers and apparently a big part of some grand scheme does not mean I am just going to work with her.

"I'm not doing this, Seth. You either find a different partner or I'm doing this on my own."

I barely hear Seth yell at me to wait and hear him out, but I let the door shut in his face. I don't care that he drove me here; I have to walk this anger off. I have half a mind to go into a Parasite neighborhood and pick a fight like I normally do since I now have an idea of how to fight with my powers thanks to Seth, but I think better of it.

Instead, I pull my phone out and pull up the GPS to see where I am, make a mental note of how to get to the main road, and walk to the one place where I know I can let my anger out and do it without the possibility of getting myself killed in the process.

I arrive at Ivan and Gray's house about thirty minutes later and I pound on the door with my fist and wait. And wait. I look to my left and the Mustang is in the driveway, so they should be home, but maybe Gray got a new car, so they're driving around in that.

I shake my head and begin to walk down the porch when the door suddenly opens behind me and I see a shirtless Ivan with only a pair of shorts on. But it's the lazy grin and the red scratches on his chest and arms that makes my cheeks heat with embarrassment even with the smoldering anger flowing through my veins when I understand what I apparently interrupted.

"Sorry. I should have called first. I'll let you get back to Gray." I say as I start to walk down the porch.

"Aiden. What's wrong?" Ivan asks, his voice holding a protective edge to it.

"It's nothing. At least nothing that will change between now and in the morning." I bite out.

"Bullshit. If it was nothing, you would have waited until morning to talk to me. Come in."

I shake my head. "I don't want to interrupt your time with your boyfriend."

"You're not." Ivan says slowly, with a look of mischief in his eyes. "Look, just get your ass in here and tell me what's wrong. I can see you're about to combust."

"Ivan, who's at the door, Baby?" Gray asks from the kitchen.

"It's Aiden." Ivan calls over his shoulder.

I roll my eyes and walk past my friend and into the living room while Gray comes out with two bottles of water. He, thankfully, is fully clothed in a t-shirt and a pair of shorts.

"Oh, I'll get another bottle of water." Gray says, but Ivan stops him with a quick kiss on the lips.

"I got it, Grayson, go sit down." Ivan says while leaning in closer to whisper into his partner's ear, but I still hear his words and I almost wish I hadn't. "If you can."

I internally groan and scrub my hands over my face while Gray smacks Ivan on the chest before sitting next to me on the loveseat and handing me a bottle of water.

"Sorry about that, Aiden. Apparently, I need to teach the Lug Nut some manners while around a visitor." Gray gives Ivan a side-eyed look.

I twist the top off my water bottle just as Ivan takes the seat across from us on the couch and his steely-gray eyes bore into my own.

"Oh come off it, Grayson. It's just Aiden." Ivan says while shaking his head before looking back at me. "So what has you looking so murderous?" He deadpans.

I sigh as I set the water bottle on the coffee table a little harder than I intended, and I shake my head at the action.

"What's wrong, Aiden?" Gray says while looking from me to Ivan.

"I met with Seth today." I begin.

"Did he try to hurt you?" Ivan asks.

I shake my head because even with the fight we had; it was all part of his grand scheme, so I don't think it was a fight to actually hurt me.

"Then spit it out, Aiden." Ivan growls as he clenches his fist in aggravation.

"She's back in town and apparently we are supposed to work together." I say.

"Who's back in town?" Gray asks.

"Over my dead body, will you work with her. She stabbed you in the back once she'll do it again." Ivan snaps.

Gray looks from me to his partner and back again. "Can someone tell me what the hell is going on?"

"Maya is here, and I guess we both are needed in what I assume is a mission to destroy The Siphon."

"I say tell both Seth and that bitch to screw themselves and we will figure this out on our own if you need to destroy that Siphon so badly." Ivan says while waving a hand in the air.

I look at my friend, and something tells me it's not that simple.

31

Gray

After Aiden left and Ivan and I turned in for the night, I settled into his bare chest and waited for the rhythm of his breathing to slow, letting me know he's asleep, which usually never takes long for him.

Once I know Ivan's asleep, I turn onto my side to face the window and I find myself thinking about Maya. About how the breakup went between her and Aiden and how to me, it's never felt right. Just as I begin to form a plan in my mind, Ivan must subconsciously feel the absence of my body against his. He turns over towards me, his muscular arms tightening around my waist, pulling my back closer to his chest. When his chin finds the spot between my shoulder and neck, he stills, falling back into a restful slumber.

As my eyes travel the expanse of his chain link wielding tattoos on his forearm, I know for sure what I'm going to do tomorrow morning. Ivan's not going to like it, but I need to help Aiden in any way I can.

Thankfully, the next morning is our day off from school, but Ivan has to go to work at his dad's factory, so I am left to my own devices today. While I'm waiting for my Keurig to finish brewing my favorite caramel coffee pod, I open the Facebook app and type Maya's name in the search bar. I hope that since she's back in town again, she's reactivated her social media.

Once my phone loads, I see a few profiles pop up, but I know I found the right one when I see a selfie of her with her water floating around her right hand in the shape of a heart.

I click on the Messenger icon and take a breath as I type the message to her.

Me

Hi Maya. I heard you were back in town. Can you meet me at the park downtown?

Maya

Why should I?

Me

Because I felt like we could always be honest with one another. And I get the feeling that there's more to be said that I know Aiden is not willing to listen to right now. So I am trying to be the voice of reason.

Maya

Gray, I don't think anyone can get through to Aiden right now.

I smile as I close out of Messenger, fix my coffee in my travel mug with a second mug for Maya, hop in my car, and drive to the park.

Once I arrive, I find a bench near a little pond and wait for Maya to show up. As she promised, twenty minutes later, I see her walking down the path, and she takes a seat next to me with a tight smile playing on her lips.

"Good morning." I smile at her while offering her the mug of coffee.

"Morning." She says softly as she takes the mug from my hand.

I let my eyes travel over her face and the rest of her body. She cut her hair, and I think the shorter length suits her, but her smile is forced, somewhat pained and that same emotion lives in her eyes rent-free. I take a sip of my coffee while looking out over the pond and I take a little note out of Ivan's book. I act like I don't care about anything in the world and let my body relax on the bench underneath me.

"So, how have you been, Maya?"

"Okay, I guess. Just taking it one day at a time, especially now." She says while taking a sip of her coffee. "What about you? Are you and Ivan still together?" She asks slowly.

"Yeah, we are. We're actually living together now; have been since we graduated high school." I look over at her and give her a full smile, just like old times. "I heard that you were the one who helped Ivan finally make his move for me. I never got to thank you for that." I tip my head in her direction, "So, thank you."

She turns her head to look at me and her gaze burns into my brown eyes. "Why are you being nice to me? I think I'd like it better if you were yelling at me." She scoffs.

"Why would I yell at you over something that I don't know all the details about?" I ask. "Will you tell me what happened three years ago? Why did you tell Aiden that you would never leave him even if he was powerless and then turn around and break his heart over the very thing you promised didn't matter?"

Maya turns her head but I still see the silver lining in her eyes with unshed tears and her bottom lip wobbles for a moment before she speaks.

"I was forced to tell him that. My dad had this gut feeling that both Aiden and I were meant to do something big. But since Aiden didn't develop powers, Dad and Seth thought I was somehow keeping him from them. So, they made us move away, but Dad had a feeling that we would be coming back in three years." Maya says, then she looks back at me with silent tears streaming down her face, "I never stopped loving him and I missed him so much that it hurt me physically every day."

I nod as I drain my coffee and twirl the empty mug in my hands for a moment before I speak. "I'll talk to Aiden for you. I'll try to convince him to at least be in the same room with you to hear Seth explain your roles in destroying The Siphon. I can't guarantee anything, but I'll do my best, Maya."

"That's all I'm asking for, Gray." Maya dries her eyes and gives me a small, wet chuckle. "We always could talk to one another so easily, couldn't we?"

"It's all because we love our guys and they are also friends. I will say, though, I'm gonna have to work on Ivan. He's totally pissed at you." I say and Maya's face falls into anguish and I mentally smack myself. "But I will get him to come around. I have my ways with him." I grin.

Maya shakes her head with a watery smile. "Thank you, Gray. You always have been a good friend."

"You're welcome. I'll be in touch. Can I have your number again?"

She nods as I pull my phone from my back pocket, and she laughs at my home screen. It's a picture of Ivan and me kissing in his kitchen the first night we moved in three years ago. No matter how many pictures we take, that will forever be my favorite because that was the first night of the rest of our lives.

Once Maya puts her number in my phone, we stand up and I pull her in for a quick hug. "I'll be in touch. Take care of yourself, Maya. I'll talk to you soon."

"Okay. Thank you for insisting we meet Gray. I'm glad that I was finally able to tell someone what really happened three years ago. Just by telling you, lifted a huge weight off my chest right now."

"You're welcome." I say as we walk away from one another and back to our respective cars.

Later that night, after I made Ivan's favorite dinner, Shepherd's Pie, and have it waiting on the table for us, he is immediately suspicious of me.

Damn him and being overly perceptive.

"What's up with you, Grayson? What did you do today? Do I have to kick anyone's ass?" Ivan asks as he makes his trademark metal crowbar and bounces it against his left palm.

"No, Baby. Can't I fix a nice dinner for my man without getting the third degree?" I playfully shove him on the shoulder as I place a steaming bowl of Shepherd's Pie in front of him.

"I mean, yeah, you can, but I can see that gleam in your eye. You're up to something." Ivan says while taking a bite of his food.

"Did you ever think that maybe I just wanted to treat the love of my life to a nice dinner?" I say as I trail my index finger down his neck, over his tattoos and I'm rewarded with his skin erupting in gooseflesh at my touch and I have to bury the dark chuckle in my throat at the pride that only my touch can make him react like this.

"Grayson, you better stop that if you want to have this dinner with me or else, you're gonna be the main course." Ivan warns.

"I can always warm the food back up." I say, my voice dropping a few degrees as I scrape my teeth over the shell of his ear.

"Okay, that's it. Move it. Bedroom. Now." Ivan orders as he drops his fork onto the table with a loud clatter and stands from his chair.

I lead him into our bedroom and as soon as he shuts the door, he's on me. His mouth devouring mine and I meet him stroke for stroke. His tongue skims over my lips and I greedily open for him while I thread my fingers through his hair. He growls into my mouth with a possessiveness that I love hearing from him.

Ivan pulls back from me enough to tug his shirt over his head and I never tire of seeing his muscular form. His broad shoulders, solid pecs, washboard abs that end in the strong V of his waist. My eyes then take in the veins traveling down his biceps and forearms that make his wielding marks flex with each movement.

I get turned on just by looking at him and I'm thankful that I ditched the jeans I was wearing earlier and swapped them for black sweats because the bulge that is slowly growing between my legs would have been painful against a zipper.

Ivan begins to lean in to kiss me again while trying to turn me towards the bed, but I have other plans. I give him a dark grin and I am the one to crash my lips to his while threading my fingers through his short, black hair. I push my chest against him and I angle him towards the mattress and when his knees meet the side; he collapses onto his back.

"Gray." Ivan says with shock, filling his voice.

"I'm feeling spicy tonight." I grin.

I'm usually fine with being his bottom, but here are nights when I feel more masculine than others, but that is usually when I've been in the gym and beat a personal record, or my jiu-jitsu class went well and I beat a stronger opponent, but tonight I know that I need to disarm him.

"Do your worst, Baby." Ivan growls.

I lean over him and press a sound kiss to his lips before I pull back enough and whisper into his ear, "Make your restraints, Babe."

Ivan's eyes blow wide for a moment, then he chuckles low in his chest. He lifts his arms over his head and I watch as the metal flows like molasses from his fingers before wrapping around the metal headboard and forming solid black chains with manacles around his wrists.

"What did I do for this treatment, Grayson?" Ivan asks as I tug my own shirt over my head and toss it to the side where the fabric lands next to Ivan's with a whisper-soft thud.

His eyes devour the exposed skin of my chest and torso, and I feel the gooseflesh flare to life at his intense gaze.

"I just missed you today, and I figured the best way to show you is to make you writhe with pleasure like you do so often with me."

I lean down again and trail my lips over the curves of his stomach and the broad planes of his chest. When I scrape my teeth over his left nipple, Ivan's groan fills the room, along with the rattle of chains as he pulls against his restraints.

When Ivan uses commands on me, like when he tells me not to touch him while he's pleasuring me, I listen like his good boy. But Ivan is not good at listening what so ever. That's how we found that he has a bondage kink, and I take full advantage of that when I am in the mood to play.

"Grayson. Stop toying with me." Ivan warns.

"Or what Ivan? I didn't tell you to remove your manacles yet. I'm not done having *my* fun with you." I croon as I press my lips to his chest and then work my way down his body, kissing that gorgeous V that dips below his pants.

"Gray!" Ivan pants.

I take my time unbuttoning the top button of his jeans and slowly pull his zipper down. Ivan bucks his hips for any kind of friction against his growing erection, but I push my hand on the top of his hip, pinning his body to the mattress.

"Patience, you Lug Nut. I'll give you exactly what you need in due time." I promise.

I tug both his jeans and boxers down in one firm movement and I free his rock-hard length to me, and I find myself smiling that I am the only one to make him like this.

"Is all this for me?" I ask in wonder.

Ivan nods frantically and I love the feeling of power that fills my chest, knowing that someone as strong and scary as Ivan can become my pleading good boy at my touch.

I wrap my hand around him and I give it a hard tug from the base to the tip and Ivan's head tips back into the mattress with a groan of pleasure.

"Who do you belong to, Ivan? Who can only touch you like this and see you look and sound like a pleading, good little boy?" I growl.

"You." Ivan pants. "Only you, Grayson."

"That's right. Only me." I reply as I slide my lips over him and devour him like he's the last meal I will ever have.

When I feel his release begin to build, I pull back and I reach into his bedside table, where I know he keeps his condoms and lube. Ivan's eyes track the movement and he pulls against the chains again.

"Use your words, Ivan." I say.

"I want to touch you while you're loving me."

I smile as I drop my pants and let him watch me cover myself with the condom, then climb back onto the mattress, hovering right over where we both want to be.

I bend down to where my mouth is a whisper away from his ear and say, "Then touch me all you like while I sink inside you, Ivan."

Just as I see him reabsorb his metal and feel his arms wrap around my neck to pull me closer to his chest, I fill him slowly; inch by glorious inch, pulling out to the tip before I thrust my hips, driving myself deeper into his body.

"Oh shit, Grayson." Ivan moans when I finally fully seat myself into him.

"I love hearing you say my name like that, Ivan." I growl as I lean in to kiss his lips.

Ivan's nails drag down my back as I pull back to the tip and thrust back into him, again and again. I trail my lips down the side of his neck and I sink my teeth into his Adam's apple, then kiss the hurt as Ivan's legs wrap around my waist, pulling me closer and deeper into him, hitting the spot that makes him chant my name with abandon as his walls tighten around me.

"You take me so well, Ivan. Are we sure I should be the bottom in this relationship?" I ask while kissing his chest.

"I'm a top, Baby. You're just a power bottom, and a damn good one." Ivan groans as I bite his left nipple while picking up one leg to drive my thrusts deeper, and I'm rewarded with a wail of pleasure from Ivan. "Yes, Grayson! Right there. Don't stop, Baby. I'm so close."

My movements become more erratic as pre-cum beads on his crown and feel my orgasm build between us.

"Come for me, Ivan. Let me see how much of a mess I can make of you while loving you like this." I grunt as I hit the spot in him that makes him shatter with his release while he continues to chant my name. "That's it. Let me have it all, Ivan Grant." I say as I wrap my hand around his erection and milk him for every drop he has to give.

"You have it. Take it all!" Ivan pleads as he bucks his hips into my thrusts, making my orgasm explode through me.

After I'm spent, I slowly pull out of him, discarding the condom in the trash before I flop onto my back and try to will my body back down to earth. Ivan chuckles beside me, and I turn my head to look at him.

"What's so funny?" I ask.

"Not funny, just it's still shocking to me how our dynamic changes based on who's railing who."

"Oh, I know. The big, bad, scary Ivan can't dare be caught begging for his orgasm. That's not allowed." I jest while playfully shoving his arm before I take his hand and lead him into the bathroom so we can both clean up.

After I cleaned us up and crash back into bed, I let Ivan hold me close to his chest as our bodies melt into one another in post-orgasmic bliss. I trace the chain link tattoo that crawls over his chest with an index finger, and Ivan shudders under my touch.

"If you don't stop that, I'm going to have *my* way with you, Grayson." He warns.

"And that would be a bad thing?" I tease.

Ivan growls as he pins me to the mattress, and I let him with a sly smile on my lips.

"You're being such a brat tonight. What's gotten into you?" Ivan asks as he kisses me on the lips.

"Nothing really, but I have been thinking." I begin and when Ivan cocks his eyebrow at me, I take a breath and I let the cat out of the bag. "I went to the park today."

"Okay." Ivan says slowly while his eyes bounce back and forth between mine.

"I met up with Maya." I say quickly, like ripping off a band-aid.

"You did what, Gray!?" Ivan snaps, and he tries to leave the bed, but I wrap my hands around the nape of his neck.

"I met with Maya and I talked to her about what happened three years ago."

He looks down at me, arms braced on either side of my head and his chest pressed against mine. "And?" Is his only response. So, I tell him about what we talked about and he listens with a quiet calm.

"And you believe her?" Ivan asks after a moment.

"Yes, Ivan."

He releases a frustrated sigh and shakes his head. "What do you want me to do?"

"Talk to Aiden. Convince him to at least hear her out."

Ivan looks at me for a minute before he chuckles and shakes his head again. "Fine. I'll talk to him tomorrow."

"Thank—" I begin, but my words are cut off when Ivan wraps his hand around my throat and I look up at him in shock.

"But not before I punish you for softening me up to where I listen to you with no objections, first."

I laugh as I thread my fingers through his hair, "Do your worst, Baby." I grin as Ivan doles out his punishment in the best way possible.

32

Ivan

I'm still pissed that Gray went behind my back and met up with Maya, but yet I know he was the best one to get her to talk about what happened and to get me to see the reasoning behind it all, too. Now to convince Aiden to listen to her.

As I pull my Mustang into a parking spot at the university, Gray and I exit the car, and just because I still want him on edge for a while, I fall into step beside him and clamp my hand around the back of his neck and he stiffens under my touch.

"I'm still pissed at what you did last night, Grayson." I whisper next to his ear, and he shivers under my hand. "I'm debating on what your next punishment should be."

I don't plan on doing anything more than what I did to him last night, but he doesn't need to know that. Bringing him to the point of his release only to slow my pace to pull him back from the edge over and over again for a good forty-five minutes before finally shoving him over like a skydiver jumping from a cliff was enough.

"Ivan." Gray whines,

"Get on to class, Baby. I'll talk to you later." I say as I notice Aiden getting out of his truck.

Gray looks from me to Aiden and I give him a small smile as if saying, *Yeah, yeah. I'm going to talk to him.*

Gray beams and I give him a playful shove towards the door. "Get, Grayson." I say darkly, but I know he sees the light in my eyes.

He gives me a wink before he darts into the door, and I have to stifle a groan at the flutter of adoration that explodes in my chest at my man's antics.

"What's got you two so happy? I can practically see the lovebirds floating above your heads." Aiden says solemnly.

Well, shit. I'm gonna have to butter him up too, since he's still in a mood.

"Just still on a high from last night." I say truthfully.

Aiden rolls his eyes as he tries to walk past me and into the main brick building, but I stop him with an arm on his shoulder.

"Aiden, can I talk to you for a minute?"

"Yeah. What's up?"

I pause when I look into his eyes. He is still fuming over Maya's reappearance in his life. But I think I know what may help him more right now before I drop the bombshell.

"Actually, meet me behind the school after your last class and before our Abilities 101. I can tell you need to release some pent-up energy." I say with a smile as I let go of his shoulder and walk with him into the main building.

Later that afternoon, I wait for Aiden to show up behind the university, where there is a medium-sized dirt-filled clearing. I picked this place so that when Aiden uses his flame to fight, he won't burn anything to a crisp.

"What are we doing here, Ivan?" Aiden asks.

"I'm helping you release some pent up anger." I say as I make a large club with little nubs near the top.

"You want to fight here? What if I hurt you?"

"You won't." I say as I will my metal to cover my skin with a sheet so thin that it's flexible.

"Okay. Don't go crying to Gray if you get hurt." Aiden shrugs as he lets a fireball dance in his right hand.

I smile and give him a 'come at me' gesture and he attacks without a thought. Rearing his right arm back to punch me in the face. I move the club to block his attack while using that point of contact as a distraction to make a medium pillar of metal shoot out from the ground and slam into his side.

"Ivan? What the hell?" Aiden snaps.

"You gotta watch your surroundings there, buddy." I say as I again find the trace elements of metal in the dirt around us to make another pillar behind him, poised to strike.

Aiden switches from his fire to his electricity in the blink of an eye, but I'm still faster. I change the properties of the pillar behind him to copper and will it to strike his left arm, discharging the current before he can even throw it my way. I think about the copper pillar bending around Aiden's arm, locking him in place, not being able to use his electricity, and I rush him.

He tries to get out of the copper restraint, even calling his fire to try to melt the material away, but I'm too close for him to melt through it and he's not powerful enough to make his fire that hot yet, so I take advantage of his shortcoming right now. I pull my arm back, hand curling into a fist and I bring it down to punch him in the face, but I pull back at the very last second so I don't hurt him too much, but his head still swings to the side at the contact.

I stand there for a moment, both of us panting for breath, but I'm not stupid enough not to have my metal just a thought away from covering my body in case he tries something off the wall.

Aiden glances up at me and I see that his eyes have changed. They are lighter. Even with the fight, they hold a joy that wasn't there this morning.

"You feeling better?" I ask.

"Yeah. I am. Now, can you let me go?" Aiden asks as he tries to pull his left arm out of the bent copper pillar.

I smile as I connect to the material and I will it to fade back into the earth. Just as I let my guard down, the little sneaky asshole charges his left arm up and lands a solid punch to my gut in the blink of an eye.

The electricity dances along my body and makes my muscles contract painfully in response, and it's all I can do just to breathe until Aiden removes his fist.

"You gotta watch your surroundings, buddy." Aiden tosses my own words back at me with a mocking smile.

"Screw you." I grind out as I take in a ragged breath. "That was a good shot, though; I'll give you that." I say once I get my wits about me.

"I'll take getting one over on you any day." Aiden replies as he runs his hand through his hair.

I shake my head and decide this is as good a time as any to drop the bomb.

"Gray, he uh, met up with an old friend of his yesterday."

"He did?" Aiden asks with confusion furrowing his brow.

"Yeah. It was Maya." I say in a rush.

"He what?! Why the hell would he do that?" Aiden growls.

"Aiden, hear me out, dude." I begin, but he cuts me off.

"No! You *both* know what the hell she did to me and Gray expects me to just let her back in my life? And you, of all people, want me to *listen* to her excuses?" Aiden seethes. "You're dumber than I thought you were, Ivan."

Aiden walks away from me with the same hard expression he had in his eyes this morning, and I know I'm losing ground, and fast.

"She didn't have a choice, Aiden!" I shout.

He just keeps walking as he flips me the bird with his right hand while a flame dances at the tip.

Aiden

I cannot believe that Ivan is actually taking Maya's side on this and that Gray talked to her yesterday. I am so pissed off right now that I'm afraid I will deck both of them for even trying to make me see whatever lies she sprouted. I almost want to skip my last class and go to the forest to blow off some steam but I have the feeling not to skip this lesson today.

"Why does he have to be in the same damn class?" I ask with a growl.

I make myself walk into Professor Jaffee's class and take my normal seat, but I keep my head down, toying with the sleeve of my shirt while I watch Ivan take his own seat out of the corner of my eye. When Professor Jaffee turns the lights down, Ivan tries to get my attention, but I give him a glare that could cut like a knife. While I can see that he wants to say something anyway, the hum of the projector turning on and Professor Jaffee's voice cuts him off again.

"Okay class, I know I have been beating this like a dead horse, but this will be the last time we discuss this." She pauses and gives the image a disgruntled look. "machine." She says, like it leaves a bad taste in her mouth. "The Siphon's main function is to steal the abilities from people, mainly from those The Parasites perceive as a threat. At least that's the way it started to function back in the late seventeen hundreds.

The way it started? Did it change somehow over the years?

"Over the years, The Parasites have started to grow desperate. They were losing more and more to their own abilities, and they started to try to change the main function of this thing."

As I watch her point to the machine, I see her wrists, and it feels like time freezes. I notice what looks like water droplets traveling from her wrist and up her forearm. It looks almost like Maya's water tattoo, but it's stark white, like Uncle Matt's lightning bolts are. With heart-wrenching clarity, I realize what this means and I find myself staring at her and I hang onto her every word.

"This other function is," she begins, and I barely see her take a breath before she continues. "Is to attempt to transplant abilities from one person to another."

I hear several students, including Ivan, suck in a sharp breath at this information, and my stomach drops. Does Seth know about this function?

"Research has found that it has been attempted several times, but never succeeds. The transfer host always dies." Mrs. Jaffee says and I notice her hardened exterior break for a moment before she puts her mask back on.

When her words fill the classroom, I hear a small whisper in my mind and somehow I know it's my own abilities that flow through me.

"Destroy and restore." They whisper in unison.

I silently nod in agreement at their words and find myself looking back at Ivan, all anger leaving my body in a rush. I nod my head once, hoping he will understand that I am willing to hear him out on what Maya had to say.

After class ends three hours later, I walk up to Professor Jaffee, who is now sitting at her desk, trying to busy herself with organizing papers while the students walk out of her room.

"Aiden, what are you doing?" Ivan asks while stopping by the door, noticing that I am not walking with him.

"I need to say something to her." I whisper to him.

He nods while he leans his back against the doorjamb, letting his long legs rest on the other side of the threshold to keep people from walking in by him and into the classroom.

Professor Jaffee looks over at me as I approach her and gives me a smile, but it doesn't reach her eyes.

"Mrs. Jaffee, can I say something?" I ask as I stop in front of her desk.

"Mr. Rivers, yes you may. What's on your mind?" She asks while trying to hide her pink nose from being on the brink of tears from the lesson.

I am careful of my word choice because I get the feeling not a lot of people know about the prophecy.

"I just wanted to let you know that I think you're brave to teach this class." I say.

Her eyes shine with tears, but also with gratitude at my words, even when she tries to brush me off. "Oh, why would you say that? Any teacher can teach this class."

"I know you have a personal beef with The Siphon." I say in a serious tone. "It's your wielding marks. I know someone personally that has the same color as you do."

As my words process in her mind, she finally lets her walls down and I place a gentle hand on her shoulder.

"You are very brave in teaching about this monstrosity. I know I wouldn't be as strong as you are." I tell her.

"Thank you, Aiden. You're very observant." Professor Jaffee says while wiping the tears from her eyes. "It was my husband that they tried to transfer my water into." She begins.

So that's why my high school teacher isn't here, and she's teaching this class instead.

I watch as she plays with the wad of tissues in her hand and I look back over my shoulder at Ivan. He nods to tell me he'll be here for as long as I need him. I pull up one of the classroom chairs next to her desk and sit in front of her, resting my elbows on my knees while pulling my sleeves up to show her my own wielding marks and give her a look that I hope shows her I want to know more. She looks over my tattoos and something almost like understanding washes over her tear-stained face.

She takes a raspy breath before she speaks again. "It was a dark, rainy evening, and we were just coming back from a date night when we were abducted. Once I woke up, I realized that somehow Victor found us. I was hooked up in a tube-like container. I remember I was still standing, but I was also being held up by something around my waist. I saw Karl across the room in the same container. Then I felt the jolt of energy in my body and it felt like it was tearing me apart from the inside out." Mrs. Jaffee says in a tight voice, trying to be strong and finish her story.

"What happened next?" I ask gently.

"I don't know how long it took for my water to be ripped from my Soul Power, but then once the pain finally stopped, I heard Karl's screams." She pauses to take another shaky breath. "I watched as my powers were forced into my husband, who was just a normal person." She starts to play with her tissue again and I put my hand on top of hers.

"Tell me what happened after that." I whisper.

"At first, I thought the crazy bastard actually did it. I watched a water tattoo appear on Karl's arms going up to his shoulder, but then after a few minutes he," She pauses again as if fighting the image that is surely burned in her mind. "The water started to make him swell, and it was coming out of every single pore and opening in him. Then he—"

I start to get the imagery of her husband's final moments and make her stop talking. "It's okay. I'm not going to ask you to keep going." The image of him bursting like a human water balloon makes my skin and stomach crawl.

"I am so sorry you had to go through that. Trust me when I say what you and Karl went through will *not* be in vain." I say with determination burning in my eyes.

She nods a silent thank you and I give her a tight smile and quietly excuse myself so she can close up class.

"Aiden?" She says my name and I stop and look back over my shoulder at her. "Thank you. No one has ever said something like that to me, and I feel you are true to your word. Please stop this from happening again and again. Please save The Protector's of Power."

I nod in her direction and walk out the door with Ivan at my side.

33

Aiden

I still can't believe I let Ivan talk me into meeting him, Gray, and *Maya* for coffee. But here I am, waiting alone in the local Starbucks with a coffee in my hand while my leg anxiously bounces on the rung of the chair I'm sitting on. And yes, I may or may not have moved the chairs where Ivan and Gray will sit to the left of me and she is alone on the other side.

Okay, yes I did. And is it an asshole move? Yeah. Do I care right now?

Big fat, NO.

I glance down at my watch, and I've already been here for fifteen minutes. Fifteen minutes too long to wait for someone who just up and deserted me over something she swore didn't fucking matter.

I'm just about to say the hell with this meeting and go to Seth's place to let him know what Ivan and I found out about The Siphon yesterday, when the door to the coffee shop dings at the arrival of new customers. My stomach sinks when I see Ivan and Gray walk in with smiles on both their faces, but my heart follows in a rush when I see Maya again.

I didn't really get a good look at her the other day, only her eyes and briefly her hair, but as I take in the rest of her body, mine comes back to life at the memory of her touch. Just as those feelings start to bloom, that little voice in the back of my head reminds me why she left and why she's back, and that makes that little blip of happiness explode like a bomb fading away in my chest. I push the sleeves of my dark purple hoodie up to my elbows like that will push the emotion filling my chest away.

I watch in silence as the three of them order their coffees along with some muffins and scones to share, courtesy of Gray's insistence. Ivan rolls his eyes as he swipes his card to pay for the order, but my eyes land on her again. She hasn't even looked in my direction once. And I would have known if she did because I've been staring at her the whole damn time.

Does she feel my gaze on her?

Is she just toying with me and purposefully ignoring me?

Is she afraid of me since we saw one another in Seth's house?

When that last thought hits me, the breath catches in my chest. I don't let myself dwell on that question as their little group joins me at the table, but I take a page out of her book and ignore her, too.

"Hey, Aiden. Sorry to keep you waiting." Gray smiles.

I take a sip of my coffee and shrug my shoulder. "It's all good. Not like I have anything going on today." I say, which is true, but my tone is flat and bored.

Gray picks up on the jab and he shoots me a stern look, but I stare right back, daring him to say something. Ivan discreetly shoulder-checks me as he sits next to me and gives me a quick, sharp look. *Knock it off,* his look tells me, and I internally groan while taking another sip of my coffee.

Gray sits by Ivan while Maya takes that single chair and hangs her purse off the back. She finally lifts her head to look at me and when our eyes meet, my heart constricts again.

Traitorous bastard.

I look down while I take another sip of my coffee and relish in the slight burn as the hot liquid rolls down my throat, making me take a much-needed breath.

As Gray offers the muffins and scones he talked Ivan into buying for us; I take a blueberry scone and wait for the conversation to start, 'cause I'm sure as hell not going to be the one to make the first leap.

"Okay, so since we have two people playing the silence game, I'm gonna talk for you both." Ivan says while looking between me and Maya.

"Ivan, you don't have to." Maya says as she straightens her shoulders, suddenly finding her voice.

I just arch an eyebrow at her. *Oh, I'm gonna love this.* I think to myself.

"Aiden." She begins. "I know I hurt you—" She starts, but I cut her off.

"Hurt me?" I scoff. "Your words fucking killed me."

"Can I talk?" She snaps and I feel her wind pick up a bit between us when a napkin lazily floats off the table.

"By all means. This oughta be good." I say as I lean back in my chair, letting my left arm hang off the back.

"Stop being an asshole." Gray says while elbowing me in the side, but I ignore him.

Maya stares at me with those sky-blue eyes that I used to get so lost in and she gives me a look that says I better keep my mouth shut.

"Again, I know what I said hurt you, but Aiden, there were things happening that I couldn't control." She explains, and her bottom lip begins to tremble. "My dad made me move away. He said that I was destined for important things in my future and I had to move away for a while."

I can't help but scoff. That's the lamest damn excuse I've ever heard. "You expect me to believe that?"

"It's the truth, Aiden." Maya says, her tone becoming hard again.

"You were eighteen, Maya. You didn't have to listen to whatever *daddy* said. If you wanted to be with me for real, we could have said to hell with your father and gotten our own place. Or hell, even moved you into my aunt and uncle's house; they wouldn't have cared." I stand up, suddenly not wanting to be in the same room with her.

I walk to the main door of the coffee shop and make it to the sidewalk before I have the three of them following me. I pause before walking the rest of the way to my truck and I turn around to tell her one more thing, but I feel something collide against my chest and that damn little seed of longing tries to flare to life in my soul as her body presses up against mine. I internally take my fire and I burn that bitch to a crisp.

"You made your choice, Maya." I growl as I push her back from me. "You lied to me. You played me like a damn fool. *You* were the one to break up with me over a fucking text message over something you *knew* was a fear of mine. I don't care what your dad told you. You could have talked to me, but instead, you took off." I say, my voice a low rumble between us.

"She didn't leave you because you were powerless, Aiden." Gray offers.

I'm about to tell him to shut up, but Ivan must see the words forming in my brain because his sharp gaze makes me bite my tongue, literally. I know Ivan would not have an issue with kicking my ass for snapping at Gray the way I wanted to. Hell, once upon a time, I would have protected this woman in front of me in the same way.

I shake my head and turn around to walk over to my Colorado, but as I put my hand on the door handle, I pause. Walking down the other side of the street are Mason and Rhett, and I get the feeling that they are more than just bullies at the university.

I look back at the group still standing in front of the coffee shop and roll my eyes, making an unfortunate decision that apparently I have no damn choice in if I want to take this monster machine down.

"I will work with you. But only to destroy that damn machine. It needs to be stopped and soon, before it takes any more lives." I say as I look at Ivan, since he knows the same disgusting truth I do.

I don't say anything else as I hop in my truck and drive away.

Mason

After we walk out of the bakery, which Rhett insisted we go to this morning to curb his 'sweet tooth'—ugh, the dude is making me seem like his personal chauffeur—we find Aiden standing by his truck and looking at his friends and a familiar woman in front of a Starbucks. I can't place her, but I feel like I know of her.

Rhett hops in the passenger side of my dark green Challenger and watches me walk around to the driver's side all the while stuffing his face with some kind of cake that makes my teeth ache just by looking at it with all the blue and white frosting that coats the thing.

"Who do you think that is?" Rhett asks, apparently not being so blind to the world around him.

"Hell if I know." I grumble as I push my finger against the start button and listen to the roar of the engine fill the cabin space. "Let's get to Victor. He's expecting us and he's gonna be pissed that we're late for our meeting. Don't be shocked if he kicks your ass, Rhett." I warn.

"Why you think I brought baked goods?" Rhett gleams wildly.

I roll my eyes, *Yeah, if you don't eat them all before we get to his hideout.*

I peel out of the parking spot along the road and head to Victor's place. Or more like his lab, that's nestled in the middle of nowhere.

After about forty-five minutes of driving, I pull into a thick forest with only enough room to drive my Challenger through. Every single time I pull up in front of this thing, I have to force myself out of the car.

The Siphon.

Perfect name for this damn thing. It siphons the life out of everything around it, and it's not even running. In pictures, this thing is terrifying, but in person. You'd have to be a soulless prick for it not to affect you.

Que my mindless partner—not by choice—to just literally skip into this machine like he's coming home to the best surprise the world could offer.

I roll my eyes as I make myself walk behind him and into The Siphon that Victor has made into his home/lab for as long as I can remember, and I have been working with him for the last two years, same as Rhett.

We walk through a long tunnel that is only as wide as the two of us as we walk shoulder to shoulder and only about three feet higher than our 6'1 and 6'3,—I'm taller, of course—height.

As we enter the main corridor, on the right, we pass the pods that are used to transfer powers from one host to another. They give me the creeps every time I see them, so I try to stay clear of them while Rhett, being the crazy asshole that he is, literally walks over to see if there is anyone inside.

I've seen these things in action, and it's not pretty. The time Victor had me and Rhett kidnap that couple, I think the man's name was Karl; I don't remember the woman's name. I try to block her face from my mind, but that image of the man still haunts me to this day. So, I steer clear of these damn things as much as I can.

"Unnatural. Stay away." My fire whispers to me.

"You think?" I scoff.

"Why do you stay?" My fire whispers at me.

"You know why." I growl, thinking of Dani.

I ignore Rhett and I continue to walk deeper into the lab, entering a control room, and there, in the middle of a mess of papers piled all around the top of the desk and floor, is Victor. The control room has a gigantic window that faces those damn pods and to the left of the window are three huge computer screens that show different data scrolling by in green font on a black background.

"Have you found anything new?" Victor asks, his voice cold and devoid of any emotion while he's plugging more information into his computer screen. The asshole doesn't even look at me when I enter.

Over the years I've been working with this maniac, I have come to somewhat understand the equation he's using to transfer the powers from one person to another, but it has failed every time, and Victor can't figure out why. I'm no mathematician, but even I can see the flaw in his logic. You can't transplant powers into someone who doesn't have somewhere to store the energy. Doesn't have a Soul Power.

I've tried to tell him this over and over, but I eventually stopped when he almost choked me out with his wind. The wildness that was shining in his eyes that day told me he wouldn't think twice about killing me. Hell, he'd barely thought once before doing it, but I didn't even let him get that far before I burned his wrist at the last minute, making him let me go. He still has that scar 'til this day.

"Nothing new this week, Victor." I say.

Just as Victor nods his head and is about to wave his hand to dismiss me, Rhett waltzes in and looks at me with a wild grin on his face.

"Oh, but there was something new today, Mason."

I give Rhett a look that could shoot daggers and kill him on the spot. I turn around and look at Victor as Rhett walks over to the desk and deposits one of those damn cakes he got from the bakery earlier.

"Tell me, Rhett." Victor urges.

"We noticed a new girl hanging around Aiden. She might be the one the prophecy foretold of." Rhett announces like he just won Victor's approval.

This isn't a game of teacher's pet, *you crazy bastard.* I think to myself.

"And why didn't you think this was important to tell me, Mason?" Victor asks as he narrows his eyes at me.

"I haven't seen her powers." I shrug nonchalantly. "So, how am I to know if it's her?"

Victor crosses the room so fast that I barely have time to call my fire to my right hand, but it's instantly snuffed out with a blast of wind.

"Do I need to remind you who you work for, boy?" Victor spits out. "Do I need to make a visit to a certain someone?" He challenges.

His threat makes my blood run cold for a moment before anger flares to life in my chest. "You stay away from her, you fucking freak." I snarl.

"Then you best do as I say." Victor says coolly. "Find this girl of Aiden's and attack her. Break him." He growls, then shoves me away roughly by the shoulder.

I don't even give them a second glance as I storm out of the control room, not even bothering to see if Rhett follows me.

34

Aiden

The next morning, I am slowly drawn out of a blissful, visionless sleep when I feel Seth probing in the back of my mind. I open my eyes and look at my alarm clock. The white digital font showing it's 5:15 in the morning.

"What are you doing waking me up this early, Seth?" I ask sleepily.

"Come by before class. I want to run a few drills with you."

I groan as I reluctantly get out of bed. When I open my bedroom door to head to the bathroom, I find the house is still quiet and dark.

Yeah, 'cause normal people are still sleeping. I think to myself as I throw on a pair of black shorts and a gray T-shirt.

I make sure to bring an extra set of clothes so I can change once Seth is finished running me through the wringer so I can head to school.

I arrive at his house at six on the dot and he meets me in the foyer before he leads me down into what I assume is the basement. There are not one but three gigantic training rooms built under his house.

I follow him into the closest one before he shuts the door behind him. I go over and tap an index finger against one of the windows and I can tell it's a mix of bulletproof glass and Plexiglas to make it a bit more flexible to different pressures that may happen in the room.

"Nice training rooms." I say, while looking around the area.

"Thanks." Seth replies, then he brings a flame to his hand, and that's all the warning I get before he comes at me.

I bring my own flame up and I imagine it becoming like a shield in that popular elf video game and trying to make my flames as solid as I can. After Seth's fist actually connects with my makeshift shield with a dull thud, I instantly drop my flame and call my lightning to force it in his face, but he teleports before I can discharge it a millisecond later.

"Good job. Keep it up." Seth coaches from behind me.

I can tell he's teleporting, but I can't keep my eyes on him; he's moving too fast. I turn around at the sound of his foot connecting with the floor, ready to send another bolt toward him, but he sucker punches me in the gut and sends an electrical pulse into my stomach.

I try to absorb his current to lessen the blow, but it sends me flying a few feet across the room, and I land hard on my back. I only have a moment to get my bearings before Seth comes at me again.

Pushing my fire to my foot, I propel myself to the left and away from his attack. Once I'm back on my feet, I throw a medium-sized fireball towards him that explodes on impact. He winces as the ball hits him in the shoulder, and I take that moment to direct my flame to my foot again to help me close the distance while I will my fire to engulf my hand, making a flaming fist and attack him with a right hook before backing up a bit to get out of his immediate reach.

He wipes his thumb across his bottom lip and it comes away bloody. Seth looks from his thumb to me before giving me a dark smile that sends chills up my spine. Then he disappears from view a heartbeat later.

When he's out of my sight, I suddenly have a thought. Can I pick up on his electrical current? We are all made up of electrical currents that control our bodies. So, I should be able to sense him.

Going against my instincts, I close my eyes and look for Seth's electrical trace, but I only pick up on the currents flowing in the lights that are in the room. I take a breath and try to ignore them; to focus on the smaller things. Sweat trickles down my back from under my shirt and then after what feels like forever, I pick up on a small pulse.

I pull my electricity to my left hand and I turn about ninety degrees to my right and when I open my eyes; Seth appears right in front of me. With a grin that was as dark as his own, I place my hand on his right arm, and with a loud crack of the dueling currents, I cancel out the charge he was about to punch me with. He looks between my hand and his, shock evident in his eyes, then a smile forms on his face as he relaxes his stance.

"Phenomenal job, Aiden!" Seth says with excitement. "How did you know where I was going to end up at?"

"I, uh, I felt for your body's electricity." I say as I rub the back of my neck with my right hand, trying to keep the embarrassment out of my voice.

"That is brilliant." Seth chuckles. "Now let me try to explain how to use both powers at the same time." He takes me to the middle of the room and has me sit on the floor. "I want you to imagine your powers, and how they are each connected to your Soul Power." Seth explains.

I close my eyes and I start to see my Soul Power, which is a bright white ball of energy. I can see my fire on the right side and my lightning on the left, but they are almost fighting for space in the sphere; both flaring and sparking off the surface.

"Now imagine that sphere being split directly in two; where each power has control over only their respective part." Seth says.

When I imagine a wall appearing between the two powers, it's almost like they become calmer, and I feel my connection to them change. Almost like I suddenly have more control. So, I test the theory. I think about both of my abilities and bring them forward. I feel the pull of my Soul Power from both sides and I am mindful to ground my electricity to my rib as I feel them get closer to my hands.

I open my eyes and glance down at my palms. On the right dancing lazily is my fire and gently arcing on my left, my electricity. Granted, they are small in comparison to what I had been able to bring forward before, but they are active at the same time, and that was the goal.

"Great job, Aiden!" Seth says with a big smile on his face.

"Thank you, Seth. But I wouldn't have come as far as I have if it wasn't for you and my friends." I say.

"It is nothing but up from here. Be sure you keep practicing, and the next time we fight, I want you to use both abilities." Seth says with a bright grin. "But you need to take it slow. If you push your powers to their max too soon, it can and will cause severe damage to your Soul Power. We need to build your stamina just like you would muscle."

As Seth leads me back up into the main house so I can get a shower, I have to force myself to stand on my shaky legs. I feel so tired, but yet it's a good feeling at the same time. It's the same after I had a hard workout session with Ivan. I feel like I've gotten stronger by what I just made my body go through. But exhaustion is still exhaustion, and I wish I could call in sick from school.

As soon as that thought hits my mind, I turn off the water and shove that temptation to the back of my mind. I know that it was not cheap for my aunt and uncle to help me pay my way through college. So, I suck it up, dry my aching body off, say goodbye to Seth, and drive to school.

The thirty-minute drive to the university does little to relieve my aching body. I groan as I walk in and as soon as I meet with Ivan and Gray, they instantly know something is up.

"You look like total shit." Gray says.

"Did you go *out* last night?" Ivan asks. Apparently, Gray doesn't know about the nighttime outings I used to do.

I shake my head no before whispering, "I went to a *friend's* house to train."

Both of them nod their heads in understanding as we continue to walk to our respective classes and it takes all I have in me not to put my head down on the desk and sleep through my classes.

Later that afternoon, I meet up with Ivan in the hallway so we both can make our way to the cafeteria, where Gray is already waiting for us since his class let out a little bit early.

"You sure you're okay, dude?" Ivan asks, seeing how tired I still am.

"Yeah, it's just Seth had me meet him this morning at six to run some drills with me, and I think I pushed myself a little too hard." I say.

As we round the corner to walk into the main hallway, we start to see people running outside with looks of panic on their faces, but I notice that some have looks of entertainment on them.

Crazy Parasites, getting off on the pain of others. I growl to myself.

Ivan and I look at one another, an unspoken understanding that we are going to follow the crowd and see what's going on. We are almost to the door when another student comes barreling in with pure, undiluted fear shining in his eyes. I grab his arm and it takes a moment for his body to stop its forward momentum to look back at me.

"What has everyone going nuts?" I ask in a hard tone.

"It's M-M-Mason. He's attacking... some girl." The guy stumbles on his words, terror lacing through each syllable.

Dread, fear, and anger fill my chest so quickly that I am out the door before Ivan can even comprehend I have moved. I slam the main door of the school open with such force that it smacks the brick wall behind it, cracking a few in the process.

At this sudden noise, everyone turns to me and through the crowd, I see Mason standing in front of someone who is bound by chains that snake around the lower tree branches. His fire is rolling in both hands and he tosses little embers toward the girl's body, just enough to scorch her clothes and enough to slightly blister her delicate skin.

The top of the person's head comes into view and I know without even seeing her face that it's Maya. Anger fills my body with such heat that I barely feel my fire roaring to life in my hand. The small gathering of onlookers backs away from me, not really out of fear, but they know I will push through them to get to Mason one way or another.

"Mason!" I roar. "Get away from her, now!" I scream at him and start to move in his direction.

"Oh, is she yours?" Mason sneers with an evil, amused look in his eyes. "I didn't know."

"Aiden! Get help!" Maya pleads, with tears rolling down her cheeks.

I give her a sharp shake of my head and then push my fire down towards my foot to help me cross the distance faster. Just as I am about to close in, Rhett comes out from behind the tree with a solid rocky fist.

"Not so fast there, buddy." Rhett sneers as he takes his fist and punches it into his open palm. "You gotta get through me first."

"With fuckin' pleasure." I growl.

I switch over to my electricity, throwing an electrified haymaker and colliding with a solid buzzing *thwack* to Rhett's face. He takes a few steps back and I know I jumbled his brains for at least a few minutes. I catch Mason coming at me out of the corner of my eye as he throws a fireball toward me. The flame is so hot that I can feel the heat coming for me from the ten-foot span that stretches between us.

I quickly make my fiery wall several layers thick so it can stop Mason's flame before it hits me. Mason takes the distraction and is quickly closing in. I drop my wall and I relish in the shocked look that floods Mason's face at the sudden change. I catch him in the stomach with my fiery fist and with my momentum, I actually throw him back a few feet away where Rhett is still reeling from my electricity.

I stand there for a few moments, still shocked at how I was able to fight these two, but then a moan from Maya brings me back to the present, and I run over to her. She's chained up to this tree by the wrists and ankles, the chains tossed over a few thick low-hanging branches.

I look over her body and I see that her jeans and shirt have burn marks all over them. Her skin is a blistery red and I know that's where the embers touched and burned her skin.

Anger swells in my chest as I look into her tear-stained face, her expression begging for my help.

"I'm here. I'm getting you out of this." I say with a touch more fear in my voice than I'm willing to admit to hearing.

I start to melt the cuffs at her wrists and ankles with my flame, being careful not to burn her. Once her feet hit the ground, I suddenly feel the electrical current of someone coming up on each side, and I know it's the duo again without even looking.

Protect.

This one word whispers in my mind and I turn around, taking a step back so that Maya is closer to the tree and protected from the assault. I know I can't fight them both at once, so I take a breath and push both of my abilities to the max.

I send a current of electricity to my left at Rhett at the same time I send a river of flames toward Mason. As I hear the crack of electricity strike its quarry and the screams of pain as my fire burns the torso of Mason, I feel pride at knowing I am using both of my powers to protect people like I always dreamed of, but then something feels off.

"Too soon." I hear a voice whisper, and then my chest starts to hurt.

No, hurt is the word I use when Seth punches me in the gut while we are doing our mock fights. This is a fiery pain that explodes in my chest, threatening to take my breath, and makes darkness want to engulf my vision.

I can make out sounds of people yelling. I think it must be the dean of the university and the campus police gathering around, but I can't focus on anything other than the unnatural burn in my chest and my body crumpling to the ground.

I barely feel Maya's hand pressed against my chest, and while her face is blurry to me, I notice the shine of tears streaming down her cheeks. I hear her screaming my name, but it's a distant echo in my darkening mind. I then see what I think is Seth looming over me, but before I can even try to form a thought, everything fades to black.

35
Seth

After Aiden left for school and I cleaned up after our fight—kid has a pretty good fighting style; my jaw is still aching from the right hook he got me with earlier—I try to relax on my couch. But something tells me to look in on Aiden.

And it's a good damn thing I did.

When I enter his mind, thanks to my mind control ability, I can feel that he's pushing his powers to the max way too soon, but I can't figure out why. The only word I keep hearing is, *protect.* And that is actually coming from his powers and not Aiden himself.

I concentrate on locating Aiden and when I figure out that he's at the university, I teleport right next to him. Once I land silently in the grass, I lift my head in time to see Aiden crumple to the ground, Maya sobbing hysterically while Gray cradles his friend's head in his lap, and Ivan standing over all of them like the sentry he is. When I rush over to the group and take one look at Aiden, I know he's in trouble.

I quickly glance between the people around him and I know none of them will leave his side, so I'm not even going to ask them to. It's been a while since I've teleported more than two people, but I know I can do it.

"Ivan, put your hand on Gray's shoulder." I instruct as I place a hand on Maya's. "I'm going to get us out of here."

I block out the sound of Maya's sobs and the chatter of the on-lookers who are still trying to get Mason and Rhett up off the ground and into the university security car. I concentrate on who I have around me and where I want to go. Back to my place, back to the living room. I feel gravity begin to shift as my teleportation power flares to life in my chest, and in the next instant, we fade into particles floating in the air and we land twenty seconds later.

But it's not in my living room. We land in the front yard but, at least it's not a mile down the road like when I was first practicing with this power back when I was younger.

"Ivan." I snap once everyone gets their wits about them. "Help me get him inside." I look at Maya, her nose and cheeks red from crying. "Maya, I need you to call Matt and Vivian. They need to know what happened. Gray, you go with her." I instruct, while looking over at him.

He gives me a sharp nod as he gently grabs Maya by the shoulders and hauls her off Aiden's still-limp body. Just as I get to my feet, Ivan's head snaps up to look at me; pure fear lights his face and it makes my stomach drop to the ground.

"Move it, Seth. Aiden doesn't have a pulse."

Maya

I watch as Seth hooks his arms under Aiden's armpits and Ivan grabs at his friend's legs and they heft his limp body from the ground. I'm frozen to the spot, so numb at what happened that I can't move. It's not until Gray pulls me along with him that I snap back into reality.

"I'll get the door for you two." Gray says as he opens the front door so Ivan and Seth can carry Aiden inside.

"We need to call Matt and Vivian." I whisper as Gray closes and locks the door behind us.

"Here, use my phone." He says as he takes his phone from the back pocket of his jeans. "They may not answer your call since you have a different number." He adds as he pulls up 'Aunt Viv' on his contact list and presses the dial button.

I take the phone from him, listening to the rings echo in my ear as he leads me back to where we hear the muffled voices of Seth and Ivan floating through the house. When we get to the threshold of the room, I can tell it's a medical room of sorts, complete with metal walls and a matching medical table. Just as my eyes take in Aiden's prone form, a cheerful voice fills my ears and I force myself to look away so I can try to keep my voice from cracking like my soul is right now.

"Gray! Hello there. How are you today?" Aunt Viv answers.

"Mrs. Rivers, it's Maya. Aiden was hurt at school today and we have him at Seth's place. You and Mr. Rivers need to get over here as soon as you can." I say, my voice trembling.

"Oh Maya! What happened?" Vivian asks as I hear her moving around in the background.

"We can explain when you get here." I say as I text her Seth's address. "I just sent you Seth's address. Please get here as soon as you can."

"Matt!" Vivian yells. Her voice is a little lower, so she must have pulled the phone away from her ear. "Move it, Aiden's hurt and he's at Seth's place." Vivian barks, her voice stronger before coming back on the line with me, "We will be there in fifteen."

"Okay." I say as I hang up the phone and hand it back to Gray.

I look back into the medical room in time to see Seth roll over what looks like a heart machine at the same time that Ivan tears Aiden's shirt down the middle, like it's made of nothing but paper.

Aiden's wielding marks are on full display, the flame and lightning designs merging in the center of his still-not-moving chest. Seth slaps some electrodes onto Aiden's chest before turning the machine on, and when the green lines appear on the screen, my stomach drops as my hand latches onto Gray's in an effort to keep my knees from buckling.

They're still straight.

"Shit." Seth swears. "Maya! In that cabinet to your right, third drawer down, are empty IV bags. I need two filled with your purified water. I'll need them once I get his heart beating again."

I nod, suddenly having a role in helping Aiden. Gray reaches for the drawer that Seth pointed out and he grabs two bags, along with the necessary tubing and needles. I take the first bag from him and I let my water come to life in my right hand. When I press my finger to the fill valve, I will it to purify into medical-grade saline like I've done countless times over the three years I've had my powers.

Just as I am starting to fill the second bag, I hear Seth's next orders ring out to Ivan.

"You breathe for him two times and then I am going to shock him, so you better be completely clear." Seth says, and Ivan merely nods and stands by his friend's head and waits for Seth's signal.

Seth straddles Aiden's stomach, careful not to be near his chest to possibly injure his Soul Power more than what it already is. I watch with bated breath as he calls his own electricity into both of his hands. The yellow and white lightning bolt tattoo appearing on his skin, and I can tell from the furrowing lines of his eyebrows that he's trying to gauge how much of a current to send into Aiden's broken body without completely killing him.

Seth then nods to Ivan to give two rescue breaths and as soon as Aiden's chest rises and falls, Ivan backs away as Seth sends the electrical current into Aiden's body. My eyes slide over at the heart monitor as it registers the jolts from the shock. We all hold our breath, hoping that the lines keep moving.

The line goes flat again.

"Again Ivan, three breaths this time." Seth instructs.

After I fill the second IV bag, Gray takes them and places them on a nearby table and he stands against my back while we watch his boyfriend and Seth work.

The front door opens a moment later and Gray turns before I do, giving a small wave to who must be Matt and Vivian walking through the door. As they join us in the doorway, Seth sends another shock into Aiden's chest. The power sparks from Seth's elbows before it goes into Aiden's body, this one a little stronger than the last.

But it still doesn't work. The lines on the monitor remain flat.

Seth lets out another curse as Ivan gives his friend three more breaths.

"Come on, damn it, Aiden." Seth growls. "You're not dying on me yet."

"Ground yourself, Seth." Matt interrupts before Seth charges up with another current.

Seth looks at Matt and gives him a sharp nod before taking a quick breath and apparently grounds himself before sending another current into Aiden's chest. This time when Seth gathers the power, all the current is forced into his hands, through his fingers, and disappears into Aiden's chest with just a quick buzz in the air.

Ivan

After Seth sends his latest shock through Aiden's chest, I can tell we all hold our breaths waiting to see if those damn lines keep pulsing after the shock fades.

But it falls flat again.

Maya and Vivian both release heartbreaking sobs as both women fall to their knees, holding onto one another for support. I'm about to breathe again for Aiden, but when Seth slowly slides off Aiden's chest to stand on the floor, I take a few steps back, the fight suddenly leaving my body and I only stop when my back hits the wall.

My legs give out and I slide down the wall, fighting back the burn of tears that threaten to spill down my face as I look at my friend's lifeless body. My eyes slide from Aiden to Gray and the fear that is filling his brown eyes and making his face look so pale makes the grief morph into anger in my chest. And when I see Maya's pain-stricken face, it takes all of one second for me to know what I want to do.

I jump to my feet, my metal itching to be released to make all of the different kinds of weapons that flash through my mind so I can beat the ever-loving shit out of Mason and Rhett for attacking Maya and fighting with Aiden.

I storm past Gray but his fingers wrap tightly around my bicep and the only reason I pause is I'm shocked at how strong his grip is on me and he's able to stop me in my anger-filled rage.

"What Grayson?" I can't help but growl.

Without taking his eyes from Aiden's body, he points at the monitor and whispers, "Look."

36

Aiden

My chest is so tight, and my whole body feels like it's on fire. Everything around me is cloaked in darkness. I want to open my eyes, but I can't.

A crackle of electricity spreads over my body, but it does nothing to erase the blackness around me.

"Heal." A gentle, silky voice says.

Then, in the center of the black void, an orange and whitish-blue sphere appears before me. I try to walk toward it, but the more I do, the more it feels like I will never reach it. Another jolt of current races through my body, and I step closer, but it's still out of reach. It's not until this phantom electricity hits me once more, now more focused on my chest instead of my whole body; I find myself standing next to this sphere, and I reach a hand out to it.

"Heal." I hear the whisper again.

This voice is different, louder this time, with more of a growl than before. Looking closer at the sphere in front of me, I see a small crack in the center that spreads over to what I now understand to be my Soul Power—my fractured Soul Power that houses my fire and electricity.

"How can I heal you?" I ask, my voice echoing in the dark abyss.

"Connect to us." The voices whisper eerily at the same time.

This is the first time I realize that both abilities have subtle tones to me. The fire is a smooth whisper while the electricity has a bit of a roughness to it. I reach out my hands again toward this sphere, resting them on either side of the hemispheres, and I think the word they have been repeating to me.

"Heal, heal, heal." I whisper.

Finally, the darkness fades away and the sound of sobbing filters into my ears, followed by a harsh pain in my chest. I force my eyes open and I'm greeted with blurry faces all around me. My eyelids close for a heartbeat before I feel a gentle caress on my cheek.

Just to open my eyes again is an effort, but when I look to my right, the face above me is clear as day compared to the others around me and her face brings a small, weak smile to my lips.

She gives me a watery smile as I whisper, "Maya." But then everything fades to black and her fingers brush against my cheek before my mind fills with nothingness.

Seth

After Aiden passes out but is stable for the most part, I can feel the shifting of worry to anger from Matt and I prepare for his onslaught of telling me off.

Matt roughly takes me by the bicep and pulls me out of the little medical room so we don't wake his nephew.

"What the hell have you been doing with him?" Matt seethes. "This should *not* have happened, Seth, if you were training him the right way!"

"We have been training! He pushed himself too hard."

"Obviously not training hard enough." Matt snaps.

"With Aiden getting his abilities so late in life, this needed to be done a certain way!" I argue.

But maybe it was too soon for Maya and Aiden to meet up again. I think to myself.

Matt sighs in aggravated defeat. "Do you think he will be okay?"

"I don't know. I think so, but we won't know until he tries to use his power again." I shake my head while looking over my shoulder at him.

"Can you still heal?" Matt asks softly.

I give a small sly smile and then turn from my long-time friend. "What kind of Mimic would I be if I can't do that?"

I walk back into the room and over to the left side of Aiden's bed since Maya is perched on the right side, still running her fingers through his hair.

I rub my hands together and tap into the special ability I have as a Mimic. Healing.

And this is a different kind of healing from those with water powers. They can heal only on a molecular level. I, on the other hand, can actually heal broken bones, skin, ligaments, and anything wrong with the body; other than the Soul Power. That is the only thing I cannot heal since the repair needs to come from the one who controls the sphere. I always found that to be a pain in the ass, but I can't help the way we were made.

Honestly, from what even I have felt myself at times, the Soul Power is built on the mental capacity of the individual. If you are strong-willed, then your Soul Power heals easier, but if you have even an ounce of fear of not being able to control your abilities for any reason, then it becomes a mind game.

Once I know that Aiden is healed from the various injuries he sustained from the fight with Mason and then from my electricity that scorched him before I could get it under control, I turn my attention to Maya for the first time and I notice the burns on her arms, legs, back and stomach. All from Mason's flames.

"Maya." I say gently to get her attention. "Let me help you with those burns. They have to be painful."

Maya nods as I grab onto her palm and will my healing ability to flow through her and watch as the burns slowly close and fade before our eyes.

"Thank you." She whispers.

I nod before turning my attention to Ivan, who is still standing beside...Gray, if I remember his name correctly, clutching Ivan's arm close to his chest like an emotional support anchor. "Ivan, help me carry Aiden into one of the guest rooms." I turn back to Maya, "Maya, if you want clean clothes, you can go into the room next door to Aiden's and change there."

She nods as Vivian steps to her side, "I'll help you, Maya." Vivian turns to look at me, "I'm glad you're alive, Seth, but this is a hell of a way to meet up after twenty-one years."

I chuckle. She always did speak her mind. " I know Viv. I'm sorry."

After Ivan and I move Aiden into the guestroom and change him into a clean pair of black sweatpants and a t-shirt, Maya comes in, pulls a chair next to his bed, and grabs his right hand, all without saying a word.

"Come on," I whisper to Ivan. "Let's leave those two be for a while."

Ivan nods as he quietly walks away from my side and into the living room where Matt and Vivian sit on the couch and Gray is pacing the length of the floor. I watch as Ivan makes his way to Gray, forcing him to stop his pacing by pulling him into his chest with a firm embrace while kissing the top of his head.

I walk into the living room, sink down onto the couch beside Matt and Vivian, and give them a tired smile as we wait for Aiden to wake up from his healing slumber.

Aiden

I am pulled out of the darkness in my mind by delicate fingers lightly brushing through my hair and the fingers on my right hand being caressed and tenderly played with.

At first, I think it's Aunt Viv because she would do the same thing when I was younger whenever I fell asleep on the couch, but when my eyes flutter open, I see the short, dark brown hair and slender form of Maya.

"Oh, Aiden." She sobs while running her fingers through my hair once more before caressing my cheek.

I find myself leaning into her touch as I remember what all happened and my eyes rove over her body. At the pink T-shirt she has on and the flawless skin that peeks out from the short-sleeves.

"Are you okay?" I ask hoarsely.

"Yes. Seth healed me after he knew you were okay."

I lose a sigh of relief, which makes my chest burn with the reminder of what I did, how close I was to a complete disaster.

"You were very brave today." Maya says while tracing her finger over the flame tattoo on my arm.

I scoff at her while shaking my head. "No." I say sharply. "No, I wasn't brave. I was stupid. I could have hurt other people. I could have hurt you." My voice drops to a whisper near the end. "Seth warned me that if I push myself too hard, I could hurt myself, but I didn't listen. I didn't care at the moment. All I knew was you were in danger and I needed to protect you, no matter the cost." I say with a trace of bitterness in my tone at what I did today. "I'm sorry that I put you in more danger." I whisper.

"Don't be sorry. I should have seen them coming. I'm the one that should be apologizing." Maya says as she drops her eyes.

"No, don't do that." I say with more strength in my voice. "This is Rhett and Mason's fault. They picked the fight, so they are to blame." I say while cupping her chin with my hand and pulling her to meet my eyes.

I give her a small smile before I cave to the need to have her close to me. To make sure she's alright. I wrap my arms around her shoulder, her head resting on my chest, and she relaxes a little. Then I feel something run through my body, but it has a coolness to it, and then

Maya begins tracing small circles on my chest; the fabric of my shirt tickling the skin underneath.

"You're still hurting." Maya whispers.

"So that's what this feeling is?" I ask mockingly with a sly smile tugging on my lips while trying to play off the burn in my chest as nothing but an ache, but with her water searching my system, I know I can't hide from her.

I try to take a breath and move a little to get a bit more comfortable, but that sends a fresh jolt of pain through my body. She instantly stops drawing on my chest with her finger and looks at me with concern filling her eyes.

"It's nothing compared to earlier." I sigh as the pain eases a bit.

One thing about this whole attack is that I've come to understand a few things about me and Maya that I was too blind to see because of my anger from three years ago. One, which I knew, I still love this woman with everything that I am. I mean, I almost killed for her. I almost died for her. And I would do it over again if it was needed. I also know that from the way she looks at me now, from the way she looked at me while hanging from the tree like a damn puppet waiting to be scorched, that she still loves me, too.

"Maya." I say and she pushes herself up enough to look into my mismatched eyes and I watch as hers light up with happiness when I say her name. "So, you were really forced to send that text and move away?"

Tears fill her eyes half a heartbeat later and she nods. "Yes. I still don't care if you have powers or not, Aiden. I love you. Always have and always will."

I feel like her words lift the boulder that has been crushing my soul little by little these past three years and I gently pull her back down to my chest while she wraps her arms around my neck. Her head fits right under my chin and I drag my stubble over her hair as she lets her body sink deeper into mine.

"I missed you so much, Baby Girl." I whisper, using her favorite nickname, and it feels so damn good pouring from my lips again.

She pulls back enough to look at my face again, and I see fresh tears in her eyes. I lift my left hand to wipe them away then slide that hand to the back of her neck, wanting to ease her in for a long-awaited kiss, but instead, she distracts me by tracing her index finger along the line of my jaw.

"This look suits you." Maya says with a smile on her lips.

As she searches my eyes, her smile falters a bit. I know she can still see the hardness of these last few years in them, and I look away from her gaze, not wanting her to see how detached I tried to be from life after our breakup.

"Aiden." Maya says while putting her index finger under my chin.

I turn back to look at her and my heart melts at the love that radiates in the smile that stretches from her lips to the corner of her eyes.

"I have never stopped loving you, Aiden," Maya confesses. "I hated what I had to do back then. I hope you can forgive me for what I said to you that broke you so badly."

"There's nothing to forgive now that we know there was a bigger reason behind what happened." I force past the knot in my throat. "I love you, Maya Harper. That has never changed." I say, while pulling her into my chest again.

I feel another twinge of pain in my chest and I am suddenly terrified that I won't be able to use my abilities, or they will tear me apart if I try to use them again. I tighten my hold on Maya to at least feel something solid in my life as that thought fills my mind.

She must notice the change in my mood because she quietly lifts her head and gives me that kiss I was trying to get from her a moment ago. As the taste of her strawberry lip gloss touches my tastebuds, I try to deepen the kiss by swiping my tongue over her lips, asking for entry, but she pulls back and puts a finger to my lips while she gives me a plump, lazy smile. I grin at her teasing and force myself to settle back down, grateful for the distraction.

She then gives me a serious look, and she flattens her hand on my chest and I know she's trying to look for my Soul Power, and I close my eyes at her touch and somehow I lead her water to the center of my chest.

"It's weird. I've never felt for anyone's powers before." She chuckles. "I believe you will be able to use your abilities again, Aiden. I can still feel them."

I grab at her hand, which is still resting on my chest, just as I start to feel darkness clouding my peripheral vision. "I hope so." I whisper as I feel my eyes get heavy.

Maya smiles and I feel her get comfortable against my side. "Rest Aiden. I will be right here."

And with that, I let the darkness take me once more.

37

Aiden

The next two days pass by in a blur. Ivan and Gray come by a few times a day, but Maya will not leave my side, and part of me likes it. It's like making up for lost time between us, but I know that she can't stay here all the time. So, I talked her into going with the guys for a bit to get something to eat or have a change of scenery.

Uncle Matt and Aunt Viv come by in the morning and stay until the evening so they can be with me and catch up with Seth now that he's come out of hiding.

This morning, I'm sitting on the corner of the mattress while I stare down at my wielding marks. I haven't even tried to use my powers since I overloaded them. Maya says she can tell my Soul Power is healed thanks to her water ability searching through my body, but I haven't had the nerve to try using them again.

Until today.

This is the first day that I am completely alone. Maya is at home with her parents for a while, after my insistence for her to leave. Ivan and Gray are at school, I think. Uncle Matt and Aunt Viv are in the living room again with Seth. So this is the best scenario to try my powers again and not risk hurting anyone. The most damage I could do is to the furniture that is spread throughout the room.

I rest my forearms on my knees and look at my right hand, at the flames that live on my skin and spiral down my arm like a snake. As I turn my hand over where my palm is up toward the ceiling, I think about my fire. There is a slight pull of my Soul Power, but it's nothing I haven't experienced before. I feel the fire snake past my shoulder, down my arm, and flow to life in my hand.

Once I have the flame dancing in my palm, I change the shape and temperature to make sure I have full control over it. After testing for a few minutes, and when I feel comfortable with the connection, I cut the flow of power, and the fire dies with a whispered whoosh and a tendril of smoke floating in the air in front of me.

I then turn my left hand over and think about my electricity. As soon as I do that, pain blooms in my chest. Images of my Soul Power flash in my mind and what looks like a small fracture in the sphere appear before me, followed by that raspy voice whispering in my mind.

"Heal."

I close my eyes, imagining the fracture again, and wonder how I can fix it. I remember one time when I was younger; I fell on the playground in grade school and ripped a hole in the knee of my jeans. When I got home later that day, Aunt Viv noticed the tear, grabbed her sewing kit and got to work on repairing the rough fabric. I remember how she deftly used the needle and thread to close the hole, almost like it was never there.

I envision the fracture before me, and I think about my lightning becoming a thread and using it like a doctor would a stitch to sew the fracture closed.

As soon as I finish the final stitch, the electrical current flows down my arm, and I quickly ground to my rib before it leaps to life in my hand. But it feels different. It's stronger than before.

"Blended." I hear the voices of my abilities whisper in my mind.

I flip over my right hand and call my fire to it. Watching both of my abilities dance in either hand, I push each power higher. My fire almost reaching the ceiling, but not close enough to burn, and my electricity is violently buzzing and arcing loudly in my hand. I feel a strength in them that I never felt before. It's almost like this fracture brought them closer to me.

Seth

After Ivan, Gray and Maya walk into my living room after I talk with Matt and Vivian for a few hours, I excuse myself so I can check on Aiden while Matt and Viv offer to make lunch for us. As I approach the open door to his room, I find him sitting on the side of the bed with both abilities roaring in his hands. I lean against the door frame with my hands in my pockets of my dark wash jeans and watch him with silent wonder.

"I know now for sure that Aiden is indeed the one we were waiting on. He is the delayed prodigy that could overpower us all." I think to myself as I watch Aiden working with his abilities, making them twist and change shape with just a thought. I smile at how far he's come, even with this latest setback.

"Now, just to train him the right way to prepare him for what's coming." I sigh inwardly as I remove my right hand from my pocket and lightly rap my knuckles on the door.

Aiden

As I sit with my powers still flowing from my hands, I hear a knock on the door. Looking over my shoulder, I see Seth standing in the doorway.

"Aiden, your friends are back, and I think we need to talk about some things."

My stomach sinks at his tone, flat and serious, but I force myself to my feet and walk behind him and into the living room. My aunt and uncle are just walking out of the kitchen with some sandwiches and chips on a serving platter and drinks for everyone present. They lead us in to the living room and set the platter on the coffee table before taking the couch.

My eyes lock onto Maya's and I notice she's sitting on the loveseat while Gray sits on one of the wingback chairs with Ivan perched on the armrest; his left arm spread lovingly yet possessively across Gray's shoulders. I take a seat next to Maya while Seth takes the spot next to Aunt Viv and Uncle Matt.

"So what do we need to talk about, Seth?" I ask.

"We need to talk about a prophecy that has been passed down for generations. And since things have finally calmed down, it's better to tell you all now what's going on." Seth says.

"Okay. Tell us everything you know." I press.

"Alright. I'm just going to get to the main point here. And I know Aiden has been having partial visions of what's going to happen, so correct me if I get anything wrong." Seth begins.

I take a breath and try to keep a level head on what I am about to hear while trying to ignore the shock on my aunt and uncle's faces at hearing I've been having visions for a while now. I don't know why that would be shocking to them on top of everything else, but I tuck that into the back of my mind to talk to them about that later.

"I'll let you know if anything seems to be different." I tell Seth.

Seth looks at us and then takes his own cleansing breath before telling us the truth. "You two are the ones The Protector's of Power have been waiting on for the last one hundred and fifty years. There is a prophecy that has been floating around that tells what is to come." Seth explains.

He gets up and opens a little door in the entertainment center and takes out this antique-looking scroll. As he unrolls the paper, the lightness I felt by getting Maya back in my life fades with the weight of what that scroll will say. As Seth takes a breath to read from the scroll, Maya's hand tightens around mine, like her touch will ground us both to what we are about to hear.

"The one to end the conflicts between The Protector's of Power and The Parasites and the only one to destroy The Siphon will be the one who was born seemingly without abilities," Seth begins. "Upon the twenty-first birthday, they will develop two abilities of flame and lightning. The one who will wield complimentary abilities of water and wind will work together to achieve the goal of destroying The Siphon once and for all, but only when the sun and moon is high in the sky and is as red as the dust of the earth. And the one who wields the flame and lightning must give everything they have in order to achieve this goal and bring peace back to the lands." Seth says solemnly.

We are quiet for a few moments, and a few things click in my head. I look over to my uncle, and I see his face turn ashen at the mention of The Siphon, and I hate to think of the pain he must have gone through at this piece of shit monstrosity.

"So that is why I was so late in getting my abilities, and why I have this deep-seeded need to destroy this machine." I say, while looking at Seth.

He nods and I can tell he has more to add to the conversation, so I wait for him to continue.

"What I can gather from the visions that Aiden's had," Seth says, pausing to think of how to say what I already know.

"Maya will make it out, but I won't." I finish for him.

"What?!" Maya exclaims and jumps up from the couch. "How do you know that?" She looks from Seth, then back to me, her eyes lingering on mine, begging me to explain.

"Aiden's part is the only variable. He has to be able to put out just the right amount of power to destroy this machine, but not to the point where he fractures his Soul Power beyond repair." Seth explains.

I think back to Uncle Matt's power being stolen by this machine, and who knows how many more people had fallen victim to this and may have even lost their lives to this damn thing.

I take a breath, then stand and walk over to her by the TV near the front of the room. I take her hands in one of mine while I hook my index finger under her chin to tilt her head to look me in the eye while giving her my sly smile that she knows so well.

"Maya, Baby, it's okay. I have seen this over and over, and it's the same thing every time." She tries to look away again, but I hold her chin firmly in my hand. "I'm okay with the outcome," I say while looking into her eyes. "I have no issues if it comes down to me dying in order to destroy this thing."

"I don't want it to come to that." Maya says, her voice breaking with unshed tears.

"Neither do I, but if it will stop more people like my uncle from having their powers stolen, I will gladly do it without a second thought." I'm still not sure where this confidence is coming from, but I'm glad that I can be strong for her at this moment.

I lead Maya back over to the loveseat and I glance over at Ivan and he gives me a firm nod knowing that we have our own information on The Siphon that we are still sitting on.

"Aiden and I have news about The Siphon that I bet none of you knew about." Ivan says.

"Ivan and I found out the other day from our Abilities 101 class that The Siphon has another function that Victor has tried to experiment with." I say with a harshness to my tone.

"That's not possible. It has no other functions other than taking powers." Seth says with a note of fear.

"Well, you're in for the shock of your life then, buddy." Ivan says in a steely tone.

"Victor has tried to transplant powers into other people." I say with disgust.

"How the hell do you know this?" Uncle Matt asks with fear and anger in his voice.

Seth suddenly rises to his feet and begins to pace the living room floor behind the couch, and I can tell he has a million things running through his mind right now, so I continue with the information I know.

"Our teacher, Mrs. Jaffee, and her husband were the most recent victims. Her water powers were taken and Victor tried to transplant them into Karl, but it failed horribly. It may have been because he was just a normal human." I say.

I spare the gory details, but I can tell everyone understands what happened to Karl.

"Are you sure this is true, Aiden?" Seth asks while staring a hole in me, as if begging me to tell him this is all a ruse.

"I wish I could tell you otherwise, but Ivan heard the whole thing, too." I say and tilt my head to my friend.

Ivan nods and gives a scornful look. "I am horrified at what I heard. I want to help Aiden and Maya in any way I can to destroy this fucking thing once and for all. I'm sorry, Seth, but your brother needs to be stopped, and fast." Ivan says.

"Yeah, I agree, Ivan." Seth pauses as he runs his hands through his hair. "Give yourself one more day of healing, Aiden, and then we start training."

38

Aiden

Later that night, Seth was confident enough in my recovery so far that I was able to go home and rest for one more day and get back into my normal routine of things. While Aunt Viv is happy that I am back home, I noticed Uncle Matt has been abnormally quiet.

I try to give him some space; after all, I'm sure it's a lot for him to take in right now. My powers and what they mean, and the new information about The Siphon. So I walk into the kitchen to help Aunt Viv with dinner, but she makes me turn around and head back into the living room to sit on the couch and rest.

"I'll make dinner myself, Aiden. You take it easy, like Seth told you." She tells me before walking back into the kitchen.

After dinner is served an hour later, we eat our chicken and steamed vegetables in pain-filled silence. Even Aunt Viv knows it's useless to talk to her husband right now. So, we eat with only the noise of our silverware clicking on the plates filling the air around us.

Once Uncle Matt finishes his last bite of chicken, he quietly excuses himself from the table, and I pick up on the anger that's been slowly forming in his features since dinner started. When he slams the garage door behind him, I look over at Aunt Viv, the sadness and heartache evident on her face.

"I'll go talk to him." I say with a small smile.

I walk over to the garage door, and when I open it, Uncle Matt is pulling tools out of his toolbox so he can work on the 1969 Mustang parked in the corner of the garage. He's been working on this thing for longer than I can remember. The cherry-red paint is peeling while dust covers the metal from years of neglect. I lean on the hood of my Colorado while crossing my arms over my chest, my wielding marks on display from the elbow down. Uncle Matt is looking at me from the corner of his eye, but he doesn't say anything, so I decide to break the never-ending silence.

"I know you're upset." I begin, but he finally speaks for the first time tonight, cutting me off before I can say anything else.

"Upset? No, I am furious. He failed you. You almost died, Aiden." Uncle Matt says harshly.

"No, he didn't." I say calmly.

"How can you say that!?" Uncle Matt yells while tossing the ratchet he was holding in his right hand onto the engine bay, the ten-millimeter socket popping off the end, only to get lost inside the mess that is the engine right now.

"He told me using my full power before I was ready was dangerous!" I roar back while pushing off my truck to close the distance between us.

"Yet, you still pushed yourself too far?! Why did you act with no regard for your own safety? For your own life, if Seth told you it was dangerous!?

"At the time, I didn't give a shit about anything else! I was only worried about Maya at that second and getting her out of those fucking chains and away from Mason's fire." I roar, my chest heaving, and Uncle Matt looks at me with shock on his face. "So when you think Seth failed me, no, I was the one that almost failed *him*. Almost failed you all." I say, with anguish in my voice.

I take a step back from Uncle Matt to lean against my truck again while tipping my head back against the curve of my shoulder and releasing a frustrated sigh.

"I messed up, but I will not allow that to happen again until I finish what I need to do." I add with determination in my voice.

Uncle Matt's face fades from anger to sadness and finally to understanding. He walks over to me while wiping the motor oil from his hands on a well-used rag.

"When did you grow up so much on me?" He asks while clamping a hand on my shoulder. I smile at him as he rustles my hair and playfully pushes me away. "Go back in the house and rest, son."

I turn, and when my hand wraps around the doorknob, Uncle Matt's voice fills the garage once more. "Aiden, I believe in you, and I know you will be able to fulfill your destiny when the time comes." Uncle Matt says, his voice tight with emotion. "And I'll pray that you come back to us in one piece."

"Thank you, Uncle Matt. I know it's gonna be a rough road, but I will see this through to the end. I promise you no one else will get hurt if I can help it." I say while opening the door and walking back into the house to rest like I've been told to.

The next morning after breakfast, I decide to drive to the forest to be alone for a while, and I want to train with my powers on my own for a bit.

I push my sleeves up to my elbows, and after I make sure that nothing is around me that I can hurt, I bring both of my powers to my hands. They flow flawlessly from my Soul Power, filled with strength and eagerness to protect whatever we can.

An hour later, the smell of charred trees and grass begins to fill my nose from both powers scorching and burning the plant life around me as I run through the many routines that Seth has been beating into my brain and replicate them with my invisible opponent until sweat begins dripping down my back and only my heavy breath filling the otherwise silent air around me. That is until I hear a twig snap behind me.

I spin around, ready to send my fire to the uninvited guest, but when I see a pair of blue eyes and shoulder-length brown hair, I stop in my tracks.

"Maya. What are you doing here?" I ask with shock filling my voice while I cut the flow to both of my abilities.

"I went by your house, and your aunt told me you came here for a while, so I figured I'd come by and see what you are doing."

"Just training, like Seth said to." I say, while taking in the destruction of my training session. "Maybe I went a little too hard." I grimace while rubbing the back of my neck.

Maya smiles as she passes me, and she walks into the middle of my makeshift training ground. She looks at the ruined plant life around her a moment before lifting her right arm, her water power flowing to life from her hand, almost flooding the area with crystal blue water that reflects the sunlight overhead.

I stare in awe as the water brings the trees, grass, and flowers back to life and moistens the dirt again, where it's something that can give life rather than the dead and hard version I left behind.

"You are absolutely incredible, you know that?" I chuckle as I walk over to her.

"I've been told that from time to time." Maya jests.

I shake my head while trying to hide my smile, but I know I fail. So I grab her hand and lead her over to a shaded area near the tree line where we can sit in the lush velvety soft grass.

I lean back against the rough bark of a tree while Maya lies down on her stomach in front of me in the grass. I watch in silence for a few minutes as she quietly makes mini tornadoes around the blades of grass with her left hand while her right hand waters a nearby red wildflower. Maya must feel my eyes on her because she lifts her head and shoots me an embarrassed smile.

"What are you staring at? You've seen me use my powers like this before."

I lift my left leg, bending it at the knee while draping the same arm over my kneecap, and try to wave off her question as the stupid thought forms in my mind.

"Come on. Tell me." Maya asks while flicking a droplet of water in my face teasingly.

I laugh at her while wiping the water from my face with my right hand, allowing myself that moment of my mental wall before I allow it to tip over.

"I was just thinking that your powers are so useful, life-giving, and helpful, while mine does nothing but destroy and kill."

"Aiden, that's not true. Once you are able to control them more, your powers can be just as helpful as mine are." She tells me with a kind smile. "Plus, have you seen the destruction that water and wind can cause?" She challenges while raising an eyebrow. "It's all in how you use them."

"Okay. You got me there." I say. "And to be honest, I'm kind of envious of how easily you use them." I confess. "I always was."

"Aiden, don't be so hard on yourself. I have had my abilities since I was seventeen. So, I had a long time to get used to them. You didn't have that luxury." Maya says. "I personally think you are making amazing strides with what you've been dealt." She says in a serious tone while sitting up and scooting closer to me.

I find myself staring into her beautiful blue eyes and without thinking; I tuck a piece of her dark brown hair behind her ear and allow my hand to linger there for a moment. To take in the feel of her under my fingers again. When her eyes flick towards my mouth, my hand moves instinctually to the back of her neck, keeping her in place. Her eyes flick back to my mismatched ones and I can see the desire slowly flare to life in those bright blues.

I slowly close the distance between us, my eyes never leaving hers. Just when I'm about a breath away from her lips, her apple scented lip gloss filling my nose, I pause. Confusion fills her eyes and I have to fight back a smirk at her reaction. I remember just how much I loved riling her up and three years apart hasn't changed that.

My eyes scan her face, lingering on her lips, before I bring my gaze back up to hers. "I'm trying to figure something out."

"What?" Maya says breathlessly, really hating the tension and distance remaining between us and my hand still wrapped around the back of her neck to keep her where I want her. So I pull her back and the aggravated groan that fills the air makes my chest swell with laughter, but I hold it in.

I look over her body again, and this time, I can't keep the sly smile from my face. "I'm trying to figure out how I should kiss you for the first time in three years."

"We already kissed back at Seth's place the other day when you were recovering." Maya says.

"But see, *you* kissed me. So, I'm trying to figure out *my* first kiss with you." I tease.

"Aiden." Maya whispers, but I can tell she doesn't know if it's a plea or a warning.

"Should I kiss you here?" I place a kiss over her right eyebrow. "Or here?" I kiss her left cheek. "Here?" I ask, my voice dropping lower when my lips skim the tip of her nose. "Or should I kiss you right...here?" I ask, my lips brushing across hers lightly as I speak.

"Aiden Rivers if you don't kiss me right now, I swear I am going to—" Maya begins, but I cut her off, my mouth colliding with hers, and as the taste of her lip gloss explodes across my tongue, it sends a shock down my spine as if she had electrical currents herself.

Even though I want to deepen the kiss, allow my tongue and teeth to explore her mouth fully to let her know just how much I truly missed her over these three long years, I make myself pull back, but I can tell the kiss sent her for as much of a loop as it did me.

She looks into my eyes and smiles again as she lets her gaze slide over my face and travel down my neck. I know she's seeing the flame tattoo that pokes out of the collar of my shirt and stops just in the middle of my neck. She goes to touch it but pauses as if that action is too bold of a request right now. I smile at her and bend my neck to the side so she can see it better while I close my eyes.

She lightly caresses my neck, her fingers tracing the flames that dance along my skin, making goosebumps come alive as she touches the marking and my body shudders under her touch.

"You are going to be so powerful once you get these under control." Maya whispers.

She looks on the other side, but my lightning doesn't travel as high, just to the base of my neck, but enough to be seen under my shirt all the same. She traces that marking too, and her touch is enough to send all the blood to pool between my legs, almost shoving me over the edge with pleasure. I force myself to pull away from her and I rub the back of my neck to ease the tension building against the zipper of my jeans.

"I better get you home." I say, my voice sounding an octave deeper than usual.

She nods and backs away with a blush on her cheeks. I take a breath and walk her back to our vehicles, helping her into the driver's seat of her Passat before we drive away to our respective homes.

Later that night, Ivan and Gray come over to hang out for a bit before dinner. It's a nice night out, so I take them out back on the patio to have a little privacy from my aunt and uncle. After I slide the door closed, Gray leads Ivan over to the porch swing and, as they both sit on the bench seat, I watch Ivan casually throw his arm behind Gray's shoulder. When he soundly kisses Gray on the lips, I think about Maya and how her lips felt against mine this afternoon. When that thought hits me, I know I have a stupid grin forming on my face that I can't hide before Gray sees it.

"What's that grin for, Aiden?" He presses with his own mischievous grin.

"It's nothing." I say, trying to play it cool.

"You were with Maya, weren't you?" Ivan asks.

"No." I lie.

Ivan hears my lie for what it is and he stands from the swing, shaking his head while he makes an iron rod the size of his forearm with his left hand and bounces it off his right.

"Are you gonna make me beat it out of you?" He asks with a playful smile while Gray shakes his head at his partner then crosses his arms over his chest, knowing that a fight is about to begin.

"I dare you to try." I say, while running off in the middle of the yard.

Ivan runs after me and just as he catches up, poised to strike, I make my firewall and instantly reach around to throw an electrical charge toward him. Ivan barely has time to change the iron pole into copper to counteract my electricity before it hits him in the chest.

I smile wickedly at Ivan and motion for him to come at me with my right hand while making my fire dance on my middle finger. He laughs and runs full force toward me.

"Just remember you asked for this, Aiden." Ivan says, but it's filled with a dark humor.

When he comes at me again with his metal rod, he tries to sweep my legs out from under me. I catch the rod with my left hand sending a current of electricity through it, shocking him enough to make him drop it while I give my fire a little flare to force him away from me, but I hold the heat back so that I don't burn him. I then hear something move behind me and I don't have to turn around to know that Ivan is making a metal pillar, poised to strike.

I give him an evil smirk while turning around, sending a river of fire hot enough toward the huge seven-foot-tall metal pillar, making it melt into the ground like it was ice.

Ivan tries to take the moment of my distraction to hit me again with his metal pole, but I can feel the electrical traces in his body move for the attack and I get the idea of making a flaming sword and point it toward him. As the sword presses into his chest, he stumbles back a few steps and when his eyes meet mine; I see the joy of the mock fight shining brightly in them.

"You're getting stronger, dude." Ivan says.

"Nah, I just got lucky. I know you could kick my ass." I reply while cutting the flow of both powers and walking back onto the deck.

"Well, you're right, but still man, if we didn't hold back I think you could give me a run for my money." Ivan says as he's still shaking the hand that was shocked a bit.

After we sit down in the patio chairs, I let out a breath and take in the nighttime sky, watching the stars flickering above me while Gray inspects Ivan for any injuries and when he's satisfied his partner is indeed alright, they settle back onto the swing, Ivan pulling Gray's body tightly against his side.

"I kissed her." I say suddenly.

The guys are looking at me dumbfounded and then Ivan has a huge smile spread over his chiseled jawline

"Ha. I knew it. You didn't have that shitty grin on your face for nothing." Ivan chuckles.

We hear the sliding door open, and Uncle Matt is standing in the doorway. "Dinners on the table."

Gray and Ivan are the first ones to jump up and run inside, and I just smile at their antics.

"Aiden." Uncle Matt says.

I stop to look at him. "Yeah?"

"I noticed your mock fight out here. You're getting good at using your abilities." Uncle Matt says. "Don't second guess your strength."

I smile at him, and I hang on to his words. "Thank you, Uncle Matt; that means a lot to me."

I pass him and walk into the kitchen to get some dinner before Gray and Ivan hog it all.

39

Mason

"Have a good time in class, Baby." I tell Dani when I drop her off at her first class of the morning.

"Thank you, Mason. You too, and stay out of trouble." Dani says while giving me a quick kiss on the lips before trying to pull away from me.

I grab her by the elbow and pin her to the wall a few feet from the door, my body towering over hers. "You like the trouble, Baby." I croon while crushing my mouth to hers, coaxing her lips to open with my tongue.

Dani melts into my chest while greedily opening up for me, and I swallow her moan to keep it between ourselves. After a moment, I make myself pull away from her when I hear more students filing into the classroom.

"I'll see you after class." I peel her off the wall, and when she walks away from me, I tap her ass as she passes by me. She squeals, and I can't help the smile that explodes on my face.

"Mason Jasper! You're gonna pay for that later." Dani warns.

"We'll see about that, Baby." I tell her with a playful wink as I walk down the hall and away from her.

My smile and playful mood vanishes like a cloud of smoke when I see Rhett waiting for me by the one class we share. I internally groan as I make my way towards him.

"You know, it wouldn't kill you to smile once in a while." Rhett grins wildly.

"Why? You don't give me anything to smile about." I snap.

"Well, you're right. And this morning is no different, I guess." Rhett scoffs. "Look at who just walked in the door."

He points over his shoulder, and I see Aiden walk in with his two friends. They are all smiles and laughter and acting like Aiden wasn't close to death three days ago.

"I can't believe he survived." Rhett says darkly, the wild grin on his face morphing into something sinister.

"What do you mean by that?" I ask, while keeping my eyes on the group in front of us.

"You didn't see it? His Soul Power cracked when he was fighting us." Rhett says. "It was just like this kid I knew a year or so ago. He was new to the Parasite group I was involved with at the time. He picked a fight with some other dude, and the kid used too much of his power. His Soul Power broke, and it killed him." Rhett turns to me with that crazed look back in his eyes. "I guess we didn't push Aiden enough that day in the courtyard with that bitch of his."

I glance back over at Aiden, and I do remember that once I stopped being burned by his fire, I watched him collapse to the ground. I didn't know exactly what happened, and I probably should have told Victor about it all. But of course, guess who ran to Victor and told him *everything* once he was able to form a coherent sentence after having his brains scrambled by Aiden's electricity?

Yup. Rhett the pet told Victor about the fight, and I got a beating for not being the one to share the information since Victor put me as the lead on this mission to stop Aiden.

I shake the memory of the beating out of my head, and I tear my gaze away from Aiden and his friend while walking away from Rhett. "Well, that just means we have to try to get him out of the picture again."

"Good idea!" Rhett says, as he skips like a young schoolboy by my side. "We need to let Victor know so we can plan our next attack."

I roll my eyes, but I don't acknowledge his statement and just keep walking down the hall.

Aiden

During lunch, Ivan finds our normal table in the corner of the cafeteria. As soon as all three of us sit down, Seth enters my mind, and I wait with bated breath to hear what he has to say.

"Good afternoon, Aiden. Why don't you and Ivan come over for a training session?"

I smile at his request, and I know Ivan will love the chance to show off in front of Seth. I lean over, interrupting a conversation between him and Gray, and flick my middle finger against his forearm to get his attention.

"Ow man, that hurt." Ivan says, his brows scrunched while rubbing at the assaulted skin.

I ignore him, and with the smile still on my face, I lean into his side and whisper, "You wanna go to *his* place and train for a bit?"

Ivan's eyes go wide and a big grin spreads on his lips. "Absolutely." He says with a smile still on his face while Gray rolls his eyes at us.

"I do not want to see you two beat the shit out of each other again." Gray cringes. "Just don't send my man back home in too many pieces, Aiden."

"I'll try not to." I say while trying to hold a grin back from Ivan's eager gleam in his eyes of the anticipated fight.

Ivan and I arrive at Seth's place and we go right down to the training rooms. Seth is in one of the bigger ones in the back, and I lead Ivan into that room.

"Hi, you two. Today is when training gets even harder. Aiden, I want you to work on using both your abilities without much thought. Right now you are still thinking about switching from one to another and I don't want you to." Seth explains. "Ivan, are you able to make your iron cover your body so you can withstand both of his powers and still allow you to move?"

"What do you think I am, an amateur?" Ivan chuckles as he coats his body almost with a second skin that I can tell is several layers thick to protect his body, but it's like a living thing and he can move normally.

"That is impressive, Ivan." Seth croons as he stands to one corner and claps his hands together once. "Okay, you two. Let me see what you got."

I look at Ivan and without warning he's charging at me; his right arm is pulled back and his fist is poised to send a right hook toward my face. I jump back and I push my fire to my foot to help me widen the distance between us quicker. At least I don't have to worry about him teleporting like Seth can.

Once I am about ten feet from Ivan, I make my firewall in front of him and then jump into the air, again using my fire to propel me like a rocket over my wall and I land behind him letting my electricity flow into my left hand. I try to punch him in the gut, but I only feel his iron skin connect with my knuckles and they feel like they are on the verge of breaking. I try to back away, but he brings his fists down in a hammer style onto my back, forcing me to my knees.

"Don't hold back Aiden," Ivan says, his voice a little darker than normal. "I know I'm not going to."

He makes an iron rod and swings it like a baseball bat, hitting me across my chest and stomach and sends me flying across the room. I collide with such force against the wall that I feel the bones in my back crack as I painfully slide down the wall, where I land on my ass with a solid thud.

I barely get my shit together before he's coming at me again, leaping at me like a madman. I make my fire wall again just in time to keep him away from me, to give myself just a few more precious seconds to recover from his attack. Ivan beats against my wall like a caveman with his club, but my fire holds strong against his onslaught. Once he figures out he's not going to break through it, he backs up about a foot and I drop the wall.

"Both powers, Aiden!" Seth snaps.

"Come on, Aiden. I can take it. Or are you scared?" Ivan taunts.

I give him a look and something in me gives and I take a step toward him, but Ivan leaps again and he raises the iron rod, readying to swing, but I block it in my left hand and let my electricity race down the rod where it rusts in Ivan's grip. I let my fire flare to life in my right fist at the same time and I make it hot enough to break through his iron skin and I sucker punch him in the gut.

This time he is the one to be sent flying back across the room and he rolls a few times before he comes to rest against the wall, smoke wafting off his stomach.

"Now that's what I'm talking about!" Ivan says as he gets to his feet and repairs the damaged iron on his stomach.

Then he comes at me again, but as he moves towards me, I get the thought to mix my abilities. I put my hands together at the wrists and let my fire and electricity flow from my hands at the same time. As I snake my fire toward Ivan, I think about Maya's little tornadoes she makes with her wind and I make my own version with flame and electricity, engulfing Ivan in an instant. I notice him try to touch the wall I created around him, but the lightning shocks his hand and he pulls it away with a curse.

While I'm making this flaming funnel, I'm keeping an eye on my Soul Power, and it feels amazing. I somehow know this is just a fraction of what I can do and that sends a new wave of confidence in me. I walk toward my creation and walk through the wall of electrified flame with both powers flowing from my hands.

Ivan notices me too late and I bring both my hands together and I shove them against his chest hard enough to send him flying through the flaming electrical wall with a yelp of pain. With a simple thought, I tear the wall down and walk over to where Ivan's trying to get back to his feet. He gives me a pained smirk, but I can tell he's enjoying every moment.

"Okay, guys. I think it's time to call it a draw." Seth says, but I can tell he is beaming with pride. "I am proud of both of you."

I extend a hand to Ivan and help him to his feet and I feel a twinge of guilt at him holding his side and I wonder if a rib was broken.

"That was a good fight, Aiden. I haven't had a fight like that in a long time." Ivan says, his voice tight from holding his side.

"Ivan, come here." Seth says.

Ivan limps over to Seth and, as he puts his hands on my friend's side, I see a little flash of greenish light and the pain instantly leaves Ivan's face.

"There, that should take care of that." Seth grins.

"Mimics are so fucking cool." Ivan beams.

"I have my moments." Seth says smoothly. "Now go home and rest. We will train more in the coming days."

Ivan and I leave his house, but before Ivan gets in his car, he stops me. "I'm happy that I can help you through this, Aiden. I've told you this before, but you are going to do great things for our people." Ivan says.

"Thanks, man. I'm glad that I can have my brother by my side to help me with all this." I say with a small smile.

"Well, someone has to keep your ass in line." Ivan chuckles, giving me a hard smack on my back and gets in his car before I can recover.

I flip him the bird with my right hand as he drives off, the sound of his tires crunching on the gravel of Seth's driveway filling the air around me.

40

Aiden

ater that night, as I'm lying in bed, my thoughts start to drift to Maya. Her beautiful dark brown hair and her smile makes my heart skip a beat. I chuckle to myself at how absurd that sounds, but it's the truth. She had my heart three years ago, and that hasn't changed now.

I remember that her birthday is coming up in two days, and my blood freezes in my veins knowing that this may be the last one I share with her. I fight against the claws of despair that threaten to take me down and think about what I can give her that will last a lifetime.

Uncle Matt's words come to mind from the other day. He said he could make shapes with his electricity. Just as that thought hits me, he knocks on the trim of my door frame and walks through the threshold.

"How did training go tonight?" Uncle Matt asks.

"It went pretty well. Gave Ivan a run for his money." I say with a slight smirk.

"That's my boy." Uncle Matt says with a chuckle.

Even though I know he's my uncle, he's been the only father figure in my life, and the look of pride beaming in his eyes makes my chest fill with happiness.

"I have a question for you." I say.

"Shoot." Uncle Matt says while pulling out my computer chair to sit at my desk.

"Do you think there's a way I can make something and keep the shape even without my power flowing into it?" I ask, while toying with my blue and black quilted comforter between my thumb and index finger.

"Do I need to ask who this is for?" Uncle Matt asks while cocking his eyebrow.

I smile at him as I run my right hand through my reddish blonde hair.

"The best way I can explain it is to figure out where you are connected to your power and wrap that connection around itself, so it's self-sustaining." Uncle Matt instructs.

I call my fire first and let it dance quietly in my hand as I try to remember what Maya likes. I smile as I recall that her favorite flower is a hibiscus. So, I make my flame take that form, which is twice the size of my hand.

Once I have the flower formed in my hand, I find what Uncle Matt is talking about. That connection between me and the flame. I take that connection and sever it, then connect it within itself. Then, I set the flower on the bed and pulled my hand back, cutting the flow of fire at the same time.

I watch as the flame-made hibiscus quietly flickers on my bed, and the little light it gives off makes shadows dance around it. I do the same with my electricity, and I make sure to pull the little arcs of current tight to keep their shape.

"That is amazing, Aiden." Uncle Matt says with awe in his voice.

"I have the best teachers to show me how to use my abilities." I reply.

"I'll let you get back to that." Uncle Matt says as he gives me an encouraging nod.

After he leaves, I get the idea of another personal touch to add, and once I make the final adjustments to the sculpture, I go to bed with a smile on my face.

On my left, I see Maya with her water power flowing from her right hand, trying to hold back a volley of rocks and dirt that I'm sure are made courtesy of Rhett while Mason is trying to burn me alive with a massive fireball he threw in my direction. I absorb his fire like it was nothing, and I send a powerful bolt of electricity toward him, hitting him square in the chest. In the distance above the pine trees, I see a blood-red moon looming in the sky, and the sight of it sends chills down my spine.

Movement out of the corner of my eye catches my attention, and I'm going for Mason again. I can actually feel the power coming from this version of me, and it's so strong—even stronger than I am now. As I walk toward Mason, I can feel that I am holding back on my electricity. Like I'm pulling it to the surface and letting it build up just under my skin. Then, as I close the distance, I let the charge go, and a violent blast throws Mason back a few feet and into a tree with enough force to crack the lumber.

Then there is a blinding flash, and the next thing I know is I'm starting to hover in the air, looking down at my friends. To the one who holds my heart. I see tears sparkling in her blue eyes. Then I look at Ivan, and I notice the determination in his gray eyes. They are the ones that give me the drive to do what I need to. I hear Mason yell a curse, and then I feel my soul power start to scream in pain at me from the power I am pulling from myself, and then everything fades to black as I begin to hear my alarm blaring at me in the real world.

I roll over and hit the alarm clock with my right hand while I throw my left arm over my eyes, letting the dream vision fade from my mind.

"Charging up my electricity, huh?" I ask myself as I lift my left arm into my line of sight, where the lightning tattoo is staring back at me.

When I walk into the kitchen a few minutes later, I fill my plate with waffles, dollops of whipped cream, and some glazed strawberries before I take my seat at the dining table where my aunt and uncle are already eating.

"I, uh, I won't be home after classes tonight." I say, after taking my first bite of waffle.

"Why?" Uncle Matt asks with a sly smile in his eyes.

I chuckle at his thoughts, but I shake my head. "I want to take Ivan to the forest and run some techniques with him." I say.

"You two, just be careful." Aunt Viv says as she wipes a non-existent crumb at the corner of her mouth with a napkin.

I see the mischievous glint leave Uncle Matt's eyes a heartbeat later and he nods once to me. I give him a small smile, and we finish our breakfast in silence.

When I arrive at the university, I find Ivan and I take him aside into a less crowded hallway. "Hey dude, can you meet me at the forest after class?" I ask in a hushed voice.

"Yeah." He replies, matching my tone. "But what for?"

"You'll find out when we get there." I say with my full voice and let some teasing humor color my words.

Ivan shakes his head and gives me an annoyed smile. "Asshole." He says, and we walk into our respective classes for the day.

After my last class, I walk out to my Colorado, toss my backpack into the bed, and drive to the little private forest to wait for Ivan to arrive. I know he was a few cars behind me when leaving the parking lot, so I put my tailgate down and wait for him.

As I wait, I find myself thinking about how far I have come in this short time. Granted, it's been hell, but I have started to control my abilities with the guidance of Seth, my uncle, and Ivan, and I'm starting to not feel as bad for playing catch-up. Plus, Maya's words come back to me that I'm comparing myself to people who have had *years* to train, and these visions I'm having are starting to give me some ideas, hence why I'm dragging Ivan here today. When Ivan's green Mustang finally pulls up beside me, I hop off the tailgate, slam it shut, and wait for him to get out of the driver's seat.

"Finally here. So what are we going to do here?" Ivan asks with anticipation in his voice.

"I want you to make some iron panels for me. I think I figured out a new trick I can do with my electricity." I begin. "I had another vision this morning." I finish with my voice dipping lower.

"Oh. What did it show you?" Ivan asks quietly.

"I think I can charge up my electricity and let a burst of it go. At least that's what it felt like in my vision." I say.

Ivan just nods his head in understanding and begins making thick iron panels while placing them on some nearby trees. After he makes three of them, he walks back over to me and gives me a thumbs up.

"Light 'em up." Ivan grins.

I give him a smile and walk forward a bit. I think back to the vision and how I could feel the power flowing through my body, and I copy it. I pull my electricity just to the tips of my fingers and to the palm of my hand, but I don't let it break through my skin. I let it keep building where I imagine it being compacted in my hand. I can feel the power gathering into my forearm, making the veins bulge from the apparent pressure. Then, as soon as I feel the pressure, I push it all forward through my hand and toward the iron panel. It shoots out with a violent electrical zap, heading straight to where I was aiming, instantly rusting the iron with a loud explosion of electricity.

"Holy shit, man!" Ivan says in both awe and terror.

"Yeah, I didn't expect it to be that loud, either. But hey, it worked." I say with a questioning smile.

"I'm backing the hell up from the next one." Ivan says in a serious tone.

I turn back to the other iron panels and charge up again, letting another blast tear from my hand and this one punches a hole right through the iron and the tree. I stare at the holes and then over to Ivan, who looks just as, no pun intended, shocked as I am.

"Remind me never to get on your bad side now." He says with forced humor.

I look at him as the shock of what I just did fades from our minds and I am suddenly itching for a fight. So, I decide to be the one to start it instead of Ivan. I can't teleport, but I use my fire to propel me so fast toward him that I know it took him a few seconds to figure out what I did.

I rear my arm back, my fire blazing to life, and as I bring it down to connect with his face, he takes a note from my book and makes an iron wall to block my punch, but I make my fire hotter and melt a hole in the metal. Drips of molten iron land on my skin, but I let little licks of fire eat them up so I don't get burned as badly.

"Oh, that was good, but not good enough." Ivan chuckles.

Suddenly, the ground around me shifts, and I realize too late that he is using the iron in the dirt to make almost a cage around me. I smirk at the thought of my own cage for him from the other day with my electrified fire tornado.

"This is cute, but the bars are too far apart, friend." I say.

Just as I am about to walk through the bars, they instantly close tighter, and when I turn around, Ivan is in the cage with me. He used the shifting of the earth and the building of the cage to attract my attention so he could get in here with me.

"Oh, shit." I say as I'm face to face with him, his full metal skin flowing over his body.

I smile wickedly at him, and we go at one another, throwing and blocking punches and kicks with ease. I can tell our fight is mainly to build muscle memory. So I don't have to really think about what punches to use and fluidly throw either a haymaker or a quick jab to the face, gut, or groin and move on to the next punch.

"Play times over," Ivan says darkly while pinning me to a corner of the cage I didn't realize was there.

He closes the distance with a powerful flex of his legs, and I know I don't have time to dodge his attack. I bring my fire and electricity to my hands and cross my wrists to block his punch. My forearms scream as his fist connects, and the pain travels up my arm and almost takes my breath.

A thought hits me just then. This is the best situation to try to use my new technique in real time. I quickly charge up my electrical blast in an instant, and I brace my left hand with my right and let the blast go.

The iron cage around me falls as Ivan is thrown about forty feet away from me, landing hard on the ground. As soon as he stops rolling, I rush over to him to make sure I didn't hurt him too badly.

"Ivan!" I yell as I approach him.

He lifts his right thumb in the air to let me know he's alive, at least. As I close the distance and stand over him, he's lying on his back while staring up into the sky, his metal skin slowly fading away as he gathers his bearings.

"Damn, dude. That is some crazy shit." Ivan breathes as he rubs his stomach, where I directed most of the blast.

I hold out a hand to him to help him up. Once he's on his feet, he lifts his shirt to check on the damage I caused. A bruise is already forming on his right side, and I cringe at the injury.

"I'm sorry, man." I begin, but he cuts me off.

"For what?" Ivan asks sharply. "This was a great exercise. I'm going to be sore as shit later, but this was great!"

"Gray is going to beat my ass and yours." I chuckle.

"I'll handle Grayson." Ivan says with a wink.

41

Ivan

After I slowly make my way to my Mustang and, as Aiden drives away in his truck, I build an internal splint to support my broken ribs before I drive home. I've had worse than this from my old man when he was training me, so I'll be fine; it's just getting past Grayson and his keen sense of knowing something is wrong is the real pain.

When I get home twenty minutes later, I'm thankful that Gray's car is not in the driveway. He told me he was going to the store at some point today, so I'm glad that he took this time to go.

I ease out of my car and walk into the house, where I toss my keys on the table beside the door. I hiss in pain at the movement and I know I need to get cleaned up before Gray gets back.

I make my way through the house and as I enter the bathroom I look into the mirror and realize how much of a wreck I am. My hair is covered with dirt and rocks, and I have dried blood in random places on my face, neck, and arms. My clothes are destroyed too. My shirt is ripped in places across my chest and back and my jeans are ripped down the legs. After my quick inventory of the damage, I can't keep the smile off my face.

"Geez, Aiden really kicked my ass today." I say as I tug my shirt over my head and toss it on the floor, along with my jeans.

Before placing my phone on the marble countertop of the sink, I decide to text Gray so I know how long I have until he gets home. I lean against the sink, crossing my legs at the ankles. The movement makes a fresh twinge of pain wash over my ribs, but I push it to the back of my mind and finish the text to Gray.

Me:

Hey Baby. Where are you? I'm home and you're not here to greet me. *Winky face emoji*

Grayson:

I'm still at the grocery store Babe. I'll be home in about 30 *Kissy face emoji*

Me:

I was beginning to think you've been kidnapped *Scared face emoji*

Grayson:

No. Plus they'd bring me back after I start talking computer geek to them. lol

Me:

Well then they would be twice as dumb, first for taking you from me, but then second for not knowing any geek speak.

Grayson:

Like you know geek speak?

Me:

Ok you got me there, but I know you. And you can speak geek to me any day of the week Baby and I'd love it. *Blue heart emoji. GIF of a man sexily smirking*

Grayson:

Ok I'm gonna need a larger graphics card… the current one cannot handle the images in my brain right now.

Me:

GIF of cartoon characters' head exploding in a ball of white smoke.

See, love that. In a total puddle right now. *Eggplant emoji. Water droplet emoji. x2*

Not a single clue what you said, but it was hot af Baby

Grayson:

OMG, Ivan Grant! You are terrible. Now let me be so I can shop in peace. I can't hide behind the cart all day.

I can't stop the laugh that bubbles in my chest at his antics, but I regret laughing when my right side flares in pain from the broken ribs. I groan, but it's worth it when I can make my man laugh.

Me:

Ok. Fine. I'll let you shop in peace. Cant say the same for when you get home though. *Imp face emoji.*

And the asshole leaves me on Read.

I shake my head, my light chuckle filling the bathroom as I turn the faucet on in the shower. While I wait, I again reinforce the internal splint around my ribs so they can begin to heal and not hurt as bad, but it does nothing for the soreness from the bruise on my skin that I'm going to have to deal with until I can heal.

Once I'm dressed, I make sure to clean up any dirt I may have brought in, and I throw my ruined clothes into the trash can in the kitchen. But knowing that Gray will be fixing dinner here soon and I don't want him to see these, I take the bag to the trash can out back.

When I come back inside, Gray is just pulling his car into the garage, so I meet him out there to help with the grocery bags.

"Hey, Ivan." Gray greets me with a smile. "Bags are in the trunk. I'll take this bag in and come out to help with the rest."

"I got it. You unload as I bring 'em in." I smile as I give him a quick kiss on the lips.

He leans into my right side and I have to hide the hiss of pain with a growl that he will think is possessiveness. And it works according to the sly grin on his face when he walks away from me.

As I gather the bags from the trunk, still being mindful of my right side, I bring them into the kitchen while Gray gets to work on unloading them and putting the groceries away. I try to help, but he waves me off.

"I got this, Babe. Go sit."

"But I want to help."

"Nope. Not in your condition."

"What do you—" I begin, but his glare cuts me off.

"I can tell you're favoring your right side by the way you had the heavier bags on your left arm, so you must have been training with Aiden. But the cameras in the hallway showed me just how messed up you are, Ivan Grant." Gray leans against the island, palms flat against the surface, and stares me down. "And let me guess, you weren't going to tell me that you got hurt today?"

"Gray, I didn't want you to get all worried over nothing." I say, now regretting the cameras he talked me into installing last week.

He storms around the island and hikes my shirt up, revealing the dark purple and blue bruise on my side. "You call this nothing, Ivan?" Gray shouts as he roughly pulls my shirt back down. His knuckles brush over my skin and I can't stop the hiss of pain bubbling from my lips.

"Gray, what do you want me to say?" I ask while pulling over the bar stool to take some pressure off my injury.

"Promise me you will stop keeping me at arm's length. Promise me that you will stop treating me like a little boy who needs to be kept in the dark." Gray pauses his rant as his gaze takes in my body, his eyes lingering on my hand caressing my side.

He slowly walks over to me while releasing an exasperated sigh. "I am not stupid, Ivan. I know you helping Aiden is dangerous, but I don't want to be kept in the dark anymore. I was going to let you three do this on your own, and I just pray that you came back after this is all said and done. But the more I thought about it, the more I decided I am not going to just wait around and wonder what is happening with you. I can fight, Ivan. I may not be as strong as you, but I can fight and I want to help you all."

I pull Gray in between my legs at the same time he takes my left hand and places it on his chest, right over his heart. I feel the organ beating against my fingertips and I grab him by the nape of his neck with my right hand, pulling his mouth down to mine in a gentle kiss.

Resting my forehead against his, I look into his brown eyes and I say, "I can't lie and say I'm not going to be terrified of you coming along, but I know at the same time I have no right to tell you to stay behind. And I'm sorry for trying to keep this from you. I just didn't want you to worry."

"We'll talk more about this in the next few days. Right now, let's get you settled and healed." Gray says as he pulls back, but not enough to completely remove himself from my embrace. "But no more hiding, do you hear me?" He asks while threading his fingers through my hair and giving it a slight warning tug.

I can't help the smile that blooms on my face, "Crystal clear, Grayson. I also want us to start sparring again. It's been a while since we've thrown down."

Gray's sexy smirk lights up his handsome face and I suddenly remember why we've backed off with our mock fights. "Baby, if you want me to get rough with you, all you have to do is say so."

"Grayson, I'm serious." I try to keep my voice even, but I know he hears a touch of something more.

"So am I, Ivan." Gray half teases with his fingers still fisted in my hair. "It can be the best of both. Teach me to get even stronger and then we can have *fun* after. Whoever loses is the bott—"

"Grayson! Shit man. You're gonna regret that challenge." I warn with a smirk.

"I'm gonna like watching you try." Gray smiles as he finally pulls away from my embrace to get back on unloading the grocery bags. "Now you go lie down in bed while I finish up here and then I'll help ice your side."

"Yeah, Babe. Ice and my arms being around you will help me in all the best ways."

Gray rolls his eyes while shooing me away. I make my way into the bedroom and wait for him to join me about an hour later with dinner, an ice pack in hand, and his warm, solid body next to mine.

42

Aiden

The next morning, while sitting up in bed, I grab my phone and dial Ivan's number to make sure he's alright from last night's training. After the third ring, he answers with a brisk, "Hello?"

"Hey man, I was just calling to make sure you're still alive." I joke half-heartily.

"You don't have to worry about me, Aiden." Ivan says in a harsh tone. "If I was that hurt, I'd go see Seth." He says with a touch of understanding at my worry. "Besides, I had a great in-home nurse." Ivan adds with humor, and I hear Gray laugh on the other side of the phone; then the sound of a bed squeaking under the weight of a body fills the background.

I roll my eyes, even though I know Ivan can't see them. "Alright man. I hear ya. I'll talk to you later." I don't want to know if Gray is getting into or out of bed with Ivan.

I hang up on him while tossing the phone on the bed, heading over to my dresser and pulling out a clean shirt and a pair of pants. After I slip into them and walk back over to my bed, I pick my phone up again to call Maya. She is quicker with her answer, and I hear her beautiful voice on the second ring.

"Hi, Aiden."

"Good Morning, Baby." I say with a chuckle. "Happy Birthday."

"Aw, you remembered." Maya says.

"Of course I did. I could never forget when your birthday is. And October fourteenth will forever be my favorite day." I say. "Because I can see you get stronger and even more beautiful each year."

Maya laughs through the phone, and it vibrates through my entire body. "You're a dork. You know that?"

"Oh well. I say what I feel, Baby. You should know that by now." I tell her while shrugging my shoulder. "Anyway, what are you doing for your birthday?" I ask while lying on the bed to stare at the ceiling.

"My parents are going to take me out to dinner later, but other than that, nothing much." Maya says.

"Why don't I take you somewhere and have lunch? Would you like that?" I ask.

"I would love that, Aiden." Maya says softly.

"Great, come by in about an hour and I will make this an afternoon you will never forget." I say with a smile, even though I know she can't see it through the phone.

After hanging up from Maya, I jump up from my bed, run into the kitchen, and start looking in the cabinets for ingredients. Aunt Viv walks in a moment later and sees me rushing around like a madman.

"Aiden, what are you doing in my kitchen?" She asks while standing near the island with her hands on her hips.

I stop in my tracks and will my heart to slow from the excitement. "Sorry, Aunt Viv. Maya's birthday is today and I want to make her something special."

"Well, geez, you don't have to act like a madman in my kitchen. Let me help you." Aunt Viv offers.

I nod my head in silent thanks to her, and we get to work. I remember that Maya's favorite food is baked macaroni and cheese, so I calmly begin to work on that dish while Aunt Viv air fries some chicken for us. One thing I cheated on a little bit was I got cupcakes from the store last night before I went to the forest with Ivan. I made sure to pick the icing in her favorite colors. The purple and white coloring twisted together in a generous three-level dollop of icing on top of chocolate cakes.

An hour later, the food is ready to go and once the insulated tote is packed; I hear a knock on the front door. I cross the living room and when I open the door I find Maya on the porch in a simple pair of blue jean capris and a purple blouse. Her dark brown hair is in a half-up-half-down ponytail that frames her face beautifully and the sight of her makes my heart stop in my chest.

"Hi there, beautiful." I say while looking her over and not even trying to be coy about it. I openly rove my eyes down her body, and I know I have a huge grin on my face, but I don't care.

"Hi, Aiden." She says with a small smile.

I move aside so she can walk into the living room, and I shut the door behind her. "I'm just about ready to go. Let me grab one more thing and then we can leave." I say while gently pressing a kiss to her cheek.

She smiles at me again and notices Aunt Viv in the kitchen, so she goes to talk to her while I sneak down the hall and into my bedroom. I shake my head at almost forgetting to get the ability-made hibiscus flowers I made for her the other night. I grab them and put them into a white gift bag that says 'Happy Birthday' in a rainbow of colors for the lettering.

I briskly walk past the kitchen so Maya doesn't see the bag and enter the garage to place it on the bench seat of my Colorado right behind the passenger seat to keep it from her view. I then go back inside and grab the tote from the island and I extend my hand for Maya.

"You ready, Baby?" I ask.

"All this just for my birthday?" She asks with a smile on her face. "Aiden, you didn't need to do all this."

"I absolutely did need to do this. You only turn twenty-one once." I say with a big grin.

She laughs and hearing it in person warms every cell in my body. I tug her off the bar stool and walk her out to my truck, all the while waving goodbye to Aunt Viv. I help Maya into the passenger seat before putting the tote in the truck bed and hopping onto the driver's side. Giving her another smile while putting the transmission into reverse, I back out onto the street and take her to the forest.

When we arrive, I open Maya's door before I grab the tote and the gift bag. I take her hand, which fits perfectly into mine, and pull her behind me, leading her to that special little clearing I found three years ago.

Back when I first found this place, I never thought I would have the chance to bring her here, and now that I am, I can barely contain my excitement.

Before we break through the line of trees, I pause mid-stride and Maya collides into my back with confusion lighting up her face. I turn, letting a sly grin pull at my lips as I slowly walk around her and cover her eyes with my right hand. The little breath she takes as I suddenly blind her makes the side of my mouth curve up into a smirk and forces blood to rush between my legs, making me so hard that I relish in the pain against my zipper for a moment.

"You are going to love this." I whisper against the curve of her ear.

I feel her shiver at my breath caressing her skin and I can't stop the full smile from forming on my face. I almost forgot how receptive she is to me and my touch. So, just to toy with her more, I press my lips to the soft spot behind her ear and she instantly tilts her head to allow me more access.

Normally, I would have taken that offering of hers and ran with it. But this is three years of pent-up longing between us, so I'm taking my time with Maya. She's going to be begging for me by the time I am finally ready to make her mine in all the ways I can imagine. I pull my mouth away from her neck and, with her aggravated groan filling the air, I walk her into the clearing.

When I walk into the center, I pull her back to my chest and remove my hand off her eyes. As she takes in the sight, her breath catches, and I know she would have stumbled back a step if I hadn't pulled her close.

In this little clearing, there are all different shades of purple wildflowers. Some just cover the ground with little flecks of green leaves poking out of the petals. Others stand tall and sway gently in the breeze, allowing their delicate scent to swirl around us. The last thing she gazes at are the lilac trees all in full bloom. The purple, white, and pink bundles make up the circle of trees around us. She looks over her shoulder at me with awe on her face, but her eyes flick to a thick purple bloom that hangs over my shoulders, and she slowly reaches up to caress the petals.

I watch as complete wonder floods her face when she takes in the forest around us again and it fills my heart with so much love for this woman that I think it may just burst from my chest. Maya turns back to me and I reach up to the bloom above my head that she was touching with my right hand. I grip the stem while I look at her with the silent question on my face.

Do you want it?

She nods once and I pluck the bloom from the tree, then hold it out for her. She places her hands over mine while gently taking in the scent coming from the flower and smiles. I find one of the bobby pins in her hair with my left hand and I tuck the flower by her right ear, pinning it in place.

"You look beautiful." I say, my voice barely above a whisper.

She just looks at me, and I can see the love shining back at me in her eyes, as she stands up on her tiptoes and gives me a kiss on the lips. Bending down to meet her so she can flatten her feet against the forest floor, I spin us where I push her back against a nearby tree.

I make myself keep the kiss somewhat tame, even though every inch of me wants to coax her lips open with my tongue so I can explore her mouth full, but I reluctantly pull back and she looks around us for a moment before her gaze lands on me again.

"How? When did you find this place?" She asks, her voice still holding the wonder of the scene.

"About three years ago." I say, swapping places with her so I'm now leaning against the tree. I pull her body flush against my front so the back of her head is on my chest and I rest my stubbly chin in her hair and say, "I didn't want to give up on the fact that we were done for. But one day I was really missing you, so I drove here and walked around aimlessly for hours and I finally stumbled on this. I knew with all the purples you would adore this place."

She pulls back from my chest to look me in the eye and I know she still sees the hurt that her sudden break-up caused and still hurts to think about it even now.

"I would sneak out here for every birthday that I missed and imagine you were with me. Imagined this." I say, pointing to the tote of food, then flicking my hand between us. "That we would have this amazing time and I could make your day special.

"Oh, Aiden." Maya whispers as she caresses my face, and rubs her thumb against the stubble on my cheek.

I take a breath and look over at a line of trees on the right side of the clearing. "Let's set this up before it gets cold." I say, while pulling her along with me.

I find a level spot that is close to the tree line and somewhat secluded before I pull out the blue and white checkered blanket that came with the tote so we can sit on it and place the food down. I pull out the chicken first and I watch as Maya gives a small grin and sniffs at the spices.

"I made your favorite side dish, too." I say with a sly smile.

"You actually cooked something?" Maya asks incredulously.

"I can cook, woman!" I say with feigned hurt at her thought of my nonexistent cooking skills.

I pull out the baking dish, remove the plastic lid and her eyes light up at the mac and cheese still bubbling a tad at one of the corners of the bowl.

"You remembered my favorite food, too." She says in shock.

I nod my head as I place the dish down on the blanket. I then pull out some plates and silverware and fill the plate for her.

"Just tell me when I have enough on your plate." I say as I scoop up a dollop of mac and cheese and set it on the plastic surface.

She tells me when, and I give her some chicken to complete the meal. Once I set her plate in front of her and filled my own, I almost forgot the tea that Aunt Viv brewed for us. I grab two plastic cups, filling them up before handing one over to Maya.

"Your Aunt's famous tea?" Maya asks as she takes a sip, closing her eyes to savor the taste.

"The one and only." I say as I take a drink and let the tea with a touch of lemon and sugar melt on my tongue.

We finally settle down to eat, and we just take in the calm, quiet around us. The slight rustle of the wind and the occasional chirp of some birds that are hiding in the tree line across from us. Once we finish eating and I put away the leftover food, I catch Maya eyeing the gift bag behind me. I give her a smile and lean over to pick it up off the ground and place it in her lap.

I lean back on my elbows, crossing one ankle over the other, and watch as she rips the purple, white, and blue tissue paper out of the bag. As soon as she sees what's at the bottom, she looks at me with tears in her eyes. She sets the bag aside and practically throws herself onto my chest. I take my left hand and hold her while keeping us both up with my right elbow.

"You don't like it?" I ask, but knowing full well it's the opposite.

"I absolutely love it, Aiden." Maya says while giving me a kiss and then she pulls away and goes back over to the gift bag.

I brush my left thumb over my bottom lip to try to hide my smile as she once again keeps me from fully enjoying her, and quietly watch as she pulls out the electrified and flame-made hibiscus flowers, but I added some extra touches.

I added leaves and stems and I also added *A.R. and M.H. Forever*, in the empty space between the flowers so that everything is connected as one large piece that expands the width of both her hands. Tears now flow from her eyes and she is slowly taking in every aspect I put into the flowers.

I'm happy to know that at least Maya will have something to remember me by once this prophecy is all said and done. She will have something of me that will last forever, even if I am no longer on this earth. When she looks at me, I am careful to school my face with the dark thoughts that are floating around in my head.

"Thank you." Maya says while wiping away a tear with her thumb. "I don't even know what to say. This is such amazing work, Aiden." She adds softly.

"You're welcome, Baby." I say as I scoot over to her. I lean against a large tree trunk behind me to pull her against my chest while we look at the piece of art I made for her together.

Just as we get comfortable in each other's arms, I start to trail light kisses down her neck. One kiss behind her ear, then the next one a little bit lower and I pause, waiting to see if she will allow me to go further. When she bends her neck to the side, I trail a few more featherlight kisses down to the curve of her collarbone. I lightly trace my left index finger over the markings of her left forearm that show little wisps of wind. The delicate clouds floating just on top of her skin, and I do the same with her right, the little droplets of water dancing around her arm.

Goosebumps come alive across her skin at my touch, and I feel her breath quicken in response. My chest burns with the desire to make every inch of her body react to mine, but that quickly disappears when both of our heads whip around at the sound of a twig snapping.

43

Aiden

The snapping twig is followed by a huge tornado made solely from chunks of rocks and red dirt. The thick line of trees at our backs makes running through the forest impossible, so Maya and I jump to our feet and prepare to fight back. She calls her water to her right hand and instantly makes a gigantic water sprout to combat the dirt funnel head-on.

Her water easily knocks down the dry earth like it was nothing, but as soon as it falls, a reddish-orange ball of flame spirals toward us. Stepping in front of Maya, I build my firewall to block the flame. When it collides with my wall, I can feel this fire is different, like it has extra force behind it, almost pushing into my barrier.

My firewall starts to bow inward from the force of this other flame, and I try adding layers to reinforce the wall, but I notice this foreign flame is almost eating away at my own. Each flicker of the darker orange against my lighter hue breaks each line of flame that makes up my wall.

I again try to replace the broken links, but it's like this flame can sense what I am doing and it flares violently, making a visible crack through my fire. Knowing I only have seconds before it shatters, I quickly push Maya down to the ground.

Just as she lands on the forest floor, my wall completely fails and I barely get the chance to turn my body away from the actual flame. The heat that flows from this fire burns my back and I have to force my scream of pain back down my throat as I collapse to one knee while the smell of burnt clothes and skin slam into my senses.

I glance over my right shoulder as the remnants of my firewall flicker out in a puff of smoke, and I watch as Mason slowly stalks toward us. His eyes are filled with malice and a grim smile dances at the corner of his lips.

"How cute, one last date before I kill you." Mason says viciously.

"Go to hell, Mason!" Maya snaps as she stands to her feet while leaning against one of the trees.

Mason just laughs darkly at her. "I'll have the most fun with you. Your vulgar words make me laugh."

I carefully get to my feet, my back pulling from the scalded skin, and I step in front of Maya. I hear her small intake of breath at the sight I'm sure my back is in, but I force the pain to the back of my mind.

"Why do you keep doing this, Mason?" I ask, trying to figure a way out of here. "What is the point of all this?"

"To remind everyone to never fuck with a Parasite." Mason croons with an evil smile as his fire flares to life in both hands.

He quickly makes another fireball and sends it flying in our direction. I take a step back, but then Maya doesn't move. I realize there is nowhere to run as this fireball comes closing in. I put us in a damn corner all because I wanted seclusion with her.

Maya's small squeak of fear rips a hole in my chest and I know I have to do something to protect her. This time, though, at least I know to protect one small part of me. My Soul Power.

I take a step forward and try to keep my mind focused on the task at hand and not the pain that I'm sure will follow.

With little thought, I extend my right hand, my fire flaring to life in my palm. As I push it to my new limits, the flame begins to lick up my forearm, mimicking the flames that are tattooed on my skin. I will my fire to become twice the size of Mason's flame and begin to mix them, much like I did with the fire from the grill. Once I start to feel my flame take over Mason's, I slowly retract my power.

I almost want to recoil at the touch of his flame against my own. Not so much from the heat, but it's the wrongness of it. It's like I can almost feel the entity that lives in the flame.

At that thought, I know I don't want to absorb it. I don't want it anywhere near my Soul Power, so I swing my arm back like a baseball pitch. I put every ounce of strength I can behind the throw and hurl the flaming ball back at Mason.

My back screams in protest at the movement, but I push through the pain as the fireball collides with Mason, throwing him backward into a nearby tree. His flame shatters into millions of little embers around him, but I don't stop the flow of my own fire. I allow it to continue and surround him, effectively pinning him to the tree.

Mason roars in anger as he tries to fight against my flames. I put my left hand over my right, snaking my electricity down the river of flame in such a lightning-quick movement that I know if I couldn't feel exactly where my current was, I'd never be able to see it with my naked eye. It hits Mason in the stomach; the loud crack at the connection and his yelp of pain fill the forest, echoing off the bark around us.

Movement out of the corner of my eye catches my attention and before I realize what is happening, Maya makes a violent tornado around Rhett. I notice the rocky sword in his hand and I know he was using that opportunity of my focus being on Mason to make an attack against me. Maya's tornado throws him about sixty feet away and he lands hard on his back. His breath wheezes out in a strained huff, but he's back up on his feet a moment later.

Maya creates something similar to a wave from the ocean about a foot off the ground and surfs over to Rhett while making what looks like a club out of ice. He sees her coming, and with an evil grin, he makes his rock sword and waits for her attack.

Just as Maya is about to close the distance, she disappears from my sight. Her skin becoming translucent with her water, and with her 'surfing,' she can almost teleport like Seth and is next to Rhett in an instant, swinging her ice club with bone-breaking force into his stomach and then to the back of the head with a loud crack.

Since I can't see her, I can only assume she got out of his reach when he strikes back at her with his rock sword and hits nothing but air. A few seconds later, she drops her translucent form and appears a few feet away from Rhett, but her stance is ready for another attack. She looks past Rhett, and with fear filling her eyes, she yells at me from across the clearing.

"Aiden, look out!"

I look over my shoulder back toward Mason as he bullrushes me. He wraps his arms around my torso, pinning my arms to my sides. I try to kick his feet out from under him. Try to pull my arms to my front, but nothing works. Before I can even think to call either of my powers to my hands, he ignites his flames on my already scorched back, and this time I can't contain the scream that tears from my throat. As the smell of charred flesh and pain assaults my brain, I desperately try to free my left arm.

If I could just get that free.

I knock Mason in the temple with my forehead, and he lets out a string of curses. As I feel him loosen his grip, I rip my left arm out from my side and charge my electricity like I've been practicing. As the charge builds, I give him a sly smile and a dark chuckle as the look of 'oh shit' fills his face.

"This is *your* reminder to not fuck with The Protector's of Power." I growl breathlessly as I release my charge.

The burst of energy forces us apart, and I push my fire to my foot to propel myself forward. I take two steps, spin on my left foot, and throw a flaming kick to Mason's face with my right. He tries to bring his own flames to his hands to block my kick, but mine are too big, too hot and I connect with his face as he spins around, landing on one knee. He slowly looks up at me while using his right thumb to wipe the blood from his lip and that's when I notice that his hands are burned, but it's not from my fire. No, it was from his own flames.

Mason lets out a furious growl and tries to come at me again. "Why won't you just fucking die?" He yells wildly.

He comes at me again, his flames flaring erratically as blood starts to trickle from his ears. This throws me for a loop and that almost allows him to land a punch to my face, but I charge up my electricity again, blasting him away from me and he lands flat on his back.

He takes a moment before he tries to get back up, but I mix my fire and electricity and make almost like a shackle across his chest to force him down to the ground. I stalk over to him, my back still screaming at me and my body starting to tremble from the exertion of the fight.

"Why do you fight like this if your own power is just going to ruin you?" I ask, my voice stronger than I feel right now.

I catch a movement in front of me and I spot Rhett. His eyes are wild from the fight and he tries to jump me when he thinks I'm not looking, but I am fed up with these two. I charge up an electrical blast, throwing him against a tree again with little effort, all the while never taking my eyes off of Mason.

"Why are you helping, Victor?" I ask again.

"What the fuck do you care?" Mason asks between breaths.

"Call me inexperienced." I shrug, and I try to hide the twinge of pain at the movement. "But I don't see the same craziness in your eyes as your buddies here." I say while pointing to Rhett, who is still reeling from my blast.

"You don't know me at all and don't fucking pretend like you understand." Mason growls as another trickle of blood slips from his ear.

"Aiden, let's go." Maya says, fear evident in her voice.

I take one look at Mason, who is still scowling at me, and I slowly walk toward Maya. She was able to snatch the bags from our little picnic area while I distracted Rhett and pinned Mason.

Forcing my legs to take one step after another, we slowly make our way back to my truck. I pause by the passenger door before I open it. I can still feel the connection to the shackles that are holding Mason down and he hasn't even attempted to move yet.

Now that the adrenaline is starting to wear off, the pain in my back is getting harder to ignore and my body is starting to shake more as the sensation builds and I can't stop the groan that bubbles from my throat as a violent tremor skates down my spine.

I look over at Maya, my eyes taking in her body to look for any injuries. "Are you okay?" I whisper.

"I'm fine, but we need to get you to Seth." Maya says, fear now filling her eyes for my well-being as she runs her hand over my face and I slowly raise my hand to cover hers.

"I need to get you home first." I say through gritted teeth when I try to push myself off the truck door, but the skin on my back pulls and the pain about takes me down to my knees.

Maya gently turns me around as she brings her water to her right hand. I can feel her fingers hovering over my damaged skin a moment before a soothing coolness spreads across my back. She made a living bandage for my back while adding just enough of a chill in the water to soothe the burn for me to drive her home. Just that alone releases some tension in my shoulders.

I smile at her, but I am barely able to help her into the passenger side of the truck. She gives me a small understanding smile and steps up on the running board. When she gets in the seat, she holds onto my hands to keep me from closing her door and I look up at her; her eyes are still brimming with fear.

"Are you sure you're okay to drive?" Maya asks softly while brushing a piece of my reddish blonde hair out of my face.

"Yeah." I simply say, my voice soft.

She releases my hands, and I shut the door. I limp around to the driver's side while keeping my hand on the hood of the truck to keep my balance. Once I get in the driver's seat, I sit there a moment with my hands on the steering wheel, as I feel my skin start to burn again and wait for the fresh wave of pain to pass.

Maya touches my back again and makes her ability-made bandage cold once more for me, and I give her a grateful smile. As I put the truck in drive, I find my connection to the shackles that are still holding Mason and I release them, knowing he won't be able to follow us, at least for a while.

44

Mason

Aiden's shackles finally release me and fade from my chest like embers on the wind, but I stay on my back for a few moments, just looking up at the sky through the canopy of trees.

His last words haunt me for some reason. What the hell does he know? He hasn't lived the life of a Parasite. He has no idea about my motives.

Rhett stumbles over to me a moment later, his wild eyes staring down at me, but he doesn't speak.

You don't have the same wild look in your eyes as your buddies here.

I shake my head as his voice fills my mind and I roll onto my knees, my head spinning from the blood still leaking out of my ears.

"Pushed too far, Mason." The raspy voice of my flame warns.

"No fucking duh." I think dryly.

Once the world stops spinning around me, I stand on shaky knees and look at Rhett. "I'm going home." I snap and limp out of the forest.

I make it to my matte green Challenger and collapse into the driver's seat. As I go to turn the ignition, I finally notice my hands. The burned skin stretching painfully at the movement. I utter a curse as I force my hand to turn the key, throw the transmission into drive, and go home.

At least Dani won't be home when I get there.

I talked her into visiting some friends out of town while I completed this attack for Victor. I wanted her safe and away from him this time. I wanted her away from me because I had a feeling I'd come back royally fucked up.

I finally pull up to our run-down townhouse in a Parasite-ridden city block on the outskirts of town thirty minutes later. As I get out of the car, using my elbow to close the door, I stumble across the dried grass, climb up the three steps onto our porch, muttering another string of curses under my breath as I slowly put the key into the door, unlock the deadbolt and walk into the foyer.

When the door closes behind me, I lean against it to catch my breath. The pounding ache in my head is getting worse, and my hands and arms are still burning from *his* fire and my own turning on me.

As I inspect the burned spot on my forearm that I can tell was from one of Aiden's attacks, I chuckle darkly, "It's hotter than last time." I say out loud to myself, the burns on my forearms almost scorching my flame markings right off my skin.

I finally push off the door and try to head into the bathroom to wash out my injuries so they can start to heal, but the rooms around me start to spin again and I barely make it to our bed before I have no choice but to collapse onto the comforter. The last thought I have before the darkness forces me under is if I don't die from my injuries, Dani is going to kill me for getting blood on her dusky purple comforter.

I don't know how much time has passed before the gentle caress of hands against my cheek pulls me from sleep. Over the smell of coppery blood, I pick up on the sweet cotton candy scent of Dani's perfume. The one that I insist she wear because it makes where we live just a bit lighter and tolerable.

"I wish you wouldn't work with Victor. Or talk me into going out of town when you go on one of his insane missions." Dani says with a touch of anger as my eyes meet hers. "You're better than this, Mason." She adds softly as she wipes the dried blood from my left hand and I try to hide the wince from her scrubbing at a piece of blood that's stuck to my skin.

I chuckle darkly at her words, "No, I'm not." I begin, "I'm no better than my father." I grunt as she finally dislodges the clot from the webbing between my thumb and index finger.

"You *are* better than him, Mason." Dani argues as she starts to work on my right hand. "You haven't let your power drive you mad." she whispers.

She finishes cleaning up my hands and forearms and then she wipes at the blood trickling from my ear. I watch in silence as her face fades from firm, indifferent concentration to anguish at my injuries. Once she's finished cleaning my wounds, I slowly take her hand in mine, bringing it to my lips to give it a gentle kiss.

"Thank you." I whisper.

"Can you get up and get a shower?" Dani asks gently.

When I sit up and turn to sit on the side of the mattress, I'm thankful that the room doesn't spin at the movement. I look at her as I nod my head before pushing off the bed to make my way into the bathroom.

After I finally get all the dirt, sweat, and blood off my body, I limp back into the bedroom in only my black boxers. I notice that the bedsheets have been changed and Dani is in one of my burgundy shirts waiting for me to slip in beside her.

I love the way my large shirt hangs on her small frame and I know that when I have her in my arms, my body encasing hers, protecting her, she looks just as small. One look at this beautiful woman in my bed is enough to send all the blood rushing between my legs, making a visible tent in my boxers.

When I slide onto my side of the bed, Dani snuggles into me and she rests her head on my chest while I get as comfortable as I can with my hands still aching from the burns from Aiden's power as well as my own.

As the pain continues to nip at the back of my mind, moments of the fight flash before my eyes like a silent movie. I can still feel remnants of the anger flowing in my bloodstream, and I think Dani can feel it too because she lifts her head and tenderly kisses one spot on my chest; the only part she gets to see.

I take in Dani's soft form against me as she rests her head against my chest again. I know I can't taint this angel beside me with my darkness. She has too much goodness in her for me to ruin it. At that thought, any desire that I felt coming to life in my blood evaporates like my fire to water.

"You know you don't have to stay with me." I say even though the words leave a bad taste in my mouth. I would lose what sanity I have left if she wasn't in my life, but I can't keep hurting her like this when I go on Victor's insane missions.

"Why would you say that?" Dani asks with a fresh wave of hurt in her voice.

"You deserve better than me, Angel." I say, using the nickname I know she loves. "You deserve better than a Parasite who is one day going to be overcome by his powers." I say while touching my right ear. Relief washes over me when my index finger comes away with no hint of crimson coating the tip.

"I would never leave you. I love you, Mason Jasper." Dani says softly as she gently brushes her lips over my burned knuckles. "I have seen some of the others." She pauses. "The ones that you claim to be part of, but you're different."

"How am I different?!" I snap, but I instantly regret it.

I start to say that I'm sorry, but she sits up, tossing a leg over my stomach where she's straddling me. The weight of her body on top of mine slowly makes the despair flowing in my veins turn molten, but I fight to keep it at bay. I can't let my desire for her, my need for something so pure, cloud my judgment. Dani then places her hands on either side of my head to bring my attention back to her as she stares down into my eyes with a stern look on her face.

"You are different, Mason Jasper, because you have control when you want to. You are different because you don't have that crazy look in your eyes like the others do. Like Rhett does." She snaps and shudders at the mention of Rhett's name on her lips, and again making that same damn statement that Aiden did.

Dani takes a breath and continues, "You are different because when I look in your eyes, I see a man that's lost. I see a man who wants to do good things, but he has always been shown violence. Your father may have been a *Parasite*." She spits, and I realize that is the first time she's said the word. "But that doesn't mean *you* are." She finishes with tears in her beautiful blue eyes.

She glances down at my chest, her eyes focusing again on the one single part of my marking that shows color, right over my heart. It's a brightly colored flame that seems to almost give off a smokey tip tethering itself to the dark flames that stop at my shoulder.

I keep this secret part of me hidden the best way that I can. If I even think that somehow my shirt is going to leave my body, I cover it either with bandages or I have Dani cover it with her makeup. No Parasite has any trace of color in their wielding marks, yet I do. I'm the anomaly that everyone seems to be able to see recently.

I sit up and wrap my arms around her shoulders, pulling her into the curve of my neck and I just hold her. Her words want to awaken something good in me, but with Victor, I know as soon as I show that goodness he will cleave it in two.

"And the final way that you are different is," She says as she pulls back to look me in the eyes. She rubs the bruise that formed after Aiden's flaming kick connected with my cheek and I wince at the touch. Dani kisses it ever so gently, and I'm afraid that my soul will splinter at her angelic touch. "That you love me. None of the others have anyone that they care for. They are too selfish, but you're not, Mason." Dani whispers. "I don't know what hold *he* has on you, but I know what you do for him is not who you are."

This woman can lay me so bare that I almost feel burned in a new way.

"You're right about that. I love you, Dani Glass, and I will protect you in any way I can, even if that means with my life." I say and I finally give in to my need, my craving for her, and give her a sound kiss.

I trace my tongue over the seam of her lips and when she eagerly opens up for me; I devour her. Her breathy moans filling the bedroom, lighting my blood with the urge to claim her with such force that I think I'd explode if I don't get her closer.

I lift my right hand to thread my fingers through her dirty blonde hair, but the strands irritate the burns and I can't stop the hiss of pain that bubbles from my throat and I'm forced to break our heated kiss.

"I'm sorry, Angel." I say as I look from her to my aching hand. "I don't think I can satisfy you the way you like it."

"Who says it has to be *you* doing all the work?" Dani says, her voice dripping with desire.

The right side of my mouth lifts up in a smirk and my eyes rove down her body, and I growl at the sight of her pebbled nipples poking against the fabric of my shirt. She pushes against my chest with enough force to tell me without words that she's in control now. As my back hits the headboard and she straddles me again, this time her ass presses right on what was a soft erection, but the presence of her body grinding against mine makes me instantly hard as steel under her.

"Dani." I growl.

Without thinking, I raise my hands to her hips to control how I want her to move against me, but she grips my wrists in her hands, not caring about the burns at the moment as she pins them above my head and I, for some insane reason, relish in the pain she inflicts.

"No touching, Mason. If your burns are so bad, then you can't use your hands." Dani says.

She releases my hands and leans down to press a kiss to my right wrist, my fingers, and over to my left wrist in an effort to soothe the hurt she caused. She continues to trail featherlight kisses down my left arm and goosebumps flare to life on my skin at her touch. When she gets to my bicep, her teeth graze against the straining muscle underneath the skin and I can't stop my hips from bucking against her hot core.

Her hands fly up to the headboard so she can keep her balance, but the glare in her eyes makes me want to do it again, but before I can, she sits up on her knees, keeping my aching hard on away from where we both want me to be.

"If you want me, Mason, you better be a good boy and stay still. I want to take my time with you."

"We know I'm bad, so why even lie to ourselves about that?" I say, but it's meant to be playful.

She smiles and I take that opportunity to plant my feet underneath my ass and thrust my hips up where she's knocked off her knees and when we land back on the bed, she's right where I want her. Pressed against my erection and this time, she is the one who can't help but grind that sweet heat of hers against me.

"Okay." Dani begins breathlessly. "You want this?" She asks as she rips my shirt over her head, showing me her soft and needy breasts.

"Always, Angel." I grin.

She slides out of her pink panties and tugs my boxers down by the waistband just enough to free my erection, then she slides down on me in one go. My head tilts back into the headboard with a solid thud as the feel of her around me overpowers any sensation of pain, and the needy moan that escapes my lips is a sound that I never thought I would make while having sex. But in my lust-filled mind, I realize that it's not *me* taking control and ravishing her, it's *Dani* using my body for her pleasure.

I make myself look at her, take in the way her hips roll and sway, taking me as deep as I can go. Her head tips back as my shaft hits her sweet spot and the moan that fills the bedroom makes me thicken even more and this time, she screams.

"Mason!"

"That's it, Baby. Ride me. Use me in any way you want, Angel. Make yourself come all over me." I say.

I know my girl has a praise kink and if I can't touch her physically, then I'll use her mind in a way my hands can't right now. I feel her walls tighten around me at my words and I know I'm close to my own climax too; I can feel it winding tightly around my spine.

"That's it, Angel. You're doing so well."

"I can't. I need more." Dani pleads.

"Well, you told me to stay still, Baby." I croon.

"When have you ever listened?!" She moans.

I chuckle, "You're right. I never listen." I say as I grab her hips, ignoring the minor twinge of pain that is buried beneath the deep-seated need to make my girl scream my name.

"Come for me, Dani." I demand as I thrust my hips into her, once, twice, hitting that magic spot as her release washes over her in waves, her inner walls milking me until my own climax hits and I roar her name at the same time she screams mine.

Once we are both spent, she collapses onto the bed, chest heaving and sweat making her skin glisten in post-bliss glory. I roll towards her, kicking my boxers off the rest of the way while being mindful of my hands as I lean over her spent body.

"You did so well, Baby." I praise while leaning down to kiss her lips.

"Are your hands okay?" She asks.

"Yeah. Still sore, but I'm okay."

"Good." Dani says lazily.

I roll over on my back while gently tugging her with me where she's sprawled on my chest. The weight of her body on mine acting like an anchor in more ways than I want to admit right now. She idly traces her fingers over that colored spot of my tattoo, lulling me into a blissful slumber, and she follows me moments later.

45

Mason

The next night, after I convince Dani that my hands are healed enough, I take the trash out to the dumpster in the alley behind our row of townhouses. I open the lid and throw the black bag into the bin, the metallic ring echoing off the bricks of the alley.

As I turn around to walk back toward the house, I hear a commotion coming from deeper in the alley, like a fight going down somewhere. I growl at the sound, wondering which group of Parasites would be this close to my house, but I know I'm in no shape to fight them, so I try to ignore them, but when what sounds like a solid punch connects with flesh followed by a yell, I know I can't leave this alone.

I storm down the alley and when I round the corner I notice three guys surrounding a younger boy, probably about sixteen, who is cowering on the ground while begging for the thugs around him to stop beating on him.

"Not right." My fire croons, and I nod in agreement.

I watch for a moment and I notice a variety of abilities being tossed around. Fire, water, and rock. All three men are still glaring at this boy with evil grins on their faces. I know these scumbags won't have second thoughts of using their powers on this kid and maybe even kill him if he doesn't fight back, but these thugs are close enough to my house, to the area that I claimed, so I used that to my advantage.

"What the fuck are you all doing in my space?" I yell and eight sets of eyes look over at me. Six Parasites and then the boys' blue eyes.

I bring my fire to my right hand even though it burns more than it normally does; I know I can't show weakness to these three or they will jump me like a hyena on a wounded lion.

"Oh, we are just showing our new friend around." The one with fire croons.

"Bullshit!" I spit as I walk toward them. "Get out of my territory right now if you know what's good for you." I growl.

The rock wielding guy takes a step toward me, and I send a small flicker of my fire to him, made to function like a grenade, but only packed with a fraction of the power that I could make it hold and let it explode in his face. A warning shot.

"You really want to push your luck with me?" I ask while I let my flame come alive in both of my hands while turning up the heat and letting a wild smile play on my lips while pushing the pain to the back of my mind.

The thugs finally back up with dark looks on their faces, knowing they're picking a fight they have no chance in hell of winning, and walk away. I take a breath while slipping my hands into the pockets of my shorts to hide my trembling fingers from using my fire too soon, and I start to walk back to the townhouse without another word.

"Thank you." The kid says.

I pause mid-step, surprised the kid was still there in the alley. I figured he would've taken that chance to run away. I look at the kid—or at least a kid to me—he's about four years younger than I am, still cowering on the ground. He's in red shorts with a white and red short-sleeved top. His blonde hair is a stark contrast to the dark alley around him, but it's his blue eyes that want to haunt me.

I can just make out the hint of the red ring beginning to form around his iris and I know he's slowly beginning to get his own powers, and he's fighting them. I walk over to the kid and I take my hands out of my pockets to kneel down in front of him. I rest one of my hands on my bent knee, not bothering to hide the burns on my skin. The kid stares at my hands with pure fear in his eyes, but I don't move them.

"What are you doing here, kid?" I ask, my voice tight, but I can't hide the touch of sadness at him being here in this neighborhood.

"I don't have anyone to help me with my abilities. I was adopted, so my parents don't know how to help me. I know I'm becoming like them." The boy says pointing to where the group of Parasites left the alley.

I run my hand over my face at his words. I think back to my own family, but mine is worse because my father did have powers. He fought his own abilities and my mother was unfortunately a love-struck fool and didn't know any better. Didn't know to get away from the abuse until it was too late and she was killed when my father went mad.

So like this kid, I didn't have any help either, but after seeing my father kill my mother, the same week I was getting my power, I told myself that *I was* still in some control, and now my flames and I have an agreement between us.

Protect those we care about. At that thought Dani's face pops into my mind and I'm glad she was in my life when I developed my powers because even though she was going through her own personal trial with the drugs her mother was slipping her, which Dani ended up addicted to for a while, we helped one another get through those dark times.

I guess that is where the colored part of my tattoo comes from. From that simple understanding between me and my power that we agree on one hundred percent, even though the entity still attacks me just like yesterday, if I use too much of its power.

"I can't help you much with tips about your powers, other than no matter how bad it hurts, don't fight it. Do *not listen* to the voices you hear. As long as you don't let them take over, you won't have anything to worry about." I say.

As I stand up, I start to walk away, but I look back at the kid and watch as understanding flickers across his face.

"Now get out of here. This place is not for a kid like you." I say.

"You don't belong here either." The boy says.

Part of me wants to laugh at him. Apparently, that is the theme for these last few hours, but something deep down stops the laugh from coming up my throat. "What's your name, kid?" I ask.

"Dylan." He says as he stands up and starts to walk away, but I notice the lingering fear creep into his eyes.

I sigh as I run my hand through my hair. "I'll take you as far as the outskirts of town. At least get you out of Parasite territory.

He nods a silent thank you and I walk him away from all this.

"What happened?" Dylan asks as he points to my hands.

I look at my right hand and a hardness settles in my tone, but it's more at my own failures. "This is what happens when you fight your powers. They can turn on you if you push them too far." I whisper.

"This is why you don't listen to the voices. I hear you have to release the ability at the right time to expel the living being of the power."

"Why didn't you do that?" Dylan asks.

"I learned that tip too late. But it's not too late for you." I say.

"How do you know?" Dylan asks with fear lacing his words.

I chuckle, stopping mid-stride. Dylan notices and turns to face me, "Because, like you said about me, you don't belong here. Only, it's true for you. You haven't settled into your power. So, you still have time."

We walk for fifteen more minutes and we reach the edge of town. It's weird to see the brightness of the town when you're on the line of something people perceive as 'evil'.

The clean streets compared to the trash-littered alleyways.

I stop at the end of the sidewalk and watch as Dylan continues to walk away from me. I find myself hoping that he gets the guidance he needs. When I see him shake his arms out like he's trying to cover an uncomfortable sensation with movement, I open my mouth before I even realize the words that are coming out.

"Find Aiden Rivers. He may be able to help you with your powers." I say as I walk away and into the shadows before he can ask any more questions.

46

Aiden

Thirty minutes of tense silence later, I finally pull up to Maya's house. I put the truck into park and begin to open my door, but Maya's hand on my arm stops me.

"I'll be okay to walk myself in, Aiden. Please, go to Seth's and let him help you."

I nod and give her a small, pained smile. "Okay. I'll let you know when I get home."

She leans over to give me a quick kiss on the cheek before she opens her door and hops out of the truck. Once I make sure she's safe inside, and with her water-made bandage on my back being the only semblance of pain relief, I make my way to Seth's.

Once I'm about ten minutes away, I reach out to him and I can somehow tell he's relaxing on the couch. His mind is still, but I pick up on enjoyment of whatever may be on TV.

"Seth, I need you. I'll be there in ten." I say.

"What's going on?" Seth asks. *"I can tell you're trying to keep me from looking too deep."*

I stare out the windshield in shock, but I realize what he's talking about. I have almost a wall up around my mind, only allowing enough room for sound or thoughts to pass between us.

"Huh, didn't know I could do that." I say in response, and I pull away from him completely as I drive down his long driveway.

Seth is waiting for me on the porch when I pull my truck up to his house. I have to take a calming breath before I can make myself open the door and step out. My back again screams at my movement, but I force myself to close my door. I try to walk to the porch where Seth is, but once the realization that Maya is safe at her home and I am in a safer area with Seth, the last bit of adrenaline fades from my veins and I stumble back onto the hood of my truck, bracing my hands on the warm metal surface. Seth mutters a curse under his breath as he rushes off the porch and I realize that my back is to him and he's seeing my injury in full HD now.

"Shit, Aiden. What the hell happened?" Seth asks in a disbelieving tone. "How the hell were you able to drive?"

"It wasn't easy." I chuckle darkly.

Seth helps me up to the porch and walks me inside his house. He takes me back to what I now know to be his medical room, to the left of the dining room. I can't stop the hiss and cries of agony as he slowly helps me take off the remaining scraps of my shirt from my scorched skin.

Then he has me lie face down on the table, and I grit my teeth at the movement so hard I think they'll break off at the gumline. I feel him disperse Maya's water, making the heat come back in full force, and I cry out at the sudden burn, gripping the table with my hands in an effort to keep still.

"Do I have to ask who did this?" Seth asks in a harsh tone as he places his hand on the center of my back, the tender flesh screaming at his touch.

"Our favorite Parasite Duo." I grit out.

Seth is quiet as he heals my back, and I slowly feel my skin start to release the heat, feel it loosen as if water is rehydrating it, and I feel my body instantly relax as the healing touch of Seth pulls away.

"You fought them, pretty much at full power, and didn't overdo it internally." Seth says, almost like he can still feel the power that flowed through my veins, but I'm not sure if his words were directed at me or just him thinking out loud.

Seth takes a step back, and I sit up on the table while rolling my shoulders to test the renewed skin on my back. Other than a few twinges of muscle pain, I am back to normal.

"I knew I couldn't make the same mistake twice." I tell him anyway. "I didn't let my Soul Power get overloaded. Plus, Maya can kick some ass." I add to try to break the hard line of his face.

Seth's green eyes drift to mine and I give him a small smile. This seems to snap him out of whatever dark place he went to.

"You're getting stronger, but with that, the attacks are more violent." Seth warns.

"I know." I say as I look down at my hands and I think about Mason and how his hands were burned from his fire.

"Mason's fire burned him." I say softly, my words bouncing off the walls and seems to hang in the air. "His ear bled too. Is that because he's a Parasite?"

Seth blows out a breath while rubbing the back of his neck and looks at me with something almost like sorrow on his face.

"Yes. Like you, if you push your power too far, it can harm you internally. For Parasites it's a little different. Their power, while it can be stronger at times, it comes at a cost. This is why most of the time they are overcome by their power." Seth explains. "They never expel that sentient being and it lives under their skin, driving them mad."

I think back to what I told Mason, how his eyes are different than Rhett's. Yes, Mason has that reddish ring round his iris, but his eyes hold a clarity that I have never seen in Rhett's.

"Do you think there would be a way to use the Siphon's power to help the Parasites? The ones that aren't too far gone?" I ask, but already knowing the answer.

"No. Once a person fights the power, they are a slave to it until their last day." Seth replies. "Why do you want to know all of a sudden?"

"I don't know. It's something about Mason that doesn't fit. I can't help but see something different in him." I say as I rub my hand over the stubble on my chin.

"I've never been close to him to see if anything is different or not. But don't let that fool you. Keep your guard up." Seth says in a hard tone.

I nod my head. "I will. Thank you for helping me, Seth."

Seth simply nods and hands me a fresh gray shirt and he smiles. "I figured that there would be times we would ruin clothing, so I have some here for you. I even included some for Maya and Ivan." He says with a smile.

"Always looking ahead, huh?" I say with a grin as I put the shirt on. Seth only nods as he cleans the medical room, throwing away my tattered shirt as I leave to go home for the night.

When I get home, I notice the house is quiet, and for the first time today, I finally look at the clock. Ten at night. I hadn't realized the hours slipping by like water in a stream. I quietly fall into bed, but before I let sleep take me, I call Maya to let her know that I'm okay now and that I'm home. She answers on the second ring.

"Aiden?" Maya answers with fear in her voice and it breaks my heart.

"Hey, Baby. I just wanted to call and let you know that I'm home and healed." I say as I run my hand through my still-damp hair.

"Seth was able to heal your back?" Maya asks, but I hear the doubt in her voice without being able to see it for herself.

"Yes. I'm fine now." I say, and I wish I could show her somehow.

I then begin to think of how Seth is able to enter my mind and I wonder if I can do that with Maya, with other people. I think of how I started talking to Seth. How I imagine him on the other end of an invisible string. I think of Maya on that string. Think of her beautiful smile, her dark brown hair, her blue eyes that I can just get lost in, almost like an ocean that pulls me under. I start to feel something at the end of that string and I understand it to be worry. I find myself smiling when I hear her voice in my head, but that quickly fades when understanding hits me.

"His back was burned so badly, I'm shocked he was able to move. I'll believe he's okay once I can see him in front of me."

Maya's words echo in my mind and my heart breaks for her worry. I try to push the feeling of my healed body towards her and at first I don't think it works, but then after a few minutes I hear her take a breath both in my head and over the phone and I smile softly.

"How did you...do that?" Maya asks over the phone.

"Took a chance on how I talk with Seth in my mind. I could hear how worried you are." I say, my voice dropping to a whisper near the end.

"I can feel you in the back of my mind. This is so weird." Maya chuckles.

"It's even weirder when you talk this way." I say to her.

I hear her make a small sound, almost like a squeak over the phone, at my voice in her mind and I can't help but send my laughter down the link I made between us. I can feel her stir in the back of my mind, and it's like she's caressing my soul.

"Is this how you do it? Just think of you and, *I guess, think the words I want to say?"* Maya asks, her voice echoing in my mind.

"That is exactly what you do, Baby." I say, and I push my joy at her voice, filling my head.

"I feel your joy. This is so odd." Maya says in awe.

Forgetting the phones in our hands, we keep talking to each other with just our thoughts.

"Seth never talked to you this way?" I ask.

"Seth did, yes, but I thought that was just him." Maya replies.

"I don't know how I can do this. Maybe it has to do with the half-visions I have. But no matter what, I love it. I love feeling you in my head when I can't be with you in person." I tell her and let the feeling of my love pour over the connection between us.

The love that even though I tried to bury it once, it would never extinguish for her. I almost feel her curl up with that emotion and I start to feel her own presence flow over my body, almost the same as she did with her water when I fractured my Soul Power not that long ago.

This phantom touch of her water is just as real. I feel her ghostly touch flow around to my back and I hear her take a breath in my mind when she finds my healed skin. I then feel relief flow through her like a balloon of worry burst at that revelation.

"I told you, Seth healed me." I say with a chuckle.

"I knew he would have, but I—" Maya says, but I cut her off before she needs to explain.

"I know. You needed to see it for yourself. I understand, Baby." I say softly.

I then start to feel sleep wanting to take her mind and I chuckle again.

"Go to sleep, Maya. It's been a long, dangerous, and tiring day. You should be able to reach out to me now that I made this link for us." I tell her. *"But for now, please Baby, get some rest. I love you."* I say as I let the feeling flow over my words.

"I love you too, Aiden." Maya whispers as she lets sleep take her from my mind.

I finally hang up my phone that lay forgotten on the mattress and I fall asleep with a content smile on my lips.

47

Aiden

The next morning, as I'm eating breakfast, I debate whether I should tell Uncle Matt and Aunt Viv what happened yesterday. I don't have to think about it long when Uncle Matt finally speaks up.

"You came in late last night." He asks with a sly smile, knowing I was with Maya for a birthday picnic.

I notice his smile and shake my head with a hint of embarrassment flushing my cheeks at the place I know his thoughts went to.

"I wish I could say it was great like that." I reply, picking up on his innuendo.

"Aiden Rivers!" Aunt Viv scolds me and then smacks Matt on the arm. "Don't encourage him."

"But when I tell you what did happen, you may wish it differently, Aunt Viv." I say as the joy leaves my face.

I tell them everything. All the good things first, on how Maya loved the secret area I took her to, but then I tell them when Mason and Rhett jumped us. I tell them how badly my back was burned, and how Maya was able to hold her own and how proud I was of her. I tell them that I was able to make it to Seth's so he could heal me, and then finally, about my new mental connection with Maya. For some reason, though, I leave out my thoughts on Mason on the differences I see in him.

"I never knew that anyone other than Seth and your mother making a mental connection." Uncle Matt says. "You are probably able to do the same because you inherited part of Avery's clairvoyance ability." Uncle Matt says.

"Maybe. I do have visions, but they are only bits and pieces." I say.

"Even your mom would have partial visions until she was able to piece everything together." Uncle Matt says.

After a few moments of silence, Aunt Viv speaks up, "You should get going, Aiden. You're going to be late for class." She says while looking at the clock.

I notice it's seven-fifteen and when I stand I place a kiss on Aunt Viv's cheek, then give Uncle Matt a light smack on the shoulder before I grab my backpack from the floor near the garage door, and hop in my truck to head to school.

I meet up with Ivan and Gray just before the start of class, thankfully. Just before we walk into the classroom, Mason and Rhett walk by us. They both are still worse for wear and I find myself trying to hide a smile at that revelation.

While Mason's ears are no longer bleeding, his hands still bear the burn marks which seem to be slowly healing, and from where my flaming kick connected to his face still shows bruising and the healing skin. Mason gives me a dirty look, but keeps walking.

Good choice buddy, I think to myself.

"Okay, why was he giving you the death stare?" Gray asks.

"He jumped me and Maya yesterday. I got in a few good hits, but most of that is from his own power." I say, trying to sound indifferent, but the thought still haunts me. "But Maya gave Rhett a good beating too." I add with a small smile.

"I can't believe he keeps coming after you." Gray says while watching them both limp down the hall.

"Well, with him knowing what Aiden is and that he's the only one that can derail their insane plans, it makes sense for them to keep attacking." Ivan says.

"And I know it will just get worse as I get stronger and as it gets closer to when it's time to destroy that *thing*." I say with a hard tone in my voice.

"We will be ready every time. So let them keep trying." Ivan says with determination burning in his eyes.

The rest of the day goes by without much thought. We don't see Mason or Rhett for the remainder of the afternoon, and that suits me just fine. When I leave the University, I decide to go to Seth's place to train more and I invite Ivan and Maya along with me. I watch as they go into a room to train together and I am glad that the friend whom I have always thought of as my brother is helping Maya get stronger.

I join Seth in the adjacent room and shut the door behind me. I want to train my electrical blast in a confined area. The other times I have used it, it's been out in the open, so it didn't matter if there was any current dispersed from the sides, but I know the more direct I can make my blast, the more powerful it can be.

As soon as I turn from the closed door, Seth immediately gets started with our training. He teleports and I instantly look for his electrical pulse and put up my firewall, making it several layers thick to keep the electrical fist at bay when he reappears before me.

When I see the shock on his face at my quick defense, I give him a small smile and let the wall down, but he teleports before I can attack him. I again track his electrical signal and I push my fire to my foot to help me close the distance he's trying to make between us and I begin to charge up my electrical current at the same time.

He tries to change his path at the last second, hoping that I'd go flying into the wall, but I bring my feet up to touch the surface and push off it, heading in the same direction I now feel his electrical pulse traveling. As he finally appears in front of me, I rear my left arm back, trying to gather all the current I can in my forearm and I bring it down toward him.

As I connect my fist to his stomach, I let the current flow out from my knuckles this time instead of my whole fist like I have been doing, and I send him flying into the wall on the other side of the room so hard that he makes a hefty dent in the plaster.

"Ow. Oh damn, when did you learn that?" Seth grunts out.

"A few days ago." I say with a sly smile, while noting that the blast was more controlled than the ones I used with Ivan and our mock fights and even better than what I used in the fight with Mason and Rhett the other day.

I go to look for Seth in the rubble of the wall, but I notice he's not there. I realize that talking to me was a distraction to make his electricity harder to trace and once I pick up on it again, he's right beside me. I cannot create my firewall in time before he makes a move of his own. He punches me in the gut and I feel whatever he hit me with fill my body, going from the center of my stomach and exploding from the inside, going down to my feet and then up to my head with such speed that I find myself wanting to curl up to keep my insides from being pulled apart.

The blast sends me flying across the room where I make my own dent into the neighboring wall. I cough as drywall dust fills my nose and lungs. The movement sending a wave of pain down my back and sides from what I can only imagine are either broken or cracked bones. I feel a trickle of something from the corner of my mouth, and when I use my right thumb to wipe it off, it comes away with a bit of crimson on the pad. I give a dark laugh at Seth for drawing blood from me.

He teleports in front of me and looks down at me with a cocky grin on his face. "That was my version." He says darkly. "How was it?" Knowing full well how I'm feeling.

"Could have been better. I'm still conscious." I say, while trying to hide my pain.

I try to move and while a new wave of pain explodes over my body; I find that I can get to my feet. I figure I need to learn how to push the pain to the back of my mind like I did while I was protecting Maya the other day. So when Seth extends a hand to help me up, I bring both of my powers just under the surface and as I grab his right hand with my left; I send a shock down his arm and make my fire tornado engulf him.

"Oh, you little tricky bastard." Seth swears.

"I never said I would play fair." I say.

I again push my fire to my foot to propel me through the firewall and I bring a normal electrical charge to my fist, ready to send a haymaker into Seth's face, but he sees me coming. He teleports while bringing both his fists together like a hammer, letting his flames dance from his fingers. He hits me in the side and I scream out in pain at the already injured bones.

With my momentum, it feels as if he hit me like I was a baseball and I go flying across the room. When I finally slam into the ground, I find myself sliding on my other injured side, so no matter what, I can't get a break. As I collide against a wall in some part of the room, I try to keep my connection to the fiery tornado, to keep Seth trapped while I get my bearings, but I can feel I'm starting to lose that connection. My flame sputters a moment later and the cyclone stops spinning to prove that point.

Seth uses a gust of wind to disburse my weakening flame as he stalks over to me and, for the second time since knowing him, fear grips my mind. I glance to the right and I suddenly see Maya on the ground next to me, but just out of reach. She's covered in blood, unmoving. Something else catches my eyes and I see Ivan's body flung over a boulder that I didn't notice was there before, staring at me from unseeing eyes. I continue to look around and I realize I'm in a forest, but I don't remember how I got here. Where is Seth's training room?

I watch helplessly as Seth picks Maya up by the back of the neck. Then The Siphon appears to Seth's right, and he takes a step toward the machine. A pod opens up at his movement towards it, and I know without a doubt he's about to place her in there.

Maya's soft cry of my name is the only thing that she can utter before being placed inside, and that breaks something in me. I feel myself begin to rally my power like I did that day when Mason strung her up in the tree, but I subconsciously know to keep my Soul Power protected, at least until the last second. I feel my body begin to lift off the ground, but it's not from me standing on my own; it's almost like an invisible force is lifting me up.

Then one thing strikes me as odd. I start to feel Seth in the back of my mind, but so far back that if I didn't know what his mind connection felt like, I never would have known he was there. Once I find his connection, the scene in front of me fades instantly. I am back in the training room and Seth is on one knee, panting before me.

"What. The fuck. Was. That?" I ask slowly while trying to get my breathing under control.

"Mimic trick." Seth pants out while tapping his temple.

"That was trippy as hell. Don't ever do that again." I say flatly.

"Noted. But I haven't tried that in a while, so I wanted to know if I still had it." Seth says with a small cocky smile tugging up one side of his lips.

"Oh, so I'm your damn guinea pig. Great." I moan as I try to roll over on my back to give my aching side a break and I let my eyes close to rest a moment.

"I also did that to see if you had the instincts to let everything go." Seth says grimly.

I snap my eyes open and I slide them over to Seth, who is now walking over to me. But after I look into his face for a moment, I notice a mix of sorrow and pride. That is when I know that I am getting closer to finishing this thing, and that calms my racing heart instantly as the heaviness sets in.

"That was a good session. It's been a while since someone gave me something to fight against." Seth says extending his hand to help me up.

I take a breath against the pain that lifting my arm wracks over my body and Seth helps me to my feet.

"How did you learn to charge up your power like that?" Seth asks while holding his stomach where the charge hit him.

I look at him from my hunched-over stance, holding a hand to my right side more than the left, and I wipe off another stream of blood from my lip before answering him. "From my visions. I can kind of tell what the future me is doing in them, and I copy it." I say with a small smile.

"Good. Keep that up." Seth says as he slaps me on the back.

I instantly go to my knees with a cry of pain and I grab at my back with my right arm.

"Really, dude?" I grit out.

Seth chuckles and that's when I know he did it on purpose and I give him the middle finger. He laughs this time, but that makes him hold his own side. I see a flash of yellow light from Seth's hand go into his body and I realize he healed himself.

"Damn Mimic's and their magic tricks." I mumble.

"What was that?" Seth asks, now back to his normal self and knowing I'm still reeling from him smacking me on the back.

"You're an asshole, you know that?" I grunt out as I stand up again.

"Yes, I know." Seth says while walking out of our training room.

"Hey! Aren't you gonna heal me?" I yell.

I limp out of the room to look for Seth, but I notice Maya and Ivan sparring in the other room. I'm happy that my brother is invested in helping both of us get stronger. I lean against the window, still holding my right side, and watch the two of them spar.

Ivan made a thick sword from his metal, and Maya has a similar weapon made of ice. It's amazing how she is able to control the element like she does. Either by adding more heat or removing it completely and letting it freeze. Other than the fight with Rhett, this is the first time I have seen her spar with anyone, and she's pretty good. I know how Ivan fights and I can see now that he's not going easy on her, but she's meeting him swipe for swipe of their makeshift blades.

She spots me in the window and falters a step, and Ivan takes this opportunity to attack. He comes in with a high arcing swing meant to disarm her, but she extends her left hand, using her wind to make a cyclone that sends Ivan flying across the room.

"She's good." Seth says, coming up behind me.

He puts a gentle hand on my shoulder this time and I feel his healing power spread through my body, making the lingering pain instantly fade. I watch in silence as he walks into the room to give them both tips, like he does with me. After Seth is finished talking with them, they all leave the training room with smiles on their faces.

"Thank you for training with me, Ivan." Maya says brightly.

"Anytime. I'm happy to help you and Aiden get strong enough to destroy that thing." Ivan says while folding his hands behind his head.

Maya turns from him and finds me still leaning against the window, letting Seth's healing power continue to flow through me to repair the remaining cracked ribs. She looks at me and her face lights up when her eyes meet mine.

She runs over to me and wraps her arms around my neck and I pull her closer to my body, taking in her sweet rose perfume. Pulling back, Maya notices my shirt is torn and dirty and worry flushes her face. She rests her right hand on the center of my chest and I can feel her searching my body with her water to make sure I'm okay.

I give her a small smile while tightening my arms around her waist. "I'm alright now, Baby. Seth healed my injuries." I tell her softly while kissing her gently on the lips; her strawberry lip gloss coating my own. I then place a kiss on her neck just below her left ear and I love the look of the lip gloss I left behind on her skin, like a tattoo.

"Aiden." Maya says while trying to wipe the imprint off her neck, her cheeks turning a shade brighter and I know it has nothing to do with the training.

I chuckle into her ear, and she stills in my arms. I swear she lets out a soft sigh as my breath caresses her heated skin. I remember that I'm in Seth's basement, and while thankfully we had a few moments of privacy while Seth was giving Ivan more tips and healing him, that little sliver of time is now long gone when Seth comes over to us, and I reluctantly let her back out of my embrace.

"You should be worried about me, Maya." Seth says while rolling his shoulders as if to work out the sore muscles. "Your man kicked my ass today."

Maya whips her head back around to me to see if what he said was true. I give her a small smile and then I hear Ivan give a disbelieving whistle from across the room. I glance over Maya's shoulder and find him looking at the wrecked room through the window.

"What did you do, Aiden?" Ivan asks with shock, filling his voice. "This room is destroyed."

Maya looks from the room and back to me and I see several emotions flash across her soft features. Worry that I may have pushed it too far again. Then she gives me a prideful look and I smile at her again in return. I shift my eyes back to Ivan as he walks over to where I am still leaning against their training room.

"Still testing out my abilities." I say to him, but even to my own ears, it sounds like a question.

"It seems like it was more of testing how much the training room could take before it fell apart." Ivan chuckles.

"He's come a long way. You all have, and I'm proud of each one of you." Seth says as he joins our little group. He then hooks each arm around mine and Ivan's neck and looks between the three of us. "Now you three get out of here and enjoy the evening." Seth says while pointing with his chin toward the destroyed training room. "Like Ivan said, I have a room to repair." He adds while letting us go and walking toward the room again.

"Do you need help?" I ask.

As Seth opens the door, he gives a small wave and says, "Nope. Mimic remember." As if that statement gives all the explanation he will ever need.

"Whatever man. Sooner or later, that excuse is not gonna work." I joke.

"Get the hell out." Seth says while trying to hide his amusement at my jab.

As we walk out of Seth's house and get ready to leave, Maya and I are standing next to her Passat, and Ivan opens the door to his Mustang but pauses before getting in.

"Hey, Man. You wanna go to the forest tomorrow and train a bit? I want to see how thick I need to make my metal to withstand your shocks." Ivan says.

"Sure thing. I'll meet ya at noon." I say as I give him a bro hug.

Ivan drives off and I turn my attention back to Maya. She's leaning against the driver's side door, her skin still flushed from training. I close the distance between us, and without much thought, I put my right knee between her legs, her little shocked breath tickling my ears as I push a piece of her dark brown hair behind her ear.

"I'm proud of you too, Maya." I say softly while looking into her gorgeous blue eyes.

"Why? I'm not that great of a fighter." Maya says, brushing off my compliment and looking away from my gaze.

I hook the index finger of my right hand under her chin, tilting her head to look at me, and when she does, I notice the pulse that flutters in her neck.

"Really? First of all, you kicked Rhett's ass the other day. I should have told you then—" I begin, but she cuts me off.

"Yeah, I understand. You had more important things to worry about." Maya says as she slides her hand under my shirt and glides up my back as a reminder of the burns that Mason caused.

I shudder at her touch and I slide my hand over the soft, yet surprisingly defined muscle of her belly, and the soft breath that escapes her throat almost unravels me. I lean closer where our lips are just a breath away and I brace my arms against the door on either side of her head, her eyes fluttering at my proximity sends the blood rushing between my legs and makes me harden painfully against the zipper of my jeans.

Her half-lidded gaze flicks from my eyes to my lips and I take that as her silent invitation for me to kiss her. I slowly lean in and I bring our lips together and she desperately opens up for me. I almost growl when my tongue finally can taste her fully and let my teeth graze and nip at her lips.

I feel her left leg lift to rub up against mine, and this brings the growl from my chest. Maya pulls her lips away at the sound with a sultry smile on her face.

"Down boy." She says, while placing a finger on my lips.

I try to playfully bite her finger, but she taps me on the nose with her index finger and I can't help the laugh that bubbles up from me. "You drive me crazy, you know that?" I ask while still chuckling.

"Then I'm doing everything right, aren't I?" Maya croons.

"Yes, you are." I say, while backing away from her and running a hand through my hair. "You better go, before it gets too much later."

"What are you afraid of? The wild animals?" Maya jokes.

I laugh as I open the driver's door of her car and she gets in; but before I close the door, I lean close again and whisper in her ear.

"I am the wild animal you should worry about, Maya."

Heat colors her neck and cheeks and I just shut her door and walk away while letting her stew over my words.

48

Aiden

The next afternoon I meet up with Ivan in the forest and this time he is the one waiting on me, but I can tell he doesn't care. While he was waiting, I noticed he's already made several iron plates, each thicker than the last, all lined up against several trees on the other side of the clearing.

Ivan notices where I am looking and he chuckles, "I kinda made estimates from the damage the room took, and made my metal thicker going down the line." He explains as we walk over to the line of trees.

"Nice." I say while rubbing my hands together. "Now, let's see how fast I can destroy them." I grin mischievously.

He gives me a vulgar gesture and I laugh him off. Walking up to the first plate, I inspect the metal and I notice it has a layer of copper in the middle to act almost as a shock absorber. So, I charge up my electricity, and just like I did with Seth yesterday, I release it through my knuckles. While it takes a moment, I am able to blast a hole through this first plate, but it did resist my current for a second, so that's promising. I look closer at the others and see that each one is indeed thicker than the last and with a larger layer of copper in the middle.

"Ivan, I think you're on to something here, dude." I say.

Ivan looks embarrassed and there is only one other time I have seen this look on his face and that's when he met Seth for the first time. I go to the last plate in the lineup and charge up my power and as I release it; I feel it cut through the first seven layers of metal, but when it hits the first layer of copper, it feels like my power is dampened.

Upon closer inspection, I notice in this plate, there are little channels where my electricity can travel and be dispersed throughout the copper and discharged once it reaches the end which is about five layers thick. I charge up again, thinking now that the copper had my electricity running through it I can now rip through the material, but again I only blast down to the copper, and my power is absorbed.

"This is the one you need to perfect, man. Maybe make more layers of copper in between every other layer, and make those channels like you did." I tell him.

I see a true smile on Ivan's face, and we both practice for a while longer. Ivan makes tweaks to his iron walls, and I try my best to break through. When we both start to sweat from the warm air around us and the exertion of using our abilities, we finally stop.

"What do you plan on doing with these types of walls." I ask, while wiping sweat from my brow.

"I wanted to be able to make a wall to withstand your shocks. That way, just in case I need to, I can make a wall to protect us from your power in the final fight." Ivan says in a grim tone.

I stare at him and my stomach tightens from his thought, but I'm glad he's thinking ahead and planning accordingly. I lean against a tree to catch my breath while Ivan starts to clean up by absorbing his metals again.

I feel a pressure on my temple and before I realize what's going on, reality begins to overlap with the vision I'm slipping into. I can still see Ivan in the real world, and he has a concerned look on his face. I try to tell him that I'm having a vision, but for the first time, I realize I can't talk while in the vision. I've never been around anyone other than Seth when I had one, so I never tried to talk. I tap my temple where the pressure is steadily building before reality fades and the vision fully takes hold.

The vision is the same as before. Maya is kicking Rhett's ass, and I'm fighting against Mason and Victor at the same time. My fire flaring toward Mason and my electricity arcing toward Victor. But one thing is new, I have never seen Ivan there before. He makes an iron rod and knocks Victor in the back of the head so I can go for Mason full force and not try to fight both at the same time.

I charge up a shock wave, sending Mason flying across the clearing and into a tree with such force it cracks in two. When I look back over my shoulder, Victor's wind is around my friend's head. Ivan is trying to desperately claw at the wind to tear open a hole. I even see him make what seems like little iron claws to try and cut through, but nothing's working and it finally hits me that Victor is going to suffocate Ivan. I run toward him, but Mason's fireball knocks me off my feet and burns my side.

From my position on the ground, I watch helplessly as Maya tries to get to Ivan. Victor attempts to push her back with a gust from his other hand, and she uses her own wind in an effort to cancel his out, but it's a stalemate. I use this moment to gather my fire in my right foot to act like a jet. I release my power with an angry growl and a moment later, I'm in the middle of the fray. Victor in front of me, with Ivan at my back. I use my shock wave to separate us, and he goes flying backward with shock evident on his face.

After he loses concentration, the wind bubble instantly disappears from around Ivan's head, and my friend crumples to the ground; lips dry and cracked. I stare at him for one, three, six seconds, but he doesn't move. I run over to check on him but I know even before I fall to my knees, my friend is dead.

I feel the anguish and pain of his death hit me like a boulder in the chest and then I lose control as anger floods my soul. A feeling of wrongness fills my head, and part of me knows I cannot lose control this way, but the feeling of loss is too great to ignore.

A pair of real hands grips my shoulders, and I am instantly brought out of the vision. I look to my right and I'm staring into Ivan's concerned, steel-grey eyes.

"What's wrong? You were screaming 'no' over and over again." Ivan asks.

"You can't come and fight with me and Maya." I say simply.

"Why not? I'm not letting you all go alone." Ivan says. "What, do I die?" He asks sharply.

I stare at him for a second and then I look away, unable to think about it again.

"You know how it happens, so stop me from getting into that situation." Ivan says matter-of-factly.

I take a breath and tell him how he's killed by Victor.

"Okay noted. But I am not going to just sit home and wait this out. I have powers and I am going to help you and Maya. There is nothing in the prophecy that says you all can't have help." Ivan says.

I smile at him, knowing he would try to come with us no matter what I would tell him.

"Why don't you really take the day off and hang out with Maya? I think she is just the type of distraction you need." Ivan says with a wink.

"You're right. I do need to spend time with her. I may not have many more chances." I say solemnly.

"Why do you say that?" Ivan asks.

"I just know, okay. But one thing though, if you can." I begin, and Ivan looks at me with the cold determination that I am familiar with.

"Anything. You name it, and I'll make sure it happens."

"Make sure, when it's time to actually destroy that damn thing, that I am in the right state of mind. Don't let me go running into it filled with anger or anguish." I say, while holding his gaze.

"Consider it done. I'll make sure you have a cool head on your shoulders." Ivan says simply and begins to walk out of the forest and I follow on his heels.

After I go home and get a well-deserved shower, I crash on the couch, stretching my body out on the soft cushions, and turn on the TV to a rock music channel. A few minutes pass and Uncle Matt comes in and sits in the armchair beside the couch.

"Rough training day?" He asks.

"Yes, and no. Training was good, we were able to get a lot accomplished. Ivan's metal can pretty much withstand my electricity, but I had a vision again." I say while covering my eyes with the crook of my left elbow, my lightning tattoo peaking out from my short-sleeved t-shirt.

Uncle Matt is quiet and waits for me to elaborate on what I saw.

"I saw Ivan die. In the vision, he tries to help me, but Victor gets a hold of him and I don't save him in time." I say, my voice cracking at the images that flood my mind.

"Did you tell Ivan?" Uncle Matt asks.

"Yeah, and he doesn't care. He says, I know the situation, so keep it from happening. His thinking is so black and white sometimes and I can't stand it." I say.

"But he is right, Aiden. That's what these visions do. They guide you in the best way they can. Trust in them and know there is a chance you can change the outcome of all this." Uncle Matt says.

I take my arm away from my eyes and look over to the armchair he's still sitting in, and understanding at my apprehension, but also determination at our success fills his features.

"Thanks, Uncle Matt." I say.

After a few moments of silence, someone knocks on the door. We look at one another, knowing we are not expecting company and I know it's not the guys or Maya. They would have messaged me before coming over.

I get up off the couch and I give Uncle Matt a look. "Stay here." I say coolly while pulling my fire to my fingers, letting him know I will protect him from whoever is at the door.

As I reach the door, I search the electrical pulse of the person on the other side and I can tell it's absolutely a stranger. I find myself relaxing a bit, knowing that at least it's not Mason or Rhett coming back for round three.

I open the door and standing on the porch is a blonde-haired kid swaying back and forth on his feet. When I look at his face, I see the fear in his eyes and the slight fleck of the reddish ring trying to creep into his blue eyes.

"I was told to find Aiden Rivers." He forces out through gritted teeth.

I nod my head, and I take a breath before I answer. "I'm Aiden. Why are you here?" I ask, fearing his answer.

"I was told to come here and ask if you would help me with my powers." The kid says. "I don't want to become a Parasite."

I see tears fill this kid's eyes and something in me hurts for him. I open the door fully, letting him in the house, but I keep my fire just under my skin in case whatever his power is, tries to surge, I can make my wall with little thought.

"What do you think your power is?" I ask.

"I don't know, but I think it may be electricity." He says. "I keep shocking everything I touch."

"Yup, that's electricity." I say with a smile, and I bring my own power to my left hand. "I got you. What's your name, kid?"

"Dylan." He says as he doubles over when a wave of pain hits him.

"Come on, let's go outside, and I'll help you through this." I say as I lead him out the back door.

"Aiden." Uncle Matt says with a warning tone in his voice.

I nod my head, knowing that it could be dangerous, but I have to help this kid from becoming one of them. As we get to the middle of the yard, I call my fire and I make it form a chamber that is about ten feet tall and about fifteen feet wide, and I pull the heat out of it while making sure to reinforce the walls to create a solid structure.

"Okay, Dylan, are you able to visualize your power?" I ask the very same thing that Uncle Matt asked me not that long ago.

Dylan nods, a piece of his blonde hair falling in front of his eyes as he tries to work through the pain that I know all too well.

"Okay. I want you to think about the electricity and how it flows through you." I tell him.

After a few minutes, he clutches his chest and I feel the electricity in the air before it discharges in the chamber. I call my own electricity forward to cancel his out.

"The voice won't shut up!" Dylan yells as he holds his head between his hands.

"Dylan, listen to me." I say, while grabbing his shoulder.

I feel the current under his skin and I have to keep mine just under the surface to be able to touch him. "You have to ignore it and clear your mind. You *have* to do that before you release it." I warn. "Look at me."

Dylan keeps his eyes closed and I give him a tiny shock of my power to get him to look up.

"Look at me." I demand again.

The fear in his blue eyes breaks my heart and I know I have to get him under control and soon.

"Take a breath and listen to what I have to say." I tell him sternly.

Dylan takes a breath while removing his hands from his head and I feel him relax just a bit.

"Alright. Now what I want you to do is to think about your Soul Power." I begin, but he gives me a look that I'm sure filled my own face back eight months ago; confusion.

I give him a small smile. "It's what gives us our power." I explain while pointing to my chest. "It's in the center of your chest. It should be shaped like a sphere."

Dylan closes his eyes and I can actually feel his electricity respond in the air to his searching, and it's so close to teetering off the edge.

"I found it." Dylan says with a bit of awe in his voice.

"Okay. Now you need to ground yourself before you let your power go for the first time." I say.

"How do I?" He begins to ask but another wave of pain hits him and he grabs at his chest again, trying to breathe through the discomfort.

I again keep an eye on the current in the air and it is starting to feel different, but I don't let the hopefulness show on my face.

"Good job, Dylan. Now what you need to do is think of your current coming from your Soul Power and connecting to something in your body. It can be anything other than the Soul Power itself or your heart. I use a rib, but that's me." I say.

Dylan again closes his eyes and I feel the current get stronger. I can only hope he grounds in time. I start to see the flickers of yellow and white currents flow over his arms and down to his fingers. He groans at another wave of pain and he discharges this time. I have to bring my own current up to cancel his out. As colors of blue, yellow, and white electricity fight for dominance in the air, the hum of the current gets to an all-time high and hangs in the space around us.

"Okay, Dylan, I think it's almost time for you to finish this." I say as I start to merge my electricity into my fire chamber to hopefully help cancel his initial burst of energy.

"I'm afraid. What if it's too late?" Dylan says with pure fear lacing his words.

"Don't you dare think that." I snap.

He looks at me with shock at my tone, and I press on.

"You came to find me, and I am *not* allowing you to leave this yard as a Parasite." I say with determination. "*You* are in control of these powers, not the other way around. Now say it."

Dylan stares at me like a deer in the headlights of a car, and I shake my head with aggravation when I feel his current change again, and then I know this power is telling him to fight back.

"Say it! Say 'I am in control of you.' Dylan." I yell.

"I am in control." Dylan whispers.

"Say it louder and believe it! I know you got this, Dylan. You don't know how close you are." I say.

"I am in control of you." Dylan says.

But his words are still not strong enough. Then a thought hits me, because it's somewhat the same thought that helped me come into my powers.

"Who do you want to protect with these powers?" I ask.

Dylan looks up and, for the first time since he's walked through the door, he smiles.

"My parents." He says. "I want to protect my parents. They adopted me, saved me from the orphanage after my real parents were killed. They protected me from nightmares and the thugs at school. I want to return the favor." Dylan says, his voice getting stronger with each word.

"Keep that thought in the front of your mind and take control." I say as I again build up the fire and electrical walls.

I just hope what I made around us will hold, because I can feel I am on the brink of my limit right now. From the training with Ivan earlier, I am about spent, but I force myself to hold on for this kid. I watch as Dylan holds his head again with his left hand and he grits his teeth together so hard that I fear they may break right at the gum line.

"Shut up! I am in control of you!" Dylan screams. "I am in control, not you!"

Then he lets his power go and at the same time I give my own power a pulse to try to cancel his out, but I am a second too late and it discharges my power flinging me back into the fiery wall behind me as his electricity fades with a crackling hiss.

My own Soul Power aches from the strain and I rub my chest while I look over at Dylan, who is on his knees and panting for breath. Luckily, my firewall is still up around us, and I push off the surface and walk over to him.

"Dylan?" I ask softly.

He looks up at me, and I look into his eyes. I collapse to my knees in front of him, my hands shaking from the amount of power I used for this.

"You did it Dylan. You are in control now." I say with a lazy, crooked smile. "You are part of The Protector's of Power." I tell him as the red ring fades from his blue eyes and a gold ring takes its place.

Dylan smiles brightly at me as tears flow from his eyes. I watch with honor as the lightning bolt tattoos cover his arms. The bright yellow and white coloring flowing across his sweat-slicked skin.

49

Aiden

"T hank you." Dylan says as we make our way back into the house.

"I don't have the time to train you right now, but I can give you some tips on how you can practice."

I can tell he wants to ask why I can't train him, but he doesn't push for the reason.

"The main thing is to keep grounded and if you can imagine your power taking shape, will it to happen." I say as I use my electricity to spell out his name. "It's as easy as that." I say with a smile.

"Yeah, says the guy who's had his power for years. I mean, what are you, twenty?" Dylan asks.

I bark out a laugh; this kid has no clue. "I am twenty-one, actually, and I've only had my power for about eight months." I say, looking him in the eye.

Shock fills his face, and I smile at him.

"You'll get the hang of it." I say. "I'll have a buddy of mine make you some light bulbs. That's good practice." I say with a mischievous smile while opening the front door. "Come by again in about three days and I'll have them waiting for you."

Dylan steps out on the porch but before he walks down the steps, I stop him as a thought hits me.

"Dylan, who told you about me?" I ask.

"I don't know his name. I met him when I went into the part of town that's run by The Parasites. I thought I was turning into one, so I might as well join them. I was scared out of my mind when three of them jumped me, but he protected me from them. His hands were burnt but, I don't know, something about him was different." Dylan explains.

I look at him in shock at what I just heard. I then shake my head in disbelief and smile at him.

"Do you know who I'm talking about?" Dylan asks, looking confused at my reaction.

"Yes, I think I do." I say, while rubbing the back of my neck. "It's getting late. You should go home. I'll see you in three days."

Dylan nods and walks down the porch, and I shut the door behind him.

"Who told him to find you?" Uncle Matt asks.

I take a deep breath in through my nose and let it out in a huff as I lean against the door to keep my knees from buckling. "I could bet money on it that it was Mason, of all people." I say.

Uncle Matt looks at me in surprise, and I nod at his reaction.

"I know. He is the last person that I would have thought to send someone to me." I say.

But that goes to prove that there is something different about him. Even Dylan said it. I think to myself.

"I'm gonna turn in for the night. I'm beat." I say as the exhaustion hits me again.

After I get another bath, I throw on a pair of black shorts, not even bothering with a shirt, and I crash into bed. Just as I am about to doze off, I start to feel something tickle the back of my mind and as I look at the trace of who is tugging at my mental connection, a slow smile spreads on my lips.

"Hey Baby." I croon towards Maya's connection.

"Hi. Wow, it worked. I didn't think it would." Maya says, her sweet voice echoing in my mind.

"Yes, it did. What are you doing?" I ask while trying to stay awake to talk to her, but the relaxing hot bath has me fighting to keep my eyes open.

"Nothing much, but it seems like you had a long day." Maya says as I feel the ghostly touch of her water course through my body. *"Why are you so tired?"*

"Ivan and I trained today. I helped him figure out how to make iron walls strong enough to take my electricity. And then this kid showed up on my doorstep, surprisingly with Mason's blessing." I say.

I tell her about Dylan and how Mason told him to find me to help him come into his power.

"So that's why I'm tired. I think I pushed myself to my limit today." I tell her.

"Get some rest, Babe." Maya says while making it feel like she ran her fingers through my hair.

At that touch, I think of what Ivan told me earlier, that I needed to take a little break and spend time with Maya.

"Can I take you out tomorrow night?" I ask.

She is quiet for a moment. I still feel her in my mind, so I know she heard the question. Then I feel what I can only think is love pouring into me from her side of the connection, and I let a lazy grin play at the corner of my mouth.

"I would love that, Aiden." Maya says softly. *"Good night, Babe."*

"Good night, Baby Girl. I love you." I say as I let my eyes close.

"I love you too, Aiden." Maya says as she pulls back from my mind and I let sleep take me then with a smile on my face.

The next evening, after I reach out to make sure Maya is still up for going out with me tonight, I pick out a pair of black jeans and a mint green button-up shirt, and then I sit on the corner of my bed to tie the laces of my black and white converse sneakers. I go into the living room to tell my aunt and uncle that I'm taking Maya to the forest.

"You better be a gentleman to her." Aunt Viv warns.

"When have I not been a gentleman to her?" I ask with a sly smile on my lips.

"You know what I mean, young man." Aunt Viv says while pointing her finger at me.

I walk over and give her a kiss. "I know Aunt Viv. I don't know what will happen, but I know I'll be careful and safe." I say.

"You better, son." Uncle Matt says with a look that means business if I take things to the next level and don't take precautions.

"I don't know if it will get to that." I begin, but again that look cuts my words short, and I just nod to him that I understand.

I take a breath and walk out the door to get in my truck and drive over to Maya's. While I don't plan on having sex with her tonight, I can't lie to myself and say that I haven't been thinking about that. I again think about what's coming and if I can have one thing before that fateful day, it would be her.

As I pull up to her house, I take a deep breath and push my desire for her deep down in my gut while I park my truck in her driveway.

I walk up to her porch and knock three times in a row on the wooden door. I wait for a few heartbeats before the door opens. The smile that spreads across my face at the thought of seeing her again fades a bit when her father is standing at the threshold instead. He smiles at me, stepping away from the door and extending an arm, telling me to come in.

I walk into the quaint living room,decorated with a brown leather sofa and loveseat along with a glass coffee table and end tables to complete the room. He sits down on the sofa while motioning for me to take the seat beside him. I take a breath before I sit down, the leather groaning at my weight.

There is an awkward silence between us before he finally breaks it. "Aiden, I want to apologize for what I made Maya do three years ago. I have partial visions, and I had a good feeling that Maya was meant to be a part of this Prophecy, but I didn't really know for sure that you were going to be a part of it until after I had her break things off with you." Mr. Harper says.

"It's alright. I understand now and the reason behind it, Mr. Harper." I say. "Thank you for making that hard decision for us. For The Protector's of Power."

Mr. Harper is shocked at my words, and he smiles at me. "You've matured a lot since the last time I saw you. I can see it in your eyes." He says.

I look away from him because I know the hardness is slowly creeping back into my eyes. The reality of each day brings us closer to the end.

"I will say, your destiny is yours to make. I have a feeling I know how your visions have been ending, and it feels like nothing is left, but it's up to you and how you control your abilities in that moment that determines if you live or not."

I look at him with shock on my face and I begin to ask him how he knows this, but when I see Maya come into the living room, my words stall in my throat and the sight of her warms my soul.

She's in a white billowing blouse, the soft plush sleeves coming just to her elbow, her wind and water tattoos seem so elegant against the fabric and she has a jean skirt on that shows her long, lean legs that are accentuated by the wedge sandals made of that faux burlap.

I openly look her up and down and I know a sly smile is playing on the corner of my mouth because her cheeks warm at my blatant staring. Mr. Harper clears his throat and I have to force my eyes away from her to look at him.

"Don't be out too late, you two, and please be safe." He says as he gives Maya a kiss on the cheek.

"Don't worry, Daddy. Aiden will protect me." Maya says while looking back at me with a wink.

Oh, fuck. Who's gonna protect you from me? I think to myself.

Mr. Harper gives me a look, and I can just imagine what he's thinking.

"Your daughter is in good hands, Mr. Harper." I say and I extend my right hand for Maya to take.

"Just be smart, you two." Mr. Harper says.

I lead Maya out the door and walk her to my truck and help her in the passenger seat. When I get in the driver's side, I take her hand in mine and I run my thumb over the back of her hand while I drive her to the forest.

50

Aiden

When we arrive at the forest thirty minutes later, I park a little farther in the wooded area because what I have planned involves the Colorado.

Once I find an area that looks to be secluded, I help Maya out of the cab to lead her to the back, near the tailgate. While keeping my right hand intertwined between her fingers, I use my left hand to lower the tailgate. When I remove my right hand from hers, I instantly feel the coolness of the evening air tickle the empty space of my flesh and she lets out a startled squeak when I grab her hips to lift her up and sit her on the tailgate.

My hands linger on her hips for a moment as she wraps her left arm around my neck. Turning my head towards her, I trail soft kisses up her velvety skin from her wrist to her elbow. I keep my lips on the skin of the crook of her arm and I look at her through half-lidded eyes. A blush colors Maya's cheeks, a sweet shade of pink and that makes my heart thunder in my chest.

I remove my right hand from her hip and I call my fire, but I keep the heat out of it, making my fire form almost like a plush comforter. The reds, oranges, and yellows filling the bed of the truck with a tangible softness. Maya looks from the bed made of fire and back to me with awe in her eyes and a loving smile playing on her soft lips.

"Come on, let's get comfortable." I say while trying to get my heart to calm down and not beat out of my chest.

She scoots onto the heatless flame and I heft myself up on the tailgate to crawl in with her. I settle down on my back and she snuggles up to my left side while resting her head in the spot between my shoulder and chest. I gently run my hand over her back while playing with her silky, dark brown hair between my fingers, and we take in the sounds of the evening.

The sound of her breathing, just barely a whisper between us. The crickets in the tree line; they're chirping in a content melody, playing off one another to see who can hit the higher note. The gentle breeze rustling the leaves of the nearby trees and on that wind, it brings with it the scent of the blooming purple lilac grove a few hundred yards away from us.

I close my eyes and almost let myself believe that the prophecy doesn't exist. That The Siphon doesn't exist, and it's just me and her on this planet and we can just stay in one another's arms until the end of time. But I can't hold on to that daydream for long. It's not a vision, but the images haunt me all the same.

The Siphon. Ivan's death warning. Mason, Rhett, Mrs. Jaffee, Uncle Matt.

They all flash through my mind and I can't stop the sigh that forces my lungs to take a breath and escapes through my nose.

Maya sits up to look at me while keeping her hand on my chest, and I try to school my expression so I don't ruin her evening, but the pleading for me to open up to her fills her blue eyes that under the moonlight, look like an endless ocean. Her dark brown hair framing her face and gives shape to the shadows that bring out her cheekbones, making her seem like an angel coming to save my soul.

And with that look, the walls that I have been building up again shatter into a million pieces and I know I will never be able to repair them.

"Please tell me what you're thinking." She says as she takes her hand from my chest and runs it through my hair, before cupping the left side of my face and running her thumb over the scruff of my beard.

"I'm fine." I say, trying to give her a sly smile.

"Aiden." She scolds.

I take a breath while looking into her eyes. "There are too many things to focus on just one." I whisper, hoping that will stop her questions.

She slides her hand down my neck and into the collar of my button-up, her fingers gliding over the lightning tattoo on my collarbone, then finally resting her hand on my broad pecs. Skin to skin. I swallow at the heat that crawls from my stomach then up my neck and seems to sit right where her hand is, right over my heart. Can she feel it thundering against my ribcage?

"Please tell me what's going through your head. Don't bottle up your feelings from me, Baby." Maya says, her voice a gentle caress.

I bring my right hand up to cover hers that's still resting on my chest and nod my head.

"I've had the vision that Ivan's going to die at Victor's hand if he joins us." I begin. "I told Ivan that I don't want him to come, but he basically said that since I know how he dies, we can stop it from happening."

"Well, he is right. You know what is coming so we can protect him." Maya says. "We can keep him safe, Aiden." she adds with determination.

"I just want to keep everyone as safe as I can." I whisper.

"We will keep everyone safe. We all will come home after this and live our lives the way we want to." Maya says.

My heart constricts at her words and I wrap my left hand around the back of her neck to tug her down to my chest while wrapping her in a tight hug.

"No matter what happens, I love you, Maya. I always have and I always will." I say, past the knot in my throat.

"You keep making it sound like you're the only one not making it out of this." Maya says softly while tracing a wrinkle on my shirt.

I lift my gaze to the dusky sky, at the stars starting to sparkle down on us, and another sigh tears through my chest.

"Why is it so easy for you to believe that you're not going to make it out?" Maya asks with sorrow in her voice, while she gathers the fabric of my shirt in her fist as if part of her wants to hear, but the other part wants to stay in ignorant bliss.

"I don't want—" I begin, but she cuts me off.

"Please tell me. Maybe I can be the one to help you, instead of you trying to save everyone else." Maya says with a smile but it doesn't reach her eyes.

"I can see myself destroying The Siphon, and I can feel the amount of power it will take to blow it up. I can feel the pain of my Soul Power fracturing again." I say, my throat dry. I force myself to swallow before continuing. "I feel the end result of releasing that much power and what it does to my body. Once I see The Siphon explode, there is nothing but blackness left." I finish and I close my eyes.

After a few minutes of silence, she lifts her head from my chest and I open one eye to look at her and when I see silver lining her eyes from unshed tears; I open both eyes to look at her fully.

"Well, *I* refuse to believe that. I just got you back after three years and I refuse to let you go that easily." Maya says with a fierceness filling her voice near the end. "I am going to be the one to fight for you." She says with a playful smile and taps the tip of my nose with her index finger.

I find myself smiling at her, at her playfulness that's slowly pushing back the darkness of my thoughts. I wrap my right arm around her waist and I flip her onto her back while my upper body hovers over her.

My arms are planted on either side of her head as a gentle breeze glides over us. I notice she shivers against the breeze, so I connect to my fire with my right hand and I give just enough heat to take the chill off while making the flames slide up to build walls around the truck and block off where the tailgate is, plus it will give us a little more privacy.

"You are getting so much better at your power." Maya says with a sultry smile on her lips. "And see, I told you, your power isn't always destructive."

I grin at her and lean down to kiss her. I planned on just giving her a gentle kiss, but when she bites my lower lip, I growl in her mouth, and I let my tongue explore her fully and she meets me stroke for stroke. I break our kiss, but I don't stop my worship of her body. I begin to trail kisses down the column of her neck, and she instantly tilts her head to the side.

Once I get to the neckline of her white blouse, I pull my lips away from her neck, which earns me a cute, frustrated growl. I chuckle as I move down the length of her body, tugging the hem of her shirt up so I can place feather-light kisses on her soft belly, all the while raising her shirt higher and higher. Her back arches from my touch and a soft moan escapes past her lips and the sound drills itself straight to my thickening shaft, making me wish I wore something other than jeans.

As I continue to lift the shirt off her body, she sits up enough for me to slip the silky fabric over her head and I toss it in the corner of the truck bed. I take in the sight of her lacy pink bra, her full breasts, her dark hair fanning out behind her, and my flames framing her face.

"You are gorgeous, Maya. I'm going to take my time claiming every. Single. Fucking. Inch of you." I growl.

She then sits up and kisses me again. I roughly run my hands up her smooth back, but I realize too late that the kiss was a distraction, and before I know it, she pulls away, and with both hands shoving against my chest, she forces me on my back. I let out a little laugh at her roughness, as I let a smile curve up the right side of my mouth.

"Oh, Maya." I breathe as she pushes her index finger to my lips to keep me from speaking more.

She then trails her right hand down my neck, over the flame tattoo that sits in the middle of my skin, sending shivers of pleasure through my already heated veins. She then glides her hands down the length of my body to the bottom of my shirt, where she then begins to unbutton it. One button at a time.

She only uses her index fingers and thumbs of both hands while she keeps her palms and the remaining fingers against my skin; running over the defined muscle of my stomach and chest so slowly that my breath catches in my throat the higher she gets. When she finally opens the last button near the top of my neck, she lets the fabric fall to either side of my body; as if I were a fish and she just fileted me wide open.

My breath comes out in ragged pants. My whole body expanding and contracting with each breath. She then leans down to trail her own tender kisses down my chest, stomach, and back again. Her teeth nip at my skin here and there, and I know I am going to be a mess of bruises, but I don't give a shit.

She continues her torture for a few more heartbeats before she makes her way to my lips, where this time she is the one to explore me. She is the one to shove her tongue against mine and I match her stroke for heated stroke while a groan that bubbles from my chest makes her smile against my mouth.

I bend my knees enough so when I sit up; she leans her back against my thighs, and I let my shirt fall off my shoulders, allowing both of my markings to be on full display for her. She unabashedly lets her eyes explore every inch of my body, and I grin at her like a Cheshire cat.

"You like what you see, Baby Girl?"

"Yes, I do." Maya says while unbuttoning my pants.

She only gets as far as unbuttoning my jeans before I use the deft fingers of my left hand to unsnap her bra. When the fabric falls past her shoulders, I take in her soft and perky skin; nipples pebbled to sharp and needy points. I pull her closer to me and I lean down, taking the left nipple between my teeth and giving it a slight tug. Maya's head tilts back as her moan fills the air around us and I growl into her flesh.

"Oh, Aiden!" Maya gasps breathlessly.

I release her nipple and kiss the soft flesh between her breasts before moving over to the other one.

"I am loving what I am seeing and hearing, Maya. You drive me absolutely crazy and it's about time I clue you in on how that feels." I tell her as I take her right nipple into my mouth and suck on it greedily as I use my forefinger and thumb to pinch and squeeze her left at the same time.

"Aiden!" She screams with need filling her voice.

I push her back down onto the fiery bed of the truck, my mouth never leaving her body, as I take my left hand and slide my jeans and boxers down my hips and off my muscular legs. Once I am fully naked before her, I pull back and her desire-filled eyes take in my whole form. She takes in a quick breath as her eyes land on my shaft, which is rock hard only for her.

"Only you could ever make me like this." I tell her as I swipe a hand over myself, dragging my fist from base to tip in a quick pump to ease some of the tension, but I can tell the movement just makes her need build for me and I can't stop the sly smile that forms on my face.

The delicate lines of her throat bob with a hard swallow and I can't stop the dark chuckle that bubbles from my chest. I lean over her, letting my crown caress her through her panties. "Do you want this, Maya?"

"Yes!" She pleads as she arches into me and I feel the wetness that has soaked through her underwear as her needy core brushes against my aching erection.

"Then we need to lose the panties, Baby Girl." I say, my voice so low it's barely audible.

I hook the index finger of my right hand into the waistband and before she can even comprehend what I did, the pink panties that was keeping me from seeing all of her, disintegrate into ash as I let my fire eat away at the fabric in a quick flash of heat.

I lean down to her, my arms braced on either side of her head, and I bring my right knee between her legs while pressing firmly against her clit. She shifts her hips against my kneecap and I suck in a breath, feeling just how hot her reaction is to me being near her, but something stops me in my tracks and I look down at her beautiful face.

"Why did you stop?" Maya whines with a concerned look on her face.

I chuckle at her, always the one to be concerned about other people before herself.

"Are you ready for this? For us?" I ask seriously.

"Aiden." She says, chuckling my name. "We are both twenty-one now. You don't have to be afraid of my father."

I think back to that night in the movie theater parking lot where we got fairly close to the first time in Uncle Matt's Outback. Back then, our clothes, while they were skewed, they were still on. I was terrified that her father was going to find out, but then she moved and I thought that was my punishment for trying to go that far, but

I know now we were too young and part of me is kind of glad that something stopped us that night.

"I loved you then, and I love you now, Aiden." Maya says. "But first." She says as she makes her water appear in her right hand and then disappear from my sight.

The next thing I know is I feel something around my shaft that is warm and, well...*wet.*

A bright smile lights up Maya's face at my shock, and if I must say horror, at the feeling and she tries to hide her laughter behind her hand.

"We gotta be safe, you big dummy." She says, while giving me this sultry look.

I chuckle, understanding that her water is acting like a condom. "Okay, smart idea."

I lean down to kiss her and as I lower my body to hers; she runs her hands through my hair, pulling me even closer. When I slowly tease her entrance with my crown, giving her just an inch, she responds by digging her fingernails into my back and I growl at the bite of them against my skin. Those are scars I would gladly keep on my skin forever.

She wraps her legs around my waist, urging me to seat myself into her, so I can love her deeper, but I force my hips to stay where they are, not giving her any more than she has at the moment and the groan of frustration that comes out of her makes me smile against her lips.

"Do you want this?" I ask as I close the gap between our bodies just a fraction of an inch, teasing her with more of me.

I swallow another moan and she arches into me, but I pull back and she actually growls at me this time, and I chuckle in response.

"And I thought I was the wild animal." I chuckle.

"Aiden." She purrs as she tightens her legs around my hips again. "I want you. Please." She begs.

"Then you will take all of me." I whisper into her ear.

I finally stop teasing her and at first, I take my time with the first stroke, letting her adjust to my size, but then something snaps between us and we love wildly. The three years of us being separated, the pain of it echoes in each renewed contact and each panted breath as the plea for me to move faster and harder pours from her lips.

Then, as if the pain of what we felt as lost time fades, I slow my pace to long, deep, languid rolls of my hips to give each of us the best time I can manage with each thrust.

"You feel so damn good, Baby Girl." I grunt as I thrust into her and trail my lips across her neck.

"Don't stop. Please. I'm almost there."

"I'm never stopping, Baby. I've waited too long to make you mine and I'm making up for lost time." I growl as I nip at her earlobe and she cries out. "Come for me, Maya."

She shatters with my name on her lips and with two more pumps of my hips, I'm following right behind her.

When we both are well-loved, which is evident in our swollen lips, the multitude of bright red scratches down my back, the bruises covering both of our necks and chests along with the satisfied ache between our legs; we lie beside one another while we try to catch our breaths.

I turn my head to look at her and I know I have this lazy smile on my face as I notice the flush to her cheeks. "Are you okay?" I ask while running my thumb over her swollen lips, still grinning that I was the one to make them like that.

She nods while I pull her to my chest, and she hooks her calf around my shin.

"Yes. I am more than okay." Maya says, satisfaction filling her voice.

I laugh and I kiss the top of her head. After a few moments of lying in each other's arms, I finally sit up to grab the phone out of my discarded pants and look at the time. It shows 11:00 pm. I sigh and I look back at her and I find her leaning on her side, her right arm in front of her just enough to cover her breasts. I almost think about going for round two with her, but I need to get her back home.

"As much as I hate to say this, I need to get you home." I say as I trail a series of kisses up that arm and ending on her lips before we reluctantly pick up our discarded clothing and get dressed.

After I reabsorb my flame, I hop out of the truck bed first and extend my arms to help Maya down, letting her body slide over mine to show her just how much I'm still reeling from her. A blush crawls up her neck, cheeks, and the curve of her ears and I give her a quick kiss on the lips before shutting the tailgate and leading her to the passenger door to help her into her seat before getting in on my side and driving her home.

I walk Maya to the front porch of her house and after another quick make-out session; I pull away and watch as she goes inside. When I finally crash on my bed forty-five minutes later, I feel sleep take me under to what I hope is a blissful dream-scape, but it's far from that.

I dream of that fateful day soon approaching. A blood-red sun and moon hangs ominously low in the sky. Ivan is grabbed by Victor just like in my earlier vision, but this time I am quicker to use my shock wave to push Victor away and save Ivan from being killed by Victor's wind. When Maya comes up beside me, I see her water flowing from her right hand and I call my lightning so we can mix our powers and send them toward Victor.

51

Aiden

I am pulled from the vision by my alarm clock going off in the background. I roll over and smack the off button with a groan before I make my way into the bathroom. I turn the water on in the sink to wash my face and as I tug my shirt off; I catch a glimpse of myself in the mirror and I pause.

Covering my neck, chest, and stomach are small circular bruises, and I can't help the smirk that my image reflects back at me.

I reach out mentally to Maya to see if she's awake and when I know she is; I ease into her mind while showing her what I'm seeing in the mirror.

"Hey, Aiden. Good morn—" Maya is cut off mid-sentence and I can tell the breath catches in her throat at what I am showing her.

"Good morning, Baby Girl. Do you see what you left on me last night?" I ask.

"Well, you didn't have a problem leaving some of your own." Maya teases as she sends me images of her neck, throat, and her soft breasts.

As the images flicker in my mind, I tilt my head back against the curve of my neck as the pressure builds between my legs and makes my boxers visibly tent with desire, and for the first time, I wish I could teleport like Seth.

"You are such a tease, you know that?" I ask as I look at myself in the mirror again. *"Just wait. I'm gonna leave bruises where only you and I will know where they are."* I say as I imagine my marks covering her thighs.

I hear her suck in a breath in my mind and I send a dark chuckle down the connection while I visualize caressing her cheek with my thumb.

When I sit at the table ten minutes later to eat a quick breakfast of pancakes and sausage, I notice Uncle Matt and Aunt Viv eyeing me. I know my hoodie doesn't hide the bruises that dot my neck in places from Maya's exploration last night, but I'm thankful my clothes hide the others on my chest and stomach.

Uncle Matt nor Aunt Viv ask me what happened last night, even though the evidence is on damming display. As I finish my breakfast, I take my plate to the kitchen and put it in the dishwasher, then I grab my backpack off the floor near the garage door. I pause with my hand on the knob, and look back at my aunt and uncle over my shoulder who are still eating, but I see them watching me out of the corner of their eye, as if waiting for me to say something. So I take a deep breath and turn to meet their sidelong gazes.

"We were safe last night." I say, smiling at remembering her water made protection over me.

Uncle Matt nods his appreciation at my words and picks up the newspaper from the table like I didn't just tell him we lost our virginity last night. I turn around and turn the knob of the garage door; the hinges creaking while it opens and I walk out to my truck. One thing is, I will never see the bed of this truck the same way again.

I will always envision the two of us there, content in one another's arms and loving each other deeply, over and over again. I pull my thoughts from last night and I jump in the cab before I'm late for class.

I meet up with Ivan and Gray in the main hallway of the university, but before I can even think about telling them what happened last night, Mason walks by me, and for the first time, he doesn't even acknowledge I'm in the hallway.

Before I can talk myself out of the thought that filters through my mind, I walk over to him, stopping him mid-stride by grabbing his bicep. He gives me a look that asks, '*what do you think you're doing?*' and I take a breath, keeping my body loose to hopefully let him know I'm not looking for another fight.

I look him in the eye a moment before I open my mouth. "Dylan's okay." I say simply.

I pause a moment before walking away, and I swear I see something loosen in his shoulders for an instant, but it is immediately replaced with the same scornful look that shows me he is all Parasite again. I turn my back to him and walk over towards my friends.

Ivan and Gray look at me like I lost my marbles and before I can tell them what that was all about I nod my head for them to follow me and as we head to our classes for the morning, I proceed to tell them about Dylan. They are floored by what I share with them and Ivan immediately agrees to make the light bulbs that Dylan will need to practice with and is even willing to meet him personally.

When lunchtime rolls around, I'm waiting for Ivan and Gray to finish up with their classes so we can grab a table and chat a bit more about what's been going on. I look up and I feel a smile spread on my lips when Maya shows up to kill some time before she meets up with Seth later.

I see her blush slightly when her eyes connect with mine and I know last night is still fresh in her mind, just like it is for me. I give her a wink and she turns even redder. I bend my head back with a bark of laughter and when her eyes land on my neck; she sees her love bites in the flesh, and it makes the blush on her cheeks reach an all-time high.

"You should have covered them up." She chuckles while taking a purple circular makeup case out of her purse. "I am the only one who gets to see them." She adds possessively.

I feel her dab what I assume is foundation on my neck, her fingers working the liquid onto my skin. My pulse flutters as her deft fingers work in the makeup, and I have to swallow down the need to growl at her touch. She smiles at me when she finishes, apparently knowing what reaction I was trying to push down, and just as I am about to kiss her, Ivan and Gray show up and we all eat with idle chatter between us.

After lunch and I come back from walking her to her car, Ivan puts me in a headlock, rubs his knuckles against my head, and then pushes me toward our next class.

"You son-of-a-bitch, when were you gonna tell us?" Ivan asks, giving me a knowing smile while tapping his neck, letting me know he noticed the change in mine. I look at him in shock and shake my head.

"Nosey bastard." I say flatly, but my eyes hold humor and he smiles right back at me.

Gray is looking between us, clueless at what Ivan is going on about until Ivan pulls him in and whispers in his ear.

I hear Gray yell, "It's about damn time, Aiden!" But I am already walking into my next class with a smile on my face.

Ivan, Gray, and I meet at Seth's place later that night and Maya is already there. I go over to give her a sound kiss on the lips, not caring anymore to hide my feelings. She places a hand on my chest to signal the same thing to the room.

"Alright, you two, enough making out. We got training to do." Ivan says while walking into a training room, but giving Gray a sound kiss on the lips before walking inside.

I smile at him and give Maya a wink before leading her into the room while Seth follows behind us.

"Seth, what is the best way for us to mix our powers?" I ask, turning back to look at him over my shoulder.

Before Seth can even answer, I see the questions form in Maya's eyes. I cup her face in my right hand and give her a small smile.

"I had another vision of our powers mixing to attack Victor." I say softly.

She nods at my explanation, and we turn toward Seth to await his instruction.

"I think you have to decide who is going to be the main power source, but don't let your powers touch or else the one that is the main line will feel the effects." Seth offers.

"Let's try it." Maya says with fire in her eyes.

I then remember the prophecy Seth told us a few months ago, but it feels like a lifetime now.

The one who will wield complimentary abilities of water and wind.

I call my fire and I point to Maya's left hand and she then allows her wind to encircle her fingers. I realize her abilities will be the better carrier of mine. Her wind can carry my fire with it and her water will carry my electricity.

"Start your wind first, and I'll mix my fire in. If I go first, you'll just blow my fire out." I say, urging her forward.

She nods her head while she effortlessly creates a medium-sized tornado in the middle of the room. I then allow my fire to snake its way into her vortex. My own fire tornado lacks the damaging power of Maya's wind, and with them together what her wind doesn't destroy, my flames will be there to finish off what's left.

"Good. Now the other two." Seth commands with his arms crossed over his chest.

We instantly cut from one power to the other. Her water also creating a vortex and I curl my electricity around the element, but I don't keep it far enough away and an electrical crack fills the room. Maya gets thrown off her feet and the yelp of pain she feels as the electrical shock flows over her body rings in my ears.

I utter a curse as I push my fire to my right foot. I just barely catch her and pivot my body behind hers in time to take the brunt of the impact against the wall. I grunt at the pain that flares across my back, but I hold on to her until she stops reeling from the shock.

"I am so sorry, Baby. Are you okay?" I ask trying to look at her hand and wishing like hell I could look into her body like she can with me through her water.

"Yeah." She groans out. "Damn, that was rough. I actually kind of feel sorry for anyone you attack with that." She says as she shakes her right hand as if that will lessen the tingling still on her skin.

I rest my forehead on the curve of her shoulder, and I tighten my arms around her waist. "I am so sorry." I whisper.

Maya turns in my arms to face me, but I keep my head low. She puts a delicate finger on my scruff-clad chin and I look into her beautiful blue eyes.

"Don't be sorry. This is what training is for. We failed, but we know now not to let them touch again." Maya says.

I nod and we help one another stand. Once we are steady on our feet, I bring my electricity to my fingers again.

"You ready for round two?" I ask with a smirk as I look over her body.

She brings her water to her fingers, and she makes me beyond happy that I wore black pants today because with that question, I feel her water condom cover my shaft. I have to fight so hard to school my face in front of mainly Seth, but I send her the feeling of what she's doing to me through our mental connection.

"You are so bad, Baby. You know how to almost drive me to my knees." I growl in her mind.

"Almost?" She croons, then makes the water ice cold.

It's all I can do to keep my knees from buckling, but I feel a shitty grin on my face before I can even try to hide it. I send her images of what I will do to her if she keeps this up. It involves my electricity, giving her little static shocks on a few choice places. Like behind the sensitive area of her ears, and the left side of her ribcage where she is just a bit ticklish, to each of her needy nipples, and that's just naming a few areas. Her face goes bright red and I can't stop the bark of laughter that comes out of my chest.

"Stop mentally fucking one another and get back to the task at hand." Seth scolds.

We smile sheepishly at him and get back to work. I hold back the voltage on my electricity until we get the hang of it and it's flawless. I feel bad for still shocking her a few times, but it's nothing as bad as the first time. Then, after Maya and I are satisfied about what we accomplished, I go over to Ivan and spar a bit with him. He tests out his new iron and copper set up as a shield and as a living skin protection and I try to push my electricity to the limit. After about an hour, we finally call it quits after we destroy this room once again and we are both heaving to catch our breath.

"I'm beginning to think you have it out for this room. It's always being destroyed." Ivan pants.

"Don't blame me this time." I force out between breaths. "You picked this room."

52

Seth

I lean against the wall as I silently watch Aiden and Ivan take one training room while Maya takes a smaller one next door, but it's Gray who I have my eyes fixated on, as he just watches Ivan in the training room. I notice his right hand balling into a fist and the muscles in his shoulders are tense and they look like they are about to rip out of his shirt.

Walking over to him, I tap him on the shoulder and he spins around with shock coloring his features. "You okay there, Gray?"

"Oh, Seth. You scared me. I didn't know you were still down here." Gray says.

I arch an eyebrow at him, letting him know I'm not going to let him dodge my question.

"I'm okay, but I feel like the odd one out here." Gray says.

"Gray, you know this is a dangerous situation. What can you do that would help them?"

"I don't know." Gray begins, "I know I don't have powers and that I'd probably be more of a pain in the ass than a help, but damn it my friends, my boyfriend, are putting their lives on the line, and what, just because I'm human I have to sit on the sidelines?" Gray says with determination in his voice, with just a touch of fear in his eyes.

"Have you talked to Aiden about this?" I ask while looking over to the training room that he and Ivan are in.

"No. I wanted to talk to you first, honestly. I know Aiden will shoot my thoughts down right away. I mean Ivan told me that Aiden didn't even want him to tag along, so I know for a fact that Aiden won't listen to me." Gray says. "Do I even stand a chance at helping them?" He asks, his voice lowering an octave as doubt sets in.

I flick my gaze over Gray's body and while he is not as muscular as Ivan or Aiden; he has this fire behind his eyes. I remember that Gray is good with computers and maybe he could be useful in helping us track the machine down once we figure out the location. Plus, I have a few other tricks up my sleeve that I have yet to share with the others.

I take a deep breath and I know once I open this door for Gray, Aiden is going to have a fit, but I understand how Gray is feeling. He feels helpless and I know that feeling all too well because of what happened twenty-one years ago. I don't want anyone to feel helpless when they are able to do something, no matter how small that task may be.

"How are you in combat?"

"Ivan and I have our own training sessions." Gray says. "And trust me, even with Ivan not using his metallurgy, we don't pull our punches."

"Alright. Come with me."

Aiden

As Ivan and I walk out of the training room, I don't see Seth or Gray anywhere and that strikes me as odd; but I figure Seth was probably showing him around the house or something. When I hear a footfall behind me a moment later, I turn to the noise to see what caused it.

Gray tosses a silver ball at my chest, and a faint beep comes from the sphere. I feel an electrical charge emanating from it before it detonates in my face so quickly that I don't have time to get my own electrical pulse up enough to cancel it fully.

The current surrounds me, making my body lock up and I'm thrown across the open area, crashing into the bulletproof window of the other training room. I crumple face-first on the floor. Every muscle is seized for a few more agonizing moments before the charge lets go of my body, but I still feel the current hovering over my skin.

Maya comes running over to me with Ivan on her heels. She starts to kneel next to me, but I give her a sharp look to keep her from touching me before I can speak my warning, and she pauses with her hand in mid-air.

"No, Baby." I grunt. "I'm still...charged."

I slowly sit up. Pain now envelops every inch of my chest and back and it's an effort to take a breath. After I am finally able to get in a sitting position and with my back still against the wall, I pull my electricity to my left hand. I look at Ivan and he knows instantly to make the wall around Maya. As soon as the wall forms, I let my power go, snaking it around the charge that still lingers on my skin. Once I have the foreign electricity surrounded by my own, I release my power with a loud crack.

After I can tell all the electricity is gone, I lean my head against the wall while trying to catch my breath; I give Ivan a slight nod, telling him to let his wall down. As soon as it drops, Maya is instantly at my side. Her hand pressing firmly against my chest sends a wave of pain flowing over my body, and I hiss a curse. I can feel her water searching my system and I know she feels the cracked and broken bones that came from mine and Ivan's training and now from my body smacking against this wall behind me.

"Oh, Aiden, you're hurt." Maya says. "Gray, what the hell was that?" She snaps as Gray and Seth walk over to us.

I look from Seth to Gray and my gaze lingers on his brown eyes that are full of fear, but I see a hint of excitement and that makes my stomach drop.

"What. The. Fuck. Was that?" I ask slowly, my eyes bouncing from both of them and landing on Seth on the last word.

Seth leans down and looks me over. "Can you move?" He asks simply.

I look at him like he's lost his damned mind. "Does it look like I can fucking move right now?" I bark.

"Gray, tell him." Seth says without taking his eyes off mine.

"Tell me what, Gray?" I ask slowly, looking around Seth at my friend.

Gray looks at me, and I see his worry at hurting me flare in his eyes. Then he looks over to Ivan for a moment and the excitement of what happened fades and it's replaced by a fire I have never seen in his eyes. Ivan glances back at Gray while running his hand through his hair and seems to give his partner a knowing smile.

"I'm going to help you all with this." Gray says finally while turning his attention towards me.

"Like hell you will." I snap.

"Aiden, shut up." Seth yells.

I look at Seth and then direct my attention to Gray and wait for him to speak.

"I want to help you guys. Just because I'm not as strong as you three doesn't mean I have to stay home and wonder which one of you will be coming back." Gray says, his voice steady and determined.

"Gray and I figured some things out, and I had some devices made for this kind of scenario." Seth says with a grin. "What he threw at you, Aiden, was a Shock Bomb. A concentrated blast that may even be a little stronger than what you can do, set to detonate at the press of a button with a three-second timer."

"Yeah, no shit, it's stronger." I say while rubbing my chest where it's still sore from the muscles being constricted and shocked.

"It has four charges and can be reloaded as well. I even have a Fire Grenade, and an Ice Blaster here too." Seth says with pride.

He shows us the other silver spheres that have designs of flames, ice shards, and a lightning bolt to show which one is which, and points to a little series of green lights that show the charge level in them, and on the Shock Bomb there is one dull area to show that charge is gone.

"How do you charge it?" Maya asks, her voice filled with awe.

"You just push your power into it." Seth replies.

He demonstrates by calling his own electric power and then actually shocking the Shock Bomb with it. The sphere absorbs the power and once it does, the green light illuminates again, showing it's fully charged. What shocks me is that it doesn't take a lot of power to fill it, but the ball makes it so condensed that it feels so much more powerful.

"That's awesome." Ivan croons.

"That's great and all, but no, Gray." I say. "You're not—" I begin, but Gray cuts me off and I look at him in shock. He's never shown anger before.

"Damn it, Aiden. Stop trying to force me away." Gray shouts.

"I'm trying to keep you alive!" I scream but instantly regret it when my back seizes up from the broken bones and strained muscles.

Maya grabs my hand in hopes of comforting me and I take a few breaths and look over to Seth with anger filling my eyes that he would allow Gray to even entertain the idea.

"What the hell are you thinking?" I ask slowly, staring him down.

"What the hell am I thinking?" Seth begins. "I'm thinking that I understand where your friend is coming from. He wants to help and protect *you*. But you keep him at arm's length because you're afraid of your own failure." Seth snaps. "I understand where he's coming from, and you want to know why?" Seth asks as he gets in my face and stares me down. His green eyes bouncing back and forth to look at my mismatched gaze, the golden ring in his eyes reflecting the light above his head.

"I felt fucking helpless at one point, too!" Seth yells. "After you were born and Victor found out that you may be the one the prophecy was talking about, he forced your parents to leave you after my own fucking brother stole Matt's power! And I stood by and did nothing! I didn't fucking fight back like I should have!"

I stare at Seth and all the anger I felt fades from my body as I see the anguish in his green eyes.

"I stood by while one friend had his powers ripped from him. I stood by while my other two had to choose to live with the devil incarnate to protect their son. In that situation, with all the types of powers I have, I felt so damn helpless that I just wanted to give up on life." Seth says, his voice dropping to a whisper near the end.

Seth then looks at Gray for a moment and then back to me. "I swore that I would never let anyone feel helpless again. So, I made those and I've given them to a few people over the years. I know they will help Gray stand by your side." Seth says while putting his hand on my shoulder to heal my broken body.

After I feel the last bit of his healing power flow over me, I stay where I am on the floor and look up at Gray. The fire is still burning in his eyes and this is honestly the first time I have seen Gray want to really fight for something. He's usually so reserved and tries to hide in the background, but with the determination burning in his eyes, I know I can't say no.

And honestly, I realize I don't want to say no.

Gray is not stupid in the least and he knows how dangerous this can be, but yet, he still wants to come. How can I say no to something so selfless? Then I laugh to myself, even though it has no humor in it. I have been selfish throughout this whole thing.

First, not wanting to have Maya involved, because of my own fear of not wanting to relive the past and fall for her again, only to have her ripped from me. Then trying to keep Ivan out of this because of my vision of his death, and now Gray because I thought his human body would make him an easy target.

Seth hit the nail on the head when he said it's all because of my own fear of failing them that I want to keep them away. But it's in our unique teamwork that we may be able to pull this thing off, destroy The Siphon, and stop Victor.

"Gray. Ivan. Maya." I say as I look at all of them in the eye as I say their name. "I'm sorry. Seth is right. I have wanted to keep you all at arm's length because I am terrified of failing you all. I want to protect you, but I realize that you all don't need that." I say softly.

Ivan stoops down to my level as Gray walks up to him and puts an arm on his shoulder, both smiling down at me, and Maya runs her right hand down my right arm with a small smile on her lips. I look at my friends; my team and I smile back at them. For the first time, I actually start to feel that even I will make it out of this too, because of their determination for my own success, and of their own burning in their eyes.

"Are you ready to stop being a one-man army and let us help you?" Gray asks with a smirk.

I chuckle while shaking my head at his words, knowing they rang true, and with a sly, crooked grin, I look at my team again and I nod.

"Yes, I would be glad to have you all at my side." I say.

Ivan extends his hand and lifts me to my feet while he stands along with me. The four of us form a circle and we hold on to each other's arms and I again look at them in turn.

"I can't wait to see the look on Victor's face when we all show up to make his life a living hell." I say.

"You lead us in, Captain, and we will make it happen." Ivan says darkly.

53

Aiden

Seth clears his throat after a few moments and we all look at him, waiting to hear what he has to say.

"I have taught you all everything you need to know. Now I will say, continue to train and make yourselves a stronger unit until it's time to end this once and for all." Seth says with pride glimmering in his voice. "I am proud of how far each of you has come and I know the world will be better once this is behind us."

"I agree." Maya says. "Let's make this something that will be told time and time again. Something that will be taught in history books of how the four of us stopped the most evil man that the world has ever known." Maya says, but she looks at Seth at her statement and realizes that she really didn't pull any punches with Seth's brother. He only nods as if to say, *I don't take offense to that. I know he's the devil incarnate.*

We leave Seth's house and when I make it to mine about thirty minutes later, beyond ready to get a cleaned up and flop in bed. I walk into the living room and I see my aunt and uncle cuddling on the couch while watching a movie. I think back to what Seth said about him failing my uncle and I know that my team is going to make things right in the world again.

"Oh Aiden, how did train—?" Aunt Viv begins to ask, then I hear her sharp intake of breath at my appearance.

I realize I didn't change out of my torn, dirty, and bloody clothes. Aunt Viv is jumping from the couch and is instantly by my side; her hands roving over my arms and shoulders.

"Are you okay? You look like a mess." Aunt Viv asks with worry in her eyes.

"Yes, Aunt Viv. I'm fine now. Seth healed me." I say, while taking her wrists in my hand and pinning them to her side with a smile. "Just another day in the training room."

As I'm lying in bed a few minutes later, and while my body is heavy with exhaustion, my mind will not let me sleep. I begin to think of my parents now that I know more about what happened to them. They didn't abandon me like I thought they did. They left to protect me.

Are they even alive now? I wonder.

With that thought, sleep is finally able to take me, but it's filled with visions of what's to come.

The four of us are walking through a forest, and just in the distance I see the blood red sun and moon hanging above the tree line, and it seems to get larger the deeper we walk in the forest, which sends chills down my spine. Then the vision jumps into the heat of the battle.

Rhett trying to bash Ivan's head in with his rock sword, but I see Gray pitch one of the silver balls into Rhett's face and a large flame ignites against his skin. I am battling with Mason, dodging his flaming fists and throwing my own toward his face.

I once again see Victor try to kill Ivan, but I am able to save my friend with what seems like practiced ease before the life can be sucked from his chest. Blackness clouds my vision once more and then I hear the burning of fire, the cracking of electricity, and the bending of metal from the machine in the distance, along with the smell of smoke, sweat, and blood on the breeze.

The next thing I know is, I am hovering about fifteen feet in the air. My powers are just about at full strength in each hand. I look back over my shoulder at my friends. Ivan leaning against a tree, holding what looks to be a broken arm. Blood and sweat coating his skin. Gray is with Seth, both of them equally torn but standing under their own power. And finally Maya.

Her dark brown hair looks black from the sweat dripping off her face, which is also covered in dirt and blood. She's on the ground trying to get to her feet, but I notice her ankle is at an odd angle so she can't stand. She reaches her hand up to me, as if begging me to end this. I turn around and I feel myself let everything go. Feel my Soul Power shatter from the force and still nothing but darkness envelops me.

Today is Sunday, and with no classes, I am free to do what I want. During breakfast, which is eaten in silence at first, but then I remember what Seth told me last night and I want to at least let my aunt and uncle know that I know some of the truth around my family.

"I know what happened to my parents." I say softly while looking down at my plate and spear a piece of scrambled egg on to one of the tines of my fork.

A fork clangs onto the wooden table, and I look up to find Uncle Matt staring at me. It was his brother, my father, that was taken from us.

"Seth told me a little bit about what happened yesterday." I offer.

"He still blames himself for what happened." Uncle Matt whispers. "It wasn't his fault."

"He needs to stop blaming himself." Aunt Viv says with sadness in her eyes while holding Uncle Matt's left hand, tracing his colorless lightning bolt tattoo that goes up his arm. "There was nothing he could have done." She adds.

"I do understand where he's coming from." I say, lifting my eyes to look at them both. "Maya, Ivan, Gray, and I will finish this, so no one else has to ever suffer like this again."

They both are shocked to hear that now Gray is involved and I tell them about our argument last night and that is when Seth told us about the demons he's been dealing with these last twenty-one years.

After breakfast, I'm sitting at my desk in my room, just staring at the black screen of my laptop. I have this feeling to start watching the phases of the moon because, in each of my visions, I've had that damned blood-filled moon hanging in the background. I had just been too focused on the bigger moving parts to notice until now.

So, I Google moon phases for the rest of the year and on November the twenty-eighth, my heart sinks to my stomach. That's when the solar eclipse happens. Only three weeks is all that is separating us from this final battle. I grit my teeth so hard that my jaw aches. I grab my phone and open the group text to my team.

I find myself chuckling at that term. My team. It sounds like we are part of the FBI or some shit. But instead of texting them, I open my mind and search for Ivan and Gray, and much like I did with Maya, I make a mental connection with them. I immediately feel Ivan's confusion and Gray's wonder at feeling me in their heads.

"Hey, you two." I say.

"This is freaky as hell, man." Ivan quips.

"I think this is cool." Gray chuckles.

"When did you figure this trick out?" Ivan asks.

"A little while back. I have Maya linked too."

"Oh, so you leave your best friends for last. Okay, I see how it is." Gray teases.

"What? I always leave the best for last, Gray. And you two are my best buds." I jest.

I can literally feel both of their eyes roll at my lame excuse and I let them both hear my laughter in their heads.

"You two are the worst." I say as I then pull Maya into our conversation, letting her know that I have Ivan and Gray connected as well.

"Well, what's with this meeting of the minds? Literally." Maya teases.

"Good one, Babe." I laugh, then my voice gets serious and I can feel my friends and girlfriend are hanging on my every word. *"I know the date that this will all go down."*

"When?" Ivan asks solemnly.

"November twenty-eighth."

"Damn, that soon, huh?" Gray asks solemnly.

"Yeah."

"Hey guys, the way I see it, we have three weeks to keep training and getting better at working with one another." Maya says.

"I also see it as a time where we all have to watch our backs. This is when people get desperate. Mason or Rhett may try to attack us again." Ivan warns, and I feel Gray and Maya nod in agreement.

"I say we all go to the forest tomorrow and train as a unit. Maybe I can ask Seth to join us and he can try to fight us all. Make it as real of a battle as we can." I say as dread fills my chest and I try to keep that feeling to myself and not let it leak to the others.

"Okay. Sounds good. I'll meet you there." Ivan says and the other chime in with their own acknowledgements.

"Now, how do we turn this off?" Gray asks.

I chuckle, *"Can you somewhat see a thread connecting the three of us?"* I ask, and I feel him nod. *"Just imagine a door to each connection and close it."*

Once Gray does that, I lose his connection, but I know I can *knock* on that door and he should open it up.

"That's so odd to feel," Ivan says, apparently sensing the same thing I can.

"It gets less and less freaky each time you do it." Maya says.

"And now that you two are connected, you can talk to each other that way, too." I tell Ivan.

"Seriously?" Ivan gasps. *"Oh, I'm gonna have fun with this."* He adds as his own connection fades with a dark ominous laugh.

"Oh, no." Maya chuckles. *"Gray is in for it now."*

"You think I should warn him?" I ask, but already knowing the answer.

"Nah. Let it be a surprise." Maya says. *"Sounds like we need some good times to focus on."* She adds, her voice going soft near the end.

"Yeah. We do." I say. *"I'll let you go. I'll see you tomorrow at the forest."* I ask.

I feel her nod. *"Of course, Aiden. I'll be there."* She says, and then she leaves my mind, shutting that invisible door behind her.

I run my hands through my reddish-blonde hair and down my face with a heavy sigh. I look over at the calendar hanging beside my desk and I take a red Sharpie from the black plastic pen holder, uncap the marker, circle that dreaded date, and write in rough capital letters.

THE SIPHON ENDS HERE.

I cross my arms while staring at the calendar, trying to will the heaviness of that date from my chest. A moment later, my bedroom door opens with a soft knock and my aunt is standing in the threshold. She takes one look at my stance and then her gaze flicks over to the calendar on my wall. She sees the words I scribbled in Sharpie and looks back at me with silver lining her eyes. I uncross my arms and open them for her, a silent invitation for me to hug her. She leans into my chest, and I wrap my arms tightly around her back.

"This will all be over soon, Aunt Viv." I say, but I also don't know what else to tell her.

I pull her back so I can look into her eyes, and I give her a soft smile. "I can't say that everything will be okay, but I can say this. I will do everything I can to come back. I think Mr. Harper is right in saying that how I end this battle is my own choice, and I have to figure out how much power it will take to destroy this thing and come back to you all." I say while brushing a tear off her cheek. "I love you, Aunt Viv."

"Love you too, Aiden." She whispers.

We stand in the middle of my room, just holding one another for a few more minutes, before she pulls back and runs her hands over my chest, resting both of them over my heart, and when she looks up at me with tears trailing through her makeup, I see her resolve. I see her faith that I will come back and she holds that like a life raft between us.

"I am not going to believe that on that date," She says as she points to the calendar, "will be the end. You are still meant for bigger things, Aiden Rivers, and I'm gonna hold you to that."

I smile and her words warm something deep in my soul.

"Thank you, Aunt Viv." I say while using the pads of my thumbs to dry her eyes.

"How about helping me with dinner?" She asks with a tearful smile on her face.

"I would love to." I reply and I walk her out of my room and softly close the door behind me.

After Aunt Viv and I fix dinner, which consists of spaghetti and garlic bread, I insist she take a seat at the dining table while I bring out the pot on a hot pad and set it in the middle of the table.

Aunt Viv lovingly fills Uncle Matt's plate, then her own, while I bring the fresh out-of-the-oven bread on the cooling rack and set that on the table as well. I fill my own plate with noodles and bread before taking my seat.

"This is amazing like always, Vivie." Uncle Matt says after his first bite.

"Well, Aiden here is getting pretty good at remembering the spices I put in it. So, we may have a competition of who can make the best spaghetti soon." Aunt Viv says, while giving me a wink.

"I could never be as good as you, Aunt Viv." I say while I take a bite, letting the Italian and garlic seasoning with just a hint of sugar dance across my tongue.

Just as we are finishing up with dinner and I clear the plates from the table to load the dishwasher, I go back into the dining room and I see Uncle Matt reading the newspaper while Aunt Viv looks at Facebook on her phone. I take my seat across from my aunt and uncle, sucking in a breath before I voice the thoughts that still have been plaguing me since I found out the end date this afternoon.

"Uncle Matt. Aunt Viv. I need to talk to you about something." I begin while rubbing the back of my neck.

Uncle Matt drops his newspaper and Aunt Viv looks up from her phone. Once she sees my face, she locks it and sets it on the table while wrapping an arm around Uncle Matt's forearm.

"I hate to say this to you guys. I know how much money you all spent on college for me, and I;m so close to finishing my degree this year, but I—" I begin, but my uncle's laughter fills the dining room, cutting off my words.

"You mean to tell me you are about to go and save the world for The Protector's of Power and you are worried about dropping out of college?" Uncle Matt asks incredulously. "I'm surprised you didn't drop out sooner, to be honest."

"We understand, Aiden. Go and do what you need to and when this is all said and done, you can pick up where you left off." Aunt Viv says with a small smile.

I keep hearing her promises of 'I can live life after all this is done.' Keep hearing my friends, my teammates tell me the same things, and I'm starting to believe it. Starting to hold on to the possibility that even I will make it to see the twenty-ninth of November all because my friends, my family will it into existence.

I grab on to that notion and hold on to it like a vice in my soul.

54

Aiden

The next morning, I go to the admissions office and sign the necessary paperwork to make the drop-out official, but that makes the heaviness in my chest set in deeper instead of lifting it.

As I'm walking out of the office, I run into Ivan and Gray in the hall, but they walk past me and into the admissions office without a word. I wait for them to come back out and when they emerge a few minutes later, Ivan throws his arm around my neck with a smile.

"Now, let's get crackin'." Ivan says with a smirk.

I smile at knowing my friends just signed their own drop-out papers too, and I pull Gray into my other side with an arm around his neck.

"You wanna see if the four of us can kick Seth's ass in the forest?" I ask.

"Hell yeah!" Ivan says with a cocky smile.

I reach out to Seth with the mental connection I have to him and ask him to meet us at the forest, then ask Maya to do the same and they both agree to meet us there in thirty minutes. I remove my arm from around Gray's neck and Ivan does the same to me and I lead us out of the university, with Ivan on my right and Gray on my left.

Just as we are a few steps from the door, I watch as Mason and Rhett come out of a classroom on the left side of the hallway and they stare us down. I know deep down I shouldn't, but I let some of my lightning skitter down my left arm while giving Mason a wicked smile and I continue to walk out of the building, not being one bit bothered to have my back to him. I hear him growl under his breath at my actions, but he doesn't do anything more.

"That was kinda reckless, Aiden." Gray says once we are out of earshot and walking towards the parking lot.

"I agree, but I liked the look on Mason's face at your challenge, Aiden. I can't wait to kick their asses for the last time." Ivan says while curling his right hand into a fist and letting some of his metal skin show across his knuckles.

"I know it wasn't the smartest thing, but I couldn't help myself." I say with a sly smile. "Now, let's get to the forest." I say while pointing my head to my Colorado and Ivan's Mustang.

After we get to the forest, I notice that Maya's Passat is parked in the grass and I only assume that Seth teleported here since I don't see his car. When the three of us walk into the clearing, I spot Maya sitting on a log talking animatedly with Seth and I can tell he's listening to her every word.

Seth's eyes drift over her shoulder as we walk up to them, and Maya turns her head to see what Seth is looking at. When she faces me, there is a purple wildflower in her hair just above her left ear and I can't help but smile as I walk up to her. I take her right hand in my left and pull her to her feet, then gently caress the flower in her hair and stare into her ocean blue eyes.

"I thought I'd take a little stroll until you all got here." She says with a small smile.

"It looks beautiful on you." I say softly, but Seth clears his throat, and that stops me from leaning into her for a kiss.

Looking over at him, he has a mixture of impatience but almost understanding at the little scene between me and Maya.

"So I'm assuming you want to know why I called you both here?" I ask, while taking a step back from Maya's side.

"That would be helpful, yes." Seth asks with a smirk.

"Smart ass." Ivan grumbles, but I see he's trying not to grin at Seth's remark as he's pulling Gray against his side.

"I want us to run a battle scenario." I say, and Seth's smile falters.

"What do you mean, Aiden?" Seth asks.

"I want you to come at us all at once. We have been practicing on a one-on-one basis. Well, now, I think we need to make it seem like an active battle, with as many moving parts as we can." I say.

"So you want me to act like Victor coming after you all?" Seth replies darkly.

"I wasn't going to say it that way, but yes, that's what it boils down to." I tell him while looking into his hard green eyes.

"Alright, but don't come whining to me when I kick your asses." Seth says as he walks to the center of the clearing a few yards away.

"How are we going to do this, Aiden? Do you have a plan?" Maya asks.

"Yup, I do. It all depends on what his first move is." I begin. *"Then we have the upper hand with this neat little trick."* I say to all of them through our mental connection while keeping Seth's side of the connection dark.

"Oh, this is gonna be good." Ivan replies, and I feel his excitement at this mock battle bubbling up in him.

"Maya, you get on his left. Gray, you get behind him. And Ivan, you're on his right." I say as we walk toward him.

I watch as my friends all take the places that I instructed them to. Seth watches them out of his peripheral vision, but never fully takes his eyes off me.

"You all ready for this?" Seth asks, his face unreadable.

"Give us your worst, Seth." I dare as I lock onto his electrical pulse so I can track him when he eventually teleports.

"Okay, you asked for it." Seth croons.

He looks between the four of us as if deciding which one to go after first, and I realize that he pulled his sleeves down so we can't see what power he's using until it's already coming at us. I growl at him and let my lightning and fire dance in both of my hands.

"We won't know what power he's using until he unleashes it." I tell my friends.

"Oh, he's sneaky." Ivan says as he activates his metal skin.

Seth then teleports, and I feel him going toward Maya's side of the clearing. I push my fire to my foot to help me close the distance and I reach out to her mind.

"On your right, about seven feet out. Send your water cyclone out." I tell her.

Maya does what I tell her and I snake my electricity out around her water like it's second nature and an instant later Seth is trapped in the middle. I continue into the cyclone, the coldness of Maya's water biting into my skin as I pass through the element. Seth grins at me, but holds his ground.

I swiftly close the six feet between us and I pull my arm back in a flaming fist, aiming for his face, but he teleports at the last second and my fist smashes into the water wall, making my flames die in my hand.

Only water made by a power can extinguish my flames.

I growl and just as I turn around to face him; he has a watery fist aiming for my face. I try to connect to the lightning that's snaking around me, but I can't force it through the water wall, or else I will shock Maya.

So instead I make a firewall to block his attack, but it's useless against the water. He makes a wave of water with his left hand, quickly extinguishing my shield. I notice too late that the knuckles of his right hand have sharp ice flecks pointing directly at me. As his fist connects with my stomach, the ice shards pierce my skin and I am thrown through the water wall and into a nearby tree. The breath is knocked out of me in a painful whoosh as I crumple to the ground.

Maya screams my name and just as I open my eyes to look at her, Seth appears in front of me. I push my fire down to my foot and take off to the right side of the forest, and just when I think I am in the clear, I feel something encircle my chest like a vice, holding me in place about five feet in the air. I feel the surprisingly gentle breeze of wind and I know that Seth is using that to keep me hanging in this space. He could also crush my chest if he wanted to, and that thought alone almost makes the panic flare in my mind if I didn't see what was coming up from behind him.

I try to push my fire toward him as a distraction, but he instantly snuffs it out with the wind that is circling around my torso. When I know the coming attack is ready to be sprung, I pull my fire just to the tip of my fingers so I can make my shield once his wind fades and I give a dark smile.

"You might want to look behind you."

Just as I say that, Gray, who has been riding on a stream of water toward us, tosses the shock grenade at Seth and it explodes two seconds later. As Seth releases the wind around my body to try and make his own firewall as protection from the ball, he fails as the blast rocks through him, sending him flying over my head and cracking not one but two trees in half.

"You okay dude?" Gray asks as he hops off the water's surface.

I rub my chest as the ache from the death grip Seth's wind had on me subsides and I nod my head. Maya and Ivan run over to us as we wait for Seth to unlock his body that I know firsthand is frozen from the shock.

"Note to self, Maya, we need to figure out a way for me to have my lightning on the inside of your water." I say as I scan the tree line. "I was a sitting duck in there. I couldn't use my fire because he was using his water against me, and if I made any new electricity, I might have shocked you if I missed an attack."

"We'll figure it out." Maya says. courtesy

"That shock was nice, Gray, but here's mine." Seth says suddenly as he appears behind us.

I look over my shoulder in shock and I mentally kick myself for not keeping his electrical pulse in my mind. Seth's yellow and black lightning dances across his fingers a moment before he flicks his wrist, sending it skittering over the ground towards us.

I begin to gather my own power to try to cancel his out, but a metal wall, courtsey of Ivan, appears in front of us and with that, the electrical pulse from Seth arcs and dies before it hits us. I find Seth's pulse again and I feel him teleporting so many times I can't keep track of him. Just as he lands in one spot, he teleports to a new one.

"Damn it. He's teleporting too quick for me to pinpoint him." I growl.

"That's right. You're not going to get me that easily." Seth says coolly from behind us.

I feel his fire flare behind me before I even turn around and I make my fire shield to protect our group, but his fire is trying to push through and I feel the shield wanting to give in.

"Gray, get the Ice Blaster now." I say.

Gray doesn't hesitate. He pokes his head around my shield, braving the heat enough to spot Seth, and with calculated aim, he tosses the ball. It lands right in front of Seth and goes off a second later. Seth's fire instantly dies, and he screams as the thousands of ice shards impale his body.

"Ivan, make your wall behind him." I order.

I push my fire to my foot just as the iron wall comes up behind a still reeling Seth and I charge up my electricity. I close the distance so fast that Seth has no time to dodge or even teleport from my attack. I drive my electrical fist into his gut and I force him into the iron wall while I let the pulse flow through him. I somehow start to feel Seth gather the energy he needs to teleport and when I grab onto his sleeve at the last second, I am pulled through space and time with him.

I feel us hit the ground again a few feet away and I instantly send a fiery haymaker into his face. He stumbles a few steps back to collect himself, panting heavily. When I feel my friends come up behind me, I instantly start giving them orders.

"Maya, get your wind tight around his chest like a fist. Ivan, try to chain him to the ground. Can you tap into the metal of his body to make the connection? Gray, you have another shock grenade ready?" I ask as I fire off question after question to my team.

Ivan and Gray nod in silent answer to my questions, but before we can even make any moves to attack, Seth teleports and is instantly behind Ivan. I watch as my friend is grabbed by the back of his neck and Seth teleports away.

I instantly look for Seth's electrical pulse and I feel him stop before he appears on the other side of the clearing. Seth leans down next to Ivan's ear and says something to him before my friend starts to grab at his throat. Pure terror fills his eyes, and I instantly know what's going on.

Seth is trying to choke out Ivan in the way that I fear Victor will.

My body feels like it's full of lead, and I don't think I will get there fast enough to cut the wind from Ivan's head.

But I have to be faster. I have to get there to save him.

I push my fire to my foot and hold it for an instant before I jet across the clearing faster than even I can comprehend, and I force myself between Ivan and Seth while charging up my electrical pulse. At the last second, I force the charge into Seth's chest to push him away. Ivan falls to the ground coughing and I reach out to Maya and send her an image of her water around Seth again with my electricity and she immediately makes her water vortex as I snake my lightning around it.

We begin to pull the two elements tighter around Seth, and just before they touch, we disconnect ourselves from them and I pull Maya into my chest to protect her from the discharge that came off the water's surface a heartbeat later. The lightning dies in the air and I release Maya from my grasp while giving her a small smile at what we did.

Through the dust that hangs in the air near the tree line, we see a figure walk toward us. I take a few steps toward Seth, figuring he called the training to talk to us like he normally does after a session. But the person who walks through the tree line isn't Seth, and my blood turns to ice in my veins.

"I see my lackeys aren't getting the job done. So I will." Victor sneers.

55

Aiden

I am shell-shocked to see Victor standing in front of us, and I have a million things running through my mind at once.

Can we end this here without even destroying The Siphon yet? Mason and Rhett can be taken care of, but him. He is the mastermind running everything.

But I can't get my body to move, none of us can. We are all stuck like a deer in the headlights of a car.

"*We have to* move, *guys.*" I urge my friends.

"*Where's Seth?*" Maya asks. "*What if he hurt him?*"

"*We can't worry about that now.*" I say.

Victor takes another step toward us and he makes an enormous tornado that is even more destructive and deadly than anything that's been seen in nature. I take a step back, and that seems to break Maya out of her trance. She makes her own tornado, and she lets her water soak through the ground at the same time so she can pick up the dirt easier, which makes her wind denser and harder to pass through. Watching her make the first attack breaks through the shock at who's in front of us and we all finally leap into action.

I rush over to Gray to recharge the Shock Grenade for him and bring my own powers to both hands and while Victor is busy with Maya; I go right for his ugly face with a flaming fist. He dodges my attack, but I pivot and send my left leg flying into his stomach with a shock that cracks off him so loudly that the trees vibrate from the sound.

Victor flies back a few feet from my kick, catches himself with his wind, and seems to be floating in the sky, watching us, trying to figure out which one to go after next. But I don't give him time to decide. I push my fire to my foot and I get up to him while building up my electricity. As I see him move toward Gray, I draw my left arm back and punch him square in the chest while releasing a shock wave through my knuckles. As my current fades, I realize with horrifying clarity, he's still in the air with me, seemingly unphased.

Then I understand that he actually stopped my shock wave with a condensed pocket of wind that dispersed the power around him. My heart sinks to my stomach and before I can even push my fire to my foot to back away, his wind tightens around my chest, squeezing so tight that stars burst at the corner of my vision and I can barely get a breath into my lungs.

"Aiden!" Maya screams, but I can't see her as darkness begins to flood my vision from lack of oxygen.

I hear a faint metallic click somewhere near me, then Gray's voice echoing in my ears. "Hey, asshole! Get the fuck away from my friend!"

Then an instant later, ice shards pepper my arms and face as the Ice Grenade goes off. Victor screams as they impale deeply into his back. With my mind hazy from the lack of oxygen, I barely comprehend when gravity around me shifts. I can't figure out why or what's causing it.

"Aiden!" Gray screams.

Once my name registers in my head, I know I'm falling, but I can't get my body to move. Internally, I am screaming for my fire to ignite in my foot and hand, but it won't work. I'm still fighting for the breath to fill my burning lungs.

Then I feel something cool and soft envelop me and gently lay me against the rough trunk of a tree for a moment before I feel something collide with my chest. The pain and sudden pressure forces me to take my first breath in what seemed like ages. I take a few more raspy breaths before I can make my eyes focus on who is around me. Maya is to my right and on my left, the one who just railed me in the chest, is Ivan.

"Are you alright?" Ivan asks while looking over his shoulder.

"Yeah. Fuck that hurt." I say while rubbing my chest and taking a few more breaths to force the stars away.

"If you can get to your feet, we gotta move." Ivan says, while taking a step away from me.

I look over his shoulder and my stomach drops when I see Gray still facing off with Victor. The brave and/or stupid bastard is still throwing those balls at him. I take one more breath and stand to my feet, testing to make sure my powers are working again. When they both flare in my hand, I look at Ivan and nod once.

"Make a wall behind him. I'm gonna fucking light him up." I say while I bring my fire around my fist and I make it as hot as I can.

Ivan nods and gives me a dark grin to let me know he's ready. I push my fire to my foot and take off toward Victor and Gray.

"Hey Victor! It's time we end this!" I yell.

Victor steps back from Gray and out of the corner of my vision, I see Maya use her water to get Gray out of the way of my attack. Just as I see Ivan's wall come up behind Victor, I pull my fire to my fist and it lights up such a dark red that even I can feel the heat of my own flame and I know it's gonna hurt like a bitch once I land my blow.

As Victor's back hits Ivan's metal wall, his green eyes fill with fear. I bring my fist down and just as I am about to connect with his chest; he disappears and my fist collides with Ivan's wall. Pain fills my hand as the bones bend at an unnatural angle and the metal starts to melt around my fire, but confusion at what just happened makes everything else seem trivial.

Victor can't teleport. I think to myself.

Just as that thought hits my mind, I feel the lightest of tingling in the back of my head and I instantly look to my left where Victor appears, and I see the sly smirk that forms on his face.

"You fuckin' sneaky bastard." I say with a small grin.

"What the fuck is going on, Aiden?" Ivan asks with pure fear in his voice.

"Oh, that's right. You all haven't seen this, have you?" I ask, my voice holding a bit of annoyance.

"Seen what?" Gray asks. "Aiden, what's going on?"

"Yeah Aiden, what's going on? Do tell your little group of weaklings." Victor sneers.

"I have to say, the acting is spot on." I tell him, and he throws his head back in a burst of laughter.

"Aiden, stop fucking around and tell us what's going on." Ivan demands.

"This is Seth, guys. It's one of his mind tricks." I say while pointing to my right temple.

My friends look at me like I have lost my ever-loving mind.

"I think you suffered some brain damage from lack of oxygen, Aiden. Either that or the flame you just made fried it." Ivan scoffs.

"Ivan, Victor can't teleport. Only Seth can. What the hell just happened a few minutes ago, just before I went in for the kill? He fucking teleported!" I yell.

"He does have a point." Maya says as she really looks at the person standing now only five feet from us.

I stare at my friends and I slowly start to see the realization hit their faces as that little tickle finds the back of their minds.

"This is all kinds of fucked up." Ivan says as he looks at Seth.

"Good ole Mimic trick. I can make you all see anything I want you to see, just as long as you don't feel me in the back of your mind. Once you see that it's an illusion, I lose all control." Seth explains.

"Which is why when he teleported, that's when I knew something was up and I saw through the illusion." I add.

"Well, I couldn't let you finish that attack, which was actually very good, Aiden. But I don't want to die just yet." Seth says. "You all worked very well together once you got over your shock."

I look at my team, taking in their tired smiles, and I agree with Seth. "He's right. We did a good job at playing off one another. And Gray, dude. You were great. Facing off against 'Victor'." I say with air quotes. "You did that alone while I was getting my shit together."

"I just didn't think much of it. I knew the grenades I had should have been enough to at least distract him until someone came to back me up." Gray says simply.

Seth closes the distance between us and heals those who need it and heals himself last. I do feel kind of guilty for how hard we went on him; but that's what happens when you fake us out and make yourself look like our enemy.

"Now go home, rest. We will talk more in the coming days. Three weeks will come faster than you all realize." Seth says and then teleports without another word.

"Well, you heard the man. Rest up and we'll figure out the next step in all this." I say as I take my hand in Maya's and give it a small squeeze.

"You got it, Captain. See ya soon." Ivan nods and walks out of the forest with Gray on his heels.

My eyes slide over to Maya and she has a small smile still playing at the corner of her lips while a bead of sweat rolls off her temple.

"You fought hard today." I whisper, while wiping the sweat from her brow.

"We'll I've had some good teachers. Seth, Ivan, and you." She says, poking me in the chest with her index finger. "Was I scared? Absolutely. Did I think for a second we didn't stand a chance? Actually, no. I believe we are stronger than *his* group. We just have to be able to act on sudden changes we didn't expect to happen." She says.

"I think that was Seth's goal today. To throw a wrench into our plan and see how we reacted." I say, while looking around the clearing. The broken and burned trees, the iron that is still poking out of the ground from Ivan's walls, and the areas of standing water puddles on the ground. "I think we did a damn good job."

Maya gives me a warm smile and I glance at her lips for an instant then back into her clear blue eyes, which seem to soften at my silent plea. I slowly lean down but keep just a breath away, and that brings an inaudible sigh from her lips and I cock one side of my mouth up in response.

"I love you, Maya, and you are a force to be reckoned with." I say.

I lean in and finally give her what she wanted. At first, her kiss is soft and teasing, but once my lips part, her tongue darts inside and I meet her stroke for stroke.

I then begin to trail kisses across her cheek, her jaw, down the soft curve of her neck and she bends to allow me more access. Pulling her in close to me while my hands roam her body, I back her into a nearby tree and I let her feel the growing, aching bulge through my jeans of how much I want round two of what we did in this forest not too long ago to happen again.

She moves her hand as if to grab at me through the rough fabric, but a snapping twig makes us jump and break apart, readying for another fight and instantly killing our arousal. What we see almost makes me want to go to my knees with delight and a bit of embarrassment.

"We just got jump scared by a freaking doe." I chuckle.

Maya laughs and takes my hand again while looking at the young white-tailed doe and her fawn happily flicking its tail and trying to graze on the grass.

"Come on, let's go before we have any other forest animals trying to take notes from us." Maya says with mischief in her eyes.

It's my turn to laugh and I lead her to her Passat, making sure she's inside safely before we both drive away from the forest.

56

Aiden

Over the next few days, I try to figure out where The Siphon is located. The internet isn't much help and neither are the libraries both at the University or the local library that have several texts on The Protector's of Power.

It's like all they know is this exists and what it does, but not the exact location. So, I put the books back on the shelves and I decide to drive over to Seth's place.

"Hey, Seth. I'm heading your way. Are you home?" I ask.

"Yeah, I'm home. What's up?" Seth asks.

"I'll let you know when I get there." I reply.

When I arrive at his house, I walk up to his recessed porch and I hear the lock of the door being turned and Seth lets me in before I can even knock. As I take a seat on the sofa in his living room, I notice his TV is showing the local sports highlights, and I can't help but grin at the screen. Seth finds me eyeing the TV and with a shake of his head, he picks up the remote control to turn it off and then looks back at me while taking a seat in one of the wingback chairs to my right.

"So, what do I owe the pleasure of this meeting?" Seth asks.

"Do you have any idea where The Siphon is?" I ask. "I have been trying to figure it out and I have no idea. There is nothing at all in the libraries or the University. Mrs. Jaffee doesn't even remember where it was. She and her husband were blindfolded when they were kidnapped." I explain while running my hands through my hair in a fit of annoyance.

"Last I heard, it was in South Bolder Park. But that was twenty years ago. I searched everywhere too, and even I couldn't find it." Seth says and is quiet for a few moments before he adds. "I don't know how Victor did it, but he somehow moved it from the location that he actually built it on, which was these grounds. The same ground where he took your uncle's powers and forced your parents to side with him." Seth says with a darkness to his tone.

"Are you serious?" I ask in shock.

"This was our parent's land. He and I grew up here. But when he only developed wind and not Mimic abilities like me, he went off the deep end. Our parents fawned and bragged about me and left him in the shadows. It wasn't until it was too late that they figure that even with one ability, he could overpower me if he wanted to. Victor ended up killing our parents, and taking over this land to make The Siphon." Seth says, pain at the memory filling his voice.

"Wow, Seth. I'm sorry." I offer.

"So after that, I met Matt, Avery, and Cole. They started to hear rumors of what was being built on my family's land and they offered to help me, but little did I know that would even drive your family apart." Seth looks away when he adds, "Your mother's last words to me after she and your father were taken and before the connection I had with them went dark was 'South Boulder Park. Please take care of my boy'."

"Well, that's not far from here. Maybe Gray can take one of his drones and fly over the park. We can find it that way." I say softly.

"I've looked over that whole park for years, and I can't find it at all. I seriously don't know how the hell Victor has hidden it all these years, but he has." Seth says with anger in his voice.

"Well, we will find it and end it soon enough." I say with determination.

"All I know is it has to be near a water source. About a mile from this house is a river. That's where the machine was originally built. So, where ever he moves it to there has got to be a powerful river nearby." Seth offers.

Later that night, as my aunt and uncle are in the kitchen cooking dinner for me, Maya, Ivan, and Gray, we are all piled in the living room. Ivan and Gray are on the couch while Maya and I take the loveseat. I lean against the arm and she lies against me with her back to my chest and I hold her waist with my left arm.

She idly traces the lines in my lightning tattoo and it's all I can do to not lean in and kiss her neck, but I know for a fact that she can feel how much her touch makes me yearn for her, and she subtly wiggles her ass against me at times to prove she indeed knows.

Finally, she rests her head on my shoulder, and I close my eyes as she gets comfortable. Then, a few minutes later, I feel myself slip into a vision.

I see the forest like I have so many times before. We walk up to that damn machine. Mason, Rhett, and Victor trying to stop us, but we're able to beat them. And as I see myself floating in the air, I look at my friends and my love one last time and I let my powers go. Let them engulf this machine to destroy it once and for all. I watch as Victor tries to stop me, but my fire actually burns his wind from the air, finds him, and engulfs him as well. I can feel my soul power aching at the energy I'm releasing, but I push past this pain, knowing that I am the only one that can destroy The Siphon and this madman. Bright flashes of white and orange erupt in my vision, then everything fades to black.

But then, as if something grabs at the back of my shirt, I am pulled backward almost. Backward in time. I see myself at the library, trying again to research the location of this machine, and Mason walks up to me with a haunted expression on his face. Then I am flashed back to the final battle. The forest remains the same, but something is off about Mason, but I can't pinpoint what it is. The images are too quick to tell if he's helping us or he's still against us.

I slip back into reality, and my head is bent backward over the arm of the loveseat. Maya's right hand is holding onto mine while her water searching inside my body as if making sure I'm okay. I slowly lift my head to give her a kiss on her temple to let her know that I'm alright, but an instant headache hits me and I bring my left hand up to my temple to rub away the pressure.

I guess the headache was brought on because whatever happened, or is about to happen, that made the future change a bit and my clairvoyance showed it to me in the same vision. She tilts her head back with a question on her lips, but I shake my head.

"It's okay." I whisper. "Nothing major has changed."

Which is true. Just because Mason and I met in a library doesn't mean anything had changed. He could have been trying to tell me to back off.

Mason

My phone buzzing on the nightstand with a text message wakes me out of a deep sleep. When it buzzes again, I gently roll Dani off my chest with a slight moan of annoyance at her sleep being interrupted and I give her a small smile and kiss her temple.

"Sorry, Angel." I croon.

She groans again and wraps her arms around my left bicep while I reach for my phone with my right hand. I see a missed call and a text from Victor, and I have to hold back a groan of my own, but my blood runs cold at his text message.

Victor

Found two new test subjects. It looks promising. Get your ass over here.

I feel my muscles tense as I read the message, and Dani lifts her head from my shoulder.

"What's wrong?" She asks with a hint of fear in her voice.

I look at her, and the apprehension in her sleepy blue eyes breaks my heart. I throw my phone on the table again and I pull her into my side. She rests her hands on my chest while her right thumb rubs over the colored part of my fiery tattoo, right over my heart, and it sends a shiver down my spine.

"Why can't you tell him to fuck off and we get out of here?" Dani asks.

I run my fingers through her silky blonde hair and I take in the rosy scent of her shampoo still lingering on the strands.

"It's complicated, but I promise you, I will be free of him one day. *We* will be free of him." I say.

If Aiden is able to take care of Victor like I think he can, then that's my ticket for a real life with Dani. I just have to keep playing along until that time comes.

"I gotta go meet up with him for a bit. I'll be back later." I say as I give Dani a sound kiss on the lips, and she moans in my mouth as she grinds her hips against me.

I reluctantly pull away, but I smack her ass playfully to let her know I will happily take her up on her offer later.

As I arrive at South Boulder Park thirty minutes later, I walk toward the river, and there, nestled in the tree line, sits The Siphon. To other people, there is nothing standing here due to the cloaking technology Victor invented. He only allows myself and Rhett to see the monstrosity hiding among the trees because he has our blood added to the recognition system.

When I walk through the main entrance, I see the low-hanging mist pooling along the floors. My stomach fills with rocks when this tells me the cooling system is running. This keeps the machine from overheating when the pods are active. I have to force back the bile that threatens to climb up my throat and push myself to enter the main transfer area.

I see Rhett first as I round the corner. He's standing over Victor's shoulder as if he's double checking Victor's calculations, and I know better than that. Rhett is so simple-minded it's laughable. But when I glance at the two pods that are lit up and see the bodies that fill up each chamber, I clench my fists in anger.

"Not right. Protect us. Protect them." I hear my flame whisper as they want to flicker to life from my fingers, wanting to tear this place apart.

I ball my fists up so tight that I feel my nails pierce the skin and the tendons of my knuckles pop from the force, all to keep my anger in check. I take a breath and force myself to join Victor and Rhett at the control panel. I glance up at the large screen in front of me and slowly take in the words that are written in a digital, blocky green font. As usual, there are no personal names, just strict facts.

2 male test subjects.

Mid-to-late twenties.

Abilities are present in both subjects.

Male in Pod #1: Water.

Male in Pod #2: Earth.

Test Method: Transferring powers from Pod #1 to Pod #2.

My knees want to give out. This is the very thing I told Victor the last time we tried to transfer powers to someone who didn't have any; didn't have a Soul Power. The images of a woman with water powers and the man that was human; the man who actually had the water tattoo appear on his arms before he exploded like a fucking bloody water balloon comes to mind.

I basically signed the death certificates of these two men before us. I told Victor that only people who had Soul Powers may have a chance of making this work. I never meant for this to happen.

"Initiating Ability Transfer in...3...2...1." Victor says, and he presses the red button in the middle of the control panel.

The machine around me begins to hum, drawing in more power while hidden mechanisms begin to whirr to life in a deafening tone. But no matter how many sounds assault my ears, I can still hear the screams from these two men. I can see the horror on their faces, while the whole time, Victor's face is unreadable like always and Rhett has this sick look of wonder if this will finally be the day the transfer will work, while I have to work past the vomit that wants to spew all over this control panel.

I involuntarily take a step back into the shadows so I can try to keep my anger and stomach in check while I helplessly watch the screen in front of us show the progress bar. And what slides across the screen makes me lean against the wall to keep my knees from buckling.

Transfer Rate: 50% Complete

Transfer Rate: 75% Complete

Transfer Rate: 88% Complete

I silently shake my head in disbelief. This might actually be happening.

Transfer Rate: 97% Complete

"The fucker might actually make this thing work." I whisper as my heart drops to my feet.

Just as it's about to hit one hundred percent, the power fails and everything whirs down until deafening silence fills the room. As I send up a silent prayer of thanks to whoever allowed this experiment to fail, Victor's growl vibrates off the metallic wall. The sound of it sends a shiver down my spine that makes me push off the wall and stand up fully on my feet.

"Damn it! We were so close!" Victor snarls while slamming a fist into the darkened control panel.

I step out of the shadows to stand next to them and stare at Victor for a moment before I make myself focus on Rhett. I can see it in his eyes that he is already scheming for another plan. I glance over to the pods, to the lifeless eyes staring back at me, and my anger flares. My flames want to claw out of my hands and burn the hell out of Victor. Burn this fucking death trap to the ground, but somehow I keep them in check.

"Victor, you need to quit now before you kill every last person on the planet. This isn't going to work." I growl, my voice dark and deep with fury.

"All he needs is more power." Rhett chimes in before Victor can respond. "You were so close this time, Victor!"

"I agree. We need to find an area with a stronger water current." Victor says while making notes in his extensive and well-used notebook. "Mason, find us another spot." Victor demands.

"You both are crazy bastards." I say in a surprisingly cool tone. "I'm done here. I'm not killing any more innocent people."

I storm out of the room, briskly walk to my Challenger, and race home to Dani. I have no clue where we will go, but we are getting out of here. Tonight.

I pull up to the townhouse, tires squealing on the driveway as I throw the car in park, and slam the door as I step out. Dani opens the front door and, somehow, in my anger-fueled movements, I gently take her arms and pull her into my chest.

"Get your important things we're getting out of here." I whisper, then I let her go so I can start pulling clothes from our dressers.

"What happened?" Dani asks, fear clouding her words as she pulls a suitcase from the closet.

"Victor just killed two more people and I'm honestly to blame for it." I snap, but she knows it's not at her. "I'm tired of seeing people die."

"Mason, Baby, you didn't kill them." Dani says.

"I might as well have!" I shout. "I told Victor that the subjects needed to have a Soul Power to have even a *chance* of the transfer happening. And what the hell does he do?! He gets two guys and tried to swap their powers! I gave him that idea! I signed their fucking death warrants!" I yell, tears stinging my eyes.

I spin around, and with a flaming right fist, I smash my hand into the wall, letting the pain cloud my thoughts for a few blissful moments. Dani comes up behind me and leans her forehead against my back while her arms wrap around my waist. I try to push her away, but she stands her ground against me.

"I don't want to burn you." I whisper.

I feel my flames going wild under my skin and I know the slightest emotional change will set my body alight. Images of my father losing his mind and burning my mother flood my mind and I close my eyes tightly to keep the memory at bay.

"No, you won't burn me. I have faith in you, Mason. You are more in control than you think." Dani says softly into my back while blindly lifting her left hand to find again where that colored flame sits over my heart.

Sometimes I hate that oddity about me, but other times it's all I can hold on to when the world around me comes closing in, like now. I lean my forehead into the wall and I take a breath at her words.

"Dani. Love and protect." My flames whisper.

I instantly feel them pull back a little as those words filter through my chaotic mind. I force myself to turn in her arms and look down at her. I see pure fiery determination in her eyes, and I give her a small smile.

"Let's get out of here, Baby." Dani croons as she gives me a solid kiss on the lips.

We grab whatever items we need and fill our suitcases within ten minutes. After she zips up the third suitcase, I gather them by the door to be able to grab them easily as we walk out. While I do that, Dani goes into our closet, to a hidden hole in the wall I had cut out within a week of us moving in and she grabs what money we had saved up from the fireproof lockbox and stuffs it into her wallet, leaving the box open on the floor. I usher her out the front door, not even bothering to close or lock it. I figure let the next poor bastard call this slump home.

I open the passenger door of my Challenger for her while I throw the three suitcases in the trunk. I glance around to make sure no one is watching us as I drop into the driver's seat and start the engine with a monstrous roar.

We get to the main stop sign of the run-down community, and I pause for a moment. We have the option to go left toward town or right for the highway. I look at Dani and I know I want to get the hell out of here as fast as possible. I get ready to turn right, but just as I am about to press the accelerator, I look in the rearview mirror and see a gigantic dark gray tornado barreling down the road toward us and my heart stops in my chest. Dani looks back when she starts to hear the wind pick up and the fear that floods her face makes my blood boil.

"Get ready to run. I'll try to hold him off." I say and I run my hand over her cheek.

"Mason, you—" She begins, but I cut her off with a look.

"Run, Angel. Please." I beg as I throw the car in park, not bothering to turn the ignition off.

She gets out at the same time I do, takes one look at the tornado, and tries to take a small step backward toward the highway, but fear freezes her in place. I allow my fire to come to my hands in a silent challenge for this bastard to come at me. I know my flames will do nothing against his wind, but if I can find him, then I can fight the source of the tornado in front of me.

The tornado keeps coming at us with no sign of stopping. The wind violently tearing at our clothes and hair as it gets closer to us. I turn my attention toward Dani and I know there is no way she can outrun this monstrous vortex.

My long legs eat up the distance between us, and I pull her into my chest. I somehow wrap my fire around us while desperately trying to pull the heat out to keep from burning at least the parts that are against her skin, while my own skin is scorched from where it's wrapped around my back, but I couldn't care less.

As I feel the wall of the tornado engulf us, we go spiraling higher into the vortex and Dani's nails dig into my skin, trying to hold tighter onto my waist. Over the roar of the wind, I hear the metallic sound of metal bending and breaking against the pressure, and I know my Challenger is destroyed.

"I love you, Dani. I'm sorry I dragged you into this." I say into her ear.

I know she hears me, because I feel her shake her head against my chest as if to say, *you didn't drag me here. I wanted to be with you.* Suddenly, the wind vanishes with such force that our ears pop at the pressure change and I feel ourselves falling. I pivot my body at the last second and take the full brunt of us slamming into the pavement.

My back screams at me in agony, but I grit my teeth against the pain and keep my arms and fire around Dani. Keeping her close to my chest. I then feel something almost like an invisible helmet glide over my head and the wind that follows threatens to take my breath. I bring my arms up, letting Dani go physically.

She sits up to back away from the sphere of wind around my head and I hope to at least keep my flames around her, but they fade from her too, as I find myself clawing at the invisible wall of wind, trying and utterly failing to tear a hole so I can breathe.

Dani stays on my waist, her legs straddling me, thighs tightening against my ribs. It's the only thing she has to keep herself locked on to me. I barely feel her balling my shirt in her small fist while she looks around to see if anyone is coming near us while I desperately try to fight against Victor's wind.

Just as my vision starts to go dark, I see a figure walk up behind her. I try to warn her, try to lift my arm to point behind her, but my body is starting to fail me. From the impact against the pavement or lack of oxygen, I don't know, but my body won't listen.

Just as Victor goes to grab her, his wind dissipates and I know it's so I can clearly hear the blood-curdling scream that rips from Dani's throat.

"Let me go, you crazy bastard!" Dani screams while trying to kick her feet into his stomach, but fails.

With every breath I take, my back screams in protest, but I force it to the back of my mind as I take in Victor holding Dani up by the back of her neck. She claws at his fingers, but she can't pry his hands off her. I try to get up. Try to go to her, but I can't fucking move.

"Trying to heal, but too much damage." My flames tell me.

"Hurry the hell up. We have to get to her." I respond.

"Look at this pretty little thing of yours. She has such a *fire* in her, don't you think, Mason?" Victor croons.

"Stay the fuck away from her." I growl as I feel my flames finally healing the broken bones in my back. I try to get up, but white hot pain fills my mind and I can't help the yelp that rips from my chest.

"Mason!" Dani cries.

"Yes, you lovely little thing, keep crying for your boyfriend. That will keep him in line for me." Victor says darkly.

"Let her go, you crazy bastard! Take me instead!" I yell as I feel more bones mending.

"Oh my boy, I am still going to use you. This beautiful creature is your reminder not to fuck me over. A bit of collateral for me to ensure you do just as I say." Victor says while looking down his nose at me.

"I'd hate to see something happen to your little girlfriend here." He adds as he slowly traces the side of her face from her temple to her jawline with a long, slender finger.

Dani tries to pull away from his touch, but with him still holding her by the neck like a damn animal, she can't move from him.

"You'll fucking pay for this." I say with venom in my voice as I feel the last bone pop back into place in my spine.

Dani somehow knows my back is healed, and I was going to try to attack because she pins me with a stare that tells me to stay down. She flicks her eyes behind me, as if telling me to *walk away. Find someone to help us.* As much as it sickens me to walk away from her and leave her in his hands, I sigh a breath through my nose and close my eyes once, telling her *I understand.*

"You act as if we have had nothing but failures." Victor begins. "But on the contrary, we have been building to our success! Death is inevitable in science. But to learn from them and make the next experiment better is the goal, my boy!" Victor says with a touch of mania in his eyes.

"You are insane." I growl.

"You will find me a location with a more powerful river," Victor says harshly, ignoring my words. "You do that and no harm will come to this beautiful creature here. You fail me, and she will be my next experiment." He adds with a voice so dark and almost hungry that my blood freezes in my veins.

"Over my dead body, will she be part of your fucked up games." I say darkly.

"That can be arranged to, my boy." Victor drawls.

I feel his wind pick up again, but not in a full-out tornado, and Victor starts to lift off the ground. I push to my feet, my back still protesting at the movement, and I try to reach for Dani. As Victor pulls her out of my reach, I see a single tear fall down her cheek and I sink onto my knees, watching helplessly as Victor floats away with her in his arms. The roar of anger that rips from my throat makes the nearby windows rattle in their panes.

After I catch my breath, I look over my shoulder in the direction that goes into town and take a final steadying breath while standing shakily on my feet.

I look back to the sky where Victor has my girl and I say to the clouds, knowing full well she can't hear them, but I have to say the words anyway. "I will get you back, Baby. I won't stop until I have you back in my arms and safe from him."

I then push my hands in my pockets and walk towards town. Towards the one person that I know will be able to help.

57

Mason

After following this strange inner need, even though I don't know why, I walk into the local library about an hour and a half later.

As I pass through the large, dark-colored faux wooden doors, the soft muttering of people milling about makes the thoughts racing through my head that much louder. I shake my head as this sensation starts to pull me to the right, where I see a hallway leading deeper into the building.

The hell with it. Let's follow this feeling. I think to myself.

I follow the directional signs for the computer room on the second floor and I open the glass-framed door, and I find one person in there. His reddish blonde hair is somewhat disheveled, as if he'd been running his hands in aggravation through the strands. I see Google is pulled up on the screen and the entry in the search bar of Location + The Siphon with zero returned results on the inquiry.

"Google ain't gonna tell you shit about the location." I say, my voice still holding onto the edge of anger as I walk up behind him.

Aiden leaps up from his seat and I can almost feel his electricity trickle over my skin in warning.

"What are you doing here?" Aiden growls.

What am I doing here? That is the question of the century. If Rhett somehow finds out about this, I know for a fact that he will blab to Victor. But I have to try this. I know for a sad fucking fact that I can't fight Victor alone. I need a team.

"I know of the place The Siphon is going to be moved to." I say. I already know where I am going to tell Victor to move this monstrosity.

Aiden's stance relaxes just a bit, and he looks me over. I didn't even realize my clothes were torn in places and I have several spots of blood dotting my back and sides.

"What the hell happened to you?" Aiden asks while waving his hand over my appearance.

"Let's just say I'm being held by the balls, so to speak, to work with Victor right now." I spit with venom.

"Why are you going to tell me where The Siphon is going to be moved?" Aiden asks. "How is it going to be moved?"

"Is there a more private place for us to talk?" I ask, while looking over my shoulder again through the glass door to see if anyone is watching.

"Yeah. Follow me." Aiden says while packing up some notebooks and pens he had laid out on the desk.

I follow him out to his Colorado and open the passenger side door while he gets in on the driver's side without a word. As he drives, I find myself absentmindedly rubbing my chest. Right over my heart where that single flame of color sits. Reminding me that Dani always said I was different. Broken, yes, but I was—I *am* different from the other Parasites. And I hold on to that like a lifeboat.

I take a deep breath to clear my mind and after a few minutes I see a forest around us and we pull up to a tall, off-set concrete-looking two-story house with an odd architectural metal beam attached to the front.

"Seth's place." Aiden offers as explanation before he gets out of the truck.

A dark green Mustang pulls up beside us and the driver, Ivan, as I recall, notices me getting out of the passenger seat of his friend's truck. He slams on the brakes and throws the transmission into park before he jumps out of the driver's seat and comes at me.

"Aiden, what the fuck is *he* doing here?" Ivan sneers.

I feel my flames want to answer to his tone, but I force them back with a clenched fist at my side.

I see the smaller guy get out of the passenger seat and, while keeping his eyes on me, he pulls his seat forward to let the last passenger out. Her I remember. Maya. The one I was forced to burn to get under Aiden's skin and hopefully make him mess up his Soul Power. Or at least that was ultimately Victor's goal without telling me.

"He wants to talk to us about The Siphon's location." Aiden says.

"How do we know he's not lying?" The smaller guy says, and I chuckle at his question.

"Cause you all would be dead by now if I wanted this to be a setup." I say.

"I feel there is something he needs to tell us. Let's just hear him out." Aiden says while looking at his friends and then back at me.

He pulls Maya against his side and kisses the top of her head. A movement that I have done time and time again with Dani. The sight threatens to rip my beating heart from my chest and I know Aiden sees it, but doesn't call me out on it.

"Let's get in here and get this over with." Ivan grumbles. "You first though, I want to keep my eyes on you."

I give him a sidelong smirk and I walk in front of the little group. Then, before I even step on the porch, the door opens and there is a man standing in the doorway. He has the same dirty blonde hair and green eyes as Victor, but these eyes are different. They are kind and soft, but they also have a hardness to them. These eyes are so different from Victor's cold and manic ones.

"Aiden said he was bringing someone to meet us. I never thought it was you, Mason." Seth says. His tone is friendly but guarded, and it's understandable.

I just nod my head and wait for him to let us in. Aiden walks by me with Maya at his side and gives me a soft smile.

"Come on. Let's talk." He says.

I walk in with them, Ivan behind me, still staring a hole in my back, and the other guy trails behind him with his hand on the small of Ivan's back. Like his touch will keep Ivan from jumping me.

"You look like you've been through the wringer." The other one says while looking me up and down.

"You could say that, yeah. Being in a tornado and then dropping probably about two hundred feet onto your back will do that." I offer as I roll my shoulder to work out the still sore muscles.

"Gray, come help me get drinks for everyone." Maya says while walking from Aiden's side and into the back of the house.

The tall ceilings, the empty room to my left, and the living room to my right makes me think this is strictly just a structure to live out of. Not a home. It kind of fits my soul. Just a vessel to use, but not something to really care about.

"Come everyone, let's sit and talk." Seth offers as he takes a seat on the wingback chairs.

I take one of the chairs near the window, still wanting to have my back covered by something solid. When Maya and Gray, now that I know his name, bring in a tray of coffee, water, and soda for us to drink, and I swipe a Dr. Pepper off the tray, pop the can, and take a heavy swig. Ivan sits beside Gray on the couch, a protective arm draped across his shoulders, while Aiden and Maya take the love seat. Again holding on to the other's hand in a way that makes my own hand feel utterly lonely.

"So now that we are all settled. Why don't you two tell us what this meeting is about?" Seth asks while looking between me and Aiden.

I toy with the pop top with my fingernail, and I look to the group before me. I can feel the camaraderie between them. And I know now that is why they have beaten me every time I've gone after them. It's not a one-person battle. They all work together. And I know I want to give them any leg up I can. Victor has got to be stopped.

"Victor is about to move The Siphon and I know where I'm going to tell him to move it." I begin.

"If you know where it is now, why not just tell us so we can destroy the fuckin' thing?" Ivan snaps.

"Cause even if I told you right where it is, you would still never see it." I say, my tone even. "Victor made a cloaking tech that is only visible to ones whose blood is listed in the system."

"Oh shit, that's some fancy stuff." Gray says in awe.

"So why can't you add our blood to the system?" Ivan demands.

"I don't have access for one, and even if I did, Victor will know I fucked with his shit." I say.

"How is he going to move it, and where?" Maya asks.

"It's going to be a bit of a drive, but I'm going to tell him to move it to Smith Falls State Park in Nebraska." I say, as I lean forward to put my soda can on the coffee table and I run my hands through my hair and let loose a breath. "Victor can teleport The Siphon from one spot to another." I say.

"He can what?" Aiden asks in shock.

"Yeah. He got the idea from you, Seth." I say grimly as I flick my eyes over to him.

"How?" Seth asks, face pale.

"That I don't know, but all I know is he said he teleported it one other time, and he got the methods from his 'fucking special brother'." I say with air quotes. "But there is a drawback from what I read in the notes. He can't activate the cloaking tech for two days because teleporting takes up so much power."

"So we attack soon after he moves it." Aiden says, looking from me and then to his group.

"Why are you telling us this?" Ivan asks. "How can we trust a Parasite?" He spits out.

"Because I've seen shit that makes me sick to my stomach, and—" I pause while rubbing at my chest again and Dani's beautiful smiling face comes to mind, then her fearful tear-stained face from a few hours ago. "He has someone I love being held against her will to force me to work with him."

"I don't buy that for one minute." Gray laughs and I can't help the flames that burst from my hands as I jump to my feet. Ivan covers himself in a metal skin while Gray pulls out a silver ball from his pocket. Aiden then gets between me and his friends while Maya and Seth stay where they are.

"You can't possibly be willing to listen to his shit, are you Aiden?" Ivan yells.

"Yeah, man. I mean, come on, it's *Mason*. The one who attacked *your* girlfriend, and then the both of you guys in the forest. How can you be so calm in all this?" Gray asks.

"Because Victor has kidnapped *his* girlfriend to make him still do the things Victor needs." Aiden says, hitting the nail on the head. "Plus, like I've always said, Mason is different, so I do actually trust him.

"Well, *I* need more than that." Ivan snarls. "What is it that makes you so damn different? Is it your good looks?"

I give him a sly smile, "Cute. Dani would say so." I begin, but my smile fades at who she is with and I decide to show them the very thing that does make me different.

I take a step back and peel off my tattered shirt to reveal my dark flame tattoos that snake up both arms, and their eyes fall on the left side of my chest at the same time. To the colorful flame that seems to dance on my skin with the tether of smoke connecting my muted gray, white, and black flames just at the tip of my shoulder and neck.

"No way. It's been years since I have seen something like that." Seth says.

"You know what that means?" Aiden asks.

"Yes. It means that while yes, he fought his powers and he still has that sentient being there, they have come to an understanding on one simple thought." Seth explains, but I cut him off to finish that statement.

"To protect those that I care about." I look at the group in front of me and I explain how a week after I met Dani, my father, who was a Parasite, finally lost his mind to the being inside and killed my mother, and how when I was getting my own powers, I figured I would be damned to the same fate as he was. But I swore that Dani would never suffer that same fate as my mother did, and my flames agreed.

"Damn, then you could be the ultimate spy." Gray says with an eagerness in his eyes.

I can't help the laugh that bubbles from my chest at his words. "Yeah Gray, I guess I would be a pretty good one." I chuckle.

I actually see Ivan's expression and stance relax a bit, but he's still guarded as he backs away to take a seat on the couch, so I do the same in my wing-back chair. I don't even bother to put my tattered and bloodied shirt back on.

Silence fills the room, only the sound of the AC system running and the fridge from the kitchen filling the void. I let them have their time to sort through things. I know I just gave them a lot to think about.

"So I think I know when game day is. Near the solar eclipse, right? But when is the exact date?" I ask as I look at Aiden and he gives me a sly smile.

58

Aiden

I take in Mason's bare chest, the single brightly colored piece of his flame tattoo and the sly smile fades from my lips as I lean my forearms on my knees and let my hands hang loosely at the wrists.

"November twenty-eighth is the date of the solar eclipse. So, you need to have Victor teleport it a day or two before, so the cloaking tech isn't running." I say.

Mason runs a hand through his hair and over his face, and I see a flare of anger flash across his features. "Damn, that's still two weeks away." Mason growls.

"I know that's not what you wanted to hear for Dani, but that's the date. I'm sorry." I say, trying to let him know I understand his unspoken words.

That's two weeks for Dani to be Victor's captive.

"As long as I do what he says, he won't hurt her." Mason says. "But that may mean I have to come after you all if I am ordered to." He adds in a rough tone.

"We'll handle it like we always have. We'll just kick your asses and send you back to him, licking your wounds." Ivan says darkly, but with a hint of humor in his words.

I look at my friend and I see the fire in his eyes and the crooked smile on his lips at the oddly friendly challenge he tossed to Mason.

"I don't doubt that Chain Link." Mason replies with a dark smile.

"Chain Link?" Ivan asks, his brows furrowing.

Mason points to Ivan's arms where his greyish white, orange, and black chain tattoo wraps around his forearms and elbows before disappearing under his short-sleeved black t-shirt.

"Dude's got jokes. Alright." Ivan chuckles.

As the sun starts to set and dusk settles on the horizon, I watch as Mason gets up off his wing-back chair and walks toward the front door. Seth stops him and hands him a heathered gray t-shirt with a soft smile. Mason takes it without a word while slipping it over his head, before looking back at us and nods his head toward our group.

"I'll try to let you know if anything changes, but I don't want any of this over phone or text." Mason says.

I smile as I say, "I have a way around that."

I open my mind up and I look for Mason's electrical pulse and I imagine a mental bridge connecting us together, much like I have done with my friends and family. I instantly feel Mason in the back of my mind, but I also feel something else from him. I can't place what it is until I focus solely on the oddity within.

"Is this a friend or foe?" The ghostly, gravelly voice asks, and I recoil from it as if it burned me.

Mason gives me a quizzical look and then realization flashes across his face as he starts to feel my presence in the back of his mind.

"Okay, that is freaky as shit. It's bad enough that I feel my flames all the time, but to feel another person?" Mason begins, but his face pales when I respond to him, mind to mind.

"I bet it's even freakier when I talk this way." I say, with humor leaking through our connection.

"Don't. Do that. Ever. Again." Mason enunciates each word.

"You can do it too, you know." I reply with a smile. "Use this connection if you need to tell us something. That way, there is no way to track our conversation." I add.

"Yeah, yeah." Mason waves us off and opens the door to walk out into the night air.

Mason

I walk outside and I remember that I don't have my Challenger anymore so I have to walk all the way to The Siphon since I'm sure by now the townhouse probably has already been claimed because we left the door wide open.

I am about halfway down Seth's driveway and I'm just about to step onto the main road when I feel someone come up behind me. I spin around, my flames roaring to life and lighting up the area around me. Once I realize who is in front of me, I let a deep growl rip from my throat

"You know better than to sneak up on me, Rhett!" I yell. "That's a damn good way to get fucking burned, dumbass."

"Why are you here at Seth's house?" Rhett asks, indifferent to the threat my flames give off.

I give a dark laugh while pulling my flames back, then shoving my hands in the pockets of my shorts. "Just sending them on a wild goose chase for when Victor teleports The Siphon. We can't have them showing up when the cloaking tech isn't running." I say smoothly.

"Where are you having Victor teleport it?" Rhett asks.

"That's for me and him to know. I don't answer to you." I snap while turning my back to him.

I take a few steps and I see Rhett's crappy 2009 Chevy S10 parked on the shoulder. I'm shocked the damn thing still runs, considering the condition that the body is in. It's a rust bucket on wheels. The once silver paint is more a dirty brown because of the rust eating away at the metal. I get in the passenger seat and wait for him to get in the driver's side and take us to The Siphon.

When we arrive at the deadly machine hidden in the forest, the only lights are the ones that come from inside the tunnel entrance. Knowing that Dani is somewhere inside this thing makes my skin crawl, and the fact that I can't do a damn thing to save her sends my blood boiling.

I hop out of Rhett's beat up truck and I stalk into the main area of the machine, the control room. There, on the old gray couch that has a few stains and tears in the fabric, is Dani. Sitting as still as I ever seen her. When she turns her head and looks at me, I see the pure fear in her eyes, but she desperately tries to school her face when she sees Rhett walk up behind me.

Glancing around the room for a moment to see if Victor is around, and I breathe a sigh of relief when he's nowhere in sight. I take a step toward Dani and the pleading in her eyes fills to the brim at my advancement toward her. It's then that I finally notice something around her wrist and I have to fight back a growl that threatens to claw up my throat.

"He seriously had to chain you like a fucking animal?" I say in a low, venomous voice as I touch the manacle encircling her small wrist.

She doesn't say a word, only leans into my touch as if that small amount of contact will protect her.

"Yes, I chained her. I had to keep that little beautiful creature from getting any wild ideas." Victor says as he walks into the control room from somewhere in the back of The Siphon.

Dani jumps at his voice filling the room and my vision goes red at the corners. I want nothing more than to tear this place apart, but I know I have to bide my time. So, I take a calming breath, give her shoulder the barest of touches, and force myself to take a few steps away from her.

"I still think that's a little overboard. Unlock her." I demand.

Victor laughs as he walks away from me and sits down at the desk in the far corner of the room. If you can call it a desk with all the papers that are scattered on top of it.

"I think if I unlock her you won't like the next place I would store her." Victor replies, like Dani is nothing but a piece of furniture to put away.

His eyes rove over Dani's slender form and then over to the left where an empty pod lies open, waiting for its next victim; and my stomach drops like a stone.

"Fine, keep her chained." I say, trying to keep my voice indifferent. I put my hands in my pockets to hide the fist I can't help but curl my hands into at the threat of putting Dani in one of those pods.

"Now, have you found a new location to teleport us to?" Victor asks changing the subject.

"Yeah. I have an idea." I reply.

Aiden

The next week and a half roll by all too quickly. It's filled with me and my teammates' training and Gray looking over the Google Earth images of Smith Falls State Park in Nebraska to see if he can find where the river cuts through the mountain. I don't hear anything from Mason, so I take that as a good thing that nothing major has changed, and that they didn't kill him. I can still feel the connection I have to him and his flame, which is still a weird thing for me to comprehend. But that's a Parasite for you, I guess.

We are still days away from making the long drive that will change the world for The Protector's of Power. I still cannot force myself to ignore the fact that I might not walk away from this, though. With that thought, I head out to the garage and hop in my truck and go to the one person that can help me with my idea. I want to leave my aunt and uncle something, so they will at least know if I am alive or not.

As I pull up to Seth's house, the dark clouds in the sky above seem to make the metal beams that offsets the concrete sides of the house look muted. I take a breath while I get out of my truck, walk up to the porch, and knock on the door. I wait a few heartbeats and the door opens and Seth lets me in without a word. We walk into the living room where Seth sits on the wingback chair and I take the love seat beside him.

"So what is this early morning visit about?" Seth asks while taking a drink of coffee from a forest green ceramic mug.

"Is there a way I can leave some of my essence in one of my abilities?" I ask.

Seth crooks a blonde eyebrow at me and I take a breath and say, "I want to leave something behind for my aunt and uncle, where if something happens to me, they won't be in the dark. It will snuff out when," I pause and force a lighter possibility, "If I were to die, they would know right then and not have to wait a day or two to see if I walk back through their door."

Seth takes another swig of his coffee and sets it down on the table. "I've never seen it done before, but I imagine it would be the opposite way you made the flowers for Maya." He says while rubbing his chin. "You keep a part of yourself connected—"

"You know about that?" I ask cutting him off, remembering the hibiscus flowers I made Maya for her birthday.

"Oh, yeah." He chuckles. "As soon as she knew you were safe, she wanted to brag about how talented you were with your abilities." Seth adds with a smile still on his face.

Heat creeps up my neck at his words, at the thought that Maya sought him out to brag about my gift to her, and then I feel a smile form on my own lips.

Of course she would. It's who she's always been. If something makes her happy, she wants everyone around her to know.

"Okay. I'll try that. Thank you, Seth. For everything. I know I was an asshole to you the first few times we met, but I am forever grateful that you helped me when I was first getting my abilities. For the way, you showed me how to use them. Pushed me past my limits to help me get to new heights." I say and I hold his gaze, his green eyes going bright with moisture.

"I will accomplish this prophecy. All the hell that you lived with for these past twenty-one years will *not* be in vain." I promise him.

Seth nods and gets up from the wingback chair, the cushion sighing as it bounces back to its original shape, and Seth rests a hand on my shoulder. "I will help you finish this in any way I can. I will go with you and fight alongside you all." Seth says.

At first, I want to tell him no, but I know I can't say that to him. He has just as much of a right in this fight as any of us. It's his brother that built this damn thing.

"Okay. I'd like to have you by our side. Remember, we leave in three days." I say, trying to force a smile.

I wave goodbye to Seth and he goes back over to his wing-back chair while grabbing his coffee cup from the center table, then takes his seat again and he gives me a small wave in return. I gently close his front door behind me and walk to my truck.

I find myself driving aimlessly around and somehow make my way to the little forest. I park my truck in the grass, kill the engine, and get out of the cab. The songs of the chirping birds hidden in the treetops greeting me like an old friend.

A little way in the tree line, I see another vehicle and I realize it's Maya's Passat, and a grin spreads over my face as I follow the trail to the one place that I know she would be at.

As I get closer, the gentle fragrance of the lilac trees in the middle of the clearing hits my nose, and I see Maya sitting on a fallen log, legs tucked under her and crossed at the ankles. Her dark brown hair is a curly sexy mess tossed to one side and flowing over her shoulder.

I have to remind myself to breathe and I swallow at the tightness in my chest and frankly below the belt too at the sight of her. I pull my phone out of my back pocket to take her picture and then I reach out to her mind.

"Hey, what are you doing?"

"Nothing, I'm just in the forest. I needed some quiet time to myself." She replies softly.

"And you didn't want your boyfriend with you?" I tease.

"I called your place and your uncle said you went to meet with Seth, so I didn't want to bother you." Maya says.

"Okay, I can understand that." I begin. *"You look* beautiful, *by the way."* I add, hearing my voice going deeper as desire floods my mind.

She looks up through the tree line as if she can sense me. We lock eyes and the smile that brightens her face is almost enough to bring me to my knees. I must send her that thought or the image of me being on my knees before her because the words that fill my head makes my erection build, pressing tightly against my jeans and a feral grin spread my lips.

"I'd love to see you on your knees, right between my legs."

"Oh Baby, don't you know it's dangerous to tease a wild animal?" I reply and she just laughs out loud.

I finally cross the clearing and, like she wanted and, I kneel before her, grabbing at her thighs, making her legs wrap around my torso. She locks her ankles at the small of my back while I run my hands up her outer thighs and only stopping when my fingers hit the log under her.

I sweep my eyes down her body; from her beautiful brown eyes, down the delicate column of her neck, over the perfect swell of her breast, and finally down the length of her belly. She lifts her right hand to run her fingers through my hair, and I close my eyes while I lean into her touch.

"Not quite what I was insinuating, but this is a *very* close second." Maya croons softly.

"Well, we could do what you want now." I say while I make my firewall go up around us with my right hand. "But I think we have scarred the wildlife enough here with our *activities*." I add with a sly smile.

She laughs and bats at my hand as if telling me to drop the firewall and I do.

"I guess you're right, but..." She lets her question hang in the air and heat blooms over every inch of my body.

"You just tell me where and I'll take you." I say, voice going deep and letting the innuendo hang as she wants to take it.

For a split second, she doesn't comprehend my words. Then she stills, and I see a blush creep up her neck and cheeks and I can't help the chuckle that escapes my chest.

I pull her into me, and nuzzle her neck. "God, you drive me crazy, and I love you for it." I whisper in her ear.

She wraps her arms around my neck and rests her chin on my head. After a few moments, she asks, "What were you doing here?"

It's my turn to go still. I pull back from her and take a cleansing breath. "I was going to try to make something for my aunt and uncle to leave them before we go." I begin, "To leave a part of myself in it so they'll know...if something happens." I force past the knot in my throat.

I brace myself for the scolding of *stop acting like you're not coming back* or *stop being a Debbie Downer*, but none of that comes.

"What were you going to make them?" Maya asks as she plays with the hair at the nape of my neck.

I have to think past the feel of her fingers and I shake my head. "I don't know. I was actually thinking about leaving them an actual flame shape. Just pull the heat out of it." I offer.

"That's a good idea." Maya replies.

I turn around and sit on the ground in front of her. She wraps her arms around my neck again while resting her hands on my chest. I lean my cheek on her left forearm and take her hand in my own while I open my right hand and call my fire.

I make it keep the flame shape, somewhat jagged and offset. The oranges, whites, and reds still dancing as if in rhythm to my heartbeat and that's when I know that is the essence I want to leave behind.

I place the little flame on the ground and I pull my fire back from my hand and I can somehow tell that this little flame will do what I want it to. It will extinguish into ash if my heart were to stop beating.

59

Aiden

After I make sure that Maya gets to her car safely, I set the living flame on my passenger floorboard and drive home. When I pull into the garage, I put my flame on the workbench near the door and walk inside to find my aunt and uncle sitting on the couch in the living room. My aunt is asleep on his chest and Uncle Matt is watching a sports recap on mute with the captions running on the screen. I walk in his line of sight so he knows it's me coming in.

"Did you get your answers from Seth?" He whispers.

I nod and give him a small smile and head to bed.

The next morning, my phone buzzing with a call pulls me from sleep. I roll over to my right, looking at the caller ID -Gray- and I pick up the phone before it goes to voicemail.

"Gray, what's up, man?" I ask groggily.

"I think I found the location. Or at least the path of the river." Gray says with excitement in his voice.

"Give me fifteen minutes to get dressed and you can come over to talk about what you found." I say while throwing the covers back, while running my right hand over my face, and scratching at my bare chest.

"Okay. Seth and Maya should be on their way too." Gray replies.

"Alright. I'll be ready." I say as I hang up and make my way over to the bathroom to get dressed in a black t-shirt and dark blue jeans.

Just as I walk into the living room fifteen minutes later, the front door opens and Seth walks in with Maya, Ivan, and Gray trailing him. They all give Aunt Viv a gentle hug as they enter the living room.

I nod my head in greeting to the guys while Maya walks over to me and I pull her in to give her a hug, then place a quick kiss on her lips. Uncle Matt calls us over into the dining room so we all can gather around and listen to Gray's findings.

Gray sets up his laptop, and he literally brought a portable projector with him to make it easier for all of us to see his report. As Aunt Viv takes her seat at the end of the table, Uncle Matt closes the blackout curtains over the window, turns the lights off, and sits beside his wife. Maya, Seth, Ivan, and I all stand around the table and we wait to see what Gray has to say.

"Okay, so I finally found the river and after some Google Earth searching, I found the spot where the current is the strongest since Mason told us The Siphon needs more power." Gray says as he pulls up some images on his laptop.

The images of a 2-D map appear on the wall after he connects to the projector with a few clicks of the integrated mouse of the laptop. I see nothing but trees in the image until Gray highlights the water hidden underneath the canopy.

"What's the best route we should go to get to this point?" Seth asks as he walks closer to the wall to get a better look at the image in front of him.

"Already figured that out." Gray beams. He taps a few commands into his PC and another screen pops up from the projector. "It's going to be a long walk, but this is the path that has the least terrain to deal with."

Gray pulls up a side-by-side window of the satellite version of the forest and a rough plain copy so we can see the lay-lines of the ground a little better.

"We park here, at the most southern part of the park, and then walk up. It's probably a five-hour walk to the river, but it's an old trail that's no longer in use." Gray says.

"Why did they stop using it?" Maya asks as she studies the maps on the wall and looks to Gray for his answer.

"That area is known for trees to randomly fall over. The soil has been barren of any life-sustaining nutrients for years, so the park shut the trail down to keep hikers safe." Gray says, then makes a few more images flash before us and I see the dates change from year to year and he says, "From the images I've found over several years the forest hasn't declined much, but they never opened the trail back up."

"I agree with Gray." Ivan begins. "This is a long way, but it's the best shot we have. Besides, I think dealing with trees trying to fall on us is a hell of a lot better than having Rhett or Victor trying to attack us if we can sneak up on them."

I notice that Ivan doesn't include Mason in this scenario, but I don't call him out on it. Instead, I turn away from the wall to address Gray.

"This is great, Gray. Thank you." I say as I look toward my friend, still leaning over his laptop.

"I told you I was gonna be the brains to your and Ivan's brawn." Gray replies with a big grin that lights his face up.

"Yeah, you did." I chuckle.

Ivan crosses the length of the dining room and over to his partner. "And I love you all the more for it, Grayson." He says as he plants a sound kiss on Gray's lips.

After a few moments of silence other than the sound of Gray packing up his laptop, Ivan speaks up.

"You guys want to run one more training exercise before we head out tomorrow?" Ivan asks while popping his knuckles.

"Sure, but I need to take care of one thing first." I begin then continue mind to mind to the four of them. *"I need to talk to my aunt and uncle about something I made for them."*

Seth gives me a slight nod while waving goodbye to Uncle Matt and Aunt Viv, who have been quietly listening to all of our conversations. Ivan and Gray follow him out, but Maya stays behind and walks over to me.

She takes the hem of my black t-shirt between her index finger and thumb, toying with it a moment before asking in a low voice, "You want me to stay with you while you tell them?"

"No, Baby. It's okay. You go ahead and start the exercise with the guys. Show them how well you can kick ass." I say with a forced grin. "I'll be by in a bit." I add as I give her a kiss on the forehead and pull her in for a quick hug.

Maya nods her head and slowly pulls away as she walks toward the front door where Seth is still waiting for her. She looks back once over her shoulder at me and I give her a wink, which makes an adorable blush creep into her cheeks as she walks through the door and I can't help the grin that curves up the right side of my lips. Seth gives me a knowing nod as he gently closes the door behind him.

Uncle Matt and Aunt Viv are still at the dining room table, the blackout curtains still closed, and I slowly pull in a calming breath through my nose.

"I have something I want to show you two." I say as I walk by them and go out into the garage and over to the workbench where I placed the flame I made yesterday.

I bring the living flame into the house and gently place it in the middle of the table, the oranges and reds of the flames dancing across the wooden surface. I walk to the opposite side of the table so I am looking at them head-on, but I don't take a seat.

"Oh, Aiden, that is amazing." Aunt Viv says with awe in her eyes.

"Well, there is a feature behind this flame." I begin. I brace my hands on the top of the chair in front of me, elbows straight, my tattoos standing out in contrast to my black shirt and the colors of the flame dancing across my skin in the partially darkened room. I point to the middle of the table with my right index finger, but I keep my palm against the curve of the chair. "That flame there is connected to me."

"What do you mean?" Aunt Viv asks, her voice barely a whisper.

I look from the flame, then to my aunt and uncle, and I take a breath. "I left a piece of myself in there, my heartbeat, basically." I say, and just as my own heart is fluttering in my chest, the flame matches what I feel. "I want to leave this here for you two. That way, you will know right away if something were to happen. It's a seven-hour drive and I don't want you all to have to wait to know what happens to me."

"I have faith that this flame will not fade. You will come back to us." Aunt Viv says with determination in her eyes.

I give her a small smile and I nod my head. "I know, but this is just like a worst-case scenario." I offer.

"We will leave this right here. It will make a nice centerpiece when you get back." Uncle Matt says with silver lining his eyes.

"Yes, it will." I say with a tight smile. "Well, I gotta go and run this last session with my team." I begin as I stand back from the chair and run my hands through my hair.

Uncle Matt stands up and offers his hand to me. I take it, and he pulls me in toward him, wrapping his other arm around my shoulders.

"Have a good session, son."

I nod at him and walk out of the dining room.

When I walk out on the porch, I find my friends all around Ivan's Mustang. Ivan's leaning against the hood with his arms crossed over his chest. Gray is closing the trunk after putting his laptop case back there, and Maya is sitting sideways in the passenger seat with her long legs stretched out in front of her.

"I could have met you guys at the forest." I say, chuckling.

"Why not go there together?" Ivan says simply as he leans forward and pushes off the hood. "Come on, let's go."

Maya stands to her feet, leans the passenger seat forward, and slips into the backseat. I follow her, settling in beside her just as Gray tilts the front seat into the upright position so he can sit down and closes the passenger door just as Ivan starts the engine.

When we arrive at the forest thirty minutes later, Seth is there waiting for us. We run drills over and over again until we are able to work seamlessly together. Maya and I work more on figuring out a way where she can leave a gap big enough for me to be able to have my electrical current inside her water cyclone without shocking her.

Time seems to fly by, but it's been a four-hour session when Seth finally calls our training to stop.

"Okay everyone, good job." Seth says with a clap of his hands, but he takes a breath before continuing, "I would make any final arrangements you need to, and then come by my place by nine tonight. We will rest there and move out first thing in the morning." Seth says in a commanding tone, then teleports without another word.

"Well, you heard the man. Let's go." Ivan says as he begins walking back to his Mustang and we all follow behind him.

Mason

These last two weeks have been absolute hell.

Victor has been keeping Dani on that damned sofa in the common area of The Siphon. I have tried to stay with her in any way I can think of. I tried to sleep on the loveseat across from her. Hell, I've even tried to sleep on the hard, dust-ridden floor, but Victor forces me out and I have been staying with Rhett.

Today is the day that Victor needs to teleport this fucking thing. I know that this is the only time Dani will be outside of this death trap. No living thing can be inside when it is teleported. I've seen the blueprints and how gravity works. Anything that is not solid metal will be torn apart.

If I can just get her away from him, we can run. Let the others run on a wild goose chase. I'll have what is most important to me by then. Let them fight their own battles.

Rhett walks out the door of his apartment and over to his crappy S10 without a word. I follow him out just as silently and get in the passenger seat; the door groaning on the rusted hinges. Rhett cranks the engine once, twice, and on the third time the engine sputters to life and he drives us to South Boulder Park in silence.

"Protect her. We must be smart." I hear my flame whisper to me and I almost hate that it can see my thoughts. I hate that it can see the two locations in my head.

"I am being smart. We are a Parasite, remember? We always fuck people over." I growl.

When we arrive at The Siphon fifteen minutes later, I roughly shut the truck door, pieces of rust flaking off at the force, and I walk into the common area of the machine. My eyes zero in right to the couch and I'm somewhat relieved to see Dani still sitting there, even if her head is hung low. I take a step toward her, but Victor clears his throat, the sound stopping me in my tracks.

"You have a location, Mason?" Victor asks, his voice emotionless as he's typing commands into the system's onboard computer.

"Yeah, I do." I reply as my eyes drift back over to Dani.

"Well, don't keep me waiting, boy. Where are we going?" Victor snaps.

As I look back over at Dani, who is still not looking at me, I know I have to get her out of here soon. I tear my eyes from her and look back at Victor. I know my gaze is as sharp as a dagger, but I don't care.

"Teleport it to Niobrara Valley Preserve." I say coldly.

60

Mason

I'm sitting in Rhett's S10 again, listening to the truck squeak and squeal as he goes over humps and defects in the road. I'm still shocked this thing hasn't broken right in half.

He's supposed to be going back to his apartment to pick up last-minute clothes and other supplies, but he makes a turn that will go to the forest that Aiden and his team go to.

"What the fuck are you doing?" I ask sharply.

"I want to make sure those assholes aren't doing anything to stop us." Rhett replies and the wildness in his gaze sends chills down my spine.

"What does it matter? The Siphon is sitting in the new spot; they'll never find it." I say as I look out the window and I close my right hand in a tight fist, knuckles popping the tighter I squeeze.

Did I make the right choice?

I look back through the windshield and I see a familiar dark green Mustang and I know it's Ivan's. I look over to Rhett and know nothing good will come from the grin that spreads on his face as he pushes the truck to a higher speed to catch up to the group ahead of us.

I feel this strange tugging in my chest again, almost like my conscience is finally catching up to my actions of twenty minutes ago.

I walk over to Dani after I tell Victor about the location to teleport The Siphon to and I kneel before her, taking her hands in mine. Her trembling fingers break something in me.

She finally lifts her head and I see fresh bruises on her cheeks. I make myself look over her body, and I see marks in the shape of his fucking hand on her throat. They are so detailed that I can see each individual finger. I notice more bruises on her arms and it's all I can do to keep my flames under my skin. She must feel this because she brings her right hand up, the chains rattling between us, and cups my cheek while running her thumb over my cheekbone.

"It's just bruises to get under your skin, Mason." Dani whispers. "He hasn't defiled me in any other way." Her eyes shine with tears and the plea for me to get her out of here. "You know I'm used to this kind of abuse. The bruises will heal—"

"I promised you that you would never have this kind of abuse while I'm around. Not by my hand or anyone else's and I keep my promises, Angel." I say with venom in my voice and I look over to Victor, who is still inputting shit into the computer.

I give her a kiss on the forehead and as I stand up; I let go of her hand so I can walk over to Victor, but I leave a bit of my fire flickering in between her feet. She looks at me with confusion on her face, but doesn't dare ask what I'm doing.

"Hey Victor, on second thought, I have a better location. Send it to Smith Falls National Park. That has a stronger river to power The Siphon."

I look back over at Dani and give her a hidden wink and flick my eyes to the floor. She looks down and sees my hidden message written in flames:

I have a plan, Angel. Trust me.

I watch silently in the passenger seat as somehow Rhett is gaining on the Mustang and I see movement in the backseat and Aiden's face appears through the rear window.

"Tell Ivan to step on it. This rust bucket can't keep up with his engine." I tell Aiden through our mental connection, or at least I hope I do. I've never used it before today.

But something must work because the Mustang shoots forward and Rhett slams his fist into the steering wheel.

"Damn it! Get back here!" Rhett screams.

"Rhett, leave them! We'll get them some other time!" I say as I grab the wheel and try to pull him off the road.

At this point, I don't care if I crash this hunk of junk. I just need them to get away. As the squeal of the tires fighting to keep hold of the pavement echoes in the cabin, Rhett lifts his left hand and points his index finger toward the road in front of us.

Before I can comprehend what he's doing, a long, pointed spear of earth and rock pierces the Mustang's engine bay, which instantly kills the engine and effectively pins the vehicle on the highway.

"Now you're not getting away." Rhett growls as he slams on the brakes and hops out of the driver's seat.

I follow him and I watch as Ivan, Gray, Aiden, and Maya all spill out from the vehicle. Ivan makes a metal rod in his right hand, Gray has some kind of silver balls in his hands, Aiden lets his flame and electricity flicker and spark down his arms and finally, Maya's right arm drips with water and I feel the wind pick up around Rhett and me.

"When are you all going to stop?" Ivan asks, looking from Rhett, then to me.

I see the minute smirk in his eyes and I let my flames flare to life in my hands, letting the anger of the last two weeks fuel the fire, but this is the first time it doesn't burn me, but I don't let that odd sensation distract me.

"When you all are dead and not our problem, Chain Link." I reply darkly.

"Well, do your worst, Flame Boy," Ivan sneers.

I laugh and I go for Ivan while I notice Rhett go for Gray. Ivan quickly makes what looks like a second skin made of iron cover his body, and I go in for a sucker punch to the stomach. I turn my flames down at the last second so I don't break his skin, but I know the impact is going to be hell on my knuckles. Ivan gives me a split-second confused look, and I let a smirk play on my lips.

"I think your friend still doesn't trust me." I send the thought to Aiden.

"He does. He was just looking for a real fight, that's all." Aiden replies.

A heartbeat later, Ivan swings an iron bar into my side, and unlike me, he doesn't pull his attack. He hits me with everything he's got and I go flying across the road and roll into the bushes.

"Damn, Chain Link! Give a guy a warning." I mumble while sending that thought to Aiden.

I feel a tickle in the back of my mind and another presence fills my head, along with a dark chuckle.

"Give me a reason to give you a warning next time, Flame Boy." Ivan responds.

"Oh no, now I got both of you in my head. Fucking great." I say and I hear both of them laugh.

I hear a buzzing crack of electricity and then Rhett's screams. I look to my left, thinking I will find Aiden, but I don't. I see the scrawny guy, Gray, with those little silver balls and Rhett's body locked up tight, pain contorting his face.

"Wow, remind me not to mess with that one." I mumble as I stand to my feet, my flames still lapping up my arms just below my elbows.

"Yeah, Gray is a badass now."

I turn toward the sweet voice and Maya stands before me with a bright smile on her face and I instinctively take a step back.

"Sorry about this, but gotta keep up the ruse." Maya says with a smirk.

Before I know what's happening, her water rushes over me with such force that I am knocked off my feet. My flames instantly dying in my hands and I can't get them to light back up no matter how hard I try.

My head goes under the surface for several long moments, my body helpless in the current and being tossed in all directions where I don't even know which way is up. The world finally stops spinning when I am pinned up against a tree and the water recedes just enough for my chin to break the surface. I don't know how, but she makes the water so cold around me that I can't stop my teeth from chattering.

Maya slowly stalks towards me, water still flowing lazily from her hand. "That is for when you and your goon tied me to that tree at the school grounds. I know you were probably made to do that, but it still pissed me off and almost cost Aiden his life." Maya says with a hardness to her eyes that I didn't know she could show.

I nod my head once at her and then, after a few painfully long minutes, she releases her water trap from the tree and I drop down into the soaked ground like a fish out of water. I watch from the ditch I'm still currently sitting in as Ivan walks over to the S10, places a hand on the hood, and gives me a sly smile.

"I'm gonna put this thing out of its misery." Ivan chuckles.

I smile and give him a nod as he connects to the metal of the truck and collapses it like he would a tin can under his foot. The whole truck crumples like an accordion. The grinding metal and breaking of springs, bolts, and glass makes my smile grow wider. I hear Rhett's screams and I make my way up the soggy embankment to act like I'm going to attack Ivan, but I still can't get my damn flames to light up.

"Damn, Maya's water is still messing with me." I say to Ivan.

"Yeah, her water can knock out all fires. You should have metallurgy. It's a better power, *after all."* Ivan taunts.

"Really, Chain Link? Say that to my fist." I snap back.

I try to go after him, but I intentionally make my punch easy to read. He builds an iron wall directly out of the road and I make my fist hit it full force; this time I know I cracked a bone.

"So readable, Mason. Do try to make the next fight a challenge, will you?" Ivan says with mock boredom.

Rhett screams again and I notice he's chained to the other shoulder of the road. He's pulling so hard against the restraints that I'm shocked he hasn't ripped his shoulders out of the joint.

"*You better get your buddy before he hurts himself.*" Ivan croons and walks away from me to join the others, who are halfway down the road from us.

"*He won't be my problem for long. That is, if you all keep up to your end of our arrangement.*" I say to both Ivan and Aiden.

"*We'll still help you get Dani back. Is The Siphon at Smith Falls?*" Aiden asks.

"*Yes, it is.*" I say without hesitation.

As Aiden leaves my mind, I feel satisfaction come from his end of our connection, which is a weird thing to experience, but Rhett's manic screaming keeps me from thinking too hard about it.

"Shut the hell up, you maniac! It's just a damn truck." I say as I walk over to him.

I finally get my fire working again now that my hands are dry, and I may or may not have burned Rhett a bit while melting off his shackles.

Oops.

61

Aiden

"**D**amn it, look at my car!" Ivan whines as we walk past his dead Mustang as it sits in the middle of the highway.

The spear made of rock and earth is still jutting through the engine bay, ending in a sharp point. The metal still creaks as it continues to cool down while oil drips down the side of the rocky structure like blood.

I hook my left arm around his neck and pull him away. "We'll have a funeral for it when we get back from saving the world if you want." I say as I reach out to Seth to see if he can teleport us to at least my place.

"Yeah, I'll be there—" Seth begins in my head and appears before us a moment later.

He takes one look at the ruined Mustang, his eyes widening at the rocky spear through the engine, and glances over to us to make sure we are okay.

"We're fine. It wasn't much of a fight." I say, waving my hand like I was swatting at a fly.

"Apparently." Seth says. "We'll hold on everyone." He adds as he grabs my shoulder and Ivan's.

I take Maya's hand in mine so Seth can teleport us while Ivan slaps his hand on Gray's shoulder. We end up at my house and Seth leaves without another word. I go in to grab my keys off the hook and I notice the house is quiet and I can't help but wonder if I will see this place again after tomorrow.

I force that thought from my mind and walk toward the garage door to go out to my Colorado, pressing my fist to the garage door opener and as it's lifting the door, I get in the driver's seat and start the engine.

When I back out, I unlock the passenger door and Maya gets in, followed by Ivan and Gray, sitting in the double seats behind me. I drop Ivan and Gray off at their place first and as I'm pulling up to their house, Gray speaks up for the first time through the entire ride.

"I tell ya, Ivan, I'm glad I bought a car a few months ago. Looks like we'll be a one car family for a while. Pity." Gray says with a smirk.

"Screw you, asshole!" Ivan says sharply as he opens the door and gets out of the cab once I pull up to the curb.

Gray just stays in his seat with a big grin on his face directed toward's his boyfriend.

Geez, he's still such a goofball. I think as I shake my head at Gray's expression.

"Let's go, Grayson." Ivan growls as he walks up his driveway, looks to where his car should be parked, and with his head hung low, he sulks onto the porch.

I chuckle at his antics, happy for the bit of humor before the coming battle. As Gray walks up behind him, Ivan turns to his partner with a chaste kiss on the cheek before looking over Gray's shoulder. Ivan and I lock eyes through my windshield, and I see the dark determination in his steel-grey eyes and I let him feel the bit of laughter filling my thoughts.

"That was my plan all along. To give this day some humor. Even if it did come from my car being destroyed by that prick, Rhett. Oh, I can't wait to beat his face in." Ivan says.

"See ya in a bit, man. You will have your vengeance soon." I say in a mocking, serious tone.

As I take Maya to her place, I interlace my fingers in hers, running my thumb over her delicate knuckles, reveling how good it feels in my hand.

"Don't go there, Aiden. Please." Maya says softly.

"I actually was not thinking about that for once." I chuckle. "But are you?" I ask, taking my eyes off the road for a few moments to gaze at her.

She looks away and tightens her grip on my hand. I realize her hand fits so well into mine. Even though mine is larger than hers, she fits perfectly in my palm. I bring her knuckles up to my lips and give her skin a feather-light kiss.

"It will be okay. We *all* will figure out what happens afterward." I say.

"Yeah. We'll figure that out afterwards." She repeats like she needs to drill the words into her heart.

I pull up to her house and I park in the driveway in behind her Passat. I get out of my seat and walk around my truck to open the door for her. Once I close her door, I don't think about anyone seeing us as I push her up against the side of my truck and drive my right leg between hers, pressing my knee against her core.

"Aiden!" Maya squeaks, her hands on my chest, trying to push me away. "We are in broad daylight!"

"What? We're old enough not to have to hide from your father. You said so yourself." I say, my voice dropping to a seductive tone.

I press my knee harder against her clit and she moves her hands from my chest to my biceps and squeezes, her nails biting into my arm for a moment. Then her eyes flutter as she takes a shuttering breath.

"You are horrible, you know that?" She says breathlessly.

I chuckle again as I remove my knee and I watch as the pleasure leaves her face and the most adorable pout forms on her lips.

"You don't know what horrible is until I take you like I plan to tonight." I say, and I know a cocky grin is playing on my lips.

At first, shock fills her face, but then longing and desire quickly replaces it. I back away from her and give her a kiss on the forehead.

"I had to get you out of your head." I whisper. "And what better way than to use me as a distraction?"

She laughs lightly as she fists my shirt in her hands. "Thank you. I knew you were always good at distracting me." Maya says as she stands on her tiptoes to give me a sound kiss.

I let her have her kiss, but then I lean in, forcing her down on the soles of her feet and sliding my left hand behind her head, grabbing a handful of her dark brown hair at the nape of her neck and I pull it just tight enough to hold her head still.

Maya lets a soft, breathy moan escape and I feel the blood rush between my legs, pressing uncomfortably against the zipper of my jeans. I force my body to pull back before I can think about tossing her in the cabin of my truck, using my fire to block the windows and just taking her in the passenger seat.

"You better get inside and get what you need done." I say reluctantly.

"Okay." She replies as she's catching her breath. "I'll meet you at Seth's place later."

I nod at her. "Okay, Baby Girl."

When she walks up to the porch, she glances back at me over her shoulder, and I give her a playful wink. Her cheeks flush an adorable shade of pink and she smiles at me as she opens the front door and walks in, closing the door with a soft click.

I force myself to get in the driver's seat again and will my heart to slow down and the raging hard on to relax before I drive off.

When I finally get back to my house, this time I notice Uncle Matt's car in the driveway and I park my truck in behind his car and walk inside. Aunt Viv is in the kitchen already fixing something for dinner and Uncle Matt is setting the dining room table for us. As I shut the door, Uncle Matt looks over his shoulder at the sound of me coming in and gives me a knowing smile.

"I'll join you all for dinner in a minute." I say softly.

As I walk past the doorway to the kitchen, Aunt Viv looks up from chopping some onions. I give her a small wave and she smiles back at me while wiping away tears due to the onion she's cutting.

Once I'm finished throwing a pair of black pants and matching shirt in my backpack, I put on a loose-fitting pair of dark blue jeans and a blue t-shirt. Pausing to look at myself in the full-length mirror I have attached to my closet door, I take in the man that's staring back at me.

In the ten months since I've gotten my powers, I have changed. Instead of the lithe build I used to have, I have solid, defined muscles throughout my body, and the tattoos that I have snaking their way up my arms and onto my neck honestly make them look bigger than they are. I also notice I have a more confident look in my eyes than I did before and even in the first few months after getting my abilities.

Even with this final battle looming in the coming hours, I feel a confidence I didn't know I would have. I might not make it out unscathed, but even now, I think all five of us will make it out alive.

I take a breath as I start to smell dinner wafting through my door and I take a step toward the threshold, but I pause mid-step. Still sitting on my desk is the CD case that Seth gave me when I was in the music store on my birthday, and beside it are the two necklaces.

I pick up the gold-plated chains and watch as they both shimmer in the light.

Flame and lightning.

I smile as I slip them over my head, letting them lie on the cotton fabric of my black t-shirt. These very necklaces are what got me started on my journey and they will see me through to the end. I know they don't have any meaning or special powers, but I don't know; it just feels right in a sense that they are a part of me as I finish this prophecy.

I finally walk into the dining room and Aunt Viv has fixed roast beef, carrots, and potatoes. The smell of the different spices and onions fills the room and makes my mouth water.

"This looks amazing, Aunt Viv." I say as I walk over to her and give her a hug.

"Thank you, Aiden. Now sit down and eat up." Aunt Viv replies in a forced, cheerful tone.

I take my usual chair across from Uncle Matt, who is waiting for Aunt Viv to take her seat so he can push in the chair for her. So I decide to remain standing until she brings in the steaming side dish of bread. She smiles at the both of us as she places the dish in the center of the table near my living flame and takes the seat next to her husband. I finally sit down too and fill my plate.

We all eat in amiable silence, with just small talk around the table like it was just another normal day to break the silence when it becomes too heavy in the air. I stare at my living flame in the center of the table and how it reacts an instant later to my own heart beating in my chest. It's the calm before the storm.

"So, when are you all leaving tomorrow?" Uncle Matt asks, pulling me out of my thoughts.

"Uh, at six I think. It's a long drive, so we are going to take turns driving Seth's car." I say.

"Why can't Seth just teleport you all there?" Aunt Viv asks.

"He could, but I insisted we drive." I begin then take a bite of food. After I swallow I say, "I need... we need him at his best to fight with us." I correct myself.

I need him at his best to heal the others when they get hurt.

"Oh, that makes sense." Aunt Viv says quietly.

We finish our meal, this time in complete silence. After we have had our fill, I clear the plates from the table and I help wash the dishes with my aunt and uncle, if anything, just to spend time with them. Even if it's just as simple as washing a dish, it's a memory for them to hold on to.

Damn it, no matter how hard I try, I still keep coming back to that thought. If I die.

As Uncle Matt is drying the last dish, the grandfather clock in the hallway chimes seven. Each toll of the bell is heavier than the last. Aunt Viv takes a step toward me and I give her a small smile, pulling her into my chest for a hug. Uncle Matt puts the last dish away and comes to stand beside his wife and puts a hand on my shoulder.

I look at him, and he gives me a curt nod, and I give him a smile in return.

"Hey," I begin as I pull Aunt Viv back to look at her now tear-stained face. I use the pads of my thumbs and wipe away her tears. "No matter what happens, know that I love you both. I know you are my aunt and uncle by blood, but I have always thought of you two as my parents." I say and then I look at Uncle Matt as I add, "I will do everything I can to come back, but you two live on knowing that everything that was lost on that day twenty-one years ago was not in vain. I *will destroy* that Siphon and make sure that Victor is not a danger to anyone ever again."

I hug my aunt and uncle one more time and I walk back into the living room as Aunt Viv finishes cleaning up the kitchen. I glance at the living flame that is still perched in the center of the dining table one more time.

"I told you once before that flame will make a nice centerpiece." Uncle Matt says.

This is his way of saying that I will make it back, and I nod. "Yeah, I may even change it up for each holiday." I say with a forced smile.

"That sounds like a great idea." Uncle Matt says. He tries to hide the silver lining in his eyes, but I see it all the same.

He pulls me in for a hug, gripping me tightly around the shoulders, and I do the same to him. He pulls away a moment later and grips the side of my face, his bland lightning tattoos peeking out from under the sleeves of his shirt.

"Don't break your aunt's heart and die on her. You hear me?" He says, his voice cracking from holding back his own tears.

"Yeah, I hear ya." I say and I take a breath. "I gotta go." I reluctantly pull back from him and take a step toward the front door.

"Aiden?" Uncle Matt says and I turn to look at him. "I love you, son."

I smile and this time I can't stop the shake in my own voice as I say. "I love you too."

62

Aiden

I arrive at Seth's house just as the sun is setting under the horizon. As I get out of my truck and walk up on the porch, I hear the rumble of an engine. I glance over my shoulder and I see Gray's dark blue Civic pull up. I lean against one wall of the porch to wait as he and Ivan get out and walk up the steps. I give them both a low-five and a somewhat rough pat on the shoulders as they pass me and walk into Seth's living room.

Just as I am about to walk in with them, another car pulls up. The gray Subaru Legacy kicks up dust and little rocks as they approach. Through the windshield, I see Mr. Harper in the driver's seat and Maya on the passenger side. When the car comes to a stop beside Gray's Civic, I walk down the steps to meet them as Mr. Harper and Maya exit the car.

Maya hugs her father while standing on her tiptoes to give him a kiss on the cheek. Mr. Harper notices me walking up to them and lets Maya go with a small smile and a gentle kiss on her forehead.

"I love you, Maya. Please be safe." Mr. Harper says.

"I love you too, Daddy." Maya replies as she walks away from her father and to my side.

I wrap my arm around her waist, pulling her closer while her father looks at me imploringly.

"Please, protect my daughter." Mr. Harper says.

"Yes, sir." I reply and I step forward to give him a firm handshake.

He walks back to his car, his hand resting on the doorhandle, takes one last look at his daughter then opens the door and slowly drives off. We watch as the dust that was kicked up from his tires settles once again before we move.

"God, that was harder than I thought it would be." Maya says while resting her head on my chest.

"I'm sure it was. It was hard for me with my aunt and uncle." I say as I kiss the top of her head.

We stand in silence for a few more minutes before we hear the front door open again, and I turn to see Ivan standing in the doorway.

"You two coming in or what?"

"Let's go." I say as I move my arm from Maya's waist, grabbing her hand and walking her inside.

When we go in, Gray has his laptop and projector set up again in the living room. It's being projected on a large whiteboard that Seth usually has downstairs in the training room. We go over the route we are going to take again when we get to Smith Falls, so we know the direction to go without question.

"How are we going to break up our driving times?" Ivan asks. "It's going to take a little over six hours to get there, according to what Gray pulled up on the maps. I can take the first two hours." He offers while taking a seat in one of the wing-back chairs.

"I'll take the next two." I say, holding my hand up lazily as I lean against Ivan's chair.

"Hey Maya, you want to split the last two and half hours with me?" Gray asks.

"Sure. I can do that. I think I'd get bored out of my mind if I drove for a solid two hours." Maya says. "An hour and fifteen minutes will be doable."

"What, are you all going to just throw me in the trunk then, since I'm not driving at all?" Seth jokes.

"If you're a backseat driver, we just might." Ivan fires back.

We all laugh at Ivan's banter, but we quickly settle into a heavy silence.

"Well, we better get to bed; six am comes quickly." Seth sighs.

We all get up and follow Seth as he shows us to our rooms. Gray and Ivan's room is the first down the long hallway. Seth shows us mine and Maya's room, which is across from Gray and Ivan's. While Seth's room is the last door on the opposite side of the hall, which is the furthest away from all of our spaces.

Gray and Ivan go into their room with a wave of goodnight and shut the doors without another word. Seth does the same and Maya and I are left alone in the hallway feeling awkward all of a sudden. Just because we had sex in the back of my pickup doesn't mean I have the right to automatically jump into bed with her without her consent, even though my words to her earlier ring through my head again.

She toys with my fingers, and I notice a hint of a blush creep into her cheeks.

"I will do whatever you want, Baby Girl." I whisper.

"*I want you, Aiden. But with the rooms being so close. I don't know.*" She pauses.

"Baby, if being loud is a concern of yours, I can easily fix that." I say, letting a sly grin play on my lips.

She opens the door and walks in, her hand still wrapped around mine, tugging me along.

"What did you have in mind?" Maya asks.

I keep walking toward her, pushing her toward the bed until her knees are against the side of the mattress. I then call my fire to my right hand, pulling the heat back and making the flame thicker, then I wrap it around the perimeter of the room, keeping it about four feet from the wall.

"Did you just make a soundproof wall?" Maya asks with astonishment on her face.

"I did." I chuckle.

While keeping her beautiful blue eyes on mine, she slips her hands under my shirt and runs her fingers over my stomach and chest and I take a shuttering breath at her touch.

"It's all you Baby. One word and I'll make you mine." I growl.

"Aiden." She pleads my name. "Please."

I instantly pick her up by her waist and she lets out a squeak at the sudden movement before she wraps her legs around my torso, locking them at the ankle. As my arms wrap around her, I let my electricity play at my fingertips in a low amperage, and I give her a little zap on her ribcage where I know she's ticklish. Her squeaky laugh is louder, and she clamps a hand over her mouth at the sound and her eyes widen in shock.

"You do remember, I owe you for that little water condom stunt you pulled in the training room downstairs a few days ago, don't you?" I ask as I zap her again.

Her face gets red as she remembers what she did and recalls all the parts of her I said I would shock.

"Aiden! Don't you dare!" Maya squeals as she tries to get out of my arms, but I see the playful smile on her face.

"You should know better than to run from a wild animal, Baby." I growl into her neck and toss her on the bed.

I peel off my shirt, tossing it into a corner of the room, and stalk her on the bed. I then take her right leg and slowly take her shoe off, tossing it behind me where it lands with a muffled thud on the carpet, then her sock.

I stroke the sole of her foot and again let my electricity trail along her skin under my finger. She tries to pull her foot away, but I hold on to it while running my fingers a few more times down her arch, her laughter bubbling up, but she tries to hold it back. I pin her foot under my arm and work on her left foot in the same manner. Taking her shoe and sock off, while trailing my electricity over the arch of her foot until she's laughing at my touch.

Once I have my fill of teasing her this way, I crawl onto the bed, my upper body hovering over hers, and place light kisses against her skin, starting from her forehead to her cheeks, and then her chin where I end on her lips. My tongue skims over the seams of her lips before darting it into her mouth to explore her fully. Just when she's getting into it, I pull back from her lips, slip my left hand under her back, and arch her up enough so I can use my right hand to pull her shirt over her head.

I slowly take in her lacy bright pink bra for a heartbeat before quickly unclasping the hooks with my right hand and gently pull the fabric away from her.

Her hands fist the sheets at her sides and I run the index fingers of my left hand through her hair, giving her another low shock behind the curve of her ear, then trail the current teasingly down the column of her neck. She bends her head back into the pillow to allow me more access and I run my finger down to the base of her neck before heading over to the other side, tracing a similar path on the opposite side before I follow the flow of her skin in between her breasts.

I cup the right one in my hand, and I growl possessively as it fits perfectly in my palm as I gently roll her peaked nipple under my thumb, all the while still sending little shocks into the taught bud.

Her breath comes out in soft moans and I feel the devilish grin starting to spread across my lips that I am the one to make her sound like this.

Now I understand that one Taylor Swift lyric that I heard non-stop on the radio. I don't know the name of it. All I know it was something about summer, but I know I'm looking up at her like a mischievous devil and that I am the only one to make her writhe like this at my touch.

I slowly lean down and take her left nipple between my teeth and bite down, but not hard enough to hurt. Just enough to know that I am indeed there.

"Oh, Aiden!" She cries out, but it's not as loud as I want her to be.

"That's not loud enough, Baby Girl." I croon against her skin before backing away.

I then unbutton her jeans and tug them down over her hips and off her legs, revealing her matching underwear to the bra that lies discarded on the floor somewhere. She goes to undo my own jeans, but I take both of her wrists in my right hand and pin them above her head.

"Not yet, Baby Girl. You'll have your fun soon." I growl.

Her breath quickens where it makes her breasts heave with each inhale, and I harden painfully against my zipper, now wishing I would have let her at least unzip me.

So to distract myself from the pain between my legs, I trail more kisses down her neck, occasionally grazing my teeth against her skin, leaving my marks behind as I work my way down her body, taking another gentle bite of her left nipple on the way across her belly, stopping just before the waistband of her panties. Then, with the index finger of both hands, I tug her underwear down her legs and toss them into the heap of her clothes on the floor.

"You are so beautiful." I say as I see every inch of her wanting more of me.

I take my left index finger and trail it along the apex of her inner thigh, and she arches into my touch.

"Eager aren't we, Baby?" I croon.

"I want you Aiden. I want all of you." Maya pleads breathlessly.

"You'll have me soon enough." I say.

I trail my finger over her thigh once more and then hover over her center.

"I want you to scream my name, Baby Girl. Don't hold back." I say.

She looks at me for a split second to see what I'm going to do and what I mean by my statement, but I don't give her much time to think before my thumb is roughly rubbing circles on her clit. She arches into my touch, but she forces her mouth to stay silent. I send a little electrical pulse into the sensitive skin and she clamps her hand over her mouth, muffling her moan.

"Ah ah." I scold her. "No covering up, Baby. Now, let's try that again."

I send another shock into her, this one just a touch stronger than the last, and she arches into my touch, grinding into my thumb, but she's still not screaming for me. I send another shock. This time, she moans my name out loud, and it's music to my ears.

"That's it Baby Girl." I praise. "Sing to me."

I do this a few more times and each time she gets louder.

"Aiden." She pleads on the edge of her release.

I then dip a finger in her center and she moans louder still. Her back arching into my touch, while her fists roughly gather the blankets above her head. I pull back to the tip of my finger and when I dip into her needy core again; I add another and she finally screams my name.

"Aiden! Oh, don't stop."

"That's it, Baby. Yell as loud as your heart desires." I croon as I work in and out again and again, and she rolls through her first orgasm.

After I withdraw my fingers, I lean in and give her a sound kiss. She forces my lips apart with her tongue and I happily let her devour me. Just like she did in the truck, she uses that kiss to distract me and she somehow pivots her hips and is now straddling my stomach. I feel her still warm center weep against my skin from my loving abuse just a moment ago.

"Now, it's my turn." Maya says breathlessly.

"Have your fun, Baby Girl." I reply.

She trails her own kisses down my neck and chest, leaving her own marks on my skin. Her love bites are still smarting as she wastes no time unbuttoning my jeans, pulling them off my hips while taking my boxers off at the same time.

I let out a sigh of relief as the pressure is no longer being held back against the zipper, but I immediately feel something wrap right back around me and it makes my breath catch in my throat. It's different from her water condom, but it's the same glorious pressure and it's all I can do not to let my eyes roll back in my head.

"I'm not one for oral, but I think this will be a close runner-up." Maya croons.

I take one look at her and I know I'm in trouble for whatever she has planned. The smirk on her face is the only thing I remember before I feel her wind tighten around me, making stars burst in the corners of my vision. I feel her power relax for a moment and before I can recover my breath, it's tightening around my shaft again. But instead of just pressure against me, it feels like it's almost pulling at the same time.

I find my own back arching off the bed in response and I can't stop the groan that slips from my throat at this sensation that is flooding my brain.

"Scream for *me*, Baby." Maya takes my own words and uses them against me.

Then she leans against my chest, trailing her lips lightly over my skin as she tightens her wind around me again, trying to milk my own orgasm from me and I can't fight the groan of her name that erupts from my lips.

"Maya! Oh, that feels so good."

She works me like this for a few more minutes, hours, years; I don't know. I've lost all track of time and space as she makes me fall apart before her. She brings me back down to Earth when she kisses me and takes my bottom lip between her teeth. Nipping and teasing at the swollen flesh.

I lock eyes with her a moment before she says, "Now, let's finish this." I feel her wind dissipate and her water forms the familiar cold, living condom around me.

I grin as I flip her onto her back. She lets out a squeal of laughter and I devour it as I crush my mouth to hers again, greedily taking in her every breath, every moan, taking every single thing I can about her and burning it into my mind.

"Ready?" I ask, my lips brushing against hers.

"Always for you, Aiden Rivers. Always." Maya says.

I use my right knee to force her legs wider so I can settle in between them before I grip her right leg and, while trailing kisses up her skin, I let it rest on my hip.

I give her one look. One moment of anticipation. One moment for us to enjoy one another for one last time.

She returns my stare as if she understands my silent thoughts and that she will cherish this moment for the rest of her days. Just like with our first time in the back of my Colorado, I tease at her entrance with the tip of my erection and she tries to buck into me, but with her leg over my hip, and my hand gripping her thigh, I keep her pinned to the bed, and let a wild smile play on my lips.

"Do you want this?" I ask as I tease her again, sliding just the tip in before pulling out.

"Yes, Aiden. Please! Please!" Maya yells.

I chuckle and I slowly seat myself inside her, filling her inch by inch. Her groans fill the room and I am so happy that I did make that firewall because the whole house would have heard that sound.

I drop her leg so I can lean into her and she wraps her arms around my neck instantly.

When I pull my hips back so I can thrust into her again, she wraps her legs around me, pulling me deeper into her sweet body and her nails dig into my back when I hit the spot that makes her feral. I rock into her, abusing that sensitive spot a few more times until she's shaking with need underneath me. Her moans and breathless voice saying my name fill my senses as her hips arch up to meet me thrust for thrust.

Maya gets me to roll onto my back and she straddles me, her knees on either side of my hips. I somehow harden even more inside her as she pulls herself just to the tip of me. Before I can wonder what she's going to do, she roughly slides back down on my length and hits that spot inside herself that has her groaning in a way I have never heard from her.

She continues that up-and-down movement and I match them with each thrust of my hips, driving myself even deeper and we both crash through our orgasms for the second time tonight.

After my head clears again, I grab her by the hips, pulling her down to my chest and flip her on her back once more, and now that I know where her sweet spot is, I hit it relentlessly. Only for an instant am I sorry she has this water condom over me. I would love to see my release pouring out of her hot and well-loved center, but I can't do that to her. Die and leave her with the possibility of a kid; that's not right. But I can't help the thought of what she would look like with my seed dripping out of her.

Once we drive out our final pleasure, I collapse beside her. Chests heaving and sweat trickling down our skin. Maya rolls onto my chest and I wrap my arm around her.

"That was amazing." She says.

"Amazing isn't the word. No word can explain the way all that made me feel." I say.

My back is burning from her nails, and my manhood is aching from the abuse I just put him through, but it's a blissful pain.

"I just hope we can walk in the morning." Maya laughs.

"Yeah." I reply as I tuck a piece of hair behind her ear. "You okay?"

"Yeah." She replies as she draws little circles on my chest with her index finger.

I match her movements and I trace her shoulder blade with my middle finger and I feel her shudder under my touch. I kiss the top of her head and wrap my arms around her, pulling her deeper into my side.

I take a deep breath, willing the words to form on my lips that I want to say to her. "Maya, I love you—" I begin, but I am cut off.

"Don't." Maya whispers into my chest. "Don't tell me you love me in a goodbye sort of way." She lifts her head to look at me in the eye.

I tug her on top of me, but just to hold her as close as I can. No desire flares from either of us. She wraps her arms under my shoulders, hooking herself around me, and rests her head on my chest again. When I feel something wet drip onto my skin, I realize she's silently crying for me, for us. I don't call her out on it, I only tangle my hands in her hair and hold her tighter.

"I love you, Baby Girl. You know that. Even before this prophecy came into our lives, back when I didn't have a lick of power, I loved you. I will always be in love with you." I pause, but I make myself continue. "I want you to promise me something."

She lifts her head, tears still rolling down her cheeks. I pull her face down and kiss each eye, the saltiness of her tears covering my tongue, then I pull back, using the pads of my thumbs to dry her eyes.

She takes a shaky breath and gives me a wobbly smile. "Anything, Aiden."

"I want you to promise me that no matter what happens tomorrow, you will continue to live your life as you want." I say. She starts to shake her head, but I give her a look that makes her stop and continue to listen. "You have amazing powers. You can help people. Don't let them go to waste over me."

"Okay." She says after a moment, her voice shaking from unshed tears. "I promise I'll live on for you, but that doesn't mean I won't stop missing you."

"I would haunt you if you ever forgot about me." I say, trying to lighten the mood.

"Oh, no. Who are you?" Maya says, a slight smile on her lips.

"Let me remind you." I say and I lightly smack her on the ass and give her another kiss.

I pull back and she glances over at the clock on the nightstand. I crane my neck to look in the same direction and I see it's eleven thirty.

"We better get to sleep." Maya says.

I extend my right arm and I let a trail of my fire flow from my hand. For flare, I let it go in the shape of a fiery dragon. We watch as it collides with the wall and once I feel the connection; I let the wall fall in a way that's reminiscent of snow over us.

Maya looks on in awe as the little embers fall around us in silence. I watch her as sleep finally takes her under and the last embers of my fire land in her hair and I pray that we all will make it out of tomorrow's battle so I can have many, many more nights like this with her.

63

Gray

After Ivan walks into our room, he steps to the side, allowing me enough space to enter, then closes the door softly behind him. As he walks past me and towards the bed, I notice the humor that was dancing in his steel-grey eyes earlier is gone, and in its place is the hard-core Ivan that strangers usually meet.

I hate seeing him closed off and quiet like this, and I know the best way to get him out of his head for just tonight.

Ivan takes a seat on the corner of the mattress and starts roughly untying his shoelaces, starting with the right one. The sound of the nylon being pulled through faux leather is the only noise in the room, and to me, it's deafening.

I slowly walk over to him while silently grabbing the back of my shirt with my right hand and pulling it over my head before tossing it on a chair that sits near the window. As I stand to the left side of Ivan, he doesn't look up at me as he toes off his right shoe and then starts to untie his left.

"Ivan." I whisper.

He pauses, the shoestring in his right hand held taut, matching the lines of his body, but he still doesn't look up at me. So I move, standing between his legs, and grab his chin, forcing his face up towards mine.

"Look at me, damn it." I say, my voice just a bit louder than a moment ago, but not commanding; it's more like a plea.

"What, Gray?" Ivan asks, his eyes searching my own.

"Don't go there. Not yet. Let me...let us be carefree for one more night. Then in the morning, you can be the brooding, scary, kick ass first, then take names later Ivan that everyone should fear."

I can literally see him processing my words as his steely eyes rove over my shirtless torso. The desire that begins to flare in their smokey depths ignites my own need for him and the way his eyes linger on the slowly growing bulge in my jeans makes me involuntarily shift to try to relieve the pressure, but Ivan's smirk at the movement only makes me grow harder for him.

"Okay. You want carefree?" Ivan asks as he grabs my hips with his large palms, and I suck in a breath at his sudden movement. "Then let's be carefree, Baby."

He pulls me toward him, and I straddle his lap in one smooth movement. His mouth immediately goes to my throat, his teeth grazing over my Adam's apple. I groan at the sensation while rolling my hips against the hardness I feel building in his own jeans.

"Grayson, stop that." Ivan pants as he trails his lips down my throat and ends in the middle of my chest. "I want to take my time with you." He adds, his breath teasing my nipple.

"I don't want to take it slow." I breathe with another roll of my hips, harder this time, making Ivan growl against my chest.

After a heartbeat, Ivan stands and I instinctually wrap my legs around his waist at the same time my arms snake around his thick neck. I nuzzle my nose into the soft spot behind his ear, but before I can even think about pressing my lips to the sensitive flesh, my body drops to the mattress. I look up and Ivan is standing there beside the bed, watching me, like he's figuring out what he wants to do.

So, like any normal human being, I provoke him into action.

"Take a picture you Lug Nut, it'll last longer."

"Let's see how long you last before you're coming down—" Ivan begins, but I cut him off, tired of waiting for him to take me.

"Stop using your mouth to talk, Ivan." I grab his wrist, pulling his body on top of mine.

Ivan's hands land on either side of my head, while his right knee is between my legs, but nowhere near where I want him.

"So demanding tonight, Baby." Ivan croons as he lifts his left hand, bracing his weight fully on his right arm, the muscles going rigid while the veins pop out against his tattooed skin.

The sight makes the breath catch in my throat, but when his left hand traces the hard lines of my neck, chest, and stomach in a feather-light caress, his touch sends a pleasurable fire right to my already aching hard on, and I turn into a pleading puddle beneath him.

Ivan's amused chuckle barely reaches my ears, and before I can snap at him for laughing, he roughly unbuttons my jeans, the zipper echoing in the otherwise quiet space between us.

As he parts the rough fabric, the build-up of pressure releases, but when Ivan grips me through my boxers with a firm hand, that pressure builds to another level, and my head tips back into the pillow with a strangled groan.

Ivan chuckles again, and this time I don't care. I don't have the mental clarity to even try to come up with a snarky remark. I just want him. And I make it clear to him as I thrust my hips against his palm, the tent in my boxers slowly growing as I move.

"Okay, Grayson." Ivan begins, "I think this little foreplay session is over, don't you agree?"

Before I can even utter a word, Ivan rips my boxers and jeans over my hips and down my legs, leaving me utterly bare to him, my erection standing proudly between us, and the look of hunger in his eyes as he takes me in, makes my tip weep with excitement.

Ivan leans down, but instead of feeling him where my body is begging for him to be, his lips trace every muscle on my stomach. Across every ab that he and I helped develop over our years of sparring together.

"Ivan." I plead when he gets to the defined V of my torso, so close to where I want his mouth, but it feels like he's a million miles away. "I thought you said foreplay was done?" I growl.

"I like to keep you guessing." Ivan says, his voice husky.

He gives me one more kiss, right at the base of my V, and in my next breath, I feel his mouth devour me in one go, his tongue teasing the underside of my shaft.

My head kicks back, bumping against the headboard with a soft thud while I clamp my hands over my mouth to keep my groan of pure desire trapped in my throat and not rattling against the walls for everyone in this strange house to hear.

Ivan hums around me, and the vibration travels right into my balls, making me jerk my hips. When I feel the crown bump against the back of his throat, pleasure coils so tight around the base of my spine, that it takes everything in my body not to spill down his throat. I don't want this sensation to end yet; I want him to work me longer, harder, but that all fades when something tickles the back of my head, but I realize it's coming from *inside* my head.

"Grayson, why are you holding back? You already taste so sweet on my tongue. Why keep me from enjoying all of you?"

Hearing Ivan's voice in my head when Aiden is not around is just as much disorienting as it is hot, and I have no choice but to come undone. I fist Ivan's short black hair at the back of his head with my left hand, while driving my hips up, forcing myself deeper. He groans against my length and I come with a shout, his name pouring from my lips as he takes every drop I give him.

"You taste like damn site Nirvana." Ivan croons.

He releases my softening and spent length with a loud pop, and through half-lidded eyes, I watch Ivan lick his lips. I groan again and with my fingers still curled around his hair; I pull him up towards me. He crushes his lips to mine, tasting the saltiness of my release on his mouth.

I go to scratch my short nails down his back but I'm met with the soft fabric of his grey t-shirt, and that's when I remember that he has had his clothes on the entire time. I fist the fabric in my hand and give it a firm tug.

"I want these off you, Ivan Grant." I demand.

"All you had to do was ask, Grayson Lukas." Ivan teases, matching my full name with his.

He sits up, his knees digging into the mattress on either side of my hips, and grabs his shirt from the hem before pulling it over his head and tossing it to the side where my jeans lie forgotten on the floor.

I let my eyes take in every inch of his broad shoulders, defined chest, and carved stomach. I'm mesmerized by the way his tattoos flex and seem to come alive as Ivan unbuckles his belt. He grips the gunmetal buckle with his left hand a moment before he rips the belt from the belt loops of his jeans, the leather snapping from the force of his movements. The sound paired with his brutal hungry expression as he looks down at me, makes me harden all over again for him.

"Unbutton my jeans, Grayson." Ivan growls low in his chest.

With trembling hands, I unbutton his jeans and slowly slide his zipper down. Ivan's head tips back as I release some of the pressure that I know his jeans were creating against him. Without taking my eyes off what I am doing, I pull his jeans along with his boxers over his hips, pushing them to the middle of his thighs, just above the bend of his knees, letting his proud, hard erection free for me to see in all its glory.

I swallow hard at the sight of him; acting like this is the first time I'm seeing him. It's still hard for me to believe that the man kneeling before me is mine and I am his. I don't think I will ever get over that feeling, and part of me hopes I never do. Because I love being consumed by every inch of him and how he reminds me that *we* belong with one another.

Ivan leans over the side of the bed, grabbing something out of his black duffel bag before sitting back up. He extends his right hand towards me and when he opens it; I see a small packet of lube sitting in his palm.

"If you want me to take you on this bed, then you better open that packet, Grayson." Ivan demands. "Lube me up so I can slide into that perfect ass of yours."

I grab the packet of lube and rip the corner off with my teeth, which earns me a hum of approval from Ivan, spurring me on. I then sit up enough where I'm within reach of his still proudly standing hard on, and empty the packet onto him. Ivan opens his mouth and I know the words that are coming next, so I don't give him the time to say them as I wrap my hand around his length and spread the lube all over his shaft, starting at the base and pulling to the crown, allowing my thumb to tease the tip once, twice, before sliding my way back down.

I don't get to a second pass before Ivan is shoving me onto my back. His large, calloused palms are on my knees, bending my legs up and spreading them wide so I am utterly open before him. With this position, he's just missing the spot we both want him to be. I can see the realization settle into Ivan's steel-grey eyes before he looks into my own.

"Guide me to where you want me, Baby Boy. And if you do, I may even give you a little surprise." Ivan croons with flaming desire.

With choppy breaths filling the space between our naked bodies, I snake my hand between our legs and guide him where we both feel his tip press against my back entrance. We hiss at the contact and my head tips back and to the side, trying to mentally prepare for the sensation of Ivan filling me like he has so many times before.

He eases in and I can't stop the groan any more than Ivan can stop his own growl. "Shit, Gray. How can you feel just as good as the first time I took you three years ago?"

"It's the same for me, Ivan." I pant. "Now stop talking and ruin me."

Ivan pulls back to the tip and with one fluid and strong flex of his hips, he seats himself inside me, making stars fill my vision as the fullness registers in my brain.

Ivan grunts as he withdraws, but before he thrusts again, he leans into my ear, his teeth scraping over the fleshy lobe, causing gooseflesh to ripple across my skin, and whispers. "I told you I'd have a surprise for you, didn't I?"

"What could you possibly give me that's better than what I have right now?" I ask as I thrust my hips to get a little friction between us.

"Oh, I think you'll like this."

I can't see what he's doing, but I can absolutely feel it. Something small, cold as ice, but hard as metal forms around the tip of Ivan's erection, and before I can even ask him what the hell he just did while *inside* me, he begins to move. Pistoning his hips in a hard and brutal motion. And the thing he made is brushing against my inner walls so fast that I feel my spine lock up from the orgasm that's quickly building.

I don't question the feeling anymore. I wrap my legs around Ivan's waist, locking them at the ankles while I thread my fingers into his hair, pulling him down to me where I can bite, kiss, and devour his neck, chest, and shoulders.

Ivan's movements begin to get choppy and erratic, and I know he's just as close as I feel. The evidence on damming display and glistening between us. He pulls back to the tip, both of us teetering on that imaginary blade of pleasure.

"Ivan, please." I beg.

He leans down, his mouth crushing a bruising kiss to mine as he whispers in my ear, "Come for me, Grayson." Just before he slams home, hitting that spot he's been teasing all evening, and I explode.

"Ivan! Oh, damn!" I scream, my release covering our chests and stomachs.

With one final thrust, Ivan's release follows next with a roar. "Gray! I love you so much."

"I love you too, Ivan." I say as he continues to rock into me, drawing out our release as much as he can. I can feel him filling me to the brim and that makes everything feel ten times better. This is the first time we are loving one another without anything between us, and I will absolutely be doing this again.

Once we are both spent, he pulls out and collapses onto his back, chest heaving, and his skin is slick with sweat. My eyes rove his body and I land on his softening shaft and what I see staring back at me makes me chuckle.

"When the hell did you get a piercing?" I ask as I stare at the circular ring around his crown. But then I whip my head back around to him, taking in the lazy, post-orgasmic smirk on his face. I smack him soundly on the chest for that look. "That's what you did while you were *inside* me?"

"Don't tell me you didn't like it." He smirks while wiping at a sticky spot on my stomach.

"You're so lucky that I love you and that I take your little bouts of insanity when they creep up."

"I'm only crazy for you, Baby." Ivan says as he pushes up on an elbow to kiss me again. "Come on, there's a shower through that door. Let's get cleaned up and get some sleep. It'll be morning before you know it."

I nod and we both get a shower together, of course. And while I'm drying off, Ivan finds some clean sheets to remake the bed before we turn in for the night, holding on to each other tightly as we anticipate tomorrow's fight of our lives.

64

Mason

After Victor transported The Siphon yesterday evening, we all have been forced to live in the command center together. At least when we walked back in, Victor actually brought a few mattresses with him, so I have been able to sleep with Dani tucked against my side, even though the damn chain is still wrapped around her wrist.

This morning, I am abruptly awoken by Victor's maniacal laughter. I sit up and instantly pull Dani close to my chest. Rhett wakes up last and groggily looks around before his eyes land on me, and I just shrug.

Victor literally runs from the pod area toward us. No, he actually damn site skips, like a kid that just found out how to steal cookies from the cookie jar when he notices we are awake.

"I have amazing news!" Victor exclaims.

"What's going on boss?" Rhett asks.

I force myself not to roll my eyes, but Dani gently scoffs at Rhett's words, and I tighten my arm around her in response.

"I think I may have figured something out!" Victor says, complete joy still lighting his eyes.

My stomach sinks at what he is getting ready to tell us.

"Come! Follow me." Victor says and turns to walk back toward the pods.

I get up, but I give Dani a stern look to stay put. She sinks back into the mattress and pulls the covers up to her chin as if that will protect her from what she may overhear.

"Bring her, Mason!" Victor snaps, his old demeanor back in place as he throws me a key to her manacles.

I force myself to swallow the growl and extend my hand toward her. She takes my hand with slightly trembling fingers and stands up. When I tuck her tightly against my side, I feel just how much she is shaking, and it breaks my heart.

"Nothing will happen to you. I swear it on my life, Angel." I whisper in her ear before giving her a gentle kiss on the top of her head as I unlock the chains from her wrists.

She nods and walks with me while I follow Victor and Rhett into the pod room.

When we walk into the room, Victor has one pod open and running. Ready to pull a power from its next victim. Next to the control pods, I see a new piece of machinery that was not there the other day. The seven-foot, silvery box-like structure with a white front sits ominously against the wall, just waiting to be turned on.

Victor walks over to the new machine and flips a switch that illuminates what I now understand to be a glass window to show off what's inside if someone would walk up next to it. Victor waves a hand with a flourish, like he's a damn game show host, and he just showed us what's behind door number two.

"This boy's and girl, is a new method of transferring that I *know* will work." Victor announces.

I take a closer look at this machine without moving from my spot near the main control panel. It looks honestly like a vending machine to me. When I look closer, there are glass jars sitting inside on metal shelves. But there's something writhing within those jars. Something that gives off different colors.

Blue, White, Brown, Gray, and Red.

When my eyes drift to the red, I get a familiar feeling, but yet it's foreign at the same time. When the understanding of what I am seeing hits me, I have to take a step back when I realize how many jars he has in this new machine.

Hundreds of jars.

"Those are all....abilities in those jars." I whisper, utter horror forcing my chest to tighten.

Blue for water.

White for electricity.

Brown for earth.

Gray for metal.

Red for fire.

"Right, you are my boy!" Victor praises.

"How did you get these?" I ask, my voice barely above a whisper.

"I told you all those failed experiments were only stepping stones in a better direction." Victor says with an evil smirk.

He's been harvesting these for years. I think to myself. *Each failed experiment, he's saved the powers like they're a collectible until he needed them again.*

"Are you able to transfer these into someone, Victor?" Rhett asks as he walks over to the machine and inspects the contents.

I glance at Dani as Rhett's words hang in the air and complete and utter fear fills her eyes.

"Yes! I just actually transferred one into myself." Victor says.

He what?

"Which one did you pick?" Rhett asks enthusiastically.

Rhett's tone makes my skin crawl. Again, he's like a kid wanting to know what kind of Pokémon card someone just pulled from their wrapper instead of someone's real ability that was ripped from their Soul Power.

Victor then raises his left hand and something red jumps into his palm. Fire.

My stomach drops, but it's not just due to the fact that he actually has another power. No, it's the wrongness of it. I don't know if it's because of the type of element he now wields, but I am able to somewhat connect with it, and it feels unstable. Like it wants to fight against him and rip him apart. Then I realize that the flame is still looking for their original host, and is fighting desperately to get back out into the sky and go back to the rightful owner.

I take another step back and push Dani up against the wall with my back. I need to keep her away from all this before Victor tries to put a power into her. She balls my shirt into her fist and my flames flicker under my skin in response to her fear.

"That is amazing, Victor! I want one!" Rhett exclaims.

"No!" I say before I think through what I'm doing.

Victor's eyes slice over to me and if looks could kill, I'd be dead where I stand. I take a breath before I continue. "The powers are still unstable. I can tell the fire is not fully yours to control, Victor." I offer.

"Nonsense! I feel great!" Victor says. "Rhett, I have a special one for you. Go get in the pod."

Rhett, like Victor earlier, literally skips toward the pod, jumps in, and closes the door behind him. He has the biggest smile on his face that I have ever seen as Victor opens the door of the vending machine like thing and it releases a blast of cold air over the floor.

He has them stabilized in a cryochamber. He then stoops down and grabs a jar from the very bottom of the machine.

The jar is clear, but there is almost like a film gathered at the bottom of the jar. Then, as if it starts to feel the heat in the air, it jumps to the top of the jar.

Victor walks over to the pod that Rhett is waiting in and he inserts the jar into another newer piece of the machine, and it houses the jar perfectly. My eyes travel over the new piece of equipment and there is a huge needle, that is just as long as the jar is waiting to be activated.

With a push of a button, the needle pierces the metal lid of the mason jar, almost touching the bottom and a whirring sound begins, signaling the machine is turned on, and the glistening substance is sucked up into the needle and into the hidden tubing within the pod.

From this angle, I can fully see Rhett standing in the pod. When Victor had someone in these fucking things before, I've been as far away as I could, but now I can see exactly what is about to happen.

Once the whirring from the jar machine stops, the pod starts to come to life, and before Dani and I can prepare ourselves, Rhett's right side is viciously impaled by an insanely large needle. It goes right between his ribs. I'm not much on the human anatomy, and I think it just barely misses his lungs, but I know it hits his Soul Power.

His screams of pain echo in the pod and I just wait for him to keel over, but he doesn't.

The pod stops whirring, and the door opens with a puff of air and we all wait with bated breath. Dani pokes her head out from under my arm, but I don't let her off the wall as Rhett finally lifts his head with a dark smirk playing on his lips.

When his eyes meet mine, I have a feeling he may try to come at me. I barely get that thought to take hold in my mind before something almost cracks in the air. I start to bring my fire to my hand to make a shield like I have seen Aiden do so many times in our previous fights, but I'm not even able to make an ember flare to life before Rhett is in my face with a rock-shaped dagger pressing into my throat.

My breath freezes in my lungs and my brain is reeling, trying to figure out what the fuck just happened. His dagger pushes deeper into my throat to the point I feel it break skin. I finally get my shit together to bring my fire to my right hand in a large arc toward him, while keeping it from Dani and forcing him to back away. He disappears and reappears next to Victor again.

He can fucking teleport now?!

I turn to look at Dani and as her face pales at what she just witnessed; I have one thought come to mind.

This needs to be destroyed, and fast.

And with that thought, I reach out to Aiden.

65

Aiden

I wake up to the sound of an alarm going off and when I open my eyes, Maya's dark brown hair fills my vision and her bare back is facing me. She stirs as the alarm finally cuts through her own sleep-filled mind. I roll over to the nightstand on my side of the bed and shut off the alarm, and when I roll back over, Maya has turned to face me.

"Morning." I say with a small smile.

"Morning." She replies.

We hear a door open and close down the hall and then a hard knock sounds on our door and then on the other across the hall.

"Time to roll, everyone!" Seth's muffled yell echoes in the room.

I take a breath and give Maya a kiss on the nose. "Let's go kick some ass today, Baby Girl." I say.

I pull the covers off us and I gather her clothes that we left discarded on the floor last night. I bring them over to her side of the bed and I kneel in front of her with her panties in my hands, waiting for her to put her legs in them while still not caring about my own lack of clothes.

"You okay?" I deliberately ask the open-ended question and I give her a smirk and wait for her reply.

"I'm fine." Maya says as she snatches her clothes from me.

She goes to get up, but she takes an awkward step and I can't help but grin at her.

"Are you sure about that, Baby Girl?" I ask, chuckling, still kneeling on the carpet.

"How are you fairing?" She shoots back a moment before she wraps her wind tightly around me.

I lean forward on my hands and try to ignore my own soreness and the pleasure her wind brings me.

"Maya stop. I don't have the firewall up." I grunt through clenched teeth as she tightens her wind around my shaft.

"You better be quiet then." She croons, and she starts to pull at me with her wind.

My head snaps up and I give her a pointed look as the pressure builds low in my spine and continues into my pelvis, but the look in her eyes stops the scolding I was about to give her and makes the pleasure trip fade away. I understand what she's doing. She's giving us something to look forward to once we *all* make it back. So, like any gentleman; I give her what she wants.

"I am so gonna punish you again when we get back. Count on it, Baby Girl."

She lets go of me, and my whole body relaxes. She leans over me, and while she's back in her bra and matching panties, she has nothing else on but a smile.

"I'm quaking in my boots. Oh wait, I'm not wearing any!" Maya jokes while wiggling her toes in my face.

"Keep it up, and I'll make sure you eat those words." I warn.

She laughs and walks across the room to pick up her jeans and t-shirt to put them on and I finally pick myself up off the floor and do the same.

After we are both fully clothed ten minutes later, we walk out and run right into Ivan and Gray as they are coming out of their room.

Gray smiles at me and Maya, but Ivan takes one look at me and the knowing smirk tells me he has an idea of what happened last night. I enter his mind before he can say anything out loud.

"Not a fucking word, dude." I warn.

"I didn't say a thing, man."

"Well, your face did." I growl.

"I didn't hear anything. Did you two leave the house?" Ivan asks, ignoring my tone.

"That's for us to know and your nosey ass to never find out." I reply with a smirk. Before I take a step, I look between him and Gray and I notice a smattering of bruises peaking out from their shirts. *"Looks like you and Gray had an* active *evening."* I tease. *"So, I doubt you would have heard anything from us,* anyway.

"Yeah. Unlike you, I don't hide my affection for my man." Ivan shoots back.

I chuckle as I take Maya's hand and pull her down the hallway and into the kitchen, where Seth is waiting for us.

"We will eat while we drive." Seth says as he finishes packing a cooler he has set up on the island.

As Ivan and Gray meet us in the kitchen, we all take one last look at one another and I give them all a grin that says let's get ready to kick ass.

We drive in the lineup that we discussed yesterday where Ivan takes the first two hours, and when he stops, I take over until it's Gray and Maya's turn to finish the last stretch of the journey, and the only sound filling the space is the rolling of the tires on the asphalt and the passing of cars beside us on the highway.

About ten minutes into Maya's drive, I lean my head back against the headrest in the hope of relaxing just a bit longer. I close my eyes for a moment before I'm surging forward in my seat with a pain-filled groan, breaking the long-hanging silence of the car. I hear the muffled shouts of Ivan, Gray, and Seth along with Maya's scream, but I can't make out their words with the pain pounding inside my head.

I lean forward with my elbows on my knees while clutching my head in my hands to try to ease the pain that feels like I'm being punched inside my brain. A moment later, Mason's presence enters the back of my mind, but I can't hear him. It's like his mind is too loud with....fear.

"Mason. You need to calm down. I can't hear you." I say.

"Aiden, what's wrong?" Maya asks finally, her voice full of worry while her head whips from the road to me and back again.

"It's Mason." I say as I rub my temple to ease the ache. "Damn, I should have trained him more on how to start a conversation this way." I add with a groan.

"Get here now. Victor is—" Mason begins, but his fear builds up again and I can't hear him.

"Mason, you have to quiet your mind. I can't hear you." I say as I try to send a calming vibe toward him.

I can feel him finally calm down a bit and the words that follow make my heart freeze in my chest.

"Victor finally figured out how to transfer powers into someone." Mason says while sending images of what he's seeing from within The Siphon.

The glass mason jars, the pods, the piece of equipment that looks like a vending machine that houses those jars.

"Maya, step on it." I say aloud. *"We'll be at the park in thirty, but it's still a five-hour hike to get to The Siphon."* I tell Mason.

"What's going on, Aiden?" Ivan asks.

I look only to Seth and I have to use all my willpower to keep my abilities in check because what was once fear at seeing the things Mason was showing me, turns to anger that Victor actually figured out how to accomplish this crazy plan of his.

"Your brother figured out how to transfer powers." I say and I show him what Mason sent me.

"I can tele—" Seth begins, but I cut him off mentally.

"No, I need you at your best to get them out when it's time for me to end this." I say.

Seth nods, "Step on it Maya."

Maya looks in her rearview mirror at Seth and then over to me. Her eyes hold the silent question of if I'm okay. I take her hand in mine and with a light squeeze; I nod my head. She releases a breath, turns back to the road and flies down the highway.

66

Aiden

We arrive at Smith Falls National Park and Maya finds the little area that we already picked out to park Seth's car in so it will be hidden from any visitors. I'm still shocked that Victor agreed to send The Siphon to such an active park when I see all the hikers going in the opposite direction from us.

Once we exit the car, I take the lead on the hike, with Seth following behind me, then Maya, Gray, and Ivan taking up the rear. I keep the mental image of Gray's map in my mind as we follow the trail that he mapped out, and we follow each other quietly for what is the first minutes into the five-hour hike.

When I look around, I can tell this trail is not kept up at all. Roots, loose rocks, and soft dirt snag our shoes and shift under our weight with each step we take. When I hear Maya's low squeak, I turn my head in time to watch Seth grab her arm in an effort to keep her from falling over a section of loose gravel. I slow my stride, falling back to the middle of our group so I can help her traverse the path while letting Seth take the lead for a bit.

Two hours into the hike, when we come across a slight turn in the path, I freeze mid-step when I start to feel the electrical pulses of someone nearby, but they're moving too fast to tell which way they're coming from. Maya looks back at me once she realizes I'm not walking beside her anymore, and just as I open my mouth to tell them about what I'm picking up on, I hear a rope being cut somewhere off to our left. My head snaps in that direction and a huge sharpened tree branch emerges from the canopy of trees above us, swinging in a vicious arc toward Maya and me. On instinct, I shove Maya to the side and into Gray's outstretched arms.

I call my fire to my right hand, readying to make my shield, but a shockwave that seems to come from the tip of the branch blasts my fire away into embers on the wind. I am utterly exposed as the branch connects with my body, impaling me about four inches deep in the lower section of my stomach. Sharp white-hot pain explodes in my body as a secondary shock wave goes off, sending me flying backward into a nearby boulder with a solid thud and a cry of pain being forced from my lips.

I slide down the boulders and I know I leave a trail of blood in my wake as I feel the irony substance gushing from the wound. When my damaged body hits the forest floor, I barely hear Maya screaming my name past the ringing in my ears as she continues to be held back by Gray and Ivan. I close my eyes, trying to shake my head to clear my ears, but I stop mid-shake when I start to feel an electrical charge snake over my skin.

My unsteady gaze slides toward the tree line and I spot Rhett with an even wilder look in his eye. I slowly sit up while lifting my left arm, pointing my trembling hand towards him; the blue and white electrical current snakes around my arm as I charge up the attack a moment before I let it go.

He somehow moves faster than I want to comprehend right now, as pain finally catches up to my rattled brain and fills every cell in my body. With my breaths echoing around me in painful pants, I try to apply pressure to my stomach to staunch the flow of blood, but I can't put enough pressure on the wound to slow the bleeding.

"Aiden!" Maya screams as she rushes over to me, applying the pressure I was not able to do myself and I can't help the scream that rips from my throat. Part of me wants to push her away, even though I know she's only trying to help.

"Move!" Seth snaps.

Maya moves enough to let Seth near me, and his healing ability flows through my broken body. Once it gets to the point where the pain is manageable and the bleeding is a little more controlled, I make him stop.

"Seth stop. I'm okay now." I grit out as I try to get up to my feet, but I stumble back to one knee.

"No, you're not healed enough." Seth says.

"You can't waste all your energy on me when they are just gonna come after me again!" I shout. "I'm fine. Let's keep going."

I try to stand up again and this time I'm able to get back under my own feet, but I try to hide the fact that my legs are still wobbly. Maya comes up to my side and the look on her face tells me that I'm not fooling her and that she's there if I decide to accept her help. I give her a small pained smile and begin to walk toward the path again, my stride slower than it was.

We walk on for three more agonizing hours. I talked Maya into getting in the middle of our group with Gray, as I take the lead again with Ivan at my back and Seth taking the rear this time.

As we slowly make our way up a slight incline, the pain in my stomach is slowly getting worse again, but I force it to the back of my mind as I start to pick up on electrical currents skittering in the air all around us. And I realized that the electrical pulse I feel is not from anything living. It's from The Siphon. I release a heavy sigh as that thought comes to mind.

We are so close to ending this.

When we get to the mid-point of the path where the incline is the steepest just before cresting over the hill, I start to stumble over the loose, rocky terrain. Ivan rushes up to the front of the line and gives me an annoyed look.

"You should have let Seth heal you more, dude." Ivan says quietly.

"I can't man. You should know why." I say.

I glance up and notice the full moon hanging low in the sky, slowly becoming redder as the minutes pass, and that sends chills down my spine.

After a few more agonizing miles, I start to see the apex of the machine jutting out from the dense line of trees that surround it. When I see the black metal with wires and pipes snaking in and out of The Siphon, I somehow find renewed strength in me to start running toward it. Ivan runs by my side with Maya, Gray, and Seth a few yards back.

As I run into a clearing, something snags on my shoe and I think it's a fallen branch, but the next thing I know is I am thrown sideways again, my ears ringing from a powerful electrical charge being detonated. The sizzling and cracking of the lingering charge skates across the dirt, rocks, and trees.

My whole body is locked up from the charge while every cell in my body is now screaming at me from the blast and from rolling so many times on the rocky ground I've lost count. My right side slams painfully into something solid, and I finally come to rest at the base of a tree.

Once the world stops spinning a heartbeat later, I go into fight mode and I am instantly on my feet, climbing back up the hillside, but what I see in front of me makes my body go numb. What I hear past the blood rushing in my ears makes my vision fill with red.

Gray's sorrowful wails and screams tear from his throat as he sits on the ground, his body rocking back and forth as he holds a bloody form in his shaking embrace. One arm is cradling their head while the other is resting on top of their chest.

"Please. Please don't leave me." Gray pleads as he glides his hand through the crimson and black hair, down the expanse of the blood-coated neck before taking the large hand and pressing it to the side of his face as tears stream freely down his cheeks.

As I step closer, I hear the gurgling whisper, "Love...you." before the final breath leaves their lungs.

I feel him slip from my mind as his body goes limp. Gray mournfully screams, cries, and pleads for the man in his arms to open his eyes.

"IVAN!" I scream as I rush over to his broken body.

While my mind is racing with what happened, my movements are calculated. I try to shake him awake, but he doesn't respond. His right arm is at an odd angle, and his left leg is torn to pieces from the blast. I lift his left arm to see if I can find a pulse in his wrist, then I move to his neck. My heart drops like a stone as I feel nothing but stillness.

"SETH!" I scream behind me, looking over my shoulder as he and Maya finally reach us.

I rip Ivan's shirt apart by the collar to expose his chest, just as Seth kneels at our side.

"Seth, heal him, please!" I beg.

Seth's energy appears, and it's the greenest aura I have ever seen him create. He looks at me and I know instantly what he's asking for. With a quick glance at Maya, she reluctantly pulls Gray away.

At first, he fights her, screaming at the top of his lungs while tears pour from his eyes. "No! Don't take me from him! Please!"

"You can't hold him while Aiden is trying to shock him. Gray, please, let them work." Maya's voice breaks, but she holds Gray back so I can do what I can.

I pull my electricity into my hand and place it on Ivan's chest, which is starting to go cold beneath my palm. I push past that sensation and when Seth finishes healing his body—visually, at least—I send a shock into Ivan's heart.

Nothing.

I pull my power again and I shock him once more.

Still nothing.

"Come on, damn it! You have to LIVE!" I scream. *This wasn't the death we prepared for.* I push into his darkened mind.

I shock him a third time, increasing the power.

As the electrical current leaves my arm and disappears into Ivan's chest, I wait with bated breath.

Wait for the rise and fall of his chest.

Wait for the lazy, cocky grin that was always on his face.

But nothing changes.

Gray rips himself from Maya's grasp and gathers Ivan's lifeless body in his arms, hot tears still streaming down his face as he gently kisses his partner's eyes, nose, cheeks, and lips as if he's committing them to memory since that's all he'll be left with.

I feel Maya come up to my side and she places a hand on my shoulder, holding it in a death grip. I cover her hand with my own and I feel the silent tears slip down my face as I take in one of my brothers lying there dead on the ground, while the other sobs his heart out at the loss of his love, and I couldn't do a damn thing to protect him. It all happened too fast.

I feel anger and sorrow start to take root and fill my chest. I move Maya's hand off my shoulder and when I get up to my feet, they somehow don't feel as shaky as I thought they would. My power responds to my anger. Flaring and crackling just under my skin, eager to be let loose on the world, and I know this is how I'm going to end this.

I need utter destruction to ease the pain I feel. And right now, I don't really care who ends up in the crossfire as long as two people make it out alive.

Just as I start to walk away, I feel a hand reach out and grab at my ankle. I'm sure it's Maya trying to stop me, so I try to pull free, but the hand holds on tight to my leg. I don't look back, though. I don't want to see the sadness or fear of me in her eyes.

I go to pull away again, but I feel something cold and solid wrap around my ankle.

67

Aiden

"You said....not to let you go....and destroy that thing...filled with anger."

I look down at the rough, strangled voice and my heart freezes in my chest. Ivan looks up at me with a tired smile on his filthy face. I feel like the weight of a mountain has been lifted off my shoulders as I collapse to my knees; the rocks biting into my skin through my jeans.

"Ivan?" I ask.

"Who'd you think it was?" He croaks. "Did he get knocked in the head that bad? Does he know who he is?" Ivan jokes as Gray showers his partner's hair, forehead and cheeks with kisses, while his watery laughter filters through the space between us.

"God, only you can joke at a time like this, Ivan." Maya groans, but she smiles at his words.

"You scared the shit out of us, man." I whisper.

"Yeah." Ivan sighs. "We didn't plan on this type of death, did we?"

"No, we didn't." I say with a somber shake of my head.

With Gray's help, Ivan sits up against a nearby boulder to get his bearings for a few minutes before he helps Ivan to his feet.

"You alright, Ivan?" Seth asks, his eyes taking in everything about Ivan standing before him.

Ivan rotates his right arm, then shakes out his left leg and smiles at us. Dirt, blood, and sweat all mixing together on his face, but it fits him somehow.

"I feel great! Now let's go and kick some ass." Ivan says as he makes his iron skin. "Probably should have had this active the whole time."

"That would have helped, Ivan." Gray scolds as he gives Ivan a mock punch on the shoulder. "Would have saved me from having a heart attack you Lug Nut."

"Live and learn I guess." Ivan says while shrugging his shoulders.

"Oh my god, Ivan." Maya rolls her eyes, but I see the playful smile she's trying to hide from him.

Seth, Maya and I begin to turn around with Gray on our heels a moment later, but when we hear Ivan's voice, we all pause, looking back at him, but his eyes are solely focused on one person.

"Grayson." Ivan says, his tone firm and all hints of humor vanish in the blink of an eye.

Gray walks back over to Ivan with a look of panic on his face. "Are you okay? Are you hurting anywhere? Do you need Seth—"

Gray is cut off mid-sentence as Ivan pulls him into his chest and kisses him soundly on the lips while he wraps his large hand around the base of Gray's neck. I want to look away, just to give them this moment of privacy, but I can't. Gray was so close to losing Ivan. Hell, he did lose him for a few minutes. And I know Ivan can still feel it in his bones. So we watch two people that are so much in love that it shines from every pore, express that emotion with every touch and every kiss.

"I am fine, Baby." Ivan says after he pulls away enough to look Gray in the eye. He uses his thumb to brush away tears from Gray's cheeks before pressing one final kiss to his forehead. "I just wanted to say I'm sorry for putting you through that, but if I ever have to go out, being in your arms for my last moments is where I'd want to be. I love you, Grayson, until my dying breath; I love you."

Gray takes Ivan's hand, kissing his knuckles lightly, and says, "I love you too, Ivan." Gray gives Ivan another quick kiss before saying, "Let's finish this so we all can go home and put this behind us."

We walk a few more minutes and the electrical pulse I feel in the air is now overwhelming, and I know it's coming from The Siphon. As we approach, we finally hear the raging river that's the power source for this machine. Through the clearing of trees, we see The Siphon and it's even worse than I thought.

It stands twelve feet high and the piping and wires that poke out from various places make it look all the more menacing. I feel my abilities surge under my skin in response to this machine like they know it's almost time to end this and are ready to get this over with. I take a step forward and allow a crack of lightning to fly off the top of my shoulder to ease the tension under my skin.

My head then whips to my left and before I see it coming, I hear the roar of fire come barreling towards us from the forest. Before it even gets near us, I know this is even hotter than what Mason's fire is, so I know it's Victor and this is the second power he's given himself.

I make my firewall in the shape of a dome over our little group, and the attack rolls right over us. I turn to my team and I reach out to them through our connection.

"No matter what happens, I am proud to have called you all my friends, my family. And I couldn't imagine anyone else being here to help me with this. I love all of you. Now, as Ivan has said, let's kick some ass."

Ivan reinforces his iron skin, Gray has the silver balls in his hands, Maya makes her ice sword, and Seth lets wind and earth play at his fingertips. I let my electricity roll down my left arm as I drop the firewall just as Victor walks out of the tree line and Rhett, with Mason at his side, emerges from The Siphon.

I look at Mason for a moment and I can tell he's fuming over something, but I don't have time to think much when Rhett makes the first move and makes a gigantic and deathly sharp piece of rocky earth shoot out from the middle of where we are standing, intent on forcing us apart. Pushing my fire to my foot, I decide to go after Victor myself, but Mason cuts me off with a wild, flaming punch.

I pull back at the last second and his fist misses me by inches. He instantly counters his attack and actually punches me right in the gut, where I was already impaled by the tree branch. His power smoldering against the flesh. I have to bite back a yelp of pain as I am flung a few feet back and forced to one knee.

"You were bleeding too much. I just cauterized your wound." Mason says.

"That's kind of you. Now we need to make this look real. Sorry." I reply.

I push my fire to my foot and bring my electricity to the tips of my knuckles that way it's a targeted attack and I punch him low in the side but it will still hurt like hell all the same, and I fling him sideways and into a nearby tree.

I then make my way over to the machine, just as I notice that Maya and Ivan are locked in a fight with Rhett and they are giving him a run for his money, but the blood that is running from Maya's temple makes my own boil. I turn back to The Siphon and Victor comes from the woods again and he has fire dancing at his fingers, but it feels wrong. Like it's fighting to get out of him.

He smiles at me as I feel the wind pick up and I know what he's trying to do; trying to gather his wind around my head. Pushing my fire to my foot, I close the distance between us with in a few heartbeats. I bring my fire and electricity to my hands, making both abilities twine together, and as I close in on him, I push both abilities into his chest, making him scream in pain as he flies into the tree line again.

When I go back toward The Siphon, Victor's running out of the forest and, just like my vision, Ivan swings his iron bar into Victor's head. Victor changes course, locking his eyes on Ivan, and just as his wind begins to encircle my friend's head.

I push my fire to my foot again, but I'm too far away. I'm not going to make it in time, and dread fills my chest. Then hands grab my shoulders, and Seth appears behind me a moment before we teleport in front of Victor and I have a heartbeat to build my electricity to make a shock wave and get Ivan away from him.

As the blast hits him, I hear Victor groan again in pain and his body slams into the side of The Siphon, making a huge dent in the metal. Smoke billows around him from, I assume, a pipe bursting from the impact.

Maya then screams from across the clearing, still locked in battle with Rhett, and Gray's throwing the silver balls, but Rhett is too fast for them to keep track of. I can feel him teleporting all over the area.

As I run over to them and I see that Maya is on the ground, and just like my vision, I see her ankle has been broken. Rage fills me and I try to focus on Rhett's electrical signal, but the bastard is moving too fast even for me to sense. I see Seth running across the clearing and I know that I can at least have him help Maya.

"Seth!" I scream.

He looks at me and he teleports over to us.

"It's okay, Baby Girl. He's gonna help you." I say as I stand near her and rest my hand on her head.

Sweat drips off my nose and I'm starting to feel the wound that Mason temporarily closed start to reopen. Seth lands beside us, panting and sweat dripping down his face, and he immediately goes to work on Maya's leg without a word.

"I still wish you'd let him—" Maya begins, but her words are cut short.

I barely pick up on the electrical current landing behind me. I turn, trying to defend against an attack that I know is coming, but I'm too slow. White hot pain flows through my back and low in my chest. The tip of a rock sword covered in my blood protrudes from my chest and I know if I wouldn't have moved that fraction of an inch, it would have cleaved right through my Soul Power.

I barely hear Maya scream my name before the weapon is withdrawn and I stumble a step backward as my blood runs freely down my back and chest. I don't know where I get the strength, but as Rhett is swinging the sword down toward my head, I turn around and I build my electricity up to the breaking point and I force my fist toward his chest and I let my power go in a deafening crack, and I know before he hits the ground on the other side of the tree line that he is dead where he lies.

I collapse to my knees and hold a hand over my bleeding chest. The sticky, coppery substance flowing through my fingers. I grit my teeth and, as Mason did for me, I make my flame flow from the inside to cover both entry and exit wounds, and I cauterize my wound enough to stop the bleeding.

I somehow force the scream to stay in my chest, but it takes me a few minutes to even out my breathing. I look at Maya and the fear in her eyes somehow makes the pain in my body feel like paper cuts. I give her a smile, and I know it's contorted with pain, but I give that smile to her anyway.

"Let's finish this." I whisper.

I then look to Gray, who had been watching this play out in front of him, as Ivan walks over and helps Maya to her feet.

"Seth, we gotta end this now. What are you doing with your brother?" I ask and I let Seth know the state of my body.

I'm weakening so fast now, and I'm worried I won't have the strength left to use my powers in full force.

"I'm right here, boy!" Victor says.

I look up and I hear a scream that makes even my skin crawl, and then I notice who Victor has at his side.

Dani.

"I've noticed that my boy Mason here has been pulling his punches with this fight. So I'm going to use my little piece of collateral here. You want her to live, you fight for me, Mason." Victor sneers.

"Seth, can you teleport?" I ask Seth, but I also push this to Mason, too.

"Yes, I'll take you and get her to Mason. I wanted to be the one to take care of my brother, but—" Seth begins.

"Once you get Dani out, I can chain him to the ground." Ivan says.

I nod once and Seth sets his hand on my shoulder. Mason's roar of pure anguish keeps Victor's eyes on him; giving us that one fleeting moment to teleport, which tears at my already broken body, but I force it to the back of my mind as I build up my electricity.

Once we land, Seth immediately grabs for Dani.

"You're coming with me, little missy." Seth says.

When he leaves and Ivan's chains appear a moment later, I let my electricity go and shock Victor, but not enough to kill him. I want him to see his creation fall at my hands.

"Reinforce his chain's Ivan. I don't want this bastard moving an inch." I growl.

More chains appear, locking into the ground and Victor pulls at them while growling in my face. A moment later, Victor's growls are cut off by wisps of wind around his head.

Seth comes up and stands beside me. "He's got enough oxygen to stay alive while you destroy this monster." He says before turning his attention to Victor. "I just have one thing to say, brother. This was not worth what you put those victims through. I told you before that I believed in the prophecy and that you were fighting a losing battle, and today that will be proven."

Victor soundlessly growls again at Seth while pulling at his chains and we just walk away from him. I limp alongside Seth and as I stare up at this machine; I notice it is eerily quiet around us. The whole forest is. The only sounds are Dani's sobbing as I see her being held tightly to Mason's chest; he gives me a firm nod as a sign of thank you for getting his girl back to him.

"You're welcome. Take care of her." I say. *"You're a good guy, Mason; don't forget that."*

"Thank you. Now, go do what you need to do and destroy this fucking thing." Mason says.

As I take in this machine for the last time, I can feel my demeanor change into what I used to be. I don't care about anything. Cold, calculated, get the thing you need to do, done.

I turn to my friends. I give Ivan and Gray a hug and then I look at Maya. I pull her to my chest and I hold her for a moment. She shakes against my broken body as tears flow down her bloodied and dirt-crusted cheeks.

I pull back from her, and I run my thumbs over her skin. "Remember me. You still have the flowers I made you for your birthday. They will last forever. I love you Maya Harper and in the time we knew one another, you have made me the happiest man alive. Live on for me." I say. I turn to Ivan, Gray, and Seth. "Make sure she's safe and she lives her life."

I give her a sound kiss on the lips and I look at her once more.

With tears in her eyes, she nods, "I love you too, Aiden Rivers, but I'm not giving up on you. You will come back to me."

I take a breath as I walk away from my team and as I step closer to this machine; I hear the roar of fire come at me, but I am in no mood to even dodge it. I lift my right hand, suck in the power and have my flames internally devour them. Victor has melted through Ivan's chains and is coming at me, but I don't care. I bring my own flames to my hands and I feel Seth's approval of what I'm about to do.

I draw my arm back and I punch Victor square in the chest, burning a hole right through him. I watch with dark satisfaction as the wild rage fades from his eyes and he collapses to the ground.

I keep walking toward The Siphon, knowing it has so many powers that have been stolen from people over the years, knowing that my uncle's power is in here. I bring my fire and electricity to my hands, pushing them to their limit, and I feel myself lift up and hover in the air.

Once I am at the same height, twelve feet in the air, I look back at my friends one last time. Ivan is holding Maya, who is silently crying, and even Ivan has wet cheeks too. Gray is on the other side of Maya, holding onto her hand for both comfort for her and for himself.

Seth is standing in front of them, and I see the look of approval in his eyes. He looks over his shoulder at Maya and she pulls herself together and she brings her powers to just below mine.

Complementary powers will be the ones to destroy this machine.

Once her water is around my electricity and her wind is around my fire, she lets her essence go and it's like they will flow along with my power, even without her command.

I take a breath and let my abilities start to flow from my Soul Power, and I keep increasing them to their limit until they each are starting to encircle The Siphon.

My Soul Power starts to ache deep in my already abused chest and I know I'm doing it the right way. I take one final look at this monster of this machine and I push all my anger that I feel into my powers. Anger at every single victim I know.

My uncle.

Mrs. Jaffee and her husband.

And all the others that I don't.

As I tick off the victims, my fire begins to get so hot that even I feel the heat and it's scorching my skin while the current of my electricity hums and cracks violently over my arm.

I force out even more power. My flame and electricity climbing up my arms to get closer to my Soul Power so they can suck more energy directly from the source.

With the new surge of power, my abilities surround the machine in an instant. The only thing I see in front of me is my fire and being fueled by the oxygen that Maya's wind is creating. My electricity, and the current being made deadlier from the water, carrying the current to each and every crevice of this machine.

I give one more final push, and the white-hot pain that is all too familiar to my Soul Power fracturing fills my chest, but I force my powers past the pain.

Then everything happens in a flash. The Siphon engulfed by my powers and explodes with such force that I feel it impact my broken body.

And then all I see is black.... just like my vision has always shown me.

68

Maya

As Aiden floats above us, it's almost like his entire being is glowing from the power he's creating. I realize it's from his Soul Power and it's practically visible in the center of his chest. The orange and blueish-white sphere almost becomes one with the powers that climb up both of his arms. Then I watch helplessly as he pushes past his limit. Hear his roar of pain fill the sky. The explosion follows an instant later.

Ivan quickly makes an iron shield to protect the four of us from the heat of the explosion and from Aiden's powers. His electricity is still arcing wildly, trying to find something to connect to and destroy while his fire is snaking around, looking for more to burn and devour.

I continue to look around, as broken parts of The Siphon fly in all directions along with dirt, rocks, and trees varying from the size of sticks to broken tree trunks.

Once everything calms down, Ivan slowly drops the iron wall from around us and I take a step forward, lifting my eyes to the sky where I last saw Aiden.

But I don't see him in the sky. Instead, I see these little spheres of different colored lights. Of blue, white, brown, grey and red, drifting on the wind a moment before they start to shoot off in all different directions, like a living kaleidoscope, leaving colored tails in their wake a moment before they disappear from my sight.

I slowly stand on unsteady feet and begin to look over the broken ground around us for Aiden. I look in a five, ten, fifteen-foot area around us, but find nothing.

"Aiden! Aiden!" I scream over and over and over again. My voice becomes raw, pleading, and almost screeching each time I scream his name into the silence around us.

At first, I think his whole being is gone, torn completely apart from the force of his powers, but then I hear Seth yell for us across the clearing a few hundred yards away.

I take one look over my shoulder to see where my only remaining friends are. Gray is leaning into his partner's side for support, while Ivan makes a splint for Gray's right knee.

"Get over here, now!" Seth screams with desperation in his voice.

Ivan nods, silently telling me he will be right behind me, and I take off. When I find Seth, his back is to us, and he's straddling something—no, someone. I stop mid-stride, Ivan and Gray almost colliding into me as I take in the broken, bloodied legs poking out from underneath Seth's body.

A crack of electricity rattles the trees around us and I jump at the sound, falling back against Ivan and Gray's chests. When their hands gently grip my arms on either side, I understand what Seth is doing.

"Shit. Come on!" Seth growls as he's trying desperately to shock Aiden's heart back into rhythm. He yells curse after curse for each failed attempt to start his heart. "Damn it, Aiden. You weren't supposed to die!" Seth bellows.

"You're a Mimic. Can't you bring him back? Can't you heal him, Seth?" Gray asks, voice breaking as tears stream down his cheeks. "You healed Ivan, now heal Aiden!"

"No one can heal a Soul Power! And Aiden's is shattered. I can feel it." Seth says with anguish.

I pull away from Ivan and Gray's grips and slowly walk over to Seth so I can stare down at Aiden's broken body. Tears well up in my eyes so thick that I can barely see him. I roughly brush them away as I kneel down beside his lifeless body and take in everything I can about the man that meant everything to me.

Eyes that were once so full of life, are now closed. Those lips that I kissed so many times, that gave me so many smiles, that caressed my skin and spoke such loving words, now lie partially open, dried, and cracked from the lack of water in his system, from him overusing his power.

Water.

I lean forward and gently caress his cheek with my right hand. My water tattoo peaking through all the dirt, blood, and grime on my skin. I take a shaky breath as I feel his skin already cooling under my touch. I close my eyes, trying to let my mind go silent and focus on my water entering through his mouth, and I find the path to his heart.

If I can get the organ hydrated, maybe, just maybe, we can get his heart beating again.

"Maya." I hear Ivan say my name, but I ignore him.

Without opening my eyes, I know Mason and Dani come upon our little group and just watch as we try to save Aiden. I feel my water rehydrating his heart, his blood, his lungs, and I look at Seth once more.

"Please, try to shock him again." I whisper the plea.

"Maya, he's—" Seth begins, but I cut him off.

"TRY IT AGAIN!" I yell.

I cannot give up on him. I promised him I wouldn't. I promised him he was going to come back with me. Damn it, I'm still waiting for him to punish me for my little stunt I pulled in the bedroom just this morning. He promised me he would make me pay for that.

He can't be gone.

Seth nods after a few precious moments and he gathers the electricity to his fingertips and lets the current go into Aiden's bare chest.

One.

Two.

Three.

Four.

Five times.

Gray falls to his knees beside me and we hold one another as we sob and mourn the loss in front of us. Ivan settles in between us, a hand on each of our shoulders, kissing the tops of both of our heads in comfort. Seth sits down on the other side of Aiden's body, his forearms on his knees in defeat. The forest around us is silent, almost like it's in mourning, too.

For several long moments, it feels like time stands still, the sound of our cries filling the air before Mason breaks the silence.

"Well, I'll be damned."

I watch as Seth looks at him with confusion.

"Look." Mason says, and he points at Aiden's body.

His broken, torn, and dirty body.

A body that is now breathing.

While it is shallow, and his breaths come with several seconds between each one, it's still the fact that his chest is finally rising and falling on its own. And while his heart is beating slowly, it's beating all the same.

I feel a smile spread across my face and I run my hands through Aiden's hair. But he doesn't stir. I look at Seth and he has that distant look in his eyes and I know he's talking to someone through a mental connection.

"I don't have enough power left to both heal him and teleport us out of here. I know someone who can stabilize Aiden until I can fully heal him."

"Let's go then." I tell him with urgency.

"I can't take you two." Seth says while looking at Mason and Dani.

"Don't worry about us. Take him and get him help." Mason barks. "Just keep us updated."

Seth nods and I give Mason a small smile before Seth teleports the five of us a moment later.

When the world settles, I look up to find the sun shining and birds chirping all around us. Looking to my left, I see a towering creme-colored stone estate with trees surrounding us in all directions. We landed in the middle of a long, circular driveway. The one-way-in, one-way-out design cuts through a lush green, well-manicured lawn. I also noticed that it's warm here. Back home it was starting to get chilly, but here, summer is still in full swing.

A door opens from the side of the estate a moment later and a tall man emerges from the doorway. His red hair pulled back onto a man-bun in the middle of his head, and beside him, is a woman with auburn hair, her soft curls cascading to her shoulders.

Spotting us in the driveway, they rush out to meet us. Both are in long opaque plastic aprons draped over their jeans and plain t-shirts, booties on their shoes, and blue medical gloves covering their hands.

"Ivan, are you able to help them carry Aiden inside?" Seth asks, sweat dripping down his nose as he's trying to catch his breath.

Ivan nods, but I can tell he is measuring up these strangers that Seth seems to know.

"Seth!" The man says. "Oh, Luna above! This is the one you told me about?" He asks, the Irish lilt in his voice becoming clearer as he gets closer to us.

He has this unnatural way about him. Every move of his body is fluid, like each one is planned and powerful. And did I mention he's tall? At least six-four and the woman beside him is quietly looking over Aiden's body, taking in all his injuries. She's shorter, coming to just under the man's arm, but she has a fierce look on her face.

"Ivan will help you carry him inside." Seth says. "I'll be there in a moment. I haven't teleported this far in a while." He pants out.

"Don't worry, Seth. You will be needed later once I complete the surgery." The man says as he looks at Ivan and smiles. "Excuse my rudeness of not introducing myself or my...girlfriend." He pauses on the word and both he and his *girlfriend* share a look and I get the feeling only they know about the meaning of his awkwardness in the moment. "We have work to get to, but I could use your help in getting him inside."

"I don't give a fuck what your names are right now. I just want you to save my brother." Ivan says. "You can tell me your life story afterward."

The man nods to Ivan and they pick Aiden up by the arms and legs and carry him into this old-looking estate, and I just sit here with Seth and Gray, who has been silent this entire time.

I just feel alone, beaten, and scared.

"He is in good hands, Maya. That doctor has *years* of medical practice under his belt." Seth offers.

I look over to him and I see a small knowing smile on his lips and I give him a slight nod. I find myself looking back to the estate as I watch Ivan and the two others go through that same side door and disappear into the building.

"Where are we?" I ask.

"We are in Montana." Seth says. "At the estate of an old friend of mine, Tobias Huntington."

69

Maya

Montana.

We are about ten hours from home. No wonder Seth had to recover from teleporting us here.

"How do you know these people?" I ask.

"These are the people that Avery, Cole, and I helped in a war that was fought here many years ago. So we go way back." Seth says.

He takes a breath, gets to his feet and extends a hand to help me up too.

"I get a weird feeling from this place." Gray says as he looks around the area.

"You may. This is a powerful household, after all." Seth says as he slowly walks toward the mansion and we follow in behind him.

Seth enters through the front door and the house is bustling with movement, but it's all orderly, so I'm not sure if this is just the norm for this place, or if it's all because of our arrival.

"Come on. There's a room down this hall we can wait in." Seth says as he leads us down a hallway, past what looks like a large dining room, where I notice a set of glass doors are wide open, leading out to a patio.

As we continue to walk deeper into the house, I notice there are two doors. One to the left of us and one straight ahead. Over that door is a bronze plaque that reads: *Surgery Suite.*

My heart stalls in my chest and I can't help but stare at the door, wondering what's happening on the other side. Gray comes up behind me and gently runs his hands down both my arms, before pulling my back into his chest.

"Come on, Maya. Let's go in here and wait." Gray says while ushering me towards where Seth is patiently waiting by another room.

He opens a solid wooden cherry-stained door before walking inside. This room looks like a normal sitting room, complete with a dark brown leather couch, loveseat, and matching chairs, along with a metal and glass coffee table with matching end tables to finish out the decor, but I can smell the antiseptic of a hospital wafting through the halls.

A few minutes later, we all hear someone knocking on the doorframe. My stomach drops, thinking it's either the young woman or the man telling us about Aiden, but we are greeted by another woman standing there instead. Her brown hair is up in a tight bun perched on the crown of her head and she has a bright smile on her face.

I glance down at her hands and she has a pewter tray filled with bottles of water, different kinds of fruits, sandwiches, and even a few slices of chocolate cake.

"You three look like you could use something to eat while you wait for your friend to get out of surgery." She says as she sets the tray on the coffee table in front of the couch. "I'm Marisol, by the way."

"Have you heard anything yet, Marisol?" I ask as I take a bottle of water from the tray.

"No. Atticus usually comes right to the family that's waiting here once he's finished with the procedure." Marisol places a hand on my shoulder and gives it a gentle squeeze. "Your friend is in good hands. Have faith in our doctor and Tamer to bring your friend back."

I don't know what a Tamer is, but Marisol seems to be a trustworthy person, so I nod my head as I allow Gray to hold me close to his side and wait for any news.

After three and a half hours of waiting, we still have no update.

Thankfully, during that time, Seth has recovered enough to heal our wounds. Once that is taken care of, Marisol shows me the girl's bathroom while someone named Teddy, a younger man that has a cocky swagger to him, shows Seth and Gray the men's bathroom where we can each get cleaned up.

Marisol sees me eyeing Teddy for a moment before the three men walk around a corner from my sight because she chuckles and says, "Don't worry about Teddy. He seems to have a big personality, but let's just say he learned the hard way to keep himself in check. He actually helps Atticus in the infirmary now. Teddy is a real hit with the children. He makes them laugh and I always say laughter is the best medicine."

I smile at her. "That sounds nice."

Just as we turn a corner, I notice two men walk in the front door dressed in what looks like Army fatigues, the deep forest green with bits of black to match the forest around the mansion. Their combat boots pound against the floor as they enter, but what shocks me is they have a huge dog at their side. It's got to be a wolf-dog hybrid, cause that thing is freaking huge.

"Is this like a government building or something? There's a lot of people around here." I ask.

"No, my dear, we are not part of any government." Marisol smiles. "But let's just say we are a part of a very large and very powerful...family."

Mafia. Okay, got it. I think to myself.

Marisol shows me the full private bathroom and walks away without another word. Once I'm alone in the bathroom, everything comes crashing back around me in full force, and I just stare at my filthy face and torn clothes in the mirror and I want to break down again. But I hold myself in check because I know what Aiden would tell me if he was here. He'd tell me to get cleaned up and let the doctors handle things. So that's what I do. I peel out of my ruined clothes and get a long, hot shower.

Once I dry off, I open the shower curtain to find a set of shorts and a pink tank top that fit me perfectly. I wonder how Marisol knew my size, but I don't dwell on that too much; I only focus on putting them on and going back into the little waiting room to wait for these strangers to tell me whether they saved my boyfriend or not.

Once I make it back to the waiting room, Seth and Gray walk in a moment later, and just as we all take a seat the door opens and the auburn-haired woman comes out, taking off her surgical hat with a tired sigh while letting her hair drape over her shoulders.

"Atticus is just finishing up the last of the stitches. You all want to come in and see your friend?" The woman asks then shakes her head while she gives an embarrassed chuckle, like she forgot something she should have known better than to forget. "My name is Quilla, by the way. Sorry I didn't introduce myself earlier, but as your friend so eloquently said, names were formalities at the time."

"I'm sorry about Ivan's remark to you, Miss Quilla." Gray begins while rubbing the back of his neck. "Sometimes my man has no filter at all, but I think that's what I love about him."

"Oh." Quilla says, eyes wide, and Gray tenses for being so open about his and Ivan's relationship with a complete stranger, and for a moment, I let my water form just under my skin just in case I need to put a bitch in her place if she says something ugly about my friends love life. But her face shines bright with a smile and I see Gray relax.

"Well, how about we take you to your loved ones, then?" She asks as she looks between me and Gray.

"Yes, please. Thank you, Quilla." I say.

Quilla nods as she takes us through the door and down a hallway and just as we walk into a bedroom, the man, Atticus, rolls a bed into the room.

"Seth, have you recovered enough to heal him?" Atticus asks.

"Not to the extent he needs right now. I'll be able to tomorrow. That's why I brought him here. So you could stabilize him until I recovered." Seth says while stepping closer to Aiden's side to inspect Atticus' work.

Ivan comes in a moment later, and he gives me a firm hug before giving Gray a quick once over to make sure he's alright, then he releases me to pull Gray's back to his chest so he can lean against the wall. Ivan is in clean clothes, as well, but unlike me and Gray being healed by Seth, Ivan is still bruised and pampering a few broken ribs he got from one of Rhett's attacks with his rock sword.

Ivan rests his chin on Gray's shoulder as he wraps his left arm around Gray's waist while offering me his right hand, a silent request for me to step closer to him. I take his offered hand, and he takes a cleansing breath before he speaks.

"He will live. Atticus and Quilla are good at what they do. Now it's just a matter of when Aiden will wake up."

I try to reach out for his mind, but all I get is the sensation of him sleeping. It feels deeper than normal sleep, though. My stomach drops at what this means, and I cover my mouth to keep the sob in my throat.

"Maya, what's wrong?" Ivan asks, his head lifting off Gray's shoulder and snapping his full attention to me.

I look at him and tears sting my eyes, then Gray touches my shoulder and his eyes search mine, pleading for me to share what I just figured out.

"He's—" I begin.

I shake my head as my legs give out. Gray helps me to the floor while Ivan limps over to my side and I just stare at Aiden in that bed. Seth looks up from Aiden's body and locks eyes with me. He looks confused at the tears silently falling from my eyes, and I force myself to say the words loud enough for all to hear.

"He's in a coma. I don't know if he ever will wake up."

"How do you know for sure?" Atticus asks.

"Seth, try to connect to his mind. See if you feel the same thing I do." I say, my voice still barely above a whisper.

Seth looks at Aiden, and his face goes from confusion to anguish.

"Fuck!" Seth says as he turns around and for the first time I've known him, he loses his temper. He shoves his fist through the wall and I hear Atticus growl, but I'm too focused on Seth to really worry about that noise from Atticus.

"Are you going to fix that?" Atticus asks with annoyance.

Seth releases a heavy sigh as he mends the hole his fist made in the wall before he looks at Atticus. "Sorry, it's just this kid can't catch a break."

"What's wrong with him?" Quilla asks.

"Maya's right. Aiden's in a coma." Seth says while running his fingers through his hair.

"Perhaps that is the best thing for him for now." Atticus says.

"How is that a good thing?!" I yell.

Atticus walks over to our side of the room and kneels before me. He takes my chin in his hand so gently it melts the anger from my chest.

"It may be a good thing so he can heal on the inside. Heal where you all get your power from." Atticus begins. "I don't know much about how your powers work, but I know it comes from a special place that is just as breakable as bone, but we cannot cast that part of your souls. Only time will heal what's inside you."

"How are you so wise?" Gray asks.

Atticus chuckles. "I have been on this earth for *many* more years than you have. So, I would certainly hope that I would sound wise at some point in my life."

"How old are you?" Gray asks again while looking Atticus up and down like he's trying to mentally calculate his age. Ivan clears his throat at Gray's perusal of the doctor, but Gray ignores his partner.

"Nay. I don't know if you're ready for that answer, yet." Atticus says teasingly as he stands to his full height while he tugs me up off the floor with him.

Quilla walks over to Atticus and smacks him on the shoulder. "Be nice, Atticus."

He leans closer to Quilla and although he whispers into her ear, I still hear what he says to his girlfriend. "What, Rosie? They have been through enough today. I was just trying to save them from the shock at my true age."

I don't get why he says that, but when my eyes fall back on Aidens' sleeping form, all I do know is I want what's best for him, and if being in a damned coma will help him, then so be it.

Gray

Once we eat a much needed dinner with Maya, I help Ivan out of Aiden's recovery room and into the bedroom that Teddy showed me after I got myself cleaned up earlier. Ivan no longer hits the bed, and he's out like a light. I try to settle in beside him, but I can't get my mind to stop turning over everything that's happened in the last five hours.

So I ease myself out of bed, pausing a moment to make sure Ivan doesn't wake up, and I tiptoe out of the room.

The sun is just starting to set, but there's still enough light to see by, so I head down the hall and past a door that's slightly ajar. I hear what sounds like plates and silverware being clung around in water, so this must be the kitchen. I open the door to get a better look at it and I just glimpse the stainless steel appliances when a few kids no older than eight rush past me and through another door that leads to the patio out back.

"Where did those kids go?" I ask myself and walk the same way they did.

Once I'm through the sliding glass door, I hear another kid whisper, "Shhh, don't let him hear you."

I look around and I see the two kids that ran past me, a red head and a brunette, huddled with another blonde boy and a gangly grey puppy.

"Oliver, stop squirming." The blonde boy says, scolding the puppy.

I walk over and stoop next to the brunette boy and ask, "Who are y'all hiding from?"

"Shhh! We're playing hide and seek!" The boy shushes me harshly, and I find myself actually wanting to keep my mouth shut.

I hold my hands up in surrender and begin to stand when I hear claws rapidly clicking on the patio behind me. I turn to see another dark grey pup barreling towards us, her tongue lolling out the side of her mouth.

"Run! He found me!"

I stare dumbfounded.

Did that puppy just talk?

I begin to turn my head to see if the other kids heard her too, but I don't get the chance when I see this huge black and brown wolf rush around the corner with a vicious growl.

The kids scream, then laugh. I'm sure as hell not laughing, though.

"Holy shit!"

I take a step backwards, but I trip over the damn planter and fall flat on my ass. As the wolf approaches me, I go to grab for my Shock Grenade, but I forgot I left them in the bedroom.

"Damn it." I mutter, before turning my attention back to the wolf. "Nice wolfie. Don't bite me, I won't taste good. I promise."

The wolf cocks his head like he's thinking about what I said.

"Gray?"

Okay... I must have a concussion, because now this animal is talking to me... And knew my freaking name.

"Gotcha!" A small voice growls just as a white puppy barrels into the side if this much larger wolf.

And they laugh.

The group of seven—three humans and four wolves—are laughing.

"I'm losing my ever loving damn mind." I say, not bothering to lower my voice.

"No, you're not, Gray." The larger wolf answers.

"Yes, I—" I stop mid sentence when Marisol comes around the corner to give the now buck-ass naked man in front of me pants to slip into.

"Teddy?" I ask in disbelief.

"The one and only." He smirks.

"How?" I ask, confusion making my voice crack.

"You want a history lesson, or the quick facts?" Teddy asks.

"Quick facts. My brain can't compute much more."

Teddy chuckles. "I like you. Come on. Follow me while I put these crazy kids to bed."

The kids gathered around us scream and laugh again as they run past Marisol and into the mansion while Teddy follows, giving the woman a kind kiss on the cheek before walking in after the kids.

Once they are all in their respective rooms, Teddy leads me to mine and Ivan's room and I pause by the threshold, seeing that Ivan is still asleep.

"So it's true. That's what you are?" I ask.

"Yup. And don't believe the movies. That shit is so farfetched, it's ridiculous." He laughs. "Biting someone to turn them. It's a bunch of bull."

I find myself smiling at him. "You're cool Teddy. Have a good night."

"You too."

I walk into the room and slip into bed beside Ivan and while he groans in his sleep; he turns over to pull me tighter against his side and his touch helps lull me to sleep, even with the crazy realization I was just bombarded with.

Maya

Later that night, after Gray and Ivan left for the night, I crawl into bed beside Aiden, and just like the night before the battle, I snuggle into his side, my head resting on his chest. I have to work to keep down the sob that wants to rip out of my chest when I don't get his strong arm wrapping around my waist, pulling me even tighter against him, or the tender kiss on the top of my head. Instead, I am rewarded only with the sound of his gentle slumbering breath against my face and his restful heartbeat drumming in my ear.

It's in this moment that I know another thing. I will never be far from his side, no matter how long it takes for him to wake up.

70

Maya

The next morning comes all too soon and reality settles in around me like a fog after a nighttime storm. I sit up to look over Aiden's body and not a thing has changed. He hasn't moved an inch. Tears prick the corners of my eyes and just as I'm about to rush out of bed to go to the bathroom for a good, hard cry, I hear a knock on the door.

"Morning." Quilla says with a smile.

"Morning." I say while wiping tears away that escaped down my cheeks.

"Talk to him." Quilla says simply as she waves her left hand and I notice the intricate black and gray tattoo with vines and flowers trailing up her forearm.

"What do you mean?" I ask.

"Talk to him as if he was awake. What would you do normally?"

I look from her, then back to Aiden and I thread my fingers through his hair, imagining him leaning into my touch. My bottom lip trembles as I say, "Good morning, Baby. Did you sleep well?"

"There you go." Quilla praises. "Remember, just because he's not awake doesn't mean he can't hear you. Trust me, the bond between loved ones can't be stopped just because the body is broken for a while. I've seen it too many times here and back in my hometown. Love is powerful and healing. So let Aiden keep feeling your love for him, Maya." She leaves without another word and I turn back to stare at Aiden for a moment and just watch him sleep.

With Quilla's words fresh in my mind, I show my love for him. I lean in and gently kiss him on the lips, just like I would normally do when I greet him in the mornings.

"I'll be right back, Baby. I'm just heading to the bathroom." I tell him as I slide off the bed and walk into the connecting bathroom.

After I settled back in bed with Aiden, I hear another knock on the door before Ivan and Gray enters the room. Ivan is holding a tray filled with breakfast foods—pancakes, scrambled eggs, and sausage—while Gray has a tray of drinks, water, orange juice, and a carafe of coffee.

"We figured that we would bring breakfast to you." Ivan says with a small knowing smile.

"Thanks, guys." I say as I scoot down near the end of the bed, where Gray sets my plate of food.

"I tell ya, this place knows how to feed its people. You should have seen the dining room and kitchen! It's huge, but so well organized." Gray exclaims.

"Yeah. I had to pull him out of the kitchen or he was going to end up cooking with the chef." Ivan grumbles playfully.

"Something is still off about this place. The people feel kinda weird here." I tell them as I take a bite of my pancake.

"Yeah, I'm picking that up too." Ivan says as he hands Gray a plate and motions for him to eat.

"I think they are in a mafia or something. I mean, a place this organized and a house this huge? Come on, they have to be *something* big." I say.

"Nope, just your average werewolf pack." Gray says jokingly.

Ivan grabs Gray's cheeks with one hand, making his face pucker like a fish as he turns Gray's head left and right in a cursory glance.

"What are you doing, Ivan?" Gray mumbles.

"Just making sure you didn't hit your head somewhere I didn't see before." Ivan replies simply.

Gray jerks his head away from Ivan's grasp, "Why the hell would you wonder about that?"

"Just making sure you don't think these guys are 'werewolves'." Ivan says while making air quotations around the word.

"Well, we aren't exactly normal humans, so why would werewolves be so impossible?" Seth says with a grin while leaning against the doorjamb with his arms crossed over his chest.

"Because we are born the way we are." I begin just as Atticus and Quilla walk in around Seth and come to the other side of Aiden's bed. "If werewolves exist, then they would have to be made, Seth. So *big* difference."

Seth just chuckles as he leaves the room and I notice Atticus' grin before he can cover it with a nervous cough.

Since we are going home in a few hours, Atticus uses that time to take Aiden back into the surgery suite to insert a feeding tube in his stomach so we can start him on a liquid nutrient diet. Once Aiden is rolled back into his room, Quilla takes me, Ivan, and Gray aside and teaches us how to disconnect the old bag from this little machine that will stand next to his bed while he's 'eating', and how to clean the port protruding from this stomach. Then she shows us how to connect new tubing, and what settings the machine should be on for his next feeding.

Once Quilla is satisfied that we understand how the feeding machine works, she then shows us a few other tasks to help Aiden while he's in this damn coma. Like inserting an IV if we ever need to, or helping him go to the bathroom with a catheter.

"Also, be sure to turn him so he doesn't get bed sores and keep his joints moving. I'll email you some exercises to do with him, too." Quilla says, her tone firm but friendly.

"Thank you." I say. "How are you so smart with all this medical stuff? You sound like you've been doing this for years."

Quilla chuckles. "Turns out it's in my blood." She shrugs a shoulder and when Atticus comes up behind her, he pulls her petite frame against his chest with a bright smile on his face. I can practically feel his adoration for this woman pouring from his body and shining in his warm emerald green eyes.

"Aye. She's an amazing Tamer and constantly gives this old man a run for his money." Atticus says, his Irish tone playful and teasing.

"I only learned from the best." Quilla quips as she turns to bat him on the nose with the tip of her finger.

I find myself smiling at their antics. At the pure love between them that reminds me so much of what I feel for the man lying in that bed who risked everything so The Protector's of Power could be safe again.

Once Seth gets back from, I'm assuming checking to make sure he has what he needs back at his place in Colorado, Gray and I gather in the hallway outside of Aiden's room waiting for Seth and Ivan to carry him out so he can teleport us home.

Just as Atticus walks up, I see a little girl quickly around a corner and she changes into a little white wolf pup before my eyes. I hear Gray chuckle as both Ivan and I just stare dumbfounded at what just happened right in front of us.

"I told you, they were Werewolves." Gray says in an I-told-you-so tone.

Seth chuckles along with Gray before turning his attention to Atticus. "Oh, Atticus, I haven't seen Tobias, Coraline, or Kai around, but please let them know I said hello."

"Both Alphas and Kai are in North Dakota at the moment with Kai's newly bonded mate." Atticus says.

"Well, tell Kai congratulations." Seth says with a small smile. "I hope to see you again on better terms, my friend."

"May the Great Luna be with you and yours." Atticus says as he bows at the waist and crossing his right arm over his chest while resting his fist over his heart.

I take one last look at Atticus and Quilla, give them a small wave before they disappear from my sight and then, in the next instant, Seth's living room is in front of me. Nothing about the space has changed from the last time I was here, but yet everything has changed.

After we got Aiden settled into bed, which Seth also adjusted to make it big enough so I could lie in it as well, I hear him call Matt and Vivian as I set up Aiden's liquid diet bag.

Ivan and Gray carry in the sofa from the living room and they set up against the long wall opposite the bed. As they both sit down beside one another, Ivan pulls Gray into his side and they both have this blank stare on their faces.

I hold on to Aiden's hand while running my thumb softly over his knuckles. "Does any of this feel real to either of you?"

"No." Ivan says, his voice low and tight with emotion. "None of this feels fucking real. Why does it still feel like we won the battle but lost the war?"

"Because we are soldiers without their leader." Gray says after a few moments. "While we did destroy The Siphon, was it all worth it to have Aiden just out of our reach?"

After a few minutes of silence, I hear a knock on the door before Vivian and Matt walk into the room. I slide off the bed, letting go of Aiden's hand to walk into Vivian's arms, and she immediately pulls me in for a tight hug.

"Seth told us that he's got a long road ahead of him." Matt says, and he puts a consoling hand on my shoulder.

I notice that something is different about him. His long sleeves are pushed up to his elbows, and I remember Aiden saying Matt always kept his sleeves down to cover his arms.

So, I let my eyes wander over his skin and I don't have to look too far. There on his arms, on full display, are colorful yellow, white, and bits of orange lightning bolt wielding marks.

Matt got his powers back.

"Oh Matt, I'm happy for you." I say with tears in my eyes as I remember the little balls of light that scattered in different directions after The Siphon was destroyed.

I go to hug him and I can tell from the water in his system that he is whole again.

"Gray." I say as I turn back to my friend on the couch. "This is how we know everything that happened was worth it." I say, pointing to Matt's arms.

"I have to get used to it again, but I have my abilities back. All thanks to Aiden's sacrifice." Matt says, his voice breaking with unshed tears.

I call my father later that day to let him know I'm back and he comes by Seth's place to see me within twenty minutes of ending the call.

"Sweetheart, I'm so happy you're back. I am so proud of you." Dad says as he pulls me in for a hug.

When his gaze lands on Aiden behind me, I tell him about Aiden's condition and my voice is surprisingly strong when I explain what all happened. I can tell that my father wants me home, but he also understands why I don't want to leave.

"I understand, Sweetheart. But remember that Aiden would not want you to waste away in here. He would want you to live your life."

"I know, but it's going to take time, Daddy." I look back at Aiden, who looks so peaceful sleeping there that it breaks my heart.

After my father leaves that night and the days slowly turn to weeks, I make sure that I am always there for Aiden at night, and talk to him about my day. I don't know if he can really hear me, but I remember Quilla's advice and I want him to know everything that happens until he wakes up.

"I got a job at the local energy plant. Since I have water *and* wind, the plant was thrilled that I was willing to join. Plus, I have a way to cheat the system. Do you remember what that is, Aiden? Of course, you do." I chuckle. "I make what they need and pull my essence out of it. So, I only have to go back once every two weeks for a replacement."

I have been keeping him clean by washing his body every day with a warm basin of water and a washcloth and then washing his hair every two days like I'm doing today.

Ivan comes by and helps me carry Aiden over to a chair that Seth created about a month ago. It looks like a salon chair, but it has rails on the side to keep Aiden upright so I can lean his head back into the sink while I gently wet his hair with the small nozzle.

As I lather the shampoo through his reddish-blonde hair, I chuckle lightly, "You love the feel of my fingers running through your hair, don't you, Aiden?" I ask. "I'm still doing that for you, Baby."

I give him a gentle kiss on the forehead, hoping and praying for any kind of response. A hint of a smile, an eye twitch, or a finger spasm. But I don't get a response at all.

"Please, Aiden. Please come back to me when you're ready." I plead. "I will wait until the end of time for you. I just want it to be when you are healed on the inside."

Once I rinse his hair of all the shampoo, I blow dry the strands before I have Ivan carry him back to bed. I then ready Aiden's liquid meal, clean off the port protruding from his stomach, which has now become second nature for me, with an antiseptic wipe before I attach the tubing, and insert the bag into the machine to start the feed. Ivan makes sure I don't need anything else before he leaves to go home to Gray for the night. I tell him no and follow him to the front door and watch him drive away.

Going back into the room, I change into my pajamas and climb into bed, snuggling up to Aiden's side and making his arm drape over my waist like I know he would do if he was here.

"Good night Aiden. I love you." I say as I give him a kiss on the lips before resting my head on his chest and letting his heartbeat lull me to sleep.

71

Aiden

My body feels so heavy that I can't even move a finger. It's like my whole being is locked away and I don't know where the key is. That thought scares me, but I'm too exhausted to hold on to the feeling.

Just before the dark haze that seems to be hanging around me takes me under again, I hear a raspy voice whisper, *"Heal"*

I begin to wonder who that raspy voice belongs to, but I can't focus on it when I hear the tone of a woman's voice that for some reason seems familiar and warms my soul even though I can't make out the words she's saying. But even her voice doesn't keep my attention for long before everything becomes quiet and dark again.

I don't know how much time passes before I start to hear things around me again. I can't understand why I feel so heavy. Why won't my body listen to me when I try to open my eyes, or move my arms or even my fingers?

I hear another voice; a male this time filter through my brain. "Hey, can you come here and look at something?"

I get the feeling his voice is familiar too, but I can't think of who it is.

"Sure. I'll be right back, Baby." She says while threading her fingers through my hair.

As her voice echoes in my head, the tone makes my chest swell with odd feelings.

Happiness and love and *home*.

She gets up off something soft around me. The word *bed* comes to mind and I want to reach for her, to keep her by my side, but I still can't get my arm to work. Before the aggravation at the lack of control over my body can fully hit me, the world fades around me again.

"Sorry, I had to help the Lug Nut with a project he's working on." I hear this woman say as she comes back into the room at some point. Then I hear another voice in the room with her. It's the one from earlier, and I find myself wishing I knew who they were. If only I could wake up and ask them their names.

"How is he?" The man asks, then pauses as his tone takes on a shocked quality. "Hang on, did you move his hand?"

"No." She says. "It may have been a spasm. He's been having them a lot lately. Quilla says it's normal for that to happen."

I feel the woman put my arm back across my stomach and I want to grab for her hand, but I can't.

"Maybe that's a good thing." He says as his footsteps leave the room. I want to follow him, to know who he is, but then everything goes dark again.

The next time I start to hear things around me, I pick up on the sounds of water running. Then someone picks me up, one strong arm under my knees while the other is supporting my upper back, and sits me in what feels like a chair. My head falls to the right side and I hear the woman's voice fill the room.

"You better get your head over here, mister, and let me wash your hair."

I can't. I'm so tired of my body not listening to me.

"There, that's better, huh?" She says as she gently sets my head on something hard and cold, but whatever it is, it cradles my neck where it won't move.

"Maya," The man's voice begins, "I'll be back in fifteen minutes. I have to pick Gray up from the airport."

"Okay. I'll probably be blow-drying his hair at that time. Is Gray coming by?"

"I'm gonna talk to him and see. It's just hard for him." He says.

Those names. Maya. Gray. I feel like I know them, but I can't put a face to the names.

Why is it hard for Gray to come by here? I want to ask, but the words are stuck in my mind.

"Tell Gray that Aiden would love to hear him come over." Maya, now that I can put a name to that voice, says.

Yeah. I want to know who he is.

A door shuts a moment later, followed by the sound of water running behind my left ear.

"Give it a minute, I need to get the water hot before I get your hair wet." Maya tells me.

I hate washing my hair in cold water.

"Okay, here it comes; don't move."

Not like I have much of a choice here.

"There, now the shampoo. This is your favorite part." She says and I hear happiness in her voice, but it's tipped in just enough sadness for me to pick up on.

Why are you sad?

"We almost had an accident at work today. A fire broke out in one of the engine rooms. Me and a few other water wielders were called in to help. Thankfully, Mason was working today, and he came to help out, too. About a dozen workers were burned."

Are you okay?

"I'm fine, don't worry." Maya chuckles. "Once the fire was taken care of, I helped the burn victims with my water until they were able to get to the hospital."

Good. I'm glad.

"So what started off as a bad day ended with us saving the plant." She says as she rinses the shampoo out of my hair, the bubbles crackling in my ears as they are rinsed away. "I'm going to go ahead and wash your body off while I'm waiting for Ivan to get back with Gray."

Okay. Why is Gray not here?

"I'm really proud of Gray. I know it's hard on him and Ivan right now, not to be living together while Gray is in college, but you know Gray, anytime he can have more training with his computers, the man is all about it. Especially since one of his PC's blew up while he was working on and it he got so pissed at not knowing what happened. So he comes back on Friday, stays the weekend, and gets back on a plane early Monday morning for his classes on Tuesday."

How much longer does he have in college? It sounds like this Ivan misses him a lot.

"Thankfully, this is Gray's last semester, so he probably has about three more months before he graduates, with full freaking honors, of course. I swear that guy does nothing half-assed." She chuckles. "Oh boy, I'm glad Ivan wasn't around to hear that. He'd be all over that perverted joke in a heartbeat."

I don't really remember him, but I find myself wanting to smile, if I could just get my damn face to work with my brain.

Once Maya seems to finish washing my body, she dries my hair with the blow dryer, and with her fingers gently threading through the strands, her touch eases me into a blissful slumber.

There is a sensation all down my right side. A gentle pressure that begins at my chest and goes down to my thigh. Someone is softly humming against my neck. The sound is the sweetest thing I could ever hear, and I start humming along in my head.

As she continues humming her song, she starts to draw little circles on my chest with what feels like a finger. I suddenly remember I love the feeling of her fingers doing that. The muscle in my neck spasms allowing my cheek to rest against the top of her head. I hear her release a contented sigh and I get the feeling she would like it if I were to run my hand up and down her back.

I try to move my right arm so I can do that for her, but it won't fucking move and I'm frankly getting tired of my body not listening to me for some reason. I try to fight against the darkness lurking around in my mind, but when I do, I get the image of chains around my body.

"Break them." I hear a smooth, silky voice whisper, and I somehow know it's from inside my head.

My own voice echoes inside my head as I let a growl of frustration tear from my throat in this dark abyss of a room as I see a flash of orange and whitish-blue chains form in front of me.

"Let me go." I say as I grab the chains with both hands and rip them apart.

At first, they don't want to give, but I pull on them again with everything I have, muscles straining from the amount of force I'm trying to use. Just when I don't think they'll give, I feel something warm up in my chest and a flare of orange appears from my right side a moment before the chains erupt in a spark of orange and blueish-white fractures of metal.

Once the shimmering pieces stop falling, the room seems to get lighter around me, and although my eyes are still closed, my body finally feels like my own.

The woman beside me is still humming, still tracing those loving circles on my chest. I think about lifting my right arm, and to my amazement, it listens. It's a jerky, harsh movement, but it's one that *I controlled.*

I slowly drag my arm down her back once while she hums a contented sigh, but when I drag my arm up her back again, the humming stops suddenly, and she jumps up into what I assume is a sitting position while her hand is still on my chest, pausing the tender way she was touching me.

"Aiden?"

I hear her say that name and I can tell it's a loaded question. At first, I don't make any connections to it.

Who is Aiden? Is it me? Is that my name?

I get the feeling that I *need* to open my eyes. To look at the face of this voice and see what she looks like. So I force them to open.

At first, everything is blurry and I can't focus on anything. I close my eyes again and when I open them once more, I finally see her face. Her dark brown hair is to her shoulders and when I look into her blue eyes, I immediately notice that her cheeks are wet, and I'm confused as to why she's crying. Confused about why I hate the look on her beautiful face.

The need to wipe her tears away fills my chest, and I lift my left arm to do just that. I don't take my eyes off hers as she leans into my touch and more tears flow from her eyes. As my gaze tracks the movement of my thumb brushing over her cheek, I notice I have a tattoo on my arm of blue and white lightning bolts snaking around the skin. Broken memories start to come back to me in such a rush that I am forced to close my eyes again.

Fire, electricity, water, and wind.

The two of us together sitting on a couch with her head on my chest.

With her in a truck bed, fire softly flowing around us while she's utterly naked beneath me, then again in a bedroom. Electricity zapping parts of her body and she's screaming the name Aiden.

With that name and how she's calling out for it, makes my heart both pound with desire and ache with hurt at the same time.

Then I remember bits of a fight with several other people, but I don't remember who they are.

One thing I do remember with vivid clarity now is destroying The Siphon, but then all-consuming darkness right after.

"I knew you'd come back to me." She says.

She gives me a gentle kiss on the cheek like she's afraid that will break me and send me back into the void. She then folds herself onto my chest and it takes everything in me to lift my right arm to hold her weakly against my body.

When my arm comes into view, I see another tattoo of a flame on my skin and for a second I have to think about what that means, but then I hear something whisper again.

"Heal."

Abilities. Soul Power. Fire and electricity.

The words float through my mind, and the marks on my skin make sense now. Wielding marks to show I can protect those I care about.

"How long have I been out?" I ask hoarsely, thinking it's been just a few days or a week.

She takes a breath and looks me in the eye with fresh tears on her face.

"Oh Aiden. Baby." She begins while threading her fingers through my hair in a way that's so achingly familiar I can't stop the groan that bubbles from my throat. "It's been a year and a half."

72

Aiden

"What?" I whisper hoarsely, fear lacing my voice.

"Yeah." She says quietly while nodding her head.

"What happened after the Siphon was destroyed?" I croak.

"There was an explosion and Seth found your body a few hundred yards into the forest. You were clinically dead." Her voice breaks at the memory. "But Seth wasn't giving up on you. So he tried to shock your heart back into rhythm, but it wasn't working. Because of you pushing your power past their breaking point, you were so dehydrated that he had no chance of restarting your heart. Once I figured that out, I added the water your body desperately needed, and Seth was able to get your heart beating again."

She runs her fingers through my hair, and I find myself wanting to lean into her touch.

She gives me a smile as she adds, "You were too injured for Seth to heal you and teleport us back home. So, he teleported us to Montana where a friend of his could perform the surgery you needed and give Seth time to recover so he could heal your body."

She then runs her hand down my neck, over the flame tattoo that still lingers on my skin, then her hand rests on my chest, right over my heart.

"I've been taking care of you from day one. Changing your port site, giving you baths, and telling you all about what I've done for that day." She says, her voice breaking with tears.

At first, and I don't really know why, but I'm mad at her for being here and not living a normal life, but then I'm glad she didn't leave my side.

"I remember you doing all that for me." I say, then I begin to wonder about something. "Hey, I have a question." She tilts her head to the side. A silent request for me to continue. "Who are you?" I ask slowly. "I feel like you're something important to me, but I don't know what."

Fresh tears fill her eyes and it makes my chest hurt like a knife was plunged into it. "I didn't mean to make you cry. If it's a bad thing to ask, don't worry about answering."

"No. No. It's okay." She says as she sniffs and wipes the tears from her eyes. "My name is Maya Harper. I'm your girlfriend."

"That explains the odd memories, then."

She chuckles, "What memories?"

"Let's just say I remember us being in the back of a truck bed and you naked beneath me." She outright laughs, and I love the sound of it. "Have I always loved your laugh?" I ask.

"Yes." Maya says while still giggling. "You do."

"Can I hold you?" I ask, even though I get the feeling I don't need to, but I do it anyway.

She grins like she knows it too, but nods her approval all the same. She snuggles into my chest and I release a sigh of relief at the pressure of her body against mine as I wrap my arm almost possessively around her waist.

"God, I have missed this. Missed you *actually* holding me." Maya whispers.

I don't say anything. Instead, I just pull her closer and rest my chin on the top of her head.

After a few minutes of holding one another, footsteps echo in the hall from the other side of the door a moment before whoever it is comes into the room.

"Hey Maya, can I have your help—" His words are cut short when we lock eyes. Shock flooding his steel-gray gaze. I don't recognize this man coming into my room, and my first instinct is to protect Maya from the intruder.

I try to sit up in bed and push her behind me, but the sudden movement is exhausting. I then remember I have powers. And if my body can't protect Maya, then my abilities can.

Images of a firewall come to my mind, so I try to create that for protection. Just when I think I'm able to make that wall, only a little spark comes out of my hand, but the fire and pain that flares in my chest makes me cry out and brings the darkness rushing over me in full force.

When I wake up sometime later, I look around for Maya, but I realize I am alone in the room. I think back to what happened when I tried to use my fire and the horrible pain in my chest. Then that man's face comes to my mind again and I begin to wonder who he is.

"Ugh, this not remembering shit I feel I should know is getting old." I say out loud to myself as I scrub my right hand over my face.

I catch a movement near the doorway and that man comes into my room again. I start to panic and try to back further into the headboard, trying to get away from him, but I don't move much; my body is too weak right now.

Is he going to try to hurt me since Maya isn't here?

He must notice the panic on my face because he takes a step backward toward the door and puts his hands up in surrender. As I look at him more, I get that feeling that I should know him, but I can't put a name to the face.

"I feel like I know you, but I can't remember you." I say.

His face goes from worry to sorrow, and he puts his hands down to the side. "My name is Ivan. I'm one of your best friends." He says.

Like his name was the key I needed; memories come flooding back.

Times in high school when we would train jiu jitsu together.

Seeing him and another guy smile lovingly at one another while we are at a restaurant, and I long to feel that emotion again when I look at them.

Him helping me train my electricity with iron plates leaning against trees.

I sink back into the bed, suddenly feeling so tired again.

"We have another friend, too. Grayson, right?" I ask as images of a guy with a nerdy smile tossing silver balls around. "Your boyfriend?"

"Yeah." Ivan smiles and nods. "Gray's been worried sick about you. He's in college a few hours away." He takes a step toward me and I smile at him as I nod my head at the memory.

"God, I feel so stupid that I can't get things straight in my head yet." Then a thought hits me. "How long was I out for this time?" I ask, fearing that another six months have gone by.

"You were out for four days." Ivan says with sorrow filling his eyes.

"Where is Maya?"

"I talked her into going to get something to eat with her family and yours while I stay here." Ivan says before taking a seat in the armchair that sits next to my bed.

He leans his forearms on his knees and I look at him for a minute, trying to figure out how to ask the question forming in my mind.

"What?" He asks.

I remember who my family is, my aunt and uncle, and I run my left hand over my face, the lightning tattoo catching my eye. "Have they been here to see me?" Wondering if they even know I'm alive.

"Yes, everyone has been here at one time or another. It's just mainly been Maya, of course, then I'm here the most to help take care of you. I think it's been too hard on your aunt and uncle to see no changes from day to day. Which I understand that. Hell, it's been hard on me." Ivan says as he runs his hand through his black faded style hair.

As I listen to this, I think that again I am so far behind on things. I didn't even finish college like my friends did. I lift my right arm to cover my eyes and that movement takes everything out of me.

Ivan seems to pick up on that and smiles. "But we can move at your pace, man. You've been out for over a year; we shouldn't throw everything at you all at once."

"You're right. One thing though, can you get a clock for me? I'm terrified that every time I go to sleep, months will pass again." I ask.

"On it dude." Ivan says.

He walks out of the room and comes back a few minutes later with a clock that already has the date on the display and plugs it in on my bedside table.

"Now get some sleep man, you look like shit." Ivan jokes with a cocky smile on his face.

I roll my eyes, "Screw you, dude. You try saving the world and see how you feel." I say, finally beginning to feel like my old self again, even though I can tell I have a long way to go.

73

Aiden

A few days go by since I've come out of my coma and Maya continues her exercises with me. She told me this Quilla woman—who, thankfully, I'm not supposed to know—gave her different exercises to help keep my joints from getting locked up from not being used. And now that I'm awake, I can try to do these exercises on my own. Lifting my legs by the knee, swinging them like a pendulum, or hinging them by the hip, lifting my entire leg off the bed before bringing it back down.

After Maya finishes with her array of leg and arm exercises she puts me through, I'm given a few hours' rest before Ivan and Seth come in and help me stand for the first time.

Even with their arms around me to support me, my legs still shake with exhaustion. I hate that I feel so weak, and I have to keep reminding myself that I have not moved for over a year, so the fact that I have any muscle mass at all is a blessing, but that's all thanks to Maya and her keeping my body moving as much as she could.

About a week after I woke up, Ivan and Maya walks in with someone I finally know right off the bat.

Aunt Viv and Uncle Matt have tears staining their cheeks the minute they see me and Aunt Viv comes right over to sit beside me on the bed while Ivan and Maya take a seat on the couch that sits against the long wall of the room.

"I knew you were alive this whole time, Aiden. The fire sculpture you made only went out once and it was the worst eight minutes of our lives until it lit back up. Even though the light it gave us was dim, I held on to the fact that you were in there." She says while tapping the middle of my chest. "You just needed time to heal."

I remember making them a small fire before I left, and I remember leaving a little piece of myself inside so that way they would know if the worst happened.

I take a moment to let my eyes wander over my aunt and uncle and they don't look any different from what I remember of them. Uncle Matt comes closer to my bedside to give me a hug once Aunt Viv moves to let him in, and when he pulls back, I notice something peeking out from the collar of his shirt. Something yellow, white and orange, but I can't make out the shape.

"What is that?" I ask, not recalling him having any tattoos like me, Maya, and Ivan.

"Oh, these?" He asks as he points to his neck.

He smiles and then tugs his shirt off, which I find to be weird, but when I see what flows over his skin, the breath freezes in my chest. These are important, but I can't remember why.

"Because of you destroying The Siphon, it somehow brought my powers back." Uncle Matt says as he shows me the brightly colored lightning tattoos that flow from the middle of his chest, branching in two directions. One goes up to the middle of his neck while the other continues down his arms and ends at the wrist.

I then have a flashback of what this other guy told us about powers being stored in jars.

Mason

"Yeah, Mason told us that Victor—right Ivan?" I ask, wanting to be sure I am remembering the names correctly. He nods, so I continue. "Kept stolen abilities in jars in hopes of transferring them to other people."

"Well, I guess once you were able to break the jars, all the stolen abilities went back to the person they were taken from." Uncle Matt says.

Stolen powers.

That phrase brought back memories that he had his powers stolen. I look back at him and his colorful markings that I recall were once white and dull.

"I'm glad that you were able to get your powers back. It makes being in this bed a little easier since it gave us another benefit." I say.

After a while, I feel myself start to nod off again. Uncle Matt and Aunt Viv give me another hug and promise to stop by more now. I smile and as they leave; I drift off to sleep again. Thankfully, it's only for a few hours at a time and days don't go by unnoticed.

Once Seth is comfortable that I am pretty much out of a coma relapse risk and with more and more memories coming back to me, he thinks I'm finally on the road to recovery.

Maya is sitting in a chair on the right side of my bed, holding my hand when we hear Seth open the front door to his house. After I hear some pleasant exchanges of hello's from Seth and the other voice, which has an Irish lilt to its tone, a tall man comes in with a shorter woman with auburn hair at his side.

I look at them wearily for a moment. I can somehow tell that they are more than what they seem.

"Aiden, this is Atticus Remington and Quilla Rose." Seth introduces them with a smile and I give them a tentative wave.

Apparently, Atticus was the one who implanted the feeding tube, which I realized I had in my stomach on day three of being awake.

As a way of distracting me from the uncomfortable feeding tube removal, Atticus says something that I never thought would come from someone who is not part of our little inner circle. "Tobias wanted me to tell you that he knows your parents would be proud of what you and your team were able to accomplish."

I look at him in shock as the pride in his voice hits my ears, but Seth steps in before I can even think of anything to say. "Your parents were friends with his, ah, boss." Seth says.

"They *are* still friends. Tobias does not think they are dead. They were too strong to be killed off." Atticus sharply replies.

"He knew my parents?" I ask.

"Aye. Coraline and myself included. I didn't really spend that much time with them; but the story goes they helped Tobias win a war that, in turn, helped him become one of the greatest leaders of Montana." Atticus says.

I smile, knowing my parents did good things before I came along.

After Atticus finishes removing the feeding tube and making sure that I am up to par on all my other vitals, he and Quilla, who has been quiet the whole time, just meticulously making notes in a small file that has my name written in perfect penmanship on the upper tab, smile and nod at me as they both leave the room.

I look at Maya for a moment when I catch her smiling at me and at my recovery so far when I hear a dog bark once in the hallway. I turn back to the sound to see who left the animal inside, and I am met with a massive red wolf with a white tuft of fur in the middle of his chest looking back at me with emerald green eyes the same shade as what I noticed in Atticus' eyes. My mouth hangs open as I watch Quilla climb on this animal's back before he takes off running through the open front door.

"What the hell was that?" I ask slowly, thinking I've lost what marbles I had left.

"Oh. They are a special group." Seth says with a chuckle. "We aren't the only beings that are not your typical human."

"Believe me, I was just as shocked to find out what they are, too." Maya says with a chuckle.

"What are they?" I ask while eyeing both Maya and Seth.

"Simple, Atticus is a Werewolf." Seth replies nonchalantly.

I stare at him like *he* is the one that lost his mind. "No way."

"Way. And there's more than just Atticus, too. But don't worry, you'll meet them soon enough, I'm sure." Seth says.

I look back to the door where I last saw the wolf—Werewolf—in the hallway and I just shake my head after a moment. "Well, just know I am *not* calling dibs on giving any of them a flea bath. I want to keep my arm thank you."

Seth smiles and before he leaves the room he says, "Glad to see you have your humor still, Aiden."

74

Aiden

The following few weeks are spent getting my body moving again. Maya helps me move my legs and arms less and less every day until I am able to move them on my own with only her verbal commands, telling me what to do. Even when I stand with either Ivan and Gray or Ivan and Seth's help, I'm able to bear more weight on my legs.

I still haven't attempted using my powers since I tried to use them on Ivan before I remembered who he was. Partly because I'm afraid that in trying to use them, they will send me back into a coma and make all the work that we've been doing the last few weeks be for nothing or that my Soul Power is so fractured that I will simply never be able to use them again.

But I try to bury that fear in the dark recesses of my mind and work on getting my body strong again, and after a few weeks of therapy, I am able to walk on my own; granted it's with a cane, but at least I am able to walk around Seth's place.

For now, until we know if I can use my powers or not, Seth wants to keep me here because his walls are made of a special material that will withstand my electricity or fire if they come out and I can't control them. That thought alone terrifies me. Not being able to control them and hurting my family, friends, and my girl.

Later that night, I lie awake listening to Maya sleep next to me. Her back is turned to me and while I find that my side is cold without her body pressed up against mine, I take this time to close my eyes and I feel for my powers for the first time in three months since I've been awake.

I can still feel them just under the surface, but it's like they are trapped with in my Soul Power. As I step closer to the iridescent orange and whitish-blue sphere, I can see that there are so many fractures scattered all over the surface that I can't even begin to count them all. No wonder it hurt like hell when I tried to use my powers.

I open my eyes, glancing over at Maya again, and she still has her back turned to me. So I slowly get out of bed, grabbing my black cane for support and I walk into the bathroom, quietly closing the door, but I don't shut it completely.

I turn the lights on over the sink and look at myself in the mirror. I still see the same man looking back at me. Same reddish blonde hair, even though it's longer and my bangs are getting in my eyes now and instead of a five o'clock shadow, I have a full beard on my face. I see the same mismatched eyes with the gold ring around them. My body is a little more lithe than I'm used to, but I know that will change the more I start moving around and once I get cleared to exercise with weights again.

With a sigh, I close the lid on the toilet, sit down, and lean back on the tank as I shut my eyes. I focus again on my Soul Power, and like that day that feels so long ago now, when I saved Maya from Mason for the first time, I hear the voices of my powers whisper, *'Heal'* over and over and over in my mind.

As the sphere appears before me again, I focus on each and every crack, imagining needles and threads the same color as the elements that flicker and arc within the transparent space, mending each fracture and becoming whole again. I watch as the end of each string from every crack vanishes and my Soul Power is finally smooth and shining again.

After what feels like only a few minutes, I open my eyes and find bright sunlight shining in my face from the little window above the tub/shower combo and Maya is sitting crossed-legged on the floor, her hand resting lovingly on my knee just looking up at me.

"You've been here for three hours, I think. I don't know how long before I got up, but I've been watching you for that long."

"I'm sorry. I didn't mean to worry you." I say as I brush a piece of her dark brown hair behind her ear.

"It's okay. Do you think you healed yourself?" Maya asks.

"I don't know." I whisper. "I am so terrified that I won't be able to either use my powers again or if I can use them, I won't be able to control them and then hurt you. I am so fucking terrified of that."

"Aiden. Baby, it's okay. You don't have to do anything you don't feel you're ready for." Maya says as she grabs my hand and pulls it to her lips, gently kissing my knuckles.

I feel her water searching my system and I lean into her, letting her water go as deep as she wants to go. "But I will say this, whatever you did, it does feel better." Maya says with a smile.

"Thank you." I say softly as we walk out of the bathroom to go back to bed and just lie in one another's arms.

When we wake up again five hours later, it's well past lunch. So, Maya decides to go to the kitchen and fix something for us while I stay in my room. After she closes the door, I gingerly get out of bed and stand in the center of the bedroom. Since I was able to fix the fractures in my Soul Power, I want to test my powers now that Maya is safely away from me.

I close my eyes and I focus on my fire. Since that was the first one to develop, it should be the easiest to call and, hopefully, control.

I feel it come to life in my Soul Power and I try to bring it to the surface. It starts to branch out from the center of my chest, snaking towards my arm, but then I feel the element snap back into my Soul Power as if it were attached to a rubber band. White-hot pain fills my entire body, and the next thing I know, I am on the floor writhing in pain while clutching my chest with my right hand.

I hear Maya laugh at something out in the hall and I can tell she's getting closer to the door. I drag in a ragged breath, fighting against the burn still flaring in my chest, and crawl back into bed. Once I'm lying down and I'm able to relax into the mattress, the pain finally subsides to a dull ache and I'm able to breathe normally before Maya enters the room with two plates filled with last night's chicken parmesan and Alfredo noodles perched in her palms. I smile at her as she hands me my plate and we eat in silence with Maya oblivious to what I just tried to do as a trickle of sweat runs down the length of my back.

Later the next day, Maya coaxes me out of my room so we can sit in the living room to watch some TV and so I can get some daylight from the large windows. I will say, it feels good to sit on a couch instead of a bed all the time.

When Maya goes into the kitchen to get us a drink after I settled on the couch, I try something with my powers one more time. Instead of trying to light my whole hand, I try to focus my fire in a smaller space. I try to light my index finger, but again, pain fills my chest, and it's actually worse trying to force it into a smaller area than using my whole hand.

I force the groan back down my throat, but can't keep the pain off my face when Maya comes back.

"Aiden, are you okay?" She asks as she sits our Cokes down to run her hand over my cheek.

"I'm fine. I guess I'm still not used to moving around, that's all." I say, trying to rub my leg like I was having a cramp.

She looks me over and thankfully she doesn't use her water to look in on me. She just gives me a small smile and hands me my Coke before she leans into my side so we watch can TV together.

As the pain slowly fades in my chest, the fear of not being able to use my abilities again grows in its place.

75

Aiden

I van comes over the next day and we talk Maya into leaving for a bit and visiting her parents. Once we are alone, Ivan takes one look at me and, just like he always does, he knows something is up. With one arch of his brow, I crack under his gaze.

"I can't use my powers." I say with sadness.

"Oh man. I'm sorry dude." Ivan says.

"And the bad thing is, I can still feel them, but when I try to use them, it feels like they want to split me in two." I say and go on to tell him about the little experiment I did yesterday.

"Maybe you just need to force them. It's like any healed injury and in order to get back on your feet, you have to push past the pain and reuse those muscles, almost." Ivan says. "Or it could just be stopped by fear. Maybe you have so much fear of hurting others or even yourself that you're holding yourself back."

As Ivan voices that reasoning, I had that exact thought, but Maya was out of the room the other day, so I wouldn't have hurt anyone. Maybe it is the fear of not being able to use them, or not being able to control them that is making things worse and keeping them locked away.

As the weeks turn into months, I am getting back on my feet day by day. Since it seems like my powers aren't coming back anytime soon, Seth releases me from his place so I can go back home. As soon as I walk in the door, it feels so good to be with my aunt and uncle again. To have Maya come over and spend time with me. Just like old times before everything went to hell.

As I am slowly working on rebuilding my body back to its original shape, another month passes and Gray finally graduates from college. So we all fly out to Texas in support of him walking across the stage to get his diploma.

As we walk into the gym that has been set up with hundreds of folding chairs and a portable stage, Maya and I meet up with Ivan who is dressed in a pair of black dress slacks and a steel gray button-up that brings out his eyes. He forgoes a tie while leaving the first three buttons undone to show off his wielding marks in a way he knows drives Gray crazy.

I still hold on to the black cane on my right side and I'm just in a pair of dark wash jeans and a white button-up shirt while Maya is in a pink dress with a flared skirt and heels to match.

As Ivan leads us to our seats near the front of the stage, Gray spots us and comes running over with a huge smile on his face.

"Ivan! You made it!"

"I would never miss my man walking across that stage on his graduation. You worked so hard on this, Baby. I'm so proud of you." Ivan says before pressing his lips to Gray's.

I notice the smug look of an older couple a few seats back and I shoot them a glare that Ivan would be proud of until they avert their gaze. I will not allow anyone to ruin this day for Gray or Ivan.

Gray pulls away from Ivan's embrace, and his face lights up as he looks over Ivan's shoulder when he finally notices me and Maya.

"Oh, my God. You brought everyone?" Gray exclaims. " I can't believe you made it, Aiden!"

"I'm not a complete cripple, Gray. I told Ivan if I could get here, I would. I might not have been awake for your entire schooling, but I'm here when it counts." I tell him as he leans in for a hug. I wrap my left arm around his shoulders and I say into his ear, "Now get your ass up on that stage so you can get back home to us and to Ivan. He's been a bore without you around all the time."

Gray laughs and I can feel Ivan's eyes on me as well as the older woman's again, so I let my own smile play on my lips. "Don't worry, man, he's still all yours. I have my sights on something a little more enticing." I say.

Gray, not knowing I'm messing with the woman behind me and thinks I'm screwing with Ivan, says, "Oh, you haven't seen his pierc—"

Ivan covers Gray's mouth, cutting him off just as he picks up on the actual target of my words. "No one needs to know about that, Grayson." Ivan says darkly as his eyes flick over my shoulder to the older couple and Gray's eyes blow wide for a minute.

"You're right. That's our little secret."

"Get up on that stage so I can scream my lungs out for you." Ivan says.

Gray, Maya, and I all chuckle at Ivan's words and he looks at us for a minute like we all just went bonkers. As Gray gives me and Maya high fives, he walks away to get in the line-up as Maya leans in to let Ivan in on the joke he unknowingly made.

"Oh shit. You all need help. Even my mind isn't in Gutterville that much, and I *live* with him."

"Happy to bring Gutterville to you any time, man." I say.

We take our seats, and we listen as the names of other students are called in alphabetical order. When we finally get to the L's and Gray's name is called, we all cheer for him. Of course, Ivan's is the loudest, and he even made a quick 'Grayson is the best' banner out of bright silver metal.

Later that night Ivan takes us out to dinner to celebrate and I offer to take care of the tab.

"No Aiden. I got this." Ivan says as the hostess takes us to a booth in the back near a large window.

"I'm sure you do, Ivan. But I want to do this. One as a congratulations to Gray, but also as a thank you to both you and Maya for taking care of me for almost two years. It's the least I can do." I take a breath and I tell my little group of friends something I've been thinking about for the last few days, "Plus, I think I'm going to sign up for online courses and finish college too."

With words of encouragement from my announcement, we celebrate Gray's achievement tonight and to my slowly building health and schooling goal.

76

Aiden

Over the next several months, on top of going to school and studying my ass off—which I'm thankful Gray is back in town to help me study—I continue to work on getting my body back in shape.

Maya and I take advantage of the warm summer air and walk through the neighborhoods that we live in. After a few weeks of this, the cane becomes a pain in the ass and I make myself use it less and less, only holding it in my hand as a reminder to keep pushing myself so I *don't* have to use that damn thing.

Once I am able to ditch the cane for good—which Ivan made a big deal out of it—he manipulated the metal to say 'fuck off', and for the first time in nine months, I wish I had access to my fire so I could have melted the damn thing. That would have been more satisfying, but my powers are still firmly locked within my Soul Power and I don't see being able to use them anytime soon.

I still think about my powers though from time to time as my walks with Maya take us around the local park and those walks soon turn into runs where we both put our earbuds in and listen to our music.

The worst part is when I think about them, I feel them come to life. I feel them fighting against the chains that I can see surrounding my

Soul Power. And when I start sparring again with both Ivan and Gray, I find myself wanting to use my powers, but I can't.

I think Ivan knows this too, and he tries to push me to the point with either a large metal club or even a sharp bright silver blade, where I would be forced to use them to protect myself, but when I do attempt to protect myself from his attack, I only create embers or a weak spark, and the pain in my chest that follows takes my breath away while darkness pools in the corner of my vision.

"You okay, dude?" Ivan asks as I collapse onto my back in an effort to slow my breathing to cope with the pain and will the black smudges to clear from my vision.

"I'll live. I think." I pant. Once Gray walks away to grab us all a bottle of water, I grab Ivan's wrist, making him look back at me. "Stop trying to make me use my powers, Ivan. They're not coming back."

Ivan stoops down beside me, his forearms resting on top of his knees, "I don't believe that. I still think you need to get out of your own fucking head, and until then, I'm going to keep pushing you."

I sit up so I can look him in the eye. "We don't know what will happen if I use my powers. I could kill you and Gray if I use them while we're training. I could blow this house apart. Do you really want that?" I growl.

"And you think I can't protect Gray and me in time? Oh Aiden, you wound me." Ivan says while placing a hand on his chest in mock pain, and I roll my eyes in agitation. "And as for this house, Seth and I can build a new one. So to me, all you're spouting is excuses about why you shouldn't use your powers. I personally think you've forgotten the real reason we have them in the first place."

Gray finally comes back in with our water and Ivan leaves my side to take one from his outstretched hand. Ivan takes the third bottle and tosses it back to me with a dark grin. I barely catch it, as Ivan says. "You've had a long enough break. Time to get back to work."

Ivan

For the next hour, I lead Gray and Aiden out back and I work him harder than I have been, to the point where Gray steps back and lets me go at Aiden full force.

Was it because I wanted to blow off some steam after hearing his excuses?

Maybe.

Okay, it absolutely was. But damn it, he needs to stop being such a hardhead.

As I continue to push him, making different iron, steel, and copper weapons or pillars erupting from the ground to attack him, I can feel little sparks of electricity skitter across my skin or just the barest flare of heat from his hand right before he either blocks me or dodges my attack completely.

Aiden's own fear is crippling him in the worst way right now, and I am determined to figure out a way to force him to face this mental handicap.

"Ivan! Come on Babe, that's enough." Gray calls from the patio. "You're gonna drive him into the ground with all the holes you have in the yard."

I pause mid-punch with spikes of iron knuckles forming on the end of my left hand as Gray's words filter into my mind. With a growl, I pull back and Aiden bends over at the waist, hands on his knees, while trying to catch his breath.

"Fine. We'll stop for today, but I want to see you tomorrow morning." I say over my shoulder to Aiden.

"Ivan! No way. You just kicked my ass and you want me back here for more?" Aiden says as he crosses the yard carefully to avoid the holes I made with my metal.

"Aiden. Go home. I'll talk to him." Gray offers before I can say anything.

Aiden looks between me and Gray before finally walking off with an aggravated huff, mumbling something about not coming back in the morning.

"Ivan." Gray begins in a chastising tone, but I cut him off.

"If you tell me to go easy on him, then don't. I'm doing this for his own good, Gray."

"Then figure out a different way to help him, because beating the shit out of him isn't working." Gray then looks over the backyard and rolls his eyes. "Plus, I don't want my yard to look like a war zone. I put too much time into it. Now fix it while I get a shower and make dinner."

"Fine." I breathe out in exasperation as I turn to walk off the patio.

"Ivan." Gray says from the threshold of the sliding patio door and I look back at him from the middle of the concrete steps. "If you work fast enough with the yard, you may still catch me in the middle of my shower." Gray winks as he shuts the door behind him.

Damn, this man knows how to turn my moods around like flipping a switch. I feel myself harden at his suggestion, and primal need courses through my veins for him. I quickly repair the yard, making sure to absorb every last trace of metal I created, and when I step inside, I hear that Gray is just turning on the shower.

I open the bathroom door to find him shirtless, his shorts hanging low on his hips.

"Took care of your precious yard, Grayson." I growl as I strip out of my clothes and pin him against the sink. "Now, let me take care of you."

I crush my mouth to his and he opens for me so I can devour him wholly, and as the taste of him explodes on my tongue, he meets me stroke for stroke. When I take his bottom lip between my teeth, his hand threads through my hair, pulling me back so he can do the same with my top lip.

His hand then glides over the hard muscles of my chest and stomach, my skin fluttering at his touch. He moves lowers still, and I am forced to suck in a breath when I feel his hand wrap tightly around my erection, his thumb toying with the piercing I left in only for him.

"Grayson." I groan.

"I love the way I can make you moan my name." Gray croons.

I stare into his eyes, and I know he can see the carnal desire in them. He smiles in challenge, and like a moth to a flame, I burn for him.

"So do I, Grayson." I rip his shorts down his legs, then I lift him up by the thighs and he instantly wraps his arms around my neck, locking his ankles around my lower back so I can walk us into the shower.

I pin him to the opposite side of the shower stall, so the water from the showerhead cascades down my back instead of hitting Gray. With his legs still tightly wrapped around my back, I slowly glide my lips across his jaw, down the side of his neck and when I get to his collarbone, I make my way back up so I can bite at his Adam's apple and the moans of pleasure that pour from Gray's throat makes me harden to the point of pain.

"Unwrap your legs, Grayson, and turn around." I demand, my voice deep with need.

He slowly drops his right leg, but he keeps his left one hooked onto my hip, and with a grin that could even make the devil tremble, Gray grinds his erection into my own and I can't stop the growl erupting from my chest any more than I could stop a hurricane.

Acting like my growl is an invitation to keep his ministrations going, Gray thrusts his hips once, twice, before I snap out of my carnal haze and glare at him. I give him a dark grin before I grab him by the throat, squeezing just enough to make his eyes glaze over as my grip slows the blood flow in his neck.

"Stop being a brat, Grayson. Put that leg down and turn around." I command, feeling the pulse in his neck going a mile a minute, and I reward him with a feral grin. "You like it when I get rough, don't you?"

Since he's not listening to me and dropping his left leg, I push it away then remove my hand from his throat to grab at his shoulder so I can turn him and roughly pin his chest against the wall while bracing my forearm across his shoulder blades, pressing him deeper into the fiberglass.

I lean into his neck, tracing my nose across his skin, and I whisper next to his ear, "You've been such a bad boy, Grayson. I don't know if you deserve to be ravaged like I was planning on doing with you." I take the teasing page from his book and I grind my aching length over his firm ass.

Gray tries to push against me, but I shove him against the wall again, making the bottle of his shampoo crash to the bottom of the tub, and this time I pin his hips with the corner of my own. Not giving him an inch to move or feel me against him.

"Ivan, please." Gray whimpers.

As much as I'm burning to be buried hilt deep inside him, I love his pleading voice even more. I grab the Axe body wash from the built-in shelf and squeeze a healthy dollop down Gray's back. I chuckle darkly against his ear when the muscles in his back quiver from the cold liquid.

"I need to get my bad boy clean. You're all sweaty and dirt is *just* caked on you." I tease as I wash the one spot of dirt on his back, which is from my filthy dirt-ridden skin since I'm covered in it.

Gray lets out a grunt of frustration at my teasing, and he knows I'm screwing with him at this point. I'm getting under his skin so much that he actually tries to push himself off the wall to face me. But I don't let him. Instead, I pull his back to my chest while calling my metal to make chains around the both of us, locking us in place so I can keep washing his body with the lingering soap on my hands.

I rub over his chest, flicking his right nipple as I make my way down to the hard lines of his stomach. Gray's head leans back on my shoulder as I head down to the defined V just above his hairline. I take his left earlobe between my teeth when I glance down and see just how needy he is for me. The evidence on damning display, ready to drip over the edge of his crown. I trail my lips down his neck while I make a small metal cup to collect the water coming from the showerhead and I hover over his erection.

"Are you going to be good for me now, Grayson?" I ask as I let the water slowly drip from a pinhole at the bottom of the cup and onto his tip.

Gray's body jerks and his groan of desire makes my spine twist with want.

"Tell me, Grayson, or we both leave this shower wet, and unsatisfied." I growl.

"Yes! God yes, I'll be good." Gray groans."Please, Ivan."

"Face the wall and spread those legs." I say as I let the chains fall from our bodies and he does as I say without a second thought.

I trail the index finger of my right hand down his spine, and gooseflesh erupts in my wake. "That's my good boy. And you know what good boys get?" He turns his head to look over his shoulder at me. I smile, "This."

I thrust into him in one powerful move, our grunts and groans roaring over the sound of the water still beating against my back and cascading into the floor of the tub.

"You take me so well, Grayson. Now, was all brattiness worth it?" I ask him as I pull out and thrust back in, driving myself deeper.

Gray looks over his shoulder at me again and with a grin, he says, "Every. Single. Time." He pushes his body into mine and we both erupt at the same time. All the pent-up longing that we created together finally boiling over.

After we come down from our post-orgasmic high, we wash one another, this time for real, and finish our shower just as the hot water runs out.

After we dry off and Gray gets dressed in nothing but gray shorts to make us dinner, I pull out my cell to make a call, and he answers on the third ring.

"Yeah, Chain Link?" Mason growls roughly.

"I want you to do something for me." I begin and I tell him about my plan that I hope and pray will work.

77

Aiden

*T*hree *months later.*

A day before finals, I ask Gray to help me study at a local coffee shop for a few hours. Thankfully, I only needed to take these two classes and then I can graduate.

"Thank you for helping me study, Gray. I appreciate it."

"You're welcome, Aiden. Training the brain to get stronger is my specialty." Gray says while tapping the side of his head.

"Well, you don't do a half-bad job of training the body, either." I say while flexing my newly rebuilt bicep.

After our argument that day in their backyard, Ivan stopped trying to push me to use my powers and only trained my body to get back in shape, along with Gray's help.

"Well, it helps when I also have a personal trainer that keeps me on my toes." Gray says while wiggling his brows.

I pause mid-drink as his words click in my mind and I just shake my head at his innuendo. "You are terrible. Why do I hang out with you again?" I ask, my voice dripping with playful sarcasm.

"'Cause I'm an absolute joy to be around and you secretly love me." Gray winks as a wicked smile plays on his lips. "I remember that time so well in the shed back in high school when you were practicing with your electricity and it almost—" He cuts himself short as if remembering that even though my wielding marks are still bright and colorful, I have not had access to them in eleven months. "Sorry, man." He says, deflating in his chair.

"You will never let me live that down, will you?" I jest, knowing he didn't mean anything by it. I mean, it's still a memory that we lived through. "Would you have rather gotten shocked? I mean, I don't think Ivan would have liked a stiff Grayson *all* the time." I say while purposefully failing to hide my smirk.

Gray picks up on my jab right away and shakes his head. "You are just as bad as I am, buddy." He points his index finger at me in a scolding gesture before picking up the trash around us while I flag the waiter down and pay for lunch.

"I learned from the worst of them." I say with a smirk on my face.

As we walk out of the coffee shop, Gray walks a few paces in front of me while looking at one of my textbooks and highlighting a line of text he feels is important. Just as he steps off the curb to head towards my truck, I hear the squeal of tires on the pavement from a few feet away.

Looking to my right, I see a dark purple Challenger flying down the road and we are helplessly in the middle of it, with Gray being the closest to the vehicle. I know we won't be able to get out of the way in time. The car's going too damn fast.

I feel my fire instinctually flutter deep in my chest. "*Protect.*"

Ah, fuck it. I think to myself.

If they are going to tear me apart, then it might as well be after protecting my friend. I pull Gray behind me and try to call my fire so

I can make a wall between us. My chest fills with white-hot pain as I feel the fire slowly trickle down every inch of my arm, but it's not enough to light my hand with the flame. I force myself through the pain with one thought flooding my mind.

Protect Gray.

I close my eyes, pushing myself harder as I feel something break deep within my chest as power flows from the center.

A heartbeat later, I hear the car slam into something. I open my eyes and even with the cracking of the hot engine not any more than eight inches from my face; I am staring at the dancing flames of my firewall.

I huff out a laugh before I stumble to my knees and my firewall slowly crumbles to embers on the wind. Still kneeling on the pavement, I hang my head while trying to catch my breath and will the darkness that threatens the edge of my vision and the lingering discomfort in my chest to go away.

"Aiden, are you okay, dude?" Gray asks with a note of fear as he shakes my shoulders. "Come on, let's get you out of the street."

He helps me to my feet and walks me over to a bench sitting on the sidewalk just a few feet away from my Colorado. Once we sit down, I rest my head in my hands and try to calm myself down.

After a few minutes, I lift my head, looking at Gray and I heave a sigh of relief that he's okay. I look back to see where the car is, but it's gone. In the haze of pain, fear, and my distorted vision, I didn't see or hear it leave or who was even driving that recklessly.

The longer I sit on the bench to get my bearings, the more I start to feel my fire coursing through my veins like I used to. Then Ivan's words from a few months ago hit me. Maybe he was right, and I was holding myself back. Maybe I had forgotten the real reason we have these powers because I was so focused on the fear of not being able to use them for myself, and I didn't think about trying them to protect others.

"You okay, man?" Gray asks again.

I look at him and I smile, "Yeah. I think I'm good."

"You used your abilities. How?" Gray asks slowly, like he's just now comprehending what happened.

I chuckle, "I think your Lug Nut boyfriend was on to something that day in your backyard." I nod my head towards my truck. "Come on, let me take you home. We've had enough excitement for one day."

As I pull up to Gray and Ivan's house twenty minutes later, I see Ivan standing in the doorway, apparently hearing us pull up. Ivan then walks down the steps and heads toward the passenger door to greet Gray as he exits the cab.

"Hey, Gray. For now, let's not tell Ivan about what happened." Gray looks at me and I'm just staring at the smug look on Ivan's face through the windshield. "Actually, hang on." I say as I feel my flame flicker under my skin in response to his gaze.

I exit the driver's seat and motion for Gray to join me.

"Hey, Babe." Ivan greets while pulling Gray in for a kiss on the cheek while keeping his eyes on me over his boyfriend's shoulder. "How was the study sesh?"

"It was good." Gray says and then looks back over at me. "What is your issue, Aiden?" He finally asks.

"You might want to move, Gray." I tell him as I walk towards Ivan.

"Aiden, wait. You don't think Ivan had anything to do—"

I cut him off. "Yes, I do."

"What do you mean, Aiden? I was home all day." Ivan says as his lips twitch with a hidden smile.

"Oh, damn it, you two. There goes my yard again." Gray sighs as he stomps off to sit on the concrete steps on the front porch.

Once Gray is out of reach, I call my fire.

While it still hurts like hell in the first few seconds after it comes to life in my hand, I'm just glad that I can call it forward at all.

"Well, would you look at that?" Ivan jests. "The Flame Boy lives."

I rear my right arm back to punch him in the face, and the crazy asshole barely covers his skin in time to block the flames. On purpose.

"Could be hotter, though. It won't melt through my metal in its current state."

"You are one crazy asshole, you know that?" I ask as I turn and try to punch him in his side and let my fire flare just a moment before impact. He grunts in pain, but the look in his eyes tells me he's enjoying this. "What if it failed and Gray was hurt?"

I feel the earth move around me and I know he has a pillar of metal poised to strike.

"I wouldn't have let that happen." Ivan says as he strikes.

I move out of the way of his pillar and, with a shout tearing from my throat; I push my fire, making it hotter. Even though I only melt halfway through his metal, I smile, knowing I was able to at least make it through the material.

"There ya go, Aiden." Ivan cheers as he watches his metal melt around my hand.

"Again, you are a crazy asshole, but I hate to admit it, but you may have been right."

"What was that?" Ivan asks, while cupping his hand around his ear.

"I'm not repeating myself, dude." I chuckle.

Gray walks over to us while rolling his eyes. "Yeah, Aiden. Don't say that again. Ivan's head doesn't need to get any bigger."

"Which—"

I cut him off. "Nope. Don't finish that fucking sentence, Ivan Grant. I'm out."

All I hear is Ivan's cackling laugh as I shut the door to my truck and drive away.

78

Aiden

Later the next afternoon, after spending three and a half hours at the university taking my finals that started this morning, I drive home. I keep the radio off and I just allow myself to think about what happened yesterday. I haven't told my aunt and uncle what happened yet. I honestly wanted to get these damn finals done before I told them anything. One goal at a time, I guess, and that was the one that was in my face.

I've been practicing with my fire in private whenever I can. Like now, I'm bringing it forward and letting it die in the center of my palm. And just like when I first developed my powers, the more I use it, the less I feel the pain in my chest. Now it's just a dull ache from not using for so long.

While I continue to practice with my fire, allowing it to flow to each individual finger, I imagine the other side of my Soul Power, my electrical half. This is the first time since I've gotten my fire back that I have looked at the sphere. Once it comes into view within my mind, my heart freezes in my chest.

Three electrical chains still keep the power locked away from me.

"Shit. You always have to be the difficult one, don't you?" I think towards the power.

It arcs within the sphere as if telling me, *get me out of here.*

I sigh as I pull into the driveway and press the button clipped to my visor to open the garage. Once I'm inside, I hear a commotion in the kitchen. When I walk in, I find both my aunt and uncle trying, and failing, to get the pilot light to catch again on the stove. The lighter that Uncle Matt is trying to use is too short for the flame to reach the pilot light.

I smile to myself as I remember the first time I used my fire to light this very stove.

Neither of them heard me come in, so I walk over and thread my right hand between them. "Looks like you need some help."

Aunt Viv looks back at me while Uncle Matt is still focused on my hand. I curl my fingers into a fist, only leaving my pinky out, and I urge the flow of fire into that single digit.

"Oh, Aiden." Aunt Viv gasps.

"When did this happen?" Uncle Matt asks.

"Yesterday." I smile and I tell them about the crack-pot plan that Ivan came up with to make me use my powers again.

"I tell ya, that kid is unhinged." Uncle Matt says, but I hear the amusement in his voice.

"Yeah, he has weird ways of making things happen, but to his credit, they end up working." I say as I shrug my shoulder.

After the stove is finally working again, I help Aunt Viv with dinner and we all eat in the dining room with idle chatter about how I felt my tests went and what Aunt Viv is reading for her next book club. I found not long after I woke up that she needed a distraction in her life when I was in the coma, so she found a local book club and they were able to help keep her in the now and not worry about the past or future when it came to me.

After dinner, I offer to clean up the kitchen for Aunt Viv, so she and Uncle Matt can relax on the couch before I head back to my room and crash onto my bed.

As I'm lying on my back staring up at the ceiling, I suddenly recall that I haven't heard or felt anyone in my head since I've been awake. I close my eyes and think about Maya, but when I try to find that familiar connection between us, I again hit that damn chain, locking in the other half of my power.

I let out a growl of frustration. I'm really getting tired of these chains.

Throwing on a T-shirt, I leave a note for my aunt and uncle on the island so they will know where I've gone when they get back from their nighttime walk around the neighborhood. As I grab my keys from the hook by the garage, I pull my phone out and text Maya.

Me:

> Hey Baby. I wanted to let you know that I'm going to the forest. I'm sorry I didn't tell you yet, but I got my fire working again and I think I'll be able to get my electricity working, but it's going to be dangerous for anyone to be around me. So please, unless you can have Ivan meet you, please stay away. I don't want you hurt, Baby Girl.

The little bubbles appear instantly, showing me she's typing a response.

I'll be there for you, Aiden. I wasn't there the first time you developed your powers, and I am not going to miss you coming back into them. Ivan will protect me. You know that. We will meet you there.

The forest is so quiet tonight. The only disturbance in the air is the chirping of crickets. After I park my truck, I walk into the center of the clearing and stand there for a few moments, remembering the times that Ivan and I trained here. The times that Maya and I came here to be alone, to tease one another, and when we loved one another in the back of my truck. Then when Mason and Rhett attacked us here before we knew that Mason was not that bad of a guy. He was just coming after us to protect Dani from Victor.

So many memories in this little forest, both good and bad.

I take a breath and call my fire to my right hand. It comes to life with hardly any discomfort. I find myself smiling at my progress when I hear a twig snap near me and I make my fire into a small wall with little thought, muscle memory taking over.

When a familiar face appears out of the tree line, I let a smile play on my lips as I drop the firewall and I walk over to Maya. When I stop at her side, Ivan comes up behind her along with Gray. Ivan makes his iron skin and slowly builds his special wall that we both worked to perfect to block my electricity from the ones we love.

I give a small smile to my friends and, with a nod of encouragement from Ivan, I walk back to the center of the forest. Just as I am about to try to call my electricity, I see Seth, along with my aunt and uncle, all break through the tree line to stand behind Ivan's wall.

Seth gives me a firm nod and I feel him in the back of my mind. *"You got this. You have come this far, Aiden, and I don't think you will fail now."*

I nod back at him and I try to push what I want to say towards him, but I don't know if they reach him, but I say them all the same.

"Thank you, Seth." I begin, and I can feel the words flow toward him, but it's only due to his own connection to me, for now at least. *"At first I thought you were this crazy dude that was stalking me, and very well could have been a mass murderer."* I say with humor in my voice and Seth chuckles, *"But I have come to respect you, and trust your judgment. Thank you."*

I look at everyone once more and then close my eyes. I look toward my Soul Power to see how my electricity is acting in this moment. It's arcing within the sphere, like it knows I'm trying to free it and it's begging for me to break the three whitish-blue chains.

I try to get a little piece to snake out past the chain, so I can ground myself, but instead of grounding, I go back to discharging like when I first started to use my ability. It cracks loudly across the clearing, barely missing a tree on the opposite side of the forest. So I know I am going to have to arc until I can break the chains inside.

I shake out my left arm, bracing for the electricity that's about to flow from me when Ivan comes up to my side, holding a thick copper rod in his hand. He smiles as he says, "Just like the first time, right?"

"Yeah, it is." I smile and take the rod from him.

I hold the rod, and I start to call my electricity full force this time. The same burning pain fills my chest just like with my fire, only it's worse. Of course, it would be. It's just like the first time I developed it. Knowing what that pain felt like, a little part of me wants to stop, but I know that I need to push past every fear to get my life going again.

After a few minutes of trying to push my electricity toward my arm, I literally feel one of the chains break and I can't help the scream that bubbles in my throat from the pain that explodes throughout my body.

Over the loud buzzing of electricity, I hear Maya scream my name. I look at her through the arcing lines of each bolt and I see her fear, but I also see determination in her eyes.

I notice how quick my breathing is becoming. It feels like I am running a marathon while standing still. I grab onto the copper bar with both hands and I try to ground myself since I was able to get one of the chains off, but it still won't reach my rib.

I imagine the remaining two chains around my Soul Power, take a final breath, and push my electricity higher. I yell out to try to cover the pain that keeps building as each chain strains against me.

The second chain finally breaks.

My legs give out, and I'm on my knees as stars begin to dance around my peripheral vision.

As I work on breaking the third and final chain, I start to lose my vision completely. When that happens, I pull what little bit of power I can control back, and my vision returns.

Now I'm apprehensive about breaking that last chain. What if that causes another coma, or worse this time?

Just as doubt starts to set in that this road of recovery may have all been for nothing, I feel a blocky hand caress my shoulder. I look back and to my surprise; I see Maya inside a copper suit that Ivan must have made for her. Her face is completely covered except for a little sliver of space for her eyes. I stare into her blue depths, silently encouraging me to break this last chain, and no matter what happens, she's there with me.

I feel Seth enter my mind again. "*Maya told me to tell you to use her as your anchor.*"

"Fuck, Baby Girl." I practically sob.

My electricity sparks around me in response to my emotions, thankfully traveling down the rod in my hand and into the ground.

"You've always been my anchor. Even before you came back into my life. Your beautiful face has always been with me." I give her a small smile and a wink. "I love you." I tell her before I take a calming breath and force this last chain open.

I imagine taking that last chain in my hands and I pull. Fire fills my chest with a renewed vigor and I scream. I scream in pain. Scream in anger. Scream in fear that morphs into determination to take control of my life again.

When the chain finally shatters, I try to tether the element to my rib to ground myself, but I don't act fast enough. A shockwave rips through the clearing as my power comes out in full force, and I watch helplessly as Maya and I are forced away from one another.

Seth teleports and catches her before she can crash into a nearby tree, but I am thrown across the clearing. I barely remember slamming into a tree before everything went dark.

79

Aiden

When I feel my hair being played with, I am pulled from the darkness of sleep and a contented sigh escapes my lips. I slowly open my eyes and Maya's tearful gaze meets mine while a wobbly smile dances on her lips. I look past her and I notice I'm back in Seth's house; then a fearful thought hits me as memories flood back into my mind.

Electricity. Us being thrown apart from the shockwave I created.

"How long have I been out this time?"

I see movement in the corner of the room and Ivan comes into view with a sly smile on his face.

"Man, it's been a while. Gray and I got married, and we adopted a kid."

"Shut up, Ivan." Maya says with a smile playing on her lips while smacking him on the shoulder.

"You are a fucking asshole, man. You are so lucky I love ya like a brother." I say, while rubbing the last bit of a headache out of my forehead. "Seriously, though. How long was I out for?" I ask.

"Just a few hours. It's early morning, around six, I think." Maya says.

I let out a sigh of relief through my nose at her words. Months hadn't passed, and I accomplished what I never thought I would get back.

My Soul Power is completely healed, and my abilities are under my control again.

After a few hours of rest, I talk Maya into seeing her parents for a while so I can head down to the training room in the basement. Just as I put my hand on the knob to walk inside, Seth comes over with a questioning look on his face.

"I just want to make sure I am back one hundred percent before I use my powers around others."

He nods, allowing me to step through the door, and he closes it without a word before standing in the middle of the large window to watch what I do.

I call my fire to my right hand and it crackles to life in my palm. I have no discomfort at all in my Soul Power and I am in complete control of it. I make it as large or as small, or as hot as I want it. I close my fist around the flame while cutting the flow from my center and it extinguishes with a whoosh.

When I call my electricity, I ground myself instantly; the arc flowing over my arm, as the crackle of energy echos off the walls. I feel a slight ache in my Soul Power, but nothing major, and again I can control it with just a thought. Making the shape of a snake around me, before I make it strike a fighting dummy in the corner and discharge as it connects with the fake flesh.

Then I call my fire again, allowing both powers to flow and I find myself smiling as they circulate through my body; it's like nothing happened to me almost two years ago now.

I relish in the sound of the crackling fire and arcing of the currents flowing around me and they feel even stronger than they were when I destroyed The Siphon. So, with that feeling, I see how far I can push them. It's like what the hell, right? Go big or die trying.

I push my powers higher and I can easily get to that same point as that fateful day two years ago and I feel myself start to lift off the ground again. I can also tell it's not a breaking point for me anymore. I have a new limit that I can work towards, and something tells me that I am going to have to find this new limit and master it.

As I am hovering about ten feet in the air, I look in the window across from me. My reflection stares back at me and my Soul Power starts glowing in my chest. I realize this is my warning sign, that I'm getting to my limit.

I instantly close off my flow of power, and my chest stops glowing; the powers fade and I land back on my feet. While I feel just a little drained, it's nothing I can't handle, and a real smile spreads across my face for the first time in two years.

The door opens and Seth stands in the threshold with his arms crossed over his chest. While his smile lets me know how proud he is of me, the shake of his head also tells me that I am a glutton for punishment and pushing myself to the brink.

I tilt one side of my mouth up at him and I shrug my shoulders. "I never know when to stop. I always have to find new limits."

"Yeah, but sometimes that's a good thing. Just don't let it go to your head." Seth says with a smile.

"I know. I just like to know that I can reach new limits to protect those who need it."

"I know the feeling. Now get outta here. I want some peace and quiet now that you're back to your old self." Seth jokes while playfully shoving me out of the training room.

Later that night, after Maya gets back from her parent's house, I take her back to our favorite spot in the forest. We lie in the bed of my truck, my flames pillowed around us just like last time, with just enough heat in the element to keep us warm. I hold her in my arms while silently looking up at the stars.

I end up telling her what I did this afternoon and while she's mad at me; she does somewhat understand. After a moment, she gives me a playful look, and I can't help but chuckle.

"What?" I ask.

"You remember what we did together once in these woods? In the back of this very truck?" Maya asks as she trails her finger over the flame tattoo covering my right arm.

It takes me a split second to remember, and a sultry smile spreads across my lips. I instantly make the fire stretch to build walls around us and I flip her on her back, pinning her arms above her head.

"I'll take that as a yes?" She asks, searching my face with a glimmer in her eyes that are filled with desire.

I chuckle again and bend down close to her cheek, my breath caressing the shell of her ear. "I remember every single second of that night, Baby Girl." I whisper.

I begin to trail light kisses across her lips and down the column of her neck. "And I have a vague memory." I begin as I run my hands up her back while hooking my thumbs around the hem of her shirt to pull it up and tug it over her head in one slow movement. "That I owe you something," I say as I trail feather-light kisses up her stomach, in between her full breasts that are still being caressed in that lacy bright pink bra, and up the column of her throat. She moans under me, making my jeans go painfully tight between my legs.

"Aiden." she whispers.

"But I can't for the *life* of me remember what it was." I growl into her neck.

"Oh well, if you don't remember, then it wasn't important." Maya says, while trying to playfully push me away.

"Oh, you are a horrible liar, Baby Girl." I say as I gently graze my teeth over the sensitive spot between her neck and shoulder.

Her sharp intake of breath and her hand gripping the fabric of my shirt makes my spine shutter with pleasure. I then move my mouth next to her ear, my breath a caress to her skin.

"I think I owe you a punishment, Baby Girl." I croon.

I unbutton her jeans and gently pull them and her panties down with one movement. I then unclasp her bra with my right hand and pull the material from her body. I kiss down her neck again, taking her left nipple in my teeth and her right hand is threading through my hair in an instant. Her breaths come in heaving pants as I continue to bite and suck at her skin.

"Aiden, please" Maya moans.

"You thought I would forget about that little wind stunt, didn't you?" I ask.

She doesn't answer me, but her fingers tighten in my hair, so I go to the other breast and I bite down, just a tad bit harder this time.

"You thought I would forget, didn't you?" I ask again, voice muffled while my teeth are still clamped around her taut bud.

When she doesn't answer me, I take my left hand and use my thumb to give her little shocks on her recently abused nipple.

"You better answer me, Baby Girl, 'cause I'm not gonna ask again." I say through my teeth again, determined not to lift my mouth from her skin.

She moans this time a little louder and finally, she says while fighting to catch her breath, "Yes! I was hoping you'd forget!"

"I will never forget what happened between us, Baby." I say as I pull away from her, making her hand fall from my hair. "Now what would be a fitting punishment, hmm?"

"You could spank me?" Maya asks innocently.

I think for a minute before I let a dark, amused smile play on my lips. "No. I have something better." I croon.

I pull my body back from her a bit and when she tries to sit up to close the distance again; I shake my head at her.

"Ah ah, Baby. Get back down there." I say as I make my fire wrap around her wrists to pull her back down and I keep the flames around her so she can't move with what I'm about to do.

I then ease her legs open and I see just how much she wants me. I slowly begin to apply pressure with my left thumb to the apex of her core, and she instantly arches into my touch. I rub rough circles against her clit and watch as her head rolls back and a soft moan escapes her lips.

I give her a bit of a shock against her sensitive flesh and smile when she screams out. I know she's close to the edge, so I back off from her completely. Maya lifts her head to see what I'm going to do next, but I just stay kneeling before her with a sly smile on my face. Confusion plays over her features for a moment as the realization of what I'm about to do hits her and before she can say anything, I slide two fingers into her core.

She instantly lets her head fall back and as I am rocking in and out of her, she grinds her hips against my hand, meeting me move for move. She tries to fight against the flame restraints, but she can't get her hands to budge. I find that spot deep inside that I know she likes, and again I get her to that blissful edge before I withdraw my fingers. She growls at me and the glare in her eyes makes me smile. I know I'm driving her crazy.

"Aiden, what are you doing?" Maya grinds out.

"Punishing you, Baby. Edging you." I growl as I grip her thighs and settle my head between her legs. "I'm going to make you a pleading mess by the time I finally give you what we both want."

I place tender kisses up her inner thigh and stop again just before I get to her sweet center.

"Aiden." Maya moans.

"Keep crying out my name, Maya. I love hearing it." I tell her as I suck hungrily on her clit and she does just that. Screams my name into the nighttime sky and I hum my approval into her needy core.

I continue to devour her, dragging my teeth over her clit, and driving my tongue deep into her sweet heat, over and over again; letting her taste fill my senses until she's trembling from the orgasm I'm slowly building within her.

But I deny her again.

Pulling away and she thrashes against the fiery bindings while trying to rub her thighs together so she can finish her own release.

"Aiden, please." Maya begs.

I lean away enough to pull my jeans off, then I'm hovering back over her, just staying high enough to keep my erection from touching her, but all the while letting her know what's there.

"Is there a problem?" I ask while looking into her eyes, my voice low and teasing.

"Yes! Yes, there is a problem!" She says with desire filling her voice.

She tries to arch her hips against mine, but I pull away, and she growls again.

I lean into her while pinning her hips down with a knee and I whisper in her ear, "Tell me, Baby Girl, what's the issue? Maybe I can fix it?" I feel her shudder under me and I kiss her neck, then smile against her skin.

"I want you. It's been so long. I want you, Aiden." Maya pleads.

With no warning, I fill her to the hilt with one thrust and her scream is music to my ears. With nothing around us, I feel her convulsing around me, almost instantly hitting her climax, but I can't have that yet.

I pull completely out of her core, forcing her to lose her orgasm.

"No!" She screams, tears beginning to form at the corners of her eyes.

I lean in, my face so close to hers that I can feel the breath panting from her nose. Her eyes lock with my mismatched gaze a moment before I lick away the tear pooling in her left eye. As the saltiness explodes across my tastebuds I fill her again, and again, and again. Edging her to the point of pain, her body thrashing against mine.

On my fourth thrust into her, her back arches off the truck bed, and when her inner walls tighten around me, it causes a violent shutter to race down my spine. I growl as I pull out of her before she can climax again, but I'm helpless to keep my own orgasm from exploding between us.

I know she realizes what happened when she fights against the flames around her wrists again and moans my name again. "Aiden, please. Let me come with you."

"What have we learned, Baby Girl?" I ask, my voice low and deep.

"Not to tease you when you can't return the favor soon after." Maya almost sobs.

"Then you better cover me with your water, Baby Girl so I can love you properly." I growl into her ear.

"I have a better idea. I can keep myself protected and still feel all of you." Maya says breathlessly.

She sends me images of her water protecting herself from the inside, and I honestly don't care what part of her body her water is between. I just know that she's protected, and that's all that matters.

"Alright, Baby Girl. You asked for this."

I roughly fill her once, twice, three times, before she's hooking her legs around my back to drive me deeper. I finally let her wrists out of my flame restraints and her arms are instantly around my neck, pulling me even closer; and we love one another with everything that has built up in the last two years.

"You feel so damn good, Baby. Look at you taking me so well." I praise.

I pivot my hips to find that special spot for her and when I hit it, her nails dig into my shoulder and I relish in the burn as they break skin. I snake my hand between us and give her clit a quick squeeze, finally letting her fall over that long-awaited edge. She screams so loud that it rings in my ears.

"That's it Baby Girl. Sing to me each time I make you come."

I then turn us around where I am the one on my back and she's straddling my hips. As Maya grinds against me, she runs her hands through her hair and down her body and I watch, mesmerized as the moon caresses her shoulders as she climaxes now for the second time.

I quickly reach out and rub my left thumb over the apex of her center again and send electrified little shocks to the already abused bud, and she rides a wave back to back, her head falling back to where she almost looks headless.

"Oh my god, Aiden!" Maya screams as she rakes her nails down my chest leaving red welts in their path.

As her scratches ignite my skin on fire, I explode again, my seed filling her to the brim and the sound that bubbles from her throat makes me pin her to the bed of the truck again, loving us both through our final waves of pleasure.

"You are so beautiful, Maya." I say as I pull out of her for the final time and we are left lying breathless next to one another.

"You make me feel beautiful." Maya whispers.

I pull her to my chest and I kiss the crown of her head. "I love you, Baby Girl. And just know I would have waited for you too if it was the other way around." I run my hand through her long hair and kiss her cheek.

"There is no one else for me, Aiden. You are my one and only. Always have and always will be." Maya says while tilting her head to look up at me.

"Absolutely, Baby. You are mine, just like I am *yours*. Forever and always."

After Maya uses her water to clean us up, we get dressed and I take her home, where we collapse in my bed together for the first time. And as I hold Maya in my arms, I listen to her steady slumbering breath and I finally let myself think about all the days and nights that we will have together for the rest of our lives and I can't wait to live through each and every single day.

80

Aiden

The next morning I'm sitting on the corner of my bed, just watching Maya sleep. Last night plays over and over in my mind and I can't stop the satisfied smile that plays across my lips.

Maya sighs in her sleep, apparently feeling me staring at her, and I want to try the last ability that I have yet to use.

Mind-speaking.

I look for her mind and realize I can find her just as easily as before, now that I don't have those chains blocking my power anymore.

"Good Morning, Baby Girl." I think in her direction.

After a moment passes, I hear her sleep-clouded thoughts fill my mind, *"Good Morning, Aiden. I haven't realized how much I've missed talking to you this way until now."*

I smile as I think about my hand caressing her face and I hear her sigh of contentment through our connection. *"I've missed this too. I'm sorry I didn't try it sooner."*

"It's okay. You've started it now, and that's all that matters." Maya replies as she opens her eyes to look at me and a small grin tugs the corner of her mouth up.

I lean in to kiss her softly, once, twice before I pull away enough to ask with my real voice, "There was actually something that I wanted to ask you."

"What's up?" Maya asks.

"Do you know where Mason and Dani are? I haven't seen him since I woke up."

"They found a house not too far from here, and I'm glad it's not where the remaining Parasites are. Ivan and I run into Mason sometimes when we go to work." Maya explains.

I'm happy to hear that Mason is making a normal living for himself now that he's no longer under Victor's thumb.

"The only thing I'm mad at him for is he didn't come to see you the whole year and a half that you were in the coma." Maya adds.

"I'm not. We weren't what you would call friends." I say.

"Speaking of, I gotta get ready to go to work. I'll see you later. Don't get into too much trouble now." Maya says with humor filling her voice.

"I make no guarantees, Baby Girl." I laugh in her mind and she rolls her eyes at me before leaving my bed to get ready to go to work.

Later that afternoon, I try to reach out to Mason and I'm able to instantly find him.

"Wow, so the rumors were true. You are alive." Mason says in greeting.

"Nice to hear from you again, *too."* I reply with a sarcastic tone.

"Are you back on your feet? I heard you weren't able to use your powers." Mason asks.

"Yeah, I'm back to my normal self now. And yes, at first I wasn't able to use my abilities. I had to heal my Soul Power more than I expected, but I was able to get them back." I explain.

"Good." He pauses for a moment. *"Tell your friends I want to meet up at Seth's place. I've been working on something over the last year and I need to talk to you all."* Mason says. *"Just tell me when it's a good time to meet up with you."*

"Alright."

"And bring your aunt and uncle. They are going to want to hear what I have to say, too." He says as I feel him pull back from my mind.

As Mason's words echo in my mind, I reach out to Seth next.

"Aiden, hello. It's nice to feel this connection again."

"Yeah. It is." I say. *"Listen, Mason wants to meet with us soon. He said he's got some information that he wants to give us. Is there a good time to meet?"*

Seth thinks for a moment before I feel his curiosity fill my mind. *"Tell him to come by tomorrow night. I'm interested in knowing what he has to share."*

I finally emerge from my room and find my aunt and uncle cuddled on the loveseat in the living room, watching some rom-com movie.

"Oh hi, Aiden. We didn't know you were up." Aunt Viv says. "We saw Maya leave, but she didn't tell us you were awake too."

"Yeah, I've been up for awhile." I say. "I, uh, I just talked to Mason, and he has some information he wants to share with me. With all of us, actually. He wants you two there as well. We are meeting at Seth's place tomorrow evening."

"Do you have any idea of what it could be about?" Uncle Matt asks as he scratches the side of his neck, right over one of the lightning tattoos.

"No idea. But the way he spoke about it, it seems important." I say.

"We will be there." Uncle Matt says.

The next evening, Aunt Viv, Uncle Matt, Maya and I all pile into his car and drive over to Seth's house. As we pull up, I see Ivan and Gray pulling up in Ivan's new black Mustang. I get out just as Uncle Matt puts the car in park and walk over to Ivan's new ride.

"So, you finally replaced the old Stang, huh?" I say as I remember the old green one being impaled by Rhett's rock spear when we were trying to run from their last-ditch effort to stop us.

"Yeah, I did, man! This one is even more badass than the last one too!" Ivan says with a smile while patting the hood of the car. "We paid Gray's car off last month and he was tired of me taking his car all the time, so I bought this one."

"You couldn't have gotten a normal sedan like mine, could you? No, you had to get the highest-end muscle car there was." Gray chastises.

"Oh, come on, you like it too. I see your face when I let it loose on the interstate." Ivan teases while poking Gray in the side.

"Oh, you mean my wanna hurl face?" Gray snaps, but I can see the hint of amusement in his eyes.

I shake my head at their banter and when I hear another engine pull up the driveway; I look over my shoulders and we see a purple Challenger pull up.

I look over at Ivan as the car flashes in my memory. This is the same one that almost ran into me and Gray. I'm about to tell him off, but the look on his face tells me he'd do it all over again to get us to this point.

Mason gets out of the driver's seat and then goes over to the passenger side to help Dani to her feet. He nods in greeting as he walks over to the six of us. I reach out to shake his hand before I give Dani a friendly smile.

"I never got the chance to tell you, but thank you for helping to save me that day, Aiden." Dani says as she leans in to hug me.

"You're welcome." I say as I pull away from her and I barely hear Mason's low growl of me touching his girl. Which I can respect.

"Come on, let's get in here and talk." Mason snaps. "We may be on a time crunch here, with what I just found out." He adds as he gently takes Dani's hand and pulls her toward the front door, the action completely at odds with his tone.

We all walk toward Seth's house and he's standing by the door waiting for us to come in. He directs us to gather in the living room, where we all take the available seats and wait for Mason to start talking.

"I don't know how else to say this, so I'm just gonna be blunt here." Mason begins. He runs his hand through his hair and lets out a frustrated breath. "Aiden, your parents are alive."

I gape at him, and before I can even say anything, Seth beats me to it.

"How do you know?"

"This was before Victor told me to start watching you." He says while pointing at me. "Avery was working with Victor before I even knew they were your parents. About eight months after I started working with Victor, I think, like you figured out, she knew I was different. So she began to show me quick images of a fight between Victor and some other man that I later figured out was Seth and that she and Cole were being held here against their will to protect their son." Mason explains.

"I remember one day, I think it was on your twentieth birthday, actually. She was arguing with Victor about visions she was having and what you were going to do to his plan. Eventually, Victor made her and Cole leave, but there was a catch. He made something like collars for them. In case he failed and The Siphon was somehow destroyed, he had a backup plan of making two of the strongest individuals in The Protector's of Power his minions to continue his legacy even after his death. Those collars give a single order and have a single feature that Victor paired with their power. To Siphon abilities and store them in jars inside some compound, and kill anyone that gets in their way. For the last year and a half, I've been infiltrating other Parasite groups to find out where they are. I don't know for sure yet their exact location, but I know they are alive and they are still being controlled." Mason says.

As his words die in the air around us, I sit there in stunned silence, part of me not believing what I'm hearing, yet somehow I know it to be the truth.

"You aren't pulling our leg, are you?" Ivan questions.

"You seriously still doubt me after all this time, Chain Link?" Mason spits.

"Sorry, but when it comes to certain things, I question anyone. Even if Seth came to us about this, I'd question him." Ivan snaps back.

"How would we even go about trying to track them down?" I ask.

"I have a few ideas on how to help with that, Aiden." An unfamiliar voice says from the doorway.

We all whip our heads to the entryway, where a group of six people stand. I recognize Atticus and Quilla right away, but the other four are strangers to me.

"Well, I'll be damned. The great Tobias finally shows his face in my humble abode." Seth croons with a broad smile on his face. " I was starting to think you didn't want to see me anymore, old friend."

"You're lucky you're my friend or I would wipe that smile from your face, Seth." Tobias says with an edge to his tone, but apparently, the joke is lost on all of us because Seth just laughs.

Ignoring Seth completely, the man, Tobias, looks at me before he speaks. "I know your parents personally, Aiden. They are also my friends and very brave in helping me fight in a war that was not theirs to fight. And when I heard of them being forced to work with the enemy to keep you safe, it hurt more than anything. I considered them my pack-mates, and they were in trouble and even I couldn't do anything to help, until now, that is."

"Who are you? Or I should ask, what are you? I can tell you are not even our type of special." I ask, while eyeing the group.

There is something about their electrical traces. It's like even though I am seeing only six people, I am sensing eleven.

"I am the alpha of the Montana and North Dakota packs. We, Aiden, are Werewolves."

I laugh at his words and even with everything that I know about abilities, even that sounds far-fetched to my ears. Then I remember back when Atticus came by to remove the feeding tube from my stomach and when he and his girl turned to leave, he turned into a wolf and Seth dropped the bombshell that they were special. I just didn't think there was a whole damn pack of them roaming around.

Tobias walks up to me but the younger man behind him, who looks to be his son from the similar features, speaks for the first time, "Father, be gentle with him."

"Oh, don't worry, Kai. I will be." Tobias says while slowly walking over to me.

He stares me down, and for some reason, I want to actually look away, and I don't like that feeling one bit. I don't like being challenged on my home turf.

I want to bring my fire to my hands as a warning to him not to mess with me, but I keep the flames just under my skin instead. Again, some deep instinct tells me not to mess with this guy unless I have to.

"Ahh, I see." Tobias croons. "As one leader to another, you know when to pick your fights. Dakota, why don't you show Aiden what we are."

"Aw, why am I always the poster girl for Were's?" She groans.

"Because you're the most beautiful out of all of us, Love." Kai says.

I note the way he looks at her and I get the feeling they are a couple from the adoration that shines in his eyes and the way he runs a finger tenderly down her arm.

I watch in utter shock as she shifts into this beautiful blondish-brown wolf. I find myself wanting to go and run my fingers through her pelt, which I am not like that with animals usually, but I stop in my tracks when I hear him, Kai, literally growl at me, and his eyes... glow.

"That's cool." I say, pointing to Dakota, "But that's fucking freaky." I add, pointing to Kai's eyes.

"Sorry for the growl, but it's just you're a foreign male, and she's my mate. No one outside of the pack touches her."

I find that odd, but yet I can understand that I wouldn't want anyone else around Maya that I didn't know.

"I can understand that, man. I'd feel the same way about my girl." I put my hands up in surrender and I back away.

Kai relaxes a bit and then I watch Dakota go around a corner with Kai right behind her with her clothes in his hand. Then a few minutes later she walks back out as a human and fully clothed.

"So what's next? How do we find my parents? How do we stop them?" I ask.

"We have two more groups that I think we need to contact, and then we can get started. The contact I personally have is someone in Utah, and that group I think will be a great asset to this mission and they just so happen to be in the FBI. Then we have someone in California that my Beta knows, and they seem to be a different kind of special as well." Tobias says with a smile on his face and determination in his dark eyes.

Epilogue-
Aiden

Later that night, after we all leave Seth's place and begin this waiting game for these two other groups to come in, I bring Maya home with me.

As we lie in my bed, I pull her close to my side, her head resting on my chest in a way that's as natural as breathing. Maya is out like a light as soon as her body relaxes against mine. But for me, sleep doesn't come, and when I start to feel the pressure of a vision begin to build in my temple, my stomach drops.

I gently roll Maya off my chest and I sit up on the side of the bed with my head in my hands and wait for the vision to begin.

I start to see what looks like random black dots and lines. They appear over and over and over in my mind and I can somehow tell what is the beginning and what is the end, but even with that, they make no sense to me at all.

Whatever these lines and dots mean, it feels important, so I make my way over to my desk, all the while having them continue flashing in my mind. As I sit down and grab a piece of paper and a pen out of the drawer, I begin to hear some kind of beeping, too. Quick sounds that then turn to longer tones. It starts to get so loud in my head;

the noises turning urgent, that I hastily write down the code that is burning behind my eyes.

.--. .- .-. .- ... .. - ./-.-. .- -- .-. / .- .-. .. --.. --- -.-

"What the hell is that, Aiden?"

Maya's voice brings me out of the vision and I look over my shoulder to her before I look back down at the paper and stare at it in confusion.

"I have not one damn clue. I can't even feel who sent this to me. It's like something is blocking me from seeing who they are. But I heard this beeping in my head too and it feels like they go together, but again, it makes no sense to me." I say as I rub my temple with my right hand to ease the headache.

"Maybe Seth will know, or that Tobias guy will know. He seems older than Atticus is." Maya says.

"You know, I can actually feel the wolves under their skin. It's such a weird thing to sense." I say.

"I have a feeling things are gonna be getting weirder and weirder as this goes on." Maya says.

I finally get the beeping to stop in my head as the dots and dashes fade. "I hope not. I just want to know where my parents are so we can save them. "

"We will get to them, Aiden. I know we will." Maya promises. "Come on, let's go back to bed. There's nothing much we can do until these other groups come to help." She says while tugging me away from my desk and back with her toward the bed.

"I know. I just hope this group is normal, and not like vampires or something. 'Cause if that shit exists, I'm out. I can't deal with all this crazy." I say.

Maya's laughter fills the room and we finally find peaceful sleep again.

The last thought I had before slumber takes me is I hope I'm not going to be too late in saving my parents from this sick, twisted fate that Victor pushed them into.

The End

Acknowledgements

I want to thank my beta readers for taking time out of their busy lives and read through this story and, like always, making it the best work I am able to create. I don't know where I would be without you all.

Kaiidth.

Kristy C.

Natascha P.

I loved seeing your reactions! From laughing and crying, to being down-right mad about what I put these characters through, and also for sharing your music ideas that made you think about certain characters! I appreciate your help and I can't wait to show you the next one!

Love you guys. OX

Other Works

Thank you for reading Fire and Water- Book 1 of The Protector's of Power series.

Please consider leaving a review on Good Reads and/or where you purchased this story from. I would greatly appreciate it!

If you liked this story, please check out my debut novel- *Everyone Has Secrets* available now on Amazon.

And if you want to know more about Dakota and Kai's story, you can find them in *The Wolf Within,* also on Amazon!

Until next time, Readers!

XO- B. M. Light